JOE COUNTRY

THE 6TH JACKSON LAMB THRILLER

'We're spies,' said Lamb. 'All kinds of outlandish shit goes on.'

Like the ringing of a dead man's phone, or an unwelcome guest at a funeral . . .

In Slough House memories are stirring, all of them bad. Catherine Standish is buying booze again, Louisa Guy is raking over the ashes of lost love, and new recruit Lech Wicinski, whose sins make him outcast even among the slow horses, is determined to discover who destroyed his career, even if he tears his life apart in the process.

And with winter taking its grip Jackson Lamb would sooner be left brooding in peace, but even he can't ignore the dried blood on his carpets. So when the man responsible breaks cover at last, Lamb sends the slow horses out to even the score.

This time, they're heading into joe country.

And they're not all coming home.

Also by Mick Herron

Jackson Lamb thrillers

Slow Horses
Dead Lions
Real Tigers
Spook Street
London Rules

Zoë Boehm thrillers

Down Cemetery Road
The Last Voice You Hear
Why We Die
Smoke And Whispers

Reconstruction
Nobody Walks
This Is What Happened
The Drop

Joe Country

Mick Herron

First published in Great Britain in 2019 by John Murray (Publishers)
An Hachette UK company

1

A CIP catalogue record for this title is available from the British Library

Hardback ISBN 9781473657441
Trade Paperback ISBN 9781473657458
eBook ISBN 9781473657472

Typeset in Garamond

Printed and bound by Clays Ltd, Elcograf S.p.A

John Murray policy is to use papers that are natural, renewable and recyclable products and made
from wood grown in sustainable forests. The logging and manufacturing processes are expected to
conform to the environmental regulations of the country of origin.

John Murray (Publishers)
Carmelite House
50 Victoria Embankment
London EC4Y 0DZ

www.johnmurray.co.uk

To Annabelle

1

The owl flew screaming from the barn, its wingtips bright with flame. For a moment, silhouetted against the blank sky, it was a dying angel, scorched by its own divinity, and then it was just a sooty husk, dropping like an anvil into the nearby trees. He wondered if it would set the wood ablaze. But the trees were thickly layered with snow, and any spark that survived the fall would be smothered on contact. He turned back to the barn in time to see the roof collapse, and a cloud of dust burst upwards. Kind of beautiful, if you liked that sort of thing. This must be what got arsonists stoked.

But he was no arsonist; just following instructions. They'd burned the barn to erase their recent presence, and it hadn't occurred to either of them that this was an extermination; that there'd be an owl inside, plus any number of mice, rats, spiders, whatever. Not that it mattered. But he should have been aware of the possibility. That way, his heart wouldn't have leaped up his throat when the burning bird emerged, desperately hunting the last few seconds of its life.

It had found them now. Up there in the great grey yonder, while its one-time home was transformed by the miracle of flame into a smoky mass.

Something gave with a crash and a heave of sparks, and that was as good a signal as any. Time to leave.

'We done?' he said.

'Not as done as that bird. What was it, a chicken or something?'

'. . . That's right. A chicken.'

Jesus Christ.

He checked the straps on his backpack, tightened the cuffs of his quilted jacket, pulled his hood up, and led the way to the footpath. Behind them smoke curled upwards, while the falling snow grew lumpier, and the world flattened to a single tone. The barn hadn't been in use, and was miles from anywhere. The pillar of smoke would rouse attention, but they'd be long gone, their tracks covered, before any professional response arrived, and there was a ready-made scapegoat here in the wilderness: kids. Country life wasn't all driving tractors and shovelling shit with happy grins. They'd be doing meth, white cider and setting fire to barns. That's what he'd have done, if forced to grow up round here.

Once the bodies were found there'd be a circus, of course, but that wouldn't happen until the flames died down. And the blood on the snow would be a muddy mess by then, trampled by the first responders.

His right cuff was too tight, so he adjusted the Velcro fastener. Better. Good jacket: kept the weather out. The woman had been wearing one similar. New-looking, though she'd managed to rip it scrambling over a fence or something, leaving a triangular tear on the right breast; a flap of fabric hanging loose, showing the spongy material beneath. As for the man, he hadn't been dressed for the cold, and would have caught his death even without intervention.

The footpath left the cover of the trees, and they were out in the open again. The weather was coming in from the coast and they were walking towards it: on the way he'd call the boss, arrange a meeting point. With any luck, the boss would have found and killed the kid this morning, but they were boots up now anyway. Sometimes jobs went south, that was all. Sometimes colleagues got killed. When it happened you chalked it down to life-lessons, then went home and waited for the bruises to heal.

His companion spoke. 'I could murder a drink.'

'Not until we're back among the lights.'

By which he meant England, obviously. There might be lights in Wales, but he wasn't convinced they weren't powered by hamsters on wheels.

A black shape flitted overhead, a bird heading home, and he thought about the owl again; how the flames were already consuming it as it fled the barn. He had a memory about owls: that they were omens of something, probably death. Most omens had to do with death, if horror movies were anything to go by.

He reached a stile and clambered over it. Behind them lay a few complicated days and a black curl of smoke etching an ideogram in the sky; ahead, a whitening landscape, and beyond that the sea. As he set off to meet it, he thought: that owl had been right on the money, even if late with its prediction. Death had visited the area, making a collection. It had had a tougher job than it might have expected, given that the opposition had been from some rejects' department: Slade House? No, Slough House . . . Slough House, because the boss had called them 'slow horses'. A harder job than expected, but it made no lasting difference.

The man was dead. The woman was dead.

Slough House was going to need some new slow horses.

Part One
Lame Ducks

Cities sleep with their lights on, as if they're afraid of the dark. Up and down their roads, clustering at junctions, streetlights make daisy chains out of the night, illuminating pavements and hiding the stars. And if, from above – from the perspective of an astronaut, say, or a reader – these chains resemble neural pathways, forging connections between a city's hemispheres, that seems an accurate picture. For a city is made of memories, stored recollections packed into boxes of stone and metal, brick and glass, and the brighter its pathways pulse with light, the stronger those memories are. On its wider, busier thoroughfares the traces of grand events linger – royal progressions, wartime rallies, victory celebrations – while the circuses where its big roads meet nurture shades of less seemly occasions: riots and lynchings and public executions. Along its riverbanks, quiet moments promenade – a hundred thousand engagements and cuckoldings – and in the explosive glow of its transport terminals, a billion arrivals and a billion departures are recalled one by one. Some of these have left scars on its memory, others a faint graze, but all contribute to the whole, for this is what makes a city: the slow accumulation of history, of a near-infinite number of happenings in a network of streets that light up at night.

But if the grandest of these memories warrant plaques and statuary, the more private are kept out of view; or at least, stored in such plain sight that they're unseen. Take Aldersgate Street, in the London borough of Finsbury, upon which the gross bulk of the Barbican squats like a toad. Even on the main drag, the dull weight of mediocrity hangs heavy: of all London's memories, this undistinguished array of shops and offices is least likely to ring bells; those bright connections, firing through the night, are at their weakest here. But briefly lit by their flare, not far from the entrance to the Underground, is a block four storeys tall, though it appears shorter.

Its pavement-level frontage comprises a black door dusty with neglect, sandwiched between a newsagent's and a Chinese restaurant; its facade is distempered, its guttering a mess, and the local pigeons have shown their contempt for it in the traditional manner. The one stab at respectability – the legend W. W. HENDERSON, SOLICITOR AND COMMISSIONER FOR OATHS tattooed in gilt on a second-storey window – has long since started to peel, and the unlettered windows above and below it are smeary and grey. The building is a bad tooth set in a failing mouth. Here is where nothing happens: nothing to see here. Move along.

Which is how it's supposed to be, for this is Slough House, and Slough House deserves no attention. Should a historian attempt to penetrate its mysteries, she'd first have to negotiate a back door which sticks in all weathers, then a staircase whose creaking suggests imminent collapse, but having done so, she'd find little to exercise her notebook: just a succession of offices equipped to face the 1990s, crumbling plasterwork, and rotting splinters in the window frames. The metallic odour of an overused kettle will taint the air, and in the corners of the flaking ceilings, mould spores congregate. She'll creep from room to room on carpets thin as motel bedsheets, place a hopeful hand on radiators that are lumps of unresponsive steel, and find no history but the desultory kind, which carries on happening out of habit alone. So she'll pack her pen away and head back down the rackety staircase, through the mildewed yard where the dustbins live, and out into the alley, then the street, then London beyond. There's plenty of history elsewhere. There are memories minted every minute in the wider world. There's no reason to waste her time on this.

And once she's gone a sigh will pass through the building, a barely noticeable exhalation that rustles papers and wobbles doors, and Slough House will know its secrets remain intact. For it has secrets: like every building in every city, Slough House is a neuron in an urban hippocampus, and retains the echo of all it's seen and heard. Memories have stained its walls and seeped into its stairwell; they reek of failure, and have been scrubbed from the public record, but they persist, and they're not for intruders' eyes. Deep within the building's bones is the knowledge that some of its rooms that held two characters now hold only one; that formerly familiar impressions – the weight of a shadow on a wall; the pressure of a foot on a staircase – occur no more. This is what memory is: an abiding awareness that some things have vanished. And this is what consciousness is: the knowledge that more absences will come.

Time passes, and the city's lights wink out as it heaves itself awake. Memories, stirred by sleep, subside with the dawn. Snow will arrive before the week's end, but today there is only cold grey normality. Soon the slow horses will troop in, and settle to the mind-numbing grind; mental forced marches through a landscape undistinguished by points of interest. With such tasks in front of them, the real challenge is remembering why they bother.

And while they do, Slough House goes about the daily chore of trying to forget.

The thing to remember about Roddy Ho – Roddy Ho remembered – was that Roddy was a spook, a spy, an agent. Roddy was a *player*.

This was why he was rustling through someone else's wastepaper bin.

True, he'd had a bad year. Kim, his girlfriend, had turned out not to be his girlfriend, and while that particular rock had been a long time falling down the well, the splash it eventually made wasn't one he'd forget in a hurry. He'd felt betrayed. Hurt. Had felt, moreover, unnerved when it had been pointed out how very nearly treasonous his actions had been – good job Lamb wasn't going to see his trusted lieutenant flushed down the pipe without a fight. But now the waters were calmer two things were certain: Kim – his girlfriend – was history, and he, the Rodster, was still the brain pumping Clever through Slough House.

. . . while the charges pertaining to your behaviour are fully investigated you will

remain assigned to . . .

But for a while, man, he'd gone to pieces. He'd let his beard go to hell, from soul patch to hipster mess. He'd crashed out of TerraWar VII on level two, so knew how Andy Murray had felt catching the early bus home from Wimbledon. And he'd barely bothered to bring the outrage when it was announced that the new Doctor would be a woman: let others fight the good fight. The RodMan had hung up his cape.

. . . shall not, until investigations have been completed to the satisfaction of this department, have contact with colleagues . . .

And if he'd been waiting for someone – probably Louisa; he'd have settled for Catherine – to take him aside and say concerned and soothing things, that hadn't happened either. Then again, this made sense. You had a wounded lion in your pack – the king of the pride; your alpha beast – you didn't fuss about it while it healed. You waited until it was strong again was what you did. And then heaved a sigh of relief that order had been restored. So that was what had been happening lately: a quiet period of recovery, respected by all around him—

. . . your salary and benefits to be frozen at their current . . .

—which was now over: he was back in the game. Women could hurt you, but they couldn't break you. Ask Batman. Walking alone was the warrior's way. And besides, in the days of Mama Internet, anyone can get laid – or at the very least, anyone had access to many vivid pictures of what getting laid looked like. So it could have been worse.

And what he was doing now, part of his recovery if you like, was regaining control of his environment. Because although a warrior walked alone, Ho had been assigned a stablemate. Alec Wicinski, the new guy's name was, or Leck – Lek? – which sounded like *Star Wars*. Two days he'd been here, and already he'd insisted Roddy move his stuff to 'his own side of the room', muttering about how this was his desk, 'for the time being'. Yeah, right. Evidently he needed a lesson about respecting his betters, which meant Roddy had to do what Roddy did best, which was saddle up, ride the

Wild Web, and find out who this Wicinski guy was, and what he'd done to warrant gatecrashing Roddy's manor.

So he'd done the obvious and dived into Service records, looking for the back story on this new comedian; info not open to casual viewers, but there was no firewall the RodMan couldn't walk through . . . Except the info didn't exist. Not just the redacted chatter about whatever mess he'd left on Regent's Park's carpet, but anything at all – no date of hire, no job description, no photo; nothing. It was like Alec (Lech?) Wicinski didn't exist, or at least, hadn't existed before setting foot in Slough House.

Which was interesting. And Roderick Ho didn't like interesting.

What Roddy Ho liked was things done properly.

But Wicinski had been getting letters, so at least somebody thought he existed. He'd sat at Roddy's other desk and read them sourly, as if they weren't just bad news but confirmation of something worse, then torn them up and tossed the bits in his wastepaper basket.

You didn't, Roderick Ho sneered, have to be Sherlock Holmes.

So he'd waited until Wicinski cleared off for the day, collected the scraps and pieced them together. Only took him forty minutes. And what he'd got was evidence, no doubt about it: a letter from HR. Stuff about not setting foot in Regent's Park, not contacting colleagues; about 'ongoing investigation'. 'Charges'. That shit sounded serious. But no clues had been offered as to the nature of his sins.

Still interesting, then. Not orderly yet.

Roddy had put the pieces back in the bin, or most of them. He was on the case now. And there'd be no stopping the Rodster, now he was back in the game.

Anyway, that had been yesterday. This morning, Wicinski had sat drinking black tea, scowling and reading another letter, pages long. You could almost feel sorry for him, if that was your bag – up to the moment, anyway, that he scrumpled the pages, tossed them into the wastebasket, and stormed out the room like a monkey with a rage on.

Ho waited, but he didn't storm back.

The pages had all landed cleanly in the basket, so props for that, but seriously, Roddy thought: the dude had looked undignified, stamping out. Gotta have respect for yourself, he thought, getting down on his knees by the bin. Gotta keep your standards up, as he started rifling through it.

He pulled out the first page, uncrumpled it.

Blank.

Odd.

He pulled out another, did the same thing.

Blank.

. . . What was Wicinski, some kind of fucked-up origami artist? Was that why he'd been sent to Slough House, for wasting paper? It took all kinds, Roddy would be first to admit, but seriously: this was weird shit and he didn't like it.

Another one.

Blank.

And then another. It wasn't until he got to the seventh sheet that Roddy found one with actual words on, and this rocked him back on his haunches a second, while he took them in.

Fuck you, you little snoop.

Now what the hell was that about?

But before he could decipher it there were other pages to uncrumple, so he plunged his hand back into the bin, touched something solid and *snap* – Roderick Ho screamed as pain ate him from the fingers up, *Jesus*, what just happened? He pulled his hand clear, throbbing in agony, and when he saw through a curtain of tears what was dangling from it, another puzzle joined the cryptic message he'd just uncovered.

Why the hell had the stupid bastard thrown away a perfectly good mousetrap?

It was funny, Louisa Guy later thought, how unused she'd become to the sound of a phone. Not a mobile, obviously, but a landline, which, with its limited repertoire, was like something from a black and white movie, in which phones were sturdy works of art, all rotary dials and clumsy black receivers. The two in her office weren't like that, were grey push-buttons, but still: it was months since her own had uttered a peep, let alone the one on the unused companion desk. She hadn't been expecting it. Apart from anything else, that desk belonged to a dead man.

The dead man was Min Harper.

The day, not halfway done, had already offered surprises, but even when new things happened in Slough House, they felt like old things. There'd been a text from River, bad news, but news that had been coming for a while, and no reply she could make could prevent its arrival. And then the new guy, Lech – Alec? – had been in the kitchen earlier. He'd looked the way any slow horse did the first few days; like someone had slapped him with a shovel. Last week, he'd been at Regent's Park, and now he was here, and the distance between the two was the kind that, if you stared into it, it stared back. Nothing she could do about that even if she'd wanted to – and there was reason to feel wary around new intake – but her inability to do anything for River Cartwright maybe softened her a bit, enough to offer advice. Not because the new guy was about to step into deep shit, but because even shallow shit got everywhere if you didn't watch what you were doing.

So she said, 'Not that one.'

'. . . Huh?'

'Not that mug.'

He'd been reaching for Clint Eastwood, which wasn't going to make anyone's day if Roderick Ho found out.

'Your office-mate gets touchy if other people use his stuff.'

'. . . Seriously?'

'Famous for it.'

'Talk about anal.'

'. . . Yeah, a word to the wise? Don't say that in front of Lamb. He'll

13

take it as an invitation.'

Which was enough to be getting on with. Any more would count as spoilers. So she just added, 'Good luck,' and carried her coffee to her office. On the way she heard a shriek from Ho's room and wondered what that was about, but not enough to go and find out.

And twenty minutes after that, the phone had rung.

For a while – five rings – she stared at the offending instrument, its *drring-drring*s churning the office air. Wrong number? She hoped so. In the animal centre of herself, was certain that no good would come of picking up. Until, from somewhere overhead, a familiar note of irritation, *Will somebody answer that fucking phone?*, so she stood at last, crossed to the other desk, and lifted the receiver.

'. . . Henderson's.'

'Is that . . . Is this Min Harper's office?'

Something inside Louisa uncurled and shivered.

'Hello?'

'Mr Harper doesn't work here any more,' she said. The words, her tone of voice, came laced with black crêpe.

'I know, I know . . . I just . . .'

Louisa waited. It was a woman's voice, about her own age, far as she could tell. Unsure of herself. Min had been dead a while. Louisa was over it, in the way you got over a childhood illness; some part of you would always be weaker, but you'd never get ill in the same way again. That was the theory, anyway. And whether it was true or not, Min wasn't coming back.

'Could you tell me why you're calling?' Louisa found herself reaching for a pen, like anybody else, in any office anywhere. A pen, a pad, the usual tools. 'Let's start with who you are.'

'My name's Clare Addison. That's my name now, I mean. But I'm Clare Harper as was.'

Louisa's pen made no mark on the paper.

'Min was my husband,' the woman said.

With power comes responsibility, along with the opportunity to stick it to those who've annoyed you on your way up. Diana Taverner wasn't gauche enough to have compiled an actual list, but like any competent First Desk, her mental envelope had several names scrawled on the back of it.

First Desk . . . Even thinking it made her smile.

When Claude Whelan had opted for retirement rather than one of the alternatives on offer – among them, the chance to be taken outside and shot – there'd been no obvious candidate for the role; or none that had survived Diana Taverner's vetting, which in at least one instance had come close to being the surgical procedure its name suggested, rather than the background check that protocol required. A potentially messy business, but as the individual in question had attended the same prep school as Oliver Nash, and had, on two occasions, attempted to flush Oliver Nash down a toilet on the grounds that Oliver Nash was a sneak and a drongo and a tool, and as Oliver Nash was now chair of the Limitations Committee, which was responsible for putting a list of potential appointees for the role of head of the Service in front of the prime minister, the whole thing was a rare example of the Old Boy network paying off in a woman's favour, and could be cited as progress if it weren't, obviously, never to be spoken of again. But as it was, everything had worked out to the satisfaction of all important parties, these being Taverner herself and Oliver Nash. Taverner had been put forward as the only available candidate in the circumstances, and the newly appointed prime minister – herself a needs-must choice, though she appeared to be the only person in the country unaware of the fact – had bestowed her blessing, and Taverner now held the office from which lesser talents had conspired to keep her for too long. And yes, of course she had a mental list of those awaiting retribution, and if some were currently off-limits, that situation would resolve itself in time. For now, she'd make do with those within reach. Hence this morning's treat: an audience with Emma Flyte, head Dog.

'This won't come as a surprise.'

Flyte gave not a flicker in response.

This was happening in Regent's Park, which was not, as the crow flies, a huge distance from Slough House, but by any other metaphor was a lifetime away. The Park was the Service's headquarters; it was where baby spooks learned their ABCs, and where flyaway spooks returned, once their missions were complete. It was where you didn't get to visit if you'd been exiled to Slough House. Once that had happened, it might as well be Oz: ruby slippers not included.

'This, ah, reappraisal of your performance.'

'My last appraisal scored me as way above satisfactory.'

'Yes, well. My predecessor was a great admirer of yours.' Lady Di let that hang for a moment. Claude Whelan had been a great admirer of a number of people, but if you were offering marks, only Emma Flyte would have scored a perfect ten. There was a girl on the hub he'd kept an eye on too – Josie, her name was – but where she scored highest was in proximity. That and the T-shirts. He'd been a good man, Claude Whelan, but thank God he'd had his flaws, else he'd still have his hand on the tiller. 'So much so, he may have allowed himself a little . . . bias.'

'And you plan to redress the balance.'

'Fair and transparent,' said Taverner. 'That's how our processes should be. Apart from all the classified stuff, obviously.'

'I was brought in because the Dogs were being used for First Desk's private purposes,' Flyte said. 'Under my watch, that's been stopped. Are you sure it's fairness and transparency you're keen on?'

Her refusal to allow the Dogs to become Taverner's poodles was the basis of the women's antagonism. That and her being younger than Taverner. Sisterhood might be powerful, but Anno Domini was a bitch.

'Let's not get bogged down in detail,' said Taverner. 'Every First Desk is a new broom, that should be obvious. And the qualities I'm looking for in the head of the internal security section aren't necessarily going to match those that so, ah, *charmed* dear Claude. That's all.'

'So you want rid of me. On what grounds?'

Beauty alone ought to do it, thought Taverner. The fact that there was no actual regulation outlawing Flyte's kind of looks didn't mean there shouldn't be: at best it was a distraction; at worst, there'd be duels fought and blood shed. Not that Flyte had ever capitalised on her appearance, but then, an elephant didn't capitalise on its size. Which didn't mean it didn't knock trees down.

'Nobody's said anything about getting rid.'

'And yet you want my performance reappraised.'

'To take recent developments into account.'

'These being . . .?'

That I'm fucking First Desk now. Did Flyte really need that said out loud?

Taverner glanced around. She hadn't changed rooms since her elevation; was still on the hub. Her predecessors had mostly occupied an upstairs office, with views of the park: sunlight and gardens, and a neverending procession of au pairs trying not to lose the kids; down here, through her glass wall, Lady Di could watch the boys and girls as they monitored the hotspots and kept the world on track. This was where the job got done. And part of the job, now, was consolidating her own position; not for the purposes of petty revenge, but to ensure that when tough decisions were needed, she could take them without a chorus of dissent in the background. That, and also for the purposes of petty revenge. Because it would be foolish to deny the satisfaction involved.

It turned out, anyway, that actual words weren't required. The look on her face was all the response Emma Flyte needed.

'Perhaps it would be simpler if I just cleared out my locker.'

'Good heavens, no,' said Taverner. 'Nobody's talking about dismissal. No, what I had in mind was a role more in keeping with our revised sense of your abilities. And not a demotion. More of a . . . sideways move.'

The glimmer of understanding in Flyte's eyes was worth more to

Taverner than a new pair of shoes.

'You've got to be kidding.'

'Oh, I don't think I am,' said Taverner. 'No, I think Slough House is the perfect place for you, in the circumstances.'

And was pleased to imagine that no hint of her triumph showed itself on her face.

Her coat had faded to the colour of dust, and wrapped within it, she might disappear on the staircase of Slough House; grow invisible against a tired carpet and age-stained walls. Did this happen to everyone? Or only to women?

rioja cabernet merlot shiraz

She wore a hat too. Not many people did these days. Hers was a dull purple – dulled by time, because it had seemed deeper, more vibrant, when she'd bought it. But maybe it was the eyes that faded, diluting all they viewed to feeble ghosts. Maybe she was wrong about her hat and coat; maybe she dazzled without knowing it. That thought almost produced laughter, an impulse easily stifled, here on the staircase. These walls had heard a lot of things, but laughter didn't figure high on the list.

burgundy barolo beaujolais

(These weren't colours, of course. Except that they were; they were reds, the colour of blood.)

Her gloves were black, mind, and her shoes. Not everything faded. But her hair had been blonde once, and while – strand by strand – it perhaps still was, when she looked in the mirror it was grey. This seemed proof enough. It had been a long time since anyone came closer to her than her own reflection.

All my colours, thought Catherine Standish. All those primary splashes life was once drenched in; it was down to shoes and gloves now. Everything else lay in shadow.

She reached her office. The room was cold, though the arthritic wheezing of the pipes meant the heating was technically on. Her radiator needed bleeding – and there it was again, blood, though this would be a watery substitute; a rusty trickle. Coat off, hat off, computer on. There were reports from Louisa Guy and River Cartwright to evaluate: Louisa's would be sketchy – she was compiling names of those who'd borrowed 'suspect texts' from public libraries – but otherwise reliable; River, on the other hand, seemed to have embarked on a work of fiction, even if that fiction was just a list of addresses. Identifying properties that were potentially hostile safe houses was his current task. The methodology involved cross-checking Council Tax payments against census forms, though the practice seemed to be that once a week River would download a bunch of random addresses and shuffle them for authenticity. Sooner or later Lamb was going to notice.

And then there was the new boy: Lech Wicinski. Also went by Alec. She wondered what mind-numbing task Lamb would find for him to do.

And wondered why she bothered wondering.

Every night for weeks she had broken her journey home to St John's Wood; had lit from the Tube one stop early, despite the chill. Snow was forecast, and the pavements were hard as iron. You felt it in each step, the bone-cold stones hammering through your frame, because this was what London did, when the weather reminded the city it was temporary: it hunched down tight. Sensible folk didn't linger when this happened. But every night Catherine braved the cold one stop early, because this way she could call in to the Wine Citadel, and buy a bottle.

sangiovese pinot noir syrah zinfandel

It wasn't really, when you got down to it, about the colour.

And it had been years since she'd enjoyed this freedom allowed most everyone else. The apparently casual nature of the transaction thrilled her. You chose your bottle and swiped your card. People did it every day, a lot of them more than once. She'd done it herself times out of mind, in the olden golden days. She'd been at Regent's Park then, a functioning alcoholic, following which, for a rather shorter period, she'd been a dysfunctional alcoholic, and then – after drying out in a Service sanatorium, courtesy of her boss, Charles Partner – a recovering alcoholic. And then that same boss, First Desk at Regent's Park, had blown his brains out in his bathtub, or that had been the story at the time.

But like a wine stain the story wouldn't go away, and every time she scrubbed it it re-emerged, its pattern different. Partner, it turned out, had been a traitor. The man who'd led the Service, and pulled Catherine back from her downward spiral, had spent a decade committing treason. This, it felt to her now, had been both a shock and a confirmation of something she'd always known: that all joes go to the well in the end. Charles's well, it seemed, had been full of money . . . What had been slower to come to light was this: that Partner had kept her on because of what, not who, she was. She'd thought herself his dedicated helper; the ever-efficient PA whose own life might have been a mess, but who ensured that his ran along straight lines. But it turned out that her chief qualification, in his eyes, was that she was a drunk, and could be trusted not to see what was happening in front of her. Every secret he ever sold had passed across her desk, her fingerprints smeared on all his crimes. Had he faced trial, she'd have been standing next to him. Her fledgling sobriety would have taken wing at that.

But he had killed himself, and here she was in Slough House, and while the other inhabitants saw it as torture, for Catherine it was a penance. Being an alcoholic was part of her make-up, its seed inside her since her teens, but she hated having been a fool. Even mindless drudgery was better than running that risk again. Even Jackson Lamb was better – his endless crudity, his animal habits.

And then the stain changed shape once more.

amarone bardolino montepulciano

It had been Diana Taverner who had told her: *There's something you really ought to know.* You had to hand it to Lady Di; when it came to breaking news, she could leave the jagged part sticking in your back. *Did you really think he'd killed himself? Surely you've worked it out by now . . .*

And of course she had; she'd known for years. Known, but never allowed the knowledge to harden and take root.

Jackson Lamb had killed Charles Partner. He'd been Partner's joe, back in the day; Partner his handler, his mentor, the maypole around which he'd danced. But he'd killed him; had shot him in his bathtub, where Catherine had found him. So there was no trial, no trauma in the tabloids; just another Service suicide, a few mumbled words, and a trip to the Spooks' Graveyard. As payment or punishment, she didn't know which, Lamb had been given Slough House, and had been squatting here since, a grim overlord to the Service's washouts; those whose careers might not have peaked with a bullet in a bathtub, but had reached a full stop nevertheless. And here she was too, every day; delivering reports to Lamb's desk, making him cups of tea; sitting with him in the dark hours sometimes, for reasons she'd never understood. She did not like him, but was bonded to him: her bogeyman and occasional saviour; and now, it turned out, the man who'd murdered her former boss. How was she supposed to feel about that?

She was supposed to keep on keeping on. She was supposed to do that one day at a time.

Catherine began going through the reports, River's and Louisa's. She'd tidy them up, print them out, staple them neatly, slide them into a folder. Sooner or later they'd wind up in Regent's Park, where for all she knew, they'd be shredded unread. Just one of the many things outside her control.

But later, on her way home, she'd buy a bottle.

If you like school you'll love work, the old line went. And it was true, thought Shirley Dander, that the one was good training for the other. If you could handle the tantrums, the malice and the potty rage in the office, education would be a breeze.

Case in point. J. K. Coe.

Coe was three-quarters psycho, if you wanted Shirley's opinion. And documented fact bore her out: he'd deliberately killed at least two people, not counting whatever he did in his free time; one of them (unarmed, manacled) here in the building; the other an admittedly harder target: a bad actor, spraying bullets from an automatic weapon. Coe had walked up and put a bullet in his head at point blank range. Even with a handgun, there'd have been a mess. With a police-issue rifle, it was modern art. Take those things, then factor in the time he'd held a blade to Shirley's own throat, and she wasn't sure why she was downgrading him to three-quarter status, unless it was professional courtesy. Most offices, a record like that, you'd be out on your arse by lunchtime. Most schools too, she hoped.

But this was Slough House, where Jackson Lamb made the rules, and provided you didn't hide his lunch or steal his whisky, you could get away with murder. There'd been at least four corpses within these walls she knew of, and she didn't work weekends. And this was the Service's backwater, where they sent you when they wanted to bore you to death. God knew what went on in Regent's Park.

So anyway, J. K. Coe and Shirley had history, which should have made it easier to have a conversation with him. As it was, it made it simple enough to find him – he was in his office – but after that it was uphill all the way.

'Quiet round here.'

If nothing else, his lack of response proved her point.

'Where's River?'

He shrugged.

When he'd first turned up, Coe had had the irritating habit of playing an invisible keyboard. He'd be at his desk, or any flat surface, and his fingers would be tapping away, spelling out whatever he was hearing in his head, which was usually piped there by iPod, but she suspected might echo round his brain regardless. He didn't do that so much any more. But he was still pretty vacant; a charisma vacuum. Didn't mean he didn't pick up information, though.

'Spoken to the new guy?'

Coe shook his head.

'You heard what he's in for?'

They always made it sound like a conviction, because that's what it was. Something that got you hard time.

But Coe shook his head again.

Shirley shook hers too: waste of fucking breath. Coe made a shoehorn look chatty. It wasn't like she wanted to be best buddies or anything. But they'd taken down bad guys together, and that should at least be worth idle conversation.

Pickings elsewhere were slim. River wasn't around, they'd established that; Louisa had made it clear she didn't want to talk; Ho was Ho; and Catherine had been strange lately, not given to chat. Sometimes, new people had that effect. They had you remembering a time when you still had hope. When you thought some mistake had been made, which might yet be rectified; that, given time, you could haul yourself out of the pit, to general applause.

After a while, you realised that all that would happen was you'd be thrown back in again.

Shirley said, 'Good talk. Let's do this again,' and left Coe to it.

Back in her own room, she had another look at her latest assignment. Lamb had had an idea not long ago; this particular gem being that your average bomb-chucking numpty (his words) was unlikely to observe the social niceties.

'This might just be me being harsh, but if your mission in life is to indiscriminately massacre your neighbours, you're probably not that bothered about paying your TV licence. Right?'

Shirley had said, 'Yeah, but don't they get taught to blend in? At terrorist school?'

'Oh, good. A volunteer.'

'No, I was just—'

23

'See, what I'm suggesting, by which I mean what you will henceforth dedicate your life to until I say stop, is what I'm going to call . . . Operation Scofflaw.'

Meaning Shirley's daylight hours were now taken up by cross-referring a register of TV licence defaulters against lists of those who'd failed to pay parking fines, child support and a million other minor offences . . .

('Wouldn't it be quicker to just take the population of Liverpool and start from there?'

'And they say I teach you nothing.')

. . . the whole shebang then, for want of a less inflammatory description, ethnically profiled. It was, essentially, classic Lamb: pointless, time-wasting and tit-blisteringly boring, with a dash of offensiveness chucked in. If it was happening to anyone else, it would be funny.

She wondered what task Lamb would find for the new guy.

And she wondered what the new guy had done to wind up in Slough House.

And then she wondered how come River was nowhere to be seen, the jammy skiver.

Good job some of us have a work ethic, she decided, making sure her office door was shut before she closed her eyes.

His grandfather was fading with the day.

River had been at his bedside since the early hours, summoned by a kind voice on his mobile: *It would be wise to get here soon.* For minutes afterwards he'd lain unhearing the words, running back the clock. He was twelve, and helping in the garden; watching worms at their incomprehensible work. On his head, the O.B.'s hat. *Don't want you catching sunstroke. Your grandmother'd have my guts.* Or twice that age and sitting in the study, rain lashing the windows, the O.B. talking him through the dark days of the Cold War. Over the years, the old man's chair had moulded itself to hold him like a hammock. River's chair was a work in progress . . . On their own darkest day, none colder, they'd buried his grandmother, Rose, and it had been the first and only time he'd seen the O.B. cry.

You built a life the way you'd build a wall, one brick on top of the other, but sooner or later, those first bricks were taken away.

He had thought about calling his mother, but for no longer than it took to shake his head. Then he'd willed himself up and into yesterday's clothes, arriving at Skylarks, the nursing home, before the sun. His grandfather had been moved into a room that was purpose-built to die in, though nobody actually said so. The lighting was gentle, and the view through the window of winter hills, their treeline a skeleton chorus. The bed the O.B. would never leave was a clinical, robust device, with upright panels to prevent him from rolling off, and various machines monitoring his progress. On one, his pulse echoed, a signal tapped out from a wavering source. A last border crossing, thought River. His grandfather was entering joe country.

Twice he took his phone out, to ring his mother. Twice he didn't. He texted Louisa, though; let her know where he was. She texted back: *So sorry*. He'd have called Catherine, but Catherine had changed lately, reverting to how she'd been in his early days at Slough House: a pale ghost, who moved through the rooms leaving no trace behind her. The previous day, alone with her in the kitchen, he'd stood close by her, reaching for milk from the fridge, and breathed in deeply: could he smell alcohol? But he caught only the herbal mix of the soap she favoured, the scent she wore.

Besides, if she'd fallen off the wagon, they'd all know about it, surely? A crash like that. Unless Catherine had done what Catherine would do, which was fall so slowly, fall so deep, that no one would notice and no one would hear.

From the bed, calm breathing.

He stood and paced the room, to keep his blood flowing. That's the kind of thought you have in a hospital room. The O.B.'s gentle exhalations, his secret murmuring, didn't waver, and seemed no different from anyone else asleep. But those familiar with death had picked up on signs River couldn't decrypt. When life was entering the final straight there were signals to read, codes to break. It was a language he didn't know yet. All the deaths he'd witnessed had happened suddenly, to healthy people.

Every fifteen minutes a nurse came in and assessed the situation. She brought River a cup of tea and a sandwich, patted his shoulder. *Are you the only family? How long have you got?* There was a mother, Isobel Dunstable, née Cartwright, who had given the Old Bastard his name, and meant it; and a father, the renegade American spook Frank Harkness, who had seduced Isobel not for love, nor even for pleasure, but to bend the O.B. to his will, perhaps the only time in his life the O.B. had been outfoxed. And never spoken a word of it, either. By the time River came to learn the truth, the old man had been lost in the twilight, unable to tell the difference between trees and shadows.

Meanwhile, Frank was in the wind, and his mother hadn't spoken to her father in years.

I just want him to be unhappy, she'd told River once. Behind the brittle levity, he'd sensed a wound still pulsing.

He dozed, so that when at last it happened, it happened without his knowing. His eyes had closed, and the images that scampered through his mind were a confused welter of loss and unhappiness. It was a noise from the corridor that brought him back, a jostled trolley, and he started at the sound, his heart hammering. It was another moment or two before he realised that the machines had changed their tune, and instead of charting progress, were transmitting the news from the other side. His grandfather had crossed the border.

River rose and kissed the old man's forehead moments before the nurse arrived.

Emma said, 'You're kidding, right?'

'Do I look like I'm kidding?'

'No offence, but it's hard to tell.'

This was true. It wasn't that Lady Di was a stoneface, and if she ever took to pulling the legs of her subordinates it would likely be in controlled conditions, with the subject fixed to a rack, but in the time Emma Flyte had been running the Dogs, she'd heard a lot of instructions that might easily have been a piss-take. It turned out that in the governance of a nation's security, many absurd situations had to be worked around: a toxic clown in the Foreign Office, a state visit by a narcissistic bed-wetter, the tendency of the electorate to jump off the occasional cliff. So sometimes a First Desk would outline an agenda and your first thought would be *Yeah, as if.*

But not this time.

'I'd have thought Slough House was on your list,' she said.

'I have a list?'

'Oh, I think we both know you have a list. And Slough House has been a thorn in your side for years, right? So here you are at last, top of the monkey puzzle tree, I'd have thought your first move would be to raze that place to the ground.'

And sow salt where it had stood. You couldn't be too careful, where Jackson Lamb was concerned.

'And instead, you're embracing its potential – oh, don't tell me. You made a deal with Lamb.'

'I'm First Desk, Ms Flyte. I don't have to make deals with anyone.'

'And I used to be a copper, Ms Taverner, and I recognise bullshit when I hear it. That's how you got rid of Whelan, isn't it? You had Lamb's help, and in return Slough House is off the hook.'

She only had to say the words aloud to recognise their truth. Back-room politics was Diana Taverner's natural habitat, and as for Lamb, he'd deal with the devil if circumstances required. Whether the devil would shake hands with Lamb was a different question. Even Satan has standards.

Lady Di had leaned back. Not a great sign. Taverner was a prowler. When someone else was in charge, she'd move around rather than sit in one place; ever-conscious, Emma supposed, of how warm flesh could be a target.

She was speaking now. 'Let's just say,' she said, 'that the higher up you move, the more your perspective changes. Slough House has been a nuisance in the past, yes. And may be again in the future, in which case I won't hesitate to trim its sails. But for the time being – let's call this a transitional phase – there are certain uses to which it can be put. Not least of which is, solving the problem of your career trajectory.' For a moment, her gaze shifted; she was looking beyond Emma, through the glass wall, at the boys and girls on the hub. A target-rich environment, Emma assumed. There were so many ways you could disappoint Diana Taverner, some of which you wouldn't know about until your head was rolling on the sand. 'So yes, as you put it, I'm embracing its potential. That's what leaders do.'

Emma shook her head.

'Something to add?'

'The Met was bad enough,' said Emma. 'But this, Jesus. You'd burn a city down to save face.'

'It would depend on the city.'

'I wish I thought you were joking.'

'This meeting seems to have become all about my sense of humour. If it'll save you time, here's my tell. When I think something's funny, I laugh. With me?'

'You remind me of someone from my old job.'

'The Commissioner, I hope.'

'No, this was a serial offender. Must have arrested him a dozen times, mostly for punching out strangers. But he never copped on that he was the one with the problem.'

'I'm going to miss our little chats,' said Diana Taverner. 'I don't often get across that end of town. It's not that the journey's tricky, it's just that it's awfully shitty over there. Unless you've a thing for street food?'

Emma Flyte smiled. 'I've eaten enough of it in my time to learn one thing. That I'll decide where I buy it.'

'That sounds like you're rejecting my proposal. But would you like to make it clearer?'

'Of course,' said Emma. 'With the greatest lack of respect, ma'am, fuck you. And fuck your job.'

And as there didn't seem much point prolonging the interview, she left.

So the day passes, as most days do, and the city sinks nightwards once more. On the guttering of Slough House, on its window panes, on the frame of the black front door which never opens, never closes, thin ice forms, and the building's only contribution to the lights that guide the city through the small hours is a laterally sliced yellow square on its upmost storey, tilted to the sky. But even as this catches the attention it winks off, and some minutes later – just enough time to allow a whisky-impaired navigation of six half-staircases, with an interval to make use of what appears from a damaged perspective to be a mobile lavatory – a heavy-coated shape emerges from the adjacent alleyway, crosses the road and disappears into the Barbican shadows, which was not the route it took the night before, and will not be its route tomorrow.

And now the building subsides, the effect of shadows cast by a passing bus. Memories stir, the residue of long brooding – the stains people leave on the spaces they've occupied – but these will be gone by morning, leaving in their place the usual vacancies, into which new sorrows and frustrations will be poured. Soon winter will shake its big stick again, not only at London but at everything in its path, and great swathes of the country will be swallowed by snow. By the time it melts, Slough House will have new ghosts.

Until then, it will do its best to forget those it already has.

3

On Saturday morning Lech Wicinski left the basement flat in Crouch End that he shared with his fiancée, intending to buy a pint of milk. There was a corner shop not two hundred yards away, but for some reason he fished his car keys from their hook in passing, and about the time he should have been sitting down to scrambled eggs he was leaving the city, heading westward, though it was some while before his destination revealed itself. For that first half hour he was driving blind, trying to reverse the clock, as if in an as yet unknown direction he'd find the misstep he'd made and untake it; return home to find everything as it ought to be, his career on track, a fresh pint of milk in the fridge. He was way too much the rationalist to think that might happen. But a human being, so, you know: *Christ.*

Traffic was sluggish: the usual weekend exodus. London's pull was a weekday force. It evened out after an hour, though, and he found himself at a stable seventy-five. It was cold and dry, the motorway verges, the fields beyond, brittle and uncared for. The cows in the fields were motionless; placeholders for actual cattle.

The previous evening he'd called Josie, one of the hub crew, and asked if she fancied a quick drink. There'd been forced cheer in his voice, a Lech Wicinski neither recognised. But it didn't matter, because all she'd said was, 'Sorry, Lech. I can't.'

shall not, until investigations have been completed to the satisfaction of this department, have contact with colleagues

He felt his teeth grinding. Forced himself to stop.

Lech had torn that letter up, dumped it in his office bin, where the prick whose office he now shared had found it. A swift lesson: life in Slough House. In the mean little shopping arcade opposite was a hardware store that sold mousetraps. *Fuck you, you little snoop.* That should lighten the atmosphere.

And just to keep things rolling along, he'd snapped the handle off Ho's Clint Eastwood mug and dumped the parts on the kitchen counter.

After skirting Oxford he left the motorway. The road narrowed, and would be leafy in summertime, but at the moment the overhead branches resembled old scars. It was potholed too, and speedbumped where it wound through villages. The cottages here enjoyed valley views and well-kept gardens, as if those who chose to live in the countryside liked to tame those parts they could. But then, who wouldn't? It was when things slipped out of control that everything went crazy.

They had found pornography on his Service laptop – child pornography.

'It wasn't me.'

Richard Pynne, his line manager – Dick the Prick, obviously, but he'd earned it – had bowed a sceptical head. 'Yes well but, Alec. There it is. For all to see.' That required a codicil: 'Or not.'

'How did you even—?'

'There are sweeps, we do sweeps. Remote sweeps. You must know about that. We issue enough warnings.'

We don't care how you get your rocks off, his words implied. Just don't be doing it with Service kit.

That had been the first he'd known of it: the Dogs arriving at his workstation, in full view of the hub, disconnecting his hardware, going through his desk. Packing everything onto those plastic trays they use at airports. What did they think he'd done? Leaked a secret, blown a whistle . . . . It had taken Dick the Prick to teach him, in one of the smaller, windowless interview rooms; the kind to which you were summoned when coffee wasn't on the agenda.

Pynne was large, and going to be larger still if he didn't start doing something about it; had long declared victory over male-pattern baldness by shaving his head, and wore thick-framed spectacles, which was all Lech was willing to admit they shared in common, though Lech himself only wore his for close-up work. Pynne was a year or two younger but on a faster track, which might have been the Cambridge degree, and might just have been that he wanted it more. Don't be fooled by the speech patterns, Lech reminded himself. That hesitancy, the repetition. He was sharp enough, Pynne the prick. One of Di Taverner's protégés.

But that was all white noise. What mattered was the impossibility of it: child porn, on Lech's laptop. Which only he used. Which he was responsible for: security, contents, the lot.

'So I'm going to have to ask you, and this is formal, it's being recorded, I'm going to have to ask you the obvious. Did you do this, Alec? Did you download this?'

'I—no! No, of course I bloody didn't.'

'And has the laptop been in your possession for the past week?'

'It's been in my possession for the past year. But I haven't been downloading bloody— Jesus, Dick, child porn? I'm engaged to be married, for God's sake!'

It sounded like a hastily concocted alibi. Men with wives, fiancées, partners – men with lives didn't do that sort of thing. Didn't use illegal pornography. Except for the ones who did, of course, but Lech wasn't one of them.

Dick said, 'If it's an error, an integrity issue – I mean integrity of the system, obviously – if that's the case, then it will all get sorted out. But in the meantime, there'll need to be an investigation, and while that's underway you can't be on the premises, I'm afraid.'

Escorted out of the building, as if he'd been caught stealing paperclips.

He turned off the road at the sign for Northwick Park.

The same morning, back in London.

Louisa, who lived out on the fringes, never came into the city at the weekend, except on those few occasions which demanded it – a date, shopping, being bored; call it every other Saturday max, or three a month at most – and yet here she was, Soho, like a mindless tourist; one among a million, even in this cheerless weather. She was wearing her new white ski jacket, and if it didn't do much for her figure she'd been glad of it walking from the Tube, with London's air a refrigerated warning. There'd been talk on the radio of a Siberian front on the way. They'd made it sound like a wartime manoeuvre.

The café windows were grey with condensation, and ghosts streamed past in an unbroken flow. Louisa wrapped both hands round her Americano, and the door opened and closed, opened and closed, and by her watch the woman should have been here ten minutes ago. If she finished her coffee, she thought. If the woman hadn't turned up by then, game over.

It wasn't like Louisa wanted to be here in the first place.

Is that . . . Is this Min Harper's office?

Something like vertigo had swamped her.

Mr Harper doesn't work here any more.

She'd been leaning against what had been Min's desk, something she had watched him do time without number. He liked to stand when on the phone; he'd had restless bones. Sitting at a desk wasn't what he'd joined the Service for. Her neither. But their careers had been derailed; Louisa's because she'd screwed up a surveillance operation that put dozens of handguns on the streets; Min because, in what had since become an accepted classic, he'd left a disk stamped Top Secret on the Underground. If there'd been other people to blame, their lives might have felt easier. As it was, both were crippled by shame and self-loathing, which was probably the igniting factor in their love affair. Which had been their business alone, she reminded herself now. Min's marriage had already been over.

My name's Clare Addison. That's my name now, I mean. But I'm Clare Harper as was . . . Min was my husband.

What Louisa figured was, it was some kind of twelve-step thing.

Clare Harper was looking for licence to move on. And part of that process was facing Louisa Guy, with whom her late husband had spent the last year of his life.

She finished her Americano and thought: there's not enough tequila in the world. Forget about coffee: not enough tequila. She didn't want to do this. Didn't want to be here. But she didn't leave, despite the deal she'd made with herself.

How old would the children be now? She'd never even met them . . . Fifteen, she decided. Sixteen? That would be Lucas. She couldn't remember the younger one's name. George? No, she was associating.

'Hello?'

Hadn't even noticed the door opening again.

'Oh. Yes.'

'You're . . .?'

'I'm Louisa, yes.' She stood. 'And you must be Clare.'

'I'm sorry I'm late.'

'No, that's okay.' There was a moment where nothing was happening; just two women, paralysed by meeting. Louisa forced her way past it: 'Can I get you a coffee?'

'Oh . . . A latte. Thank you.'

First contact survived, Louisa rejoined the queue, and like a spy studied Clare Harper in the mirrored wall. Except not Harper: Addison. Either way, she was about Louisa's age, a little older; so call her thirty-nine, or thirty-eight and three-quarters for solidarity's sake. She was a brunette, her hair tapered close to the neck but longer in the front, a style Louisa had tried herself a couple of years back, but didn't entirely get on with. Wearing jeans and a loose green sweater, which in other circumstances Louisa might have asked where it came from. She didn't think, though, that they were about to become best buddies. She thought they were here so Clare Addison could stomp on her a bit before moving on. But Louisa wasn't here to be anyone's bunny, or even to talk about Min: she was here to say *Yes, that was me*. Give

Clare Addison a face to go with the name, just like Louisa herself had one now. Closure worked both ways.

When she returned to the table Clare was sitting, hands clasped in front of her. Louisa said some words: she wasn't sure what – have you come far?; something like that. Clare was nodding, or shaking her head, and Louisa noticed tight lines around her mouth, the way her eyes flickered left to right, as if she were expecting somebody else. The tension seemed unnecessary. Whatever was going to happen, the worst was in the past. Wounds healed.

She made to say more words, useful ones this time, but Clare was already speaking.

'You worked with Min, right? At this place – Slough House?'

'That's what they call it.'

'It's where they assigned him after he messed up that time.'

'Yes,' said Louisa. She didn't understand why the woman was going the long way round. What did she want, a day-by-day account of their affair? Because screw that. She was prepared to offer sympathy, but wasn't about to bare her soul. 'Clare, I don't know how much Min told you about me, or about Slough House, but you have to understand there are some things I can't talk about.'

'He didn't tell me much. Just that it was a punishment posting, which I'd already worked out. And he didn't talk about his colleagues at all. That's why I rang his old number. I didn't know who to ask for, otherwise.'

'You didn't . . .'

'He talked about your boss, a dreadful man. Is he still there?'

'Oh yeah.'

'But I couldn't remember his name.' Clare's eyes became still at last, and she focused on Louisa. 'And you were in the same office? On the next desk?'

'It's an old-fashioned set-up,' she heard herself saying. 'Not open-plan or anything.' Her voice faded away at the impossibility of putting Slough House into a modern office context. 'He didn't talk about any of us?

His colleagues?'

'We weren't together long, after he was posted there. He was in such a state. He couldn't believe he'd messed up so bad.'

'No . . .'

'He heard about it on the radio, you know. On *Today*. An item about a classified disk being found on the Tube. They were on to the weather before he realised it was him they were talking about.'

One of those moments when the floor drops away. Louisa had once seen a photograph of a construction site in China; a huge development that razed a neighbourhood, though one homeowner had refused to sell up. So his house remained intact while all around was dug away, leaving it perched on a pillar of earth a hundred metres high. She remembered looking at the picture and recognising it: no ground beneath your feet, save the space you occupied. Min had felt the same. It wasn't so different now, she supposed, except that she'd got used to it.

She didn't want more coffee; would be buzzing the rest of the morning. Gave her something to do with her hands, though.

'Clare—'

'I need your help.'

'Why? What's wrong?'

'It's Lucas. Our son. Min's and mine.'

'Lucas? What's he done?'

'He's disappeared,' said Clare. 'I've no idea where he is.'

A rusting green skip sat parallel to a length of wooden fencing, which looked twenty minutes' effort away from being in the skip itself. This side of the fence was a row of garages, some with their doors rolled up, revealing workshop interiors, and overalled men tinkering with engines. From behind the thinly wooded area to Lech's left came the sound of traffic, but here, in this low-key industrial estate, the cars were mostly sick or injured. This was where you'd come if you were rebuilding an American classic, or had recently flogged a car to death and were disposing of the body. A metal sign read POWDER COATING FABRICATION SHOT BLASTING, and it briefly amused him that, while he understood what each word meant, he had no clue what they signified.

Life was coding; was hidden messages. You knew what was going on or you didn't.

Lech had parked on a grassy verge, and was walking through the estate called Northwick Park. A memory of mist hung in the air, and the ground was slick with leaves and the occasional fat black slug. Thrusting his hands into his pockets, he skidded briefly, then righted himself. A plane passed overhead, flying low; a two-seater, by the look. He didn't know aeroplanes. His grandfathers, who'd both lived here, wouldn't have recognised it either. But they'd have known what kept it in the air, and have held their breath at the memory of flight.

There were brick huts with corrugated roofs; some ivy-trailed, some barred up. Originally a hospital for American troops, the estate became a refuge for displaced Polish people in the war's aftermath, and looking at it now in the bleak winter light, he couldn't help wondering how it had felt: refugees turning up from concentration camps, from a broken Europe, to find this bleak estate; its squat huts their new homes. There'd been watch towers and barbed wire fences. It can't have looked like freedom.

But freedom was measured, he supposed, by what you were leaving behind. Both his grandfathers had left Poland before the occupation; had served in the RAF, one a pilot, the other ground staff. They'd fought the war under foreign skies, but in time those skies had come to be their own. Maybe the skies hadn't felt the same way. The war over, the men had chosen to stay and raise their families among fellow Poles, other ex-servicemen, until Northwick Park shut down in 1970. Both sets of grandparents, by this time in-laws, went to live on the south coast then, and family holidays for young Lech in the eighties had been seaside jaunts: ice cream and sandcastles. Poland was a name on the news, it was footage of unrest and cold-looking buildings, and he'd bridled against his ethnic heritage, hating the way it marked him as different, and had insisted on Alec, wouldn't answer to Lech. His parents hadn't fought him on the issue. Families from that end of Europe had learned to play the waiting game centuries ago. Give it time, give it time.

He had dark curly hair, and by five of an evening, looked like he'd gone two days without a shave. His genetic inheritance, he supposed. That, and a bone-bred pessimism: if you expected things to get worse, history would prove you right. And then, of course, there was the expectation of betrayal. Which was working out fine too.

A few short weeks back Lech had been an analyst on the hub, Regent's Park's centre of activity, where the brightest and best were called to arms. He'd had all the usual training, but had never been out in the field. The nearest he'd come to an op was sitting in the back of the van while someone else kicked a door down. Afterwards, he'd be brought out to look at what had been found behind the door, or to offer a plausible reason as to why there was nothing behind the door after all, or occasionally to point at a different door and explain that that was the one he'd meant. This happened often enough that it had its own column in the budget. Analysis suited Lech; it gave him an excuse to brood. Not that he was sullen; he just liked to work things out, discover what was ticking. Plagued by insomnia, he'd pound the city streets, something he likened to taking London's back off and exploring the workings. His fiancée, Sara, was used to waking in the dark to his absence, and would tell him, not entirely joking, that this would obviously cease once they were married. That was what life was: you worked, sometimes you couldn't sleep, and your future was already being shaped. Until something crashed into it and knocked everything out of true. A phrase that brought to mind Jackson Lamb.

Lamb was the head of Slough House, though you'd be forgiven for thinking him the belly. And yet, when Lech replayed their first encounter, he wondered how much to trust that initial judgement. Lamb was gross, sure – corpulent – though somehow not as obese as he appeared, as if the impression he gave of spilling out of his chair even while motionless was engineered. But when Lech had blinked and looked again, he hadn't been able to tell where that thought had come from. Lamb was fat, that was all, and had a cruel look pasted across his damp-looking features. His hair, what was left of it, might have a blond tint if it were clean; his toenails might not be poking through his socks if he cut them. This last observation was impossible to avoid, Lamb's shoeless feet being on his desk. He still wore his coat, however. The thought processes of a man who'd relax with his shoes off, his coat on, were foreign territory to Lech. Then again, the thought processes of Jackson Lamb, as revealed by their subsequent conversation, were probably *terra incognita* to the psychiatric profession as a whole.

'Oh, goodie fucking gumdrops,' he said, when Lech stepped into his room. 'Fresh meat.'

'I was assigned here temporarily,' Lech said. 'While some HR issues are sorted out.'

'HR issues,' Lamb repeated slowly. 'Not heard it called that before.' He removed his feet from the desk with surprising agility, produced a cigarette out of nowhere, lit it, farted, reached into his desk drawer, removed a bottle of whisky he slammed onto his desk top, farted again, and said, 'I don't have any bad habits myself, so maybe I'm over-censorious. But seriously, kiddy porn?' He unscrewed the cap on the bottle. 'You're the six-foot Pole I wouldn't touch that with.'

Lech Wicinski, who was five eleven, felt his teeth clench. 'I was told all details were sealed. You're not supposed to know that.'

'Yeah, a list of things I'm not supposed to know but do would be nearly as long as the list of things I know but couldn't give a toss about. Currently, you're at the top of both. And a thing you should know about me is, I hate lists.' He blew out smoke Lech hadn't noticed him inhaling. 'The ones I don't screw up and throw away, I feed into the shredder.'

Lech glanced around. The further reaches of the office were cloaked in shadow, but he couldn't make out anything that might be a shredder.

'Yeah, okay, smartarse. I improvise.' There was a dirty glass among the rubbish on his desk, and Lamb poured whisky into it; what might have been a triple, if your idea of a single was a double. 'Says on the paperwork you go by Alec. But your signature reads Lech. I'm guessing you reckoned a little ethnicity wouldn't do any harm at this stage of your career, eh? This stage being the bit right before it runs off a cliff.'

'I answer to both.'

'How very broad-minded of you. But then, we've already established your lack of boundaries.'

'My lawyer—'

'Your lawyer is a figment of your fucking imagination. No way are the Park gunna allow you a brief, not until they've decided what the outcome's gunna be. And as long as I'm popping your balloons, nobody gets assigned here temporarily. What you see is all you get. So let's make everything simple, yeah? You spend the rest of your career pushing whatever paper I see fit to send your way, or you trot off now and jump in front of a bus. I'd use the pedestrian bridge, I was you. But wait until after six, there's a sport, because it does fuck up the traffic.'

'The issue's being investigated. I'll be cleared. Because I didn't do anything.'

Jackson Lamb farted again. 'Me neither. And yet here we both are.'

'Are you always this unpleasant?'

Lamb shrugged. 'It's not an exact science.' He dropped his cigarette into a half-empty teacup. 'And you can drop the wide-eyed innocence. Here in Slough House, you're always guilty of something. Of being in Slough House, if nothing else.'

Lech stared.

'And one more thing. I don't want to have to tell you to fuck off every time I want you to fuck off. So learn to read the signals and just fuck off at the appropriate moment, right? Of which this is one. So fuck off.'

If you expected things to get worse, history would prove you right, Lech remembered. You didn't always have to wait for history, either. Sometimes the present stepped up and got on with the job.

When he'd left Lamb's room, the woman in the office opposite glanced up from her desk. There might have been sympathy on her face, but if so it was only there for a moment.

I didn't do it, he wanted to scream.

But isn't that what the guilty always said?

That advice about stepping in front of a bus, he'd thought. Let's not rule that out altogether.

For the moment, though, he trudged on through the fallen leaves of Northwick Park.

In the café the usual noises continued, but were blotted out by Clare's words. Louisa put her mug down. Min's son, Lucas, whose name she'd heard many times, but whom she'd never met. Missing. And here was his frightened mother.

She said, 'Have you been to the police?'

'Well of course I've been to the police! You think you were my first option?'

'Sorry. Sorry. What did they say?'

Clare Addison calmed as suddenly as she'd erupted. 'No, I'm . . . They took details. They've put him on a register or whatever . . . A missing persons list.'

'How old is he?'

'Seventeen.'

Seventeen: Jesus. Where did the time go? But his mother didn't need to be asked that.

Louisa said, 'He's a minor. Aren't they treating it with urgency?'

Clare looked away, towards the door. Someone was coming in, or going out. It didn't matter which. She said, 'He's had some . . . issues. In the past.'

'He's run away before?'

'He had difficulties. When Min left. And when he died.'

'Of course . . .'

'There was trouble at school, and he took off for a few days. But that's all it was, a few days.'

'And the police looked for him then?'

'There was a bit of a palaver. And there was some, well. Drugs. Cannabis, that's all.'

'Did they prosecute?'

'No, thank goodness. It was just a small amount. And that was two years ago.'

'When he was fifteen.'

God, shut up. This isn't a maths lesson.

'Yes,' Clare said. 'And after that, he . . . Things got better. I came down on him hard of course, but that's what he needed, what he wanted, really. And he settled down. Sixth-form college now. He's been doing really well.'

'But now he's disappeared?'

'And the police think he's done another bunk, that he's off getting high in some squat or other, but he isn't, I know he isn't.' Clare broke off and stared into her lap. It was a second or two before Louisa realised she was crying.

She reached awkwardly across, and laid a hand on the woman's shoulder.

Clare said, 'He's been gone three days.'

'What happened? Did he . . .' Did he what, she wondered. What did teenagers do? If her own experience was anything to go by, nothing they wanted their mothers to know about, but they were past that stage. Here his mother was, in tears, looking to a stranger for help. And it only then struck her what was going on: Clare wasn't here because Louisa and Min had been lovers. She was here because Louisa was a spook, and might have access to

43

uncommon search engines, to special forces. Clare was a frightened mother, with no space to be anything else. And desperate too, turning to Min's old colleagues for help.

'He's like his dad,' Clare said at last.

'Headstrong?' said Louisa, unable to help it. 'Prone to . . . charging off?'

'You knew him, didn't you?' Clare reached into a pocket and produced a tissue; blew her nose noisily. 'Sorry.' She lifted her cup, set it down. Brushed at her hair with a hand. 'Yes. He gets it into his head to do something, it's hard to dislodge.'

'What did he get it into his head to do?'

Clare didn't know.

But what had happened was, a few days previously, Lucas hadn't come home from college. A telephone call had established that he hadn't made it as far as college that morning, either. Clare had called the police, whose response was initially alert, but became significantly more lax once details were gathered.

'He'd taken some money from his savings account.'

'How much?'

'A few hundred pounds.'

Louisa nodded, trying to keep all expression from her face. The kid had been minted; he had a history of skipping out and getting wasted. There was only one box left unchecked:

'Does he have a girlfriend?'

'He's not just sloped off to shack up with a girl. He wouldn't do that. He wouldn't do that without letting me know.'

'I'm sorry, I'm just asking the obvious questions, that's all . . . Did he take anything other than money?'

Again the door opened, closed; again Clare looked up. It was as if she expected him to walk in and plonk himself down next to her. As if this nightmare she was living through could be wiped away as easily as that; the way real ones were, when you opened your eyes.

'A rucksack,' she said. 'Just a small one.'

Louisa mentally filled it with the things a teenage boy might think essential – a mobile phone, charger, condoms. Dick Whittington for the twenty-first century. She took a deep breath, and said what needed saying. 'I'm sorry, but it's pointless kidding around here. He left of his own accord. You must see that.'

'But why?'

'That's not for me . . . Clare, I'm sorry.' She'd apologised more this past ten minutes than in the past two years combined. And all for stuff that was less her fault than it was her business. 'But it's a good thing. If he left of his own free will, under his own steam, then he'll come back when he's ready. I'm sure he will.'

Yeah, right, because she was an expert.

She said, 'You should go home. Wait there. He'll turn up soon.'

Clare threw her a look. 'You think I'm making a fuss about nothing.'

'I read some stats not long ago,' Louisa said. Her job was all stats; she couldn't avoid them. 'Ninety per cent of missing teens come home inside of three days.'

She was pretty sure that's what she'd read.

'His three days are up.'

'Which is why you should be at home.'

'He said he wasn't worried about a student loan any more.'

'. . . Okay . . .'

Clare shot her a look. 'You don't think that's significant?'

'I don't think anything. I don't know what you mean.'

'It's something we've talked about, the cost of a degree. I've told him I'll help as much as I can, but he knows he's going to have to take out a loan. And he's been, well, not obsessing about it exactly. But it keeps coming up. He wants to travel, wants to go the States, but he's also aware that everything costs so much. But suddenly he's saying it's not a problem.'

Louisa didn't know how to respond. She said, 'What about his brother? You have two boys, right?'

'Andrew. He's two years younger.'

'And he doesn't have any idea where Lucas might have gone?'

'He says not. They fight like cat and dog half the time. They'll grow out of it, but . . . No. He has no idea.'

'And where did Lucas's savings come from? Does he have a job?'

'Not during term time. But he was working over Christmas. We were in Pembrokeshire. In Wales?'

Yeah, thanks, thought Louisa.

'We go there often, family holidays. We started when Lucas was two. So we've made friends down there, and . . .'

The way she tailed off made Louisa wonder whether any particular friend came to mind. But not her business.

'And he was working there?'

'I know someone runs a catering business, he takes on part-time help. And it pays well. So Lucas usually does a few jobs when we're down there. It's cash in hand, so . . .'

She looked up once more as the door jangled again. Despite everything, it was getting on Louisa's nerves. She said, 'Clare? He's not about to walk in. If you're expecting him, it's your home he'll turn up at.'

'It's not that, I just . . . Oh, I'm just feeling paranoid. These past few days. As if I'm being watched.'

'. . . Really?'

'I'm all over the place. It's nothing.'

Louisa finished her coffee. She played it out for a few seconds, hunting for an escape clause. She'd come expecting a showdown, or perhaps a tearful encounter and a few shared memories. But Clare had no idea she'd been more to Min than a colleague, and her missing son was a teenager with a couple of ton in his backpack and a history of going walkabout while stoned. It didn't feel like anything she should be getting involved with.

Her stonewalling technique might need working on. Clare said, 'I shouldn't have bothered you. Not on your weekend.'

'It's no bother.'

'You're right. He'll turn up. Or he won't. But that's no concern of yours, is it?'

She gathered herself together and stood.

'He'll be fine,' Louisa said. 'I'm sure he will.'

'You're sure,' said Clare. 'That's okay, then.'

'What is it you expected me to do?'

'You work for the security services,' Clare said, a bit louder than Louisa would have preferred in a crowded café. 'I thought you might think of something. Not as a favour to me, or even to Lucas. But you were fucking Min, weren't you? I'd have hoped that counted for something.'

This time, the door slammed instead of just clicking shut. But then, Clare put some shoulder into it.

Excellent Saturday morning so far, thought Louisa. But as she was in town anyway, she might as well get some shopping done.

Lech remembered the memorial as soon as he laid eyes on it. It was a shrine, almost; a drystone alcove, under a tree. There was a statue of the Virgin, of course, and vases of flowers, and saucers holding unlit candles. He wondered about lighting one, but didn't have a match, and anyway, it wouldn't flicker for a moment before the wind put it out of its misery. Besides, who was he kidding? He read the inscription, or started reading it, then hurried to the end, cherry-picking words: *To commemorate the Polish ex-servicemen who lived here with their families from 1948 to 1970.* Ordeal, deportation, Allied victory. And everything that followed, including, eventually, him.

He could hear shouting from the garages, horseplay, and he closed his eyes, pretending that this was a normal day, and the impulse that brought him here a Saturday whimsy. Sara would be wondering where he was. If he turned his phone on it would confirm this, with a series of irritated chirrups.

But Sara, at least, believed in him – or would do, if she knew what was going on, which she didn't. He'd explained that it was stuff, that's all; a protocol issue; that he'd been seconded to an office near the Barbican for the time being. Even he hadn't known what 'protocol issue' meant.

The thing is, they found child porn on my laptop. So everyone's a little tetchy. You want to catch a movie, or shall we have an early one?

Someone had stubbed out a nearly complete cigarette on the stonework, and left it nestled in a rift. He looked at it for a moment or two, then walked on.

When he ran his mind over the weeks prior to the cataclysm, one thing stuck out. He'd done a favour for an acquaintance, a Service drone called John Bachelor, who worked the milk round, nannying superannuated spooks. Just because you'd put your life on the line back in the Dark Ages didn't mean you could get to Sainsbury's on your own here and now. Spooks got old too. So other spooks who were never much cop were assigned to hold their hands, or do their shopping for them. That had been Bachelor's role: a straight-to-DVD career. Lech had met him just once before, at the funeral of one of his grandfather's comrades. It seemed, in retrospect, an appropriately Polish encounter; they'd spent an afternoon drinking, talking about someone neither had known especially well, who was dead. And months later there'd been a bill to pay, because Bachelor had asked a favour; that he run a name through the Service search engines; a name, it turned out, that was flagged – a person of interest. Which meant Lech was trespassing. So he'd shut the search down and waited for shit to fall from on high, which he'd expected to take the form of a finger-wagging email, or a visit from a Dog. But nothing happened. Bachelor had rung a day or so later, calling it off; whatever had sparked his need had died down. And that was it: maybe nothing of consequence, except it was the only thing out of the ordinary in the period before the shitstorm.

No way of chasing it up now, either. He was tainted twice over, a pervert and a slow horse, and doors were closing, every way he looked. Any further research, he'd have to use chicken entrails and a dowsing rod.

There was a glitter of wings as a pigeon took to the air.

Lech turned his phone on and checked his screen. Four unread texts and seven missed calls. All from Sara, who was unaware he was a hundred miles away.

As he walked back to his car, passing the shuttered huts, their barred windows, he tried to think about his grandparents again; about the lives they'd made after all they'd come through. Object lesson in overcoming adversity.

But mostly he was thinking about Slough House.

4

Mondays are bastards, through and through; Thursdays are waiting days, neither one thing nor the other. Fridays: everyone knows what they're like. But this Wednesday, the day of the funeral, had stepped outside the calendar, and had no borders River could see. Dressing had been like putting on a costume for a role he hadn't rehearsed. And the feeling in his stomach, a Sunday-night anxiety, had been with him on waking and continued to grow. It made little sense – the bad thing had already happened. Still, he felt as if he'd been diagnosed with a condition that was serious and complicated, but about which he remembered nothing. He'd just have to wait and see.

The O.B. had spent his retirement years in Kent, but would be buried in London, as Rose had been. The memory of that day was one River kept sealed, and he and the old man had rarely talked of it. But it had been there in their silences; in the gaps between the stories his grandfather told. When River arrived at the house unexpectedly, he had sometimes felt he was interrupting a conversation; that even now, with Rose in her grave, the pair shared secrets. Not all spies' partners knew the truth, that their other half lived on Spook Street. But Rose had always been in the know. She'd held the door open between her husband's different addresses, allowing him to step into the light when the day's dark deeds were done.

But all that was long ago. For the last year of his life, his grandfather's conversations had had no anchor, and whether he'd been talking to Rose, who was absent, or River, who was not, made no difference; he would drift with the prevailing current, his conversation spinning into eddies or battering invisible rocks. All his life, River had heard tales from the old man's past, the failures, the victories, the stalemates, and he had learned to read between the lines enough to tell which was which. But no longer. The scraps he heard now were remnants from a shot memory; tattered flags blown by conflicting winds. You'd need a map to know which side the old man had been on. Which might have been the last secret he needed to impart to his grandson; that in the end, all lines blurred. That no day had firm borders.

But but but. This day had come.

So had his mother.

He hadn't been sure she'd turn up. Their phone conversation, the day the O.B. died, had been one of tortured small talk, 'So apart from that, how are you?' being his mother's most memorable contribution. She was currently 'wintering' in Brighton, a term he'd only heard her use in Mediterranean contexts before, and he wondered if she were lowering her ceilings; whether the comfort the late Mr Dunstable had left her in had begun to leak at the seams. He hoped not. River hadn't lived with his mother since he was seven, when she'd left him at her parents' door, and his fading memories of the life they'd shared were scrappy and unfulfilled. Until lately, when he'd thought about those years, the context had been one of bad parenting, but now he thought about how unhappy she must have been, how desperate. He didn't think she'd survive another taste of that. He was pretty certain he wouldn't survive hearing about it.

So it was a relief when she arrived at St Leonard's in a taxi she'd evidently hired on the south coast: evidence of economy measures – travelling by train, or, God forbid, coach – would have indicated not merely penury but a character transplant. He'd seen enough of that with the O.B.

He'd been waiting at the roadside end of the gravel drive, next to the eight-foot hedge that shielded the chapel from view. Once she'd waved her car off she hugged him, and he felt for a moment that life could have been different. But only for a moment, and only until she spoke.

'How did you get to be so *big*?' she complained. 'Having a son your size. It's very ageing.'

'Yeah, I'm sorry about that.'

'I don't suppose it's entirely your fault.'

There were times he could admire his mother's self-absorption: it was a rare example of her showing total commitment. 'You decided to come, then.'

She looked around. She was holding a single lily wrapped in cellophane, and now the hugging was done she resumed a two-handed grip on it, as if it were an assault weapon. 'Where is everyone?'

'The service doesn't start for forty-five minutes.'

'You said eleven sharp!'

'And it's quarter past now,' he explained. 'Which is why I lied.'

Cruel as it was to deprive Isobel of her big entrance, he felt he had enough to cope with already.

'I suppose you think that was clever.'

He kind of did, but could see it wasn't an argument he'd win in a hurry. 'I wasn't sure how long you'd be able to stay. And I thought you might want a chance to talk.'

'I think we both know where you get your deviousness from.' She stroked his cheek. 'It's a good job you inherited some of my charm along with it.'

That was another debate he wasn't about to get involved in.

She tucked her arm through his. 'Come on, then. Let's look at the final resting place. Plot, I should say. Yes, in his case, definitely a plot.'

He'd give her that one, though he was pretty sure she'd worked it out on the journey. But he was glad, even so, that she was here, and they walked round the side of the chapel together.

'Wonder if he'll jump in the grave.'

'This isn't *Hamlet.*'

'Does that happen in *Hamlet?*' said Lamb. 'I was thinking of *Carry On Screaming.*'

They were in the back of a taxi, Lamb taking up seventy per cent of the available space, and Catherine wishing the day over. She didn't like funerals – who did? – and hadn't known David Cartwright in any meaningful sense. Once or twice long ago she'd encountered him, or taken minutes at a meeting he'd attended; and much later, she'd had the brief keeping of him while River feared his life was at risk. He'd been lost to dementia by then, and if it were true that such conditions reveal the secret self, David Cartwright had been mostly cunning and fear, the two sides of his nature entwined and snapping at each other like fox cubs. She shook the memory away; pictured, instead, the bottle she'd buy on her way home, then squashed that thought too. Sitting next to Lamb, your secrets weren't safe. He had a way of seeing inside your head, and holding what he found up to the light, for his amusement.

She just hoped he wasn't going to talk about death the whole journey.

'So when you cop it,' he said, 'how'd you want to go? Buried, cremated or eaten by cats?'

'I don't keep cats,' she said.

'You don't have to. Crafty bastards, cats. They'll find a way in.'

'Can we talk about something else?'

Lamb cast her a malevolent look. 'Why not? Heard any good jokes lately?'

'If life's taught me anything, it's that we won't find the same things funny.'

It had also taught her that when she least wanted Lamb's company, she'd end up in the back of a cab with him. Like those cats he thought crafty bastards, he responded to being shunned by singling you out for attention. 'Oh, I don't know,' he said. 'Here's a good one. Guess how our new recruit pissed on his chips?'

Lech Wicinski. Catherine had assigned him to Roderick Ho's office; both Louisa and Shirley had space, but Shirley could be volatile on days ending with y, and Louisa had made it clear she didn't want to share. It was like wrangling teenagers. But as to how Wicinski had blotted his copybook, Catherine didn't know and didn't want to. Apart from anything else, mere blots didn't warrant Slough House. Most recruits had set fire to their copybook, shoved it through First Desk's letterbox, then tried to douse the flames by urinating through the slot.

She said, 'Disciplinary files are supposed to be sealed. You'll have HR on your case if you start talking about your team's misdemeanours.'

'Really? I never knew that.' He considered for a moment. 'Good job I'm the soul of discretion, or things could have got embarrassing.'

'Imagine.'

'But anyway, they caught him with child porn on his laptop.'

Catherine Standish closed her eyes.

'I know, right? Time was you could pass it off as an allergy to pubic hair. But these days, you want to see pubic hair, you've really got to go looking. If the *Daily Mail*'s to be believed.' He adopted a pious expression. 'Personally, I wouldn't know. But anyway, yeah, Lech Wicinski. He's Polish, by the way.'

'I did not know that,' she said, in a flat tone.

'Well, smarten up. The name should've been a clue. I'm not saying all Poles are kiddy fiddlers. Wouldn't hire one as a baby-sitter, though.'

The idea of Lamb being in need of a baby-sitter, for any reason whatsoever but especially one involving an actual baby, was too upsetting to contemplate. Which was why Catherine responded, rather than allowing the moment to drift away at its own speed. 'He doesn't look the type.'

'And what does the type look like?'

He had a point. They didn't all sport tracksuits and medallions.

She said, 'That's a criminal offence. How come he's been assigned to us?'

'Maybe they think I'm collecting the set.' He counted off on his fingers. 'Fuck-ups, basket-cases, druggies and drunks. Now a kiddy porn peeper. When I've got a dog-botherer, I win a case of cutlery.'

'And what would you do with cutlery? You mostly eat with your fingers.'

'You're very confrontational lately. I have to walk on eggshells, God knows why. You're too old to be on the rag.' He sniffed suspiciously. 'Don't tell me you're hitting the bottle.'

'You're asking me? You wouldn't be able to work it out for yourself?'

'You alkies can be devious. It's the reason no one trusts you.'

She said, 'As long as we're on the subject, I hope you don't plan to drink during the actual ceremony. Those who are genuinely grieving might take it the wrong way.'

'There's no point having a hip flask if you don't use it.'

'That's not a hip flask. It's a small bottle.'

'Jesus. Who put you in pedants' corner?' Lamb produced the offending bottle, unscrewed the top and took a swallow. 'And a less tolerant man would take issue with that. Genuinely grieving, I mean.'

'You're not seriously going to pretend you're mourning his passing. So why are you even here?'

'You're expecting me to say, to make sure the old bastard's dead, aren't you?'

She didn't reply.

'And well, yeah, that's part of it. Okay, so he was off his head the last year, but if I'd done half what he got up to I'd pretend to go doolally too, in case the busies turned up with a charge sheet and a bucket full of questions. So maybe he was on his game the whole time, and he's faked his death. He'd not be the first.'

She stared at him, mouth not entirely closed.

'We're spies, Standish. All kinds of outlandish shit goes on. You want some of this?'

She shook her head.

'Like I said, devious. A blind man could tell you do.' He put the bottle away, but its odour lingered in the air, and caught the back of her throat.

'You hated him.'

56

'I hate a lot of people. Doesn't mean I won't get lonely when they're all dead.'

You're lonely now, she thought but didn't say. You're lonely now.

'And what about Wicinski? Lech.' She had to force herself to use his name. Some allegations tainted every syllable, even when they were just that: allegations.

'There's an ongoing investigation, unquote,' Lamb said. 'While facts are assessed and outcomes determined. Unquote.'

'So he wasn't actually caught red-handed?'

'One-handed, you mean. But no. His laptop's guilty as charged, but his dick's still in the dock.'

'Which means, for the moment at least, we regard him as innocent. Unless I'm misremembering the basic principles of British justice.'

'Your faith in human nature really pisses me off, you know that?'

'As good a reason as any for clinging onto it.'

The taxi gave a lurch as it pulled away from a set of lights, and the motion made everything drunken for a second: Catherine was in a strange loose place, and rattled around, unanchored. And then the moment passed, though the taste at the back of her throat remained, as it likely always would. The taste she'd never forget, and would always be straining to remember.

She blinked, and her vision blurred. She blinked again, and it returned.

On her way home, she'd buy another bottle. Meanwhile, there was a funeral to get through. She hoped that would happen without Jackson Lamb causing any gross moments.

And she hoped River didn't jump into any graves.

Which didn't seem likely, but Lamb had a point.

All kinds of outlandish shit went on.

The funeral was in Hampstead. St Leonard's was a discreet brick building in a quiet close: services on alternate Sundays, though the alert might notice that these seldom came to pass. Perhaps this was a sign of dwindling congregations; perhaps an indication that the powers that be considered this particular enclave well served already, and that other, less moneyed areas might benefit more from the Church's resources. But it was true that, if regular services were not on the menu, St Len's put on a lovely funeral. The graveyard at its rear was a calm oasis; each corner with its own tree, its own bench. Sitting there, you could forget there was a city mere streets away. You could bask in the quiet company of the dead.

And if it seemed strange that most of the buried had no obvious local connection, there were few to keep track of such oddities. Funerals are private affairs, and never more so than at the Spooks' Chapel, where many cover stories had been laid to rest and last words said over careers that had blossomed in dark corners, some so successfully that even close friends and family remained unaware of their true nature. But, as Jackson Lamb had been known to remark, suits' bodies were easier to find than those of joes, and messy ends didn't lead to tidy burials. So inside the chapel, on the west wall, were plaques to the memory of those who hadn't made their way home, a display some called the Last Dead Letter Drop. The names on the plaques weren't always those their owners had been born with, but there was a case for saying that the name you died with carried more weight. The identity you never let go of; that, in the end, let go of you instead.

Though of course, thought River, the O.B.'s identity had slipped away from him before he gave up breathing.

His mother at his side, he walked among the gravestones towards a freshly dug hole. It was cold, because how could it be anything else? And the ground was hard, which meant someone had had a job of it; clearing a space for David Cartwright. Did you tip gravediggers? River couldn't recall the subject coming up.

Isobel's grip on his arm tightened. 'I know you think I hated him.'

'Well, yes. But only because you told me you hated him.'

'It was complicated.'

River knew how complicated it was. His mother, though, didn't know he knew that, or he didn't think she did. That was how complicated it was: people not knowing how much other people knew they knew. It was possible that other families were like this; ones without spies in them.

He said, 'I'm glad you're here.'

'He'd lost his mind, hadn't he?'

'There were . . . glimpses of him. Right to the end.' This was a lie. The last sight he'd had of his grandfather – the man, not the shell – had been months ago.

And he wasn't sure why he didn't say as much. His mother didn't need her feelings tiptoed round. She hadn't spoken to her father in years. When she'd called him the Old Bastard, she'd meant precisely that. It was River who'd diluted the words; doused their spite with affection.

On the other hand, since learning what had driven father and daughter apart, he was less inclined to blame his mother. Things had happened to Isobel that had been part of a game she hadn't known she'd been drafted into. She had lost her heart, and borne a son, to Frank Harkness, an American spook, though 'lost her heart' was a kind way of phrasing it. In reality Harkness had stolen it, then traded it back to David Cartwright for various favours. Had he not done so, River's life would have taken a very different course – he'd have been a soldier in another man's army – so he supposed he couldn't complain that things had worked out as they had, but he was aware that the bargain had been a foul one, and Isobel's heart had not been returned intact. Certainly it never opened in her father's direction again. It probably explained why River himself had always felt his mother's absence, even on those occasions when she was present. Like now, approaching the O.B.'s grave.

It was next to Rose's, of course, on whom the earth had settled. They stopped beside it, and Isobel placed the lily on the headstone.

'A lily for Rose,' she said, and again River had the feeling he was an audience for a rehearsed moment.

While she stood contemplating her mother's resting place, or planning her next gesture, River looked into the hole that would soon accommodate his grandfather. The O.B. had filled the space a father might have done in River's life, while his actual father pursued a mad crusade. That venture had come to an end now, or River assumed it had. But with Frank, who knew? He was out in the world somewhere, and pretty certainly hadn't hung up his sword and shield. Though whatever use he was putting them to was probably confined to the shadows.

He looked at his mother, who was dabbing her eyes with a tissue, and tossed a mental coin: benefit of the doubt.

'Are you okay?'

'Oh . . . I'll be fine.'

'He loved you, you know. They both did.'

'I never had cause to doubt my mother's love.'

Which sounded like it had been put through translation software. But again: benefit of the doubt.

His mother had taken hold of his arm again, and he led her away, along the path to its far corner, where it curved and headed back towards the front. But she paused there and reached into her bag, from which she produced cigarettes and a lighter.

'You're still doing that?'

'You're my son, not my GP.'

'And what does your GP have to say about it?'

Isobel lit a cigarette, and watched smoke float into the branches overhead. 'I'm sure I can't imagine.'

From where they were standing they could see past the body of the chapel to the drive, where a limo was pulling up. River supposed he should be there to greet arrivals, but wasn't sure of the protocol. When you buried a grandfather, people queued to shake your hand. Did the same hold true when you buried a spy? Or was that an occasion for furtive glances, mumbled code? Whatever the case, River abandoned all thought of it when he saw who was emerging from the limo: Lady Di Taverner, newly appointed First

Desk, and the woman responsible for his exile to Slough House.

Down the road, a man sat in a car. His hazard lights were flashing, as if to indicate a temporary, unwilled stop, and he was talking on his phone, or seemed to be. His lips were moving; the phone was near his mouth. Even so, his presence earned a tap on the window.

He flipped a switch, and the glass rolled down.

'Can I ask if you're going to be long, sir?'

This from a handy-looking gent in an overcoat. The man said, ''Scuse one sec,' into his phone, securing it between chin and shoulder while he produced an ID card which he flashed at the intruder with something between a squint and a smile: *You're just doing your job, mate, we both know that.* The newcomer took the card, studied it a moment, and handed it back with a nod. As he walked back the way he'd come, the car window hummed upwards again.

Out loud, the man in the car said, 'And don't you just feel like you've had a narrow escape, buddy? One of you Dogs gets a long hard look at a CIA pass, the next words you hear are usually "black, two sugars".'

This might have earned a chuckle if there'd been anyone on the other end of the phone.

He carried on chatting to nobody while a limo pulled onto the chapel's drive: long, black, funeral issue, fuck knows why. You might as well turn up in a clown car, have everyone tumble out in a heap. Make no difference to the dead. But instead, from the back of this limo emerged a woman; from the far side, a man.

That the American could identify both should have been a problem, but the people it should have been a problem for were happy with a squint and a smile and a fake ID. The pair from the limo disappeared from view. Another car was arriving; there'd be a fleet of the damn things soon. He wondered how many of their occupants felt genuine stirrings of sorrow. Let's face it, an ancient spook like David Cartwright, if people had the nerve to offer the tribute he deserved, as many would be taking a leak on his coffin as removing their hats. You didn't end a life on Spook Street without more enemies than friends; not if you'd done things properly. On the other hand, Cartwright was a legend, and it's always sad when legends die. It underlines the fact that shit like death can happen to anyone.

Place was a security nightmare, though – they called it the Spooks' Chapel, which summed it up: why didn't they pitch a neon sign out front? He'd just watched the Park's First Desk arrive, followed by Oliver Nash, head of the Limitations Committee, who, okay, wasn't going to sell tickets on his own, but if you were in the know – if you knew who pulled the levers on this secret train they rode – you'd definitely want to target, if you were a bad actor. One well-timed intervention and you could take out the whole of the Service's top tier, and much of its dead wood, without pausing between breaths. But then, that was the trouble with England – with Britain – it was so in love with its myths and legends, it couldn't see what a ball and chain they were. No, if you wanted to stay ahead of the bad guys, you had to cut history loose. That was his considered opinion. He had memories – who didn't? – but his baggage was all carry-on; he could walk away from any identity he'd ever had without a backward glance. He certainly wouldn't hang around to bury his dead. And if he did, he wouldn't bury them in a tourist attraction. The Spooks' Chapel. You might as well print pamphlets.

Some of this he said out loud, into the dead phone, and if anyone was watching they'd note his animation and assume he was talking to someone he could pull rank on: an underling or a girlfriend, not a boss or a wife. And maybe, thinking he was CIA, they'd assume he was here to pay his respects to a one-time hero of a rival service, because they were all in this together, even if only one of them was going into a hole today. So yeah, that's what they'd think; that he was representing the Company, and he'd hang up his call and dip his head when they carried the coffin inside.

But he wasn't here to pay respects.

He was here collecting faces.

And this, anyway, solved River's protocol problem: if they stood right where they were they could watch arrivals without having to worry about whom to acknowledge, whom to discreetly ignore. Lady Di, for instance, and the tubby man she'd come with: what Lamb would call a suit, by which Lamb meant it was only the pinstripes holding him upright. Whoever he was, Lady Di was a difficulty. Responsible for River's exile, because though – on paper – he'd crashed King's Cross, a messed-up training exercise of a kind no junior spook could walk away from, the mess-up hadn't been of his making but hers. History now, but it still churned River to see her.

His mother was regarding him, an odd expression on her face. 'Are you all right, dear?'

'It's my grandfather's funeral.'

But she'd followed the direction of his scrutiny. 'Oh, I say.' She watched Taverner walk the gravelled path to the chapel door. 'A little . . . *mature* for you, dear.'

'She's . . .' He hesitated, but what the hell. His mother was a Service child. 'First Desk. That's why she's here.'

'Well, she's nicely turned out, I'll give her that. But you ought to set your sights on someone your own age.'

'I'm not—'

'Or your own wage bracket. That's Chanel she's wearing.' She eyed her son critically. 'Whereas, well, not to criticise. But where did that suit actually come from? A garage forecourt?'

'They had a surprisingly wide selection.'

'You're going to need that sense of humour if you don't start earning money soon. And who's this?'

This was Louisa Guy, who saw them and sketched a wave, but went straight inside. River was glad to see her. She hadn't known his grandfather, and hadn't come because he was a Service legend: she'd come because River was a friend, and if River drew up a list of his current friendships, he'd be chewing his pencil once he'd written her name. But he was also happy she'd headed in. Friend didn't necessarily mean he wanted her to meet his mother. There were some conversations you didn't want to have.

And some you couldn't avoid.

'A little more your league, dear.'

'She's a colleague.'

'Like I say.'

'It's a funeral, Mother. Not a speed-dating group.'

'Just as well. You're not exactly in a hurry, are you?' She wrapped both hands round his elbow. 'But I don't mean to pressure you. If there's anything you want to tell me, just come out and say it. Your grandfather was an old reactionary, but I've always had very liberal views.'

'I'm not gay.'

'Well, if you're sure.'

'And if I was, why imagine I'm fixated on Di Taverner?'

'It's a not uncommon pattern. But don't forget, dear. Liberal views.'

His sexual identity, income bracket and dress sense having been taken care of, River wondered whether they could now focus on the morning's actual business. He looked away. Frost had rimed the headstones' edges, and crystallised the bouquets that graced some graves; it had captured, too, a hundred spiderwebs, transforming them to works of antique beauty: jewellery fit to adorn the Egyptian dead. Not that the O.B. would have considered himself a pharaoh. But he'd have enjoyed advising one; whispering strategies into the ear of power. That would have been his role whatever his era.

The lily his mother had placed on Rose's stone had been glazed already by the light, and might have been sculpted there. River wished – he didn't know what he wished. He felt an unanchored yearning; a desire that things weren't like this. But he couldn't wish his grandparents alive. He couldn't face watching them die again.

He felt a tug on his sleeve: his mother. A taxi had arrived.

'And that's him, is it?'

It did not surprise him that Isobel should so easily recognise a man she'd never met.

'That's Jackson, yes.'

'I thought he was supposed to be some kind of master spy.'

'I'm not sure anyone's ever decided what kind of spy he is.'

'A badly dressed one, that's clear. Does he realise it's a funeral?'

'I'm pretty certain it was mentioned on the invite.'

Catherine was with Lamb. She seemed grey, a creature of the weather. Funerals had that effect, unless there was something else going on.

'We should make our way inside,' he said. Just saying the words shifted something inside him: this was really happening, a memory he'd never lose. Today he was burying his grandfather.

They walked back the long way round, and passed the waiting grave once more. River had the feeling it should have had more to say for itself; should have been an empty, yawning terror. But it was only a hole in the ground, and that somehow made it worse.

Louisa had passed a man in a car up the road, perfectly placed to clock attendees, but if he was anyone to worry about the Dogs would have sorted him out. Though they were Dogs without a walker at the moment – she'd heard from Emma Flyte at the weekend. Louisa had been in the shower, and the call had gone to voicemail. Emma sounded pissed but against a quiet background.

I just got screwed. Does that make me a member of your club?

A pause, a swallow.

Yeah, well, anyway. I told Taverner to fuck off, so I'm now what they call looking for a new position. Should be fun.

Another pause.

So give me a call sometime. We can swap notes on what it's like being booted out of Regent's Park. It's Emma, by the way.

Louisa had already gathered that much.

She wished she'd been there, to see Emma give Taverner the finger.

Who was here, of course, duty-mourning. There were others she half-recognised too, faces glimpsed back in the day, riding the lifts to the Park's top floors. If things had been different, River Cartwright would have been down the front; chief mourner and heir apparent. As it was, he was loitering under a tree, with a woman Louisa supposed was his mother. He'd slip in soon, and make his way to the front, but it wasn't like the great and good would be lining up to offer their sorrows. The way things might have been. A funeral a pretty obvious occasion to flip through that book of swatches.

But enough of other people's problems. What should she do about Lucas Harper?

You were fucking Min. I'd have hoped that counted for something.

She hadn't been, of course. Well, she had been, but that wasn't what it had been about; she had loved him, he had loved her, they'd have shared their lives, or made the attempt, if he hadn't died. So where did that leave her? Not in Clare Harper's debt, that was certain. Addison. Whatever. So why was it niggling at her, this feeling that she'd turned her back when she should have offered a hand? Min's boys had been a fuzzy image on the periphery of their relationship, part of his life she had no access to. She hadn't hassled him to make introductions; had assumed that that would happen sooner or later, mentally filing it as an ordeal her future self would handle. And here she was: her future self. Niggled at by responsibilities a younger Louisa had avoided.

But Min's son had left home, that was all, taking his savings with him. A bad idea, but at seventeen a lot of bad ideas had a certain attraction. Louisa could think of a few she'd had herself; Clare too, probably. But there was no doubt Clare was suffering. Louisa thought of the way she'd startled every time the coffee shop door opened. It was natural, to become paranoid at such times. She'd spend her nights awake, blurry with fear. It would be like grief.

Whose soundtrack started even as she had the thought; something grey and sonorous from the organ above. It seemed designed to mark time;

not so much its current passage as those stretches forever gone. It made her think of Min, of course. She hadn't attended his funeral. Too angry. If she had, she'd have met – or seen – Lucas; would have a mental picture of him based in reality, instead of imagining a younger Min; the same half-smile; the same look of concentration when sending a text or checking a score. She had a whole catalogue of images to flick through, from a relatively short time together. What would a lifetime's memories look like? It was already too late to tell.

If Min hadn't died, they'd have lasted – sitting here at someone else's postscript, this felt like a truth. They could have shared a life together, once they'd swallowed the bitter pill about their careers, and jumped ship – happy-ever-afters weren't much of a thing around Slough House: you couldn't have the one within the other. Too late now. And Louisa could feel herself getting into the funeral vibe; tears ready to flow, though misattributed tears; nothing to do with the deceased . . .

River walked past, arm in arm with his mother, and the music grew louder, and the service was ready to begin.

He'd seen the face he had come to collect, he was ninety per cent sure of that. Had taken a photo. So what he should do now was leave, but something was holding him in place; the sense of unfinished business. That was always the way with funerals, except in those rare cases where you were burying someone you'd killed yourself. That was less of a joke than it might have been if someone else had made it but he thrust the thought aside as he turned his hazard lights off, put his phone away, climbed out of the car.

The Dog who'd checked him out earlier watched as he approached but didn't challenge him; nodded, rather, from his sentry position by the hedge. Jesus, mate. Do your job. An organ was droning. They'd be lined up in pews now; heads bowed, attention elsewhere. Instead of joining them, he skirted the building and found the graveyard, in the far corner of which a hole was waiting. He lit a cigarette, thinking about those he'd seen heading into St Len's earlier. River, of course, and his mother. Isobel had aged gracefully, presumably at the same speed as himself, though she'd taken care to slow down on the curves, or had some first-class mechanics hammering the dings out every other lap. As for River, he was still young enough to take the knocks and stay standing, or get back on his feet afterwards. A nice trick, soon lost. River would learn.

He inhaled, breathed out; the smoke torn apart on the wind. He should leave, he reminded himself, but approached the graveside anyway.

Some of the others, he could put a name to. The fat, badly dressed man: that would be Jackson Lamb. Fat didn't mean soft, if the stories were true. He'd worn a sly smile, as if finding grim humour in the surroundings, and not only because it was a boneyard. No, Lamb looked the type who'd find grim humour in a kindergarten; who'd find most things blackly funny because of who he was, and what he'd been through; because otherwise he'd sit up at night wondering whether to put a bullet through his brain. He'd had a woman with him, one of his crew. They called them the slow horses. Slough House/slow horse; it was clever, in that very English way; the kind that expressed itself in word play and crossword clues, and was fuck-all use. Look at the Dog out front. Though to be fair, David Cartwright would have had that slacker on a charge.

David Cartwright, though, was beyond any such measures, as the waiting grave underlined. There was no stone yet, of course. Names, dates, came later. The first order of business was planting the dead. Any moment now the chapel's back door would open, and the bearers would carry him out, and that would be the last touch of daylight he'd know. Comes to us all in the end.

But at least I outlived you, you old bastard, thought Frank Harkness, as he tossed his still burning cigarette into the grave.

The funeral was the usual mess: litany and music interrupting a stream of disconnected memories. River felt actively present one minute out of two.

The music had been chosen by Rose Cartwright, long ago. Her husband might have the nation's security in his keeping, she'd once confided in River, but anything more important fell into her domain. River had retrieved the instructions from the drawer where she'd filed them and emailed them to the funeral director, but had no memory of the titles; no idea what he'd been listening to. Throughout, he'd kept glancing at his mother. Widowhood had bestowed respectability, but the role of grieving daughter seemed beyond her, at least where her father was concerned. At Rose's interment there had been feeling. But here and now, she seemed wooden; almost bored. As if this final duty were a chore.

And now they were outside, and the coffin being lowered into the ground. There was a good crowd, thirty or more; many of them unknown to him. He expected their names would strike bells though; among them some who had figured in the O.B.'s tales; stories of labyrinthine deviousness; of actions carried out to convince others that certain knowledge was in our possession, or not in our possession; that certain facts held sway, or never had. A wilderness of mirrors, the land of spooks. Nothing you saw meant what it seemed, apart from those times when it did. Telling the two apart was the tricky bit. Knowing which was real, which the reflection.

Ashes to ashes.

Diana Taverner had nodded at him; had switched her phone to silent as a mark of respect, and hadn't sent more than three emails since the service began. Jackson, too, was uncharacteristically restrained, meaning he hadn't started a brawl yet. He'd subjected Isobel to one of his visual audits, though: a frank appraisal which in some men might have indicated sexual interest, but with Lamb, thank God, was transgressive in a different way: he was measuring her like a joe does a contact, wondering if she could be trusted. River could have saved him the effort. The coffin touched earth, and the world blurred. That was it, then. He raised his eyes skyward to a mass of cloud, then turned to his mother again, who didn't look back; he blinked twice, then saw in the far corner of the graveyard a leafless tree sheltering a bench, and a figure upon it, watching him.

He blinked a third time, but the figure didn't disappear.

It was Frank Harkness.

'Okay, so he didn't jump in the grave,' Lamb said later. 'But, you know. Next best thing.'

Which was that River had leaped over it, scattering those on the other side, who included Lady Di, Oliver Nash, the vicar, and an elderly woman who, it turned out, had been one of the O.B.'s neighbours, and under the impression that David Cartwright had been a big wheel in the Department of Transport. Given that, she handled it rather well; better, anyway, than Nash, who windmilled backwards before falling over a headstone. River was history by then; had vanished round the far side of St Len's, giving chase.

'Dear God,' Catherine said.

Louisa appeared at her side. 'Was that who I think it was?'

'I didn't get a good look. You're not going to follow?'

'In these heels?'

Lamb said, 'Well, supercalifragilisticfuckmealadocious. And people say funerals are glum affairs.' He slotted a cigarette into his mouth.

Alone among the company, Isobel Cartwright seemed unaffected. She remained standing by the grave with her head bowed, her eyes closed. Those around her shifted away a little. This specific situation might not be covered in etiquette manuals, but common sense suggested breathing space.

With Diana Taverner conducting operations, and a fresh-faced Dog taking an arm apiece, Oliver Nash rose from the grave. Not his own, but even a resurrection by proxy must feel like a second chance. 'I thought mourners were supposed to rend their own garments,' he snapped. He freed his arms from his helpers' grip and bent to check a split seam. 'Not bystanders.'

Taverner came to join Lamb. When she spoke, her lips hardly moved. 'Why do I sense your hand in this?'

Lamb saw no reason to adjust his volume. 'Because you have a nasty fucking mind?'

'One of your crew just made a circus out of a Service funeral. Why would he do that?'

'I wouldn't rule out instructions in the will.' Lamb lit his cigarette: decorum had clearly sailed. 'The old bastard had a sense of humour, after all.'

'You're sure about that?'

'Hell, he rescued Cartwright's career. He was either having a laugh or losing his marbles long before anyone noticed.'

Taverner said, 'Who was under that tree?'

'Grim reaper?'

The funeral was breaking up, the way a wedding might if someone dropped the just-cause-and-impediment bomb. The more obvious Service retirees slipped away, to avoid a debriefing, or just on general principles. Not being near an ongoing scene was second nature to joes and handlers alike. Those who'd known the O.B. as a retired civil servant, on the other hand, were clearly awaiting an explanation, ideally one involving twisted family secrets. Taverner, well practised at screwing lids down tight, passed among them: grandson, always unstable; unhinged by grief, poor thing. If River's mother caught this, she didn't allow it to ruffle her. She might have been a solitary mourner at an ancient grave.

From somewhere distant, as if playing on a different channel, came a chorus of vehicular complaint: a screaming of brakes, a wailing of horns.

'Does it count if it's interrupted?' Lamb asked Catherine. 'I mean, is he properly buried yet or do we have to start again?'

'That was River's father, wasn't it?' Catherine was better than Taverner at speaking without seeming to, no one but Lamb could have caught her words. You'd have thought she'd had less practice, but a closeted alcoholic picks up tricks.

'Yep.'

'Was he there the whole time?'

'He was behind the tree to start with. I assumed he was having a piss. Not everyone treats sanctified ground with respect.' He belched smoke. 'That was before I clocked who it was.'

The tree was fifty yards away, and the figure had been wearing a cap pulled low. It was easy to forget that Lamb hadn't always occupied an office, with the blind down.

'Someone should go after River.'

'And spoil his fun?'

Catherine thought: the last time they met, River's father had dropped him in the Thames. Any reunion they were having wouldn't involve hugs and tears.

Oliver Nash was smoothing things over with the vicar; something about the stresses and pressures of spook life. Nash would know about such things. He had the figure of a man who watched a lot of TV.

Louisa said, 'Why do you think he came? He must have known he'd not be welcome.'

'If Frank Harkness only went places he was welcome,' said Lamb, 'he'd have the social life of Julian Assange.'

'He had history with David Cartwright,' said Catherine. 'Is it so strange he'd want to see him buried?'

'Yes.'

'Not to mention Isobel. Maybe he wanted to see her again. I'm talking about human responses here. I appreciate that it must sound like Mandarin to you.'

Lamb replied with a mellifluous jangle of syllables, then tossed his cigarette away. It bounced off a nearby headstone, and dropped into a tin pot. 'That's the only Mandarin I know,' he said. 'And if the answer's more than twenty quid, you've priced yourself out of the market.'

Calling Lamb's bluff would be a full-time occupation, and unlikely to pay off in the long run.

Catherine said, 'And then there's River.'

'Who wants to kill him,' Louisa said.

'And who has a tendency to walk into a trap when one's offered.'

'Except when he runs,' said Louisa.

Lamb said, 'If Harkness wanted to set a trap for River, he'd not have picked a public occasion. He might be a show-off, but he's a professional and values his skin. No, he was here for something else, and given his track record, we should probably be bothered by that.'

'Maybe River will catch him and make him tell,' said Louisa.

'Yeah,' said Lamb. 'And we can all live happily ever after.'

Louisa looked to the corner around which River had vanished. 'I wish I'd worn different shoes,' she said.

'Imagine how I feel,' said Lamb, rummaging for another cigarette.

Harkness was still rounding the chapel when the Dog who'd approached him earlier stepped into his path. The movement the American made might have been interpreted as reaching for his credentials, though in fact he was positioning his elbow to jam into the Dog's throat. He didn't make clean contact, but the beauty of brute force is, you don't have to. The Dog dropped like an autumn apple, and Harkness was round front of St Len's, skirting its high hedge, then on the street again, heading for his car.

It had been bad tradecraft, but hell: watching his son help shoulder his grandfather's coffin was circle-of-life stuff. Last time he'd seen River the boy had been a mess, but not giving an inch – there was a steel core there. If he'd been in Frank's keeping he'd have been something to see by now, and who knew what the future held? But there'd need to be drastic changes first. Step one was River leaving Slough House, and putting that loser crap behind him. Then Frank would be waiting, ready to show him step two. He was nearly at his car now, had unlocked it on the move, so was perfectly placed to half-turn and crouch just as his son reached him, full tilt; nearly soundlessly but *nearly* was the key; *nearly* would get you killed. As it was, it got River a brief moment of unassisted flight as Frank's shoulder came up and Frank's

73

left arm gripped his right elbow, twisted and threw. The kid landed okay – needed work, but he wasn't a civilian – but even so Frank was in the car before he was back on his feet. Tough love. He pulled away while fastening his belt, already thinking about the journey ahead, already consigning River to the back pocket of his mind, when the car rocked like someone had dropped a dog on it, and Frank blinked, and River was sprawled on his bonnet, teeth bared.

For a second they were staring into each other's eyes, father and son. He'd been right about the steel core. Either that, or River was a fucking nutcase. Then he slammed on the brakes, just before the junction, and a passing car screamed its head off as River tumbled onto the road.

Frank thought for half a moment about opening the door, letting River climb in. It could be that easy. They could drive off and sort everything out somewhere down the line, this father–son thing they had going on. The main problem was he'd have to batter River into submission first, which would be time-consuming, and besides, there was movement back at the chapel: more Dogs, unless they'd learned their lesson on that score, and sent out the vicar instead. Time to move. All around them cars had stopped, sensing an incident in progress, and a chorus was warming up: the beeping and blaring of confused traffic. River was upright but swaying, and reaching a hand out to bang on the glass, unless he was hoping for support. But more tough love, son: Frank pulled away before River made contact, swerved round the stationary vehicle ahead, and turned right, away from the centre. He'd collected the face he'd needed to see, and if he saw it again, he'd take action.

Meanwhile he'd concentrate on doing what he did best, and disappear.

5

That afternoon, at Slough House, Lamb held what he insisted on calling a post-mortem.

'Get it?' he'd asked Catherine.

Who didn't bother hiding her sigh. 'Can you try using a little tact in front of River?'

'I'm not the one played leapfrog with his dead grandpa.'

The slow horses were trooping up the stairs; those who'd not been at the funeral picking up on the vibe that it hadn't gone by the book, and even Wicinski, the novice, aware something odd had happened. Less than a week in residence, and that bar was higher by the day.

There wasn't much room in Lamb's office, but, as Lamb was fond of pointing out, you didn't hear him complaining. So they arranged themselves as best they could, while Lamb sprawled in his chair with his feet on his desk. He'd had something involving prawns and rice for lunch, judging by the Rorschach stains on his shirt, and excavated fugitive scraps from folds and crevices as he spoke. River was his first target. 'Great show. Couldn't have been more fun if you'd booked a stripper. Come to think of it—'

'That was my mother.'

'Pity.' Lamb moulded his findings into something the size of a grape, and levered it into his mouth. 'Don't suppose Daddy stopped for a chat on his way out?'

'He was in a bit of a rush.'

Everything had been a rush, in fact, once River had returned from the wars. Those who'd remained at the graveside, nailed in place by embarrassment, waited while the obsequies were completed, and then their exodus was swift and uncomplicated. The look Diana Taverner shot him was almost visibly directed through a sniper's scope; the now torn suit she left with, River had identified as Oliver Nash, chair of Limitations, and thus string-puller in chief to the Service as a whole. Well, on paper. But any reality which involved pulling strings and expecting Di Taverner to dance was going to find itself fake news in a hurry. The chances of Nash winning that contest was on a par with Lamb deciding the morning's events were best forgotten about.

Speaking of whom, he'd adopted a mournful expression, and looked like a solemn hippo regretting a heavy night. 'I mean, I'm not a stickler for manners, fuck knows, but even I wouldn't turn a sorrowful occasion into a hit-and-run opportunity. Not without serious provocation.'

'Harkness being there was serious provocation,' River said.

'I can see "Daddy" might be a stretch,' Lamb said. 'But "Harkness"?'

'Mr Harkness.'

Next to River, Lech Wicinski shifted, a man ill at ease. In the cluster by the door, he was the one around whom space had appeared: his history had gone round Slough House swiftly as a diuretic, and no one wanted to get close.

He said, 'Do I need to be here for this? I've no idea who any of these people are.'

'Somewhere you'd rather be?' Lamb asked. 'Knock yourself up.'

'. . . I think you mean out.'

There was an embarrassed pause, broken by River. 'He's suggesting you screw yourself.'

'I'm glad someone's paying attention,' said Lamb. He shifted to brace an unshod foot against his desk. Experience had determined that this posture increased the volume of his eructations, and the gathered crew hunched, trying to dull their hearing without resorting to fingers in ears, a defensive strategy known to upset Lamb. 'What did you have in mind, one of those classes where they address deviant behaviour? Because if you want to go celebrity spotting, do it in your own time. But while you're in Slough House, you stay where you're fucking put. Clear?'

He lowered his leg. The fart never came.

As if none of that had happened, Shirley said, 'Harkness was there? The one sent the psycho to kill us?'

Still looking at Wicinski, Lamb said, 'New viewers start here.'

Shirley said, 'He didn't try to kill anyone this morning, did he?'

She sounded like she'd sulk if he had: another treat missed.

Lamb said, 'Well, he bounced Cartwright off his car, but let's face it, that doesn't necessarily speak to evil motives. But he was hanging around while what passes for the great and the good were all in a bunch, so who's to say he didn't have designs on mass slaughter?' He fumbled at his crotch to general alarm, but he'd merely found a sliver of red pepper. 'Nah, just kidding. Cartwright took after him with all the grace of a septic iguana. If he'd been there to toss a bomb, he had time to toss it. Trust me on that. I know a tosser when I see one.'

River all but lip-synched that last line, thinking: *I've been here too long.*

Earlier, Louisa had grabbed five minutes with him: still in his funeral blacks, trousers gaping at the knee. 'You okay?' she'd asked. And then amended herself: 'I mean, given you're not okay, are you okay?'

'Had better days.'

'Why'd you think he was there?'

'God knows.' Though River had a shortlist of reasons: so Frank could lay eyes on his son, and his son's mother; so Frank could see the old man put in the ground – that one rang true. Sentiment wasn't Frank's style, but keeping score was in character. So yeah, that, or else this: Frank had some other reason all of his own. In which case, they'd have to just wait and see.

'What about your mother?'

'. . . What about her?'

Louisa said, 'You know, did she have much to say on the subject?'

Like: goodness gracious me, there's the man who pretended he loved me, and got me pregnant, and all so my father would bankroll his mad spook scheme, hatched in a French chateau.

No, none of that came up.

Instead, River and his mother had stood by the grave, River's knees pulsing where they'd scraped along the road, his heartbeat back to normal but heavy with grief and a confusion of other emotions. He should have been boiling with rage, but wasn't quite. Rather, he felt as if a fuse had been lit, and that his father's reappearance heralded some major shift, the way the grey vault of sky promised snow. When it came, it would cover everything. Nothing would be missed.

He said, 'She's spent so long pretending he doesn't exist that she didn't even see him. That's how she acted, anyway.' Acted with her silent posture; with her frozen refusal to notice his escapade. Right up until she was getting into her taxi, when she'd hugged him tighter than normal. *This was his fault*, she'd said, and he'd known she'd meant the O.B.; her father, not his. It was possible she was right, but difficult to discern what difference it made. He shook his head for Louisa's benefit. 'Don't know whether to go into therapy or write a sitcom.'

'Your grandfather was proud of you.'

River looked up, down, all around. Slough House. Words weren't necessary.

'Yeah, okay. But you haven't given up, have you?'

'I've given it some thought.'

He was giving it more now, by the look of him. Louisa would be worried, if she didn't have troubles of her own. And didn't have to pay attention to what Lamb was saying, because he tended to notice when you wandered, and that was never fun.

'Apparently he had CIA ID,' he was saying now. 'Which must be harder to say than to fake, because our Frank soiled his pants with the so-called Cousins about the same time he soiled Cartwright's mother's sheets. No way is he holding legitimate paper.' He tossed the fragment of red pepper into the air, and snapped like a pike taking a fly. 'Now, maybe he turned up at the funeral for old times' sake, but my feeling is, he doesn't scratch his arse without a hidden agenda. And given that his last appearance involved redecorating our walls, I'm not inclined to shrug him off. Which is why I'm looking at you, Scissorhands.'

Roddy Ho said, 'What?'

Ho had his fingers bandaged, Louisa noticed, though she didn't care why. True, he'd been less of a dick this last little while, but that might have been because being more of one was a stretch even for him.

'You're awake. Good. Because what we've got ourselves here is a mystery, and as with any mystery, you have to address the four Fs.'

No one dared ask.

'Who the fuck, what the fuck, where the fuck and why the fuck,' Lamb continued. 'Fake paper or not, Harkness must be leaving a trail. What's he calling himself, what's he up to, where's he gone, and why now? I'm reliably told you can't use a public pissoir these days without showing up on You-Bend or whatever it's called, and if I want someone to follow digital breadcrumbs, who better to ask than our own little digital detective? Whose digits, I notice, are looking mangled. Stick them somewhere you shouldn't?'

'Accident,' said Ho.

'Sorry to hear it,' said Lamb. 'So. River's daddy. Where do you start looking?'

'Car,' said Louisa, River and Shirley as one.

'He drove away in a car, and while Cartwright here was too busy playing Starsky and Hutch to get his number plate, there'll be CCTV footage, even if the Dogs didn't think to make a note of it. But I suppose, having lost their head, they'll have trouble licking their balls, let alone doing their job.'

'Emma's gone?' asked River.

'That got your attention, didn't it? Yeah, Flyte's history, and she was oh-so-nearly one of the gang. Pity. She'd have brightened this place up no end. Not that I'm objectifying her, you understand, but she's a right cracker. And some of us have a sense of aesthetics.' He slipped a hand down his trousers and scratched vigorously. 'You still here?' he asked Ho. 'Find the car. It'll be hired, under an alias, but that'll be a start.'

'Why not stolen?' Shirley asked.

'To avoid unnecessary attention. Any more questions?'

'Yeah, what's Starsky and Hutch?'

Ho left, having to sidle round Wicinski, who refused to move. Something going on there; Louisa hoped she wasn't going to be forced to pick sides. Roddy Ho versus a kiddy porn user: it'd be like choosing between Jeremy Clarkson and Piers Morgan in a bare-knuckle death-match. There ought to be a way both could lose.

'Meanwhile,' said Lamb. He eyed River, Louisa, Shirley and Coe, his gaze somehow drifting over Catherine and Lech. 'You lot can walk back the cat. We can assume Harkness's base of operations is Europe, because he's about as welcome in the States as a turd in a martini. Which means European arrivals, planes, trains and ferries. Do we still have that face recognition malarkey?'

Louisa said, 'Yes, but it's so old it mostly recognises eighties pop stars. It'd be quicker walking the streets with an e-fit, asking passers-by.'

'Ho's kit's faster,' River put in. 'Why can't he do that?'

'Because Ho's looking for the car,' Lamb said.

'He could multitask.'

'Multitask? He couldn't charge his phone while having a dump.'

Coe said, 'Last time we saw Harkness, he was running his own private French Foreign Legion. It's more likely he was dropped off on a beach than he walked through border control.'

'You know, mostly I forget you're here, and when you do speak I wish you weren't. Maybe he crawled under the wire, yes, but since we lack the ability to run a trace on uncaught illegal immigrants, let's just do what we can, yes? Unless you have a better idea?'

Coe shrugged.

River said, 'The Park keep tabs on entry points, and their recognition software's up to date. If he came in through channels, they'll already know.'

'But they're not likely to share that with us, are they? On account of, you know, you lot being not only surplus to requirements, but an actual hindrance and embarrassment.'

'Last time he showed, we were his target,' River insisted. It was no warmer in Lamb's office than anywhere else in Slough House, but Louisa could see his temperature rising; a pink flush creeping upwards from his collar. 'If they know what he's up to now, they should keep us in the loop.'

'We've talked about your proximity to loops before,' said Lamb. 'And you're no nearer one now than you were then. So let's do things my way, shall we?' He adopted a martyred expression. 'I mean, just for a fucking change? Planes, trains and ferries, then. On your bikes. In fact, there's an idea. Add bikes to that list. Just in case.'

'What about me?' Wicinski asked.

'What about you?'

'What do I do?'

'You sit in your office and try not to think about children. And if you do, you try not to fiddle with yourself while doing so. Or is that too big an ask?'

'I am not a paedophile!'

'The thing is, there's no way to make that statement sound convincing. Funny, that.'

Louisa didn't want to look Wicinski's way, but couldn't help it. The man's face had turned grey, which wasn't the colour she'd have expected. Neither anger nor embarrassment; rather, the expression you might see on someone looking into a pit, the bottom of which was out of sight, and whose edges were starting to crumble.

Lamb broke wind loudly.

Nobody moved.

'Did I misfart? That's your signal to leave.'

They left; mostly back to their offices, though Louisa followed

Catherine into her room. It seemed as if Catherine hadn't noticed; her back to Louisa, she began straightening files that didn't need straightening. A lock of her hair had come loose from its ribbon, and Louisa had to quash an urge to reach out, undo the bow, and see Catherine come undone. Except, it occurred to her, that's what she was already seeing. Catherine with a hair out of place was as familiar a sight as Jackson Lamb handing cake round at Christmas. But before she could utter this, or something like it, Catherine turned, her hands full of folders; using them, Louisa thought, as a shield, a barrier. She regarded Louisa calmly, then said, 'Are you sure you want to hang around up here? When he's on a crusade, it's best to make yourself scarce.'

Louisa reached into her back pocket and pulled out the sheet she'd printed off earlier. 'Funny you should bring that up. I need to take some leave.'

'There's a form on the intranet.'

'Yes.' Louisa waved the paper in her hand. 'I've filled it in.'

'Well, then.'

'. . . Are you okay, Catherine?'

'Me? Yes, I'm fine. Thank you for asking. You want me to get Lamb to sign off on that, I expect.'

'He doesn't like it when we take time off. You know that.'

'And I don't like being the buffer between him and the rest of you. But I don't suppose you know that because it's never occurred to you to think about it.'

'. . . Jesus, where did that come from?'

Catherine shook her head. 'Nowhere. Never mind. Here, give it to me.'

She almost didn't want to now, but not quite as much as she didn't want to head back into Lamb's office and put it on his desk herself. She held it out, and Catherine whipped it from her hand with the air of one removing a sharp object from an infant's grasp.

Job done, but she couldn't leave it at that. She watched Catherine place her form on top of a pile of other papers, marvelling a little at how perfectly aligned this new addition was, with no apparent effort on Catherine's part. And then watched Catherine notice her stray strand of hair, and tuck it behind her ear pending major reconstruction.

She said, 'Maybe you should think about taking some leave yourself.'

'And do what?'

'Just get away. Go somewhere warm.'

'Is that what you're doing?'

Louisa glanced towards the window. Soon there'd be snow, if the radio's dire warnings came true; the sort that lingered for days, making castles out of parked cars and hillsides out of hedgerows. All very well if you had somewhere to be, and could afford to put the heating on. For those on the wrong side of closed doors, possibly lethal.

Maybe Min's son was having the time of his life; bedding down in a warm room with a girlfriend or two and a pizza menu. But if not, if he was out there on the streets, she owed it to Min to find him. Or maybe not Min; maybe she owed it to herself, to keep being the person Min would have wanted her to be. She didn't exactly know, but it was what she seemed to be doing regardless.

'No,' she said. 'I just need some time to myself, that's all.'

Catherine stared, as if she'd announced a desire for some agonising luxury or other. Then said, 'I'll have him sign it. When do you want to start?'

'Right away,' said Louisa.

'You're supposed to give at least as much notice as the length of leave requested, you do realise that?'

Why'd you think I want you to hand him the form, Louisa thought, but didn't say. 'Thanks, Catherine. I owe you one.'

'You owe me more than one,' said Catherine softly as Louisa disappeared downstairs. She added another form to the stack requiring Lamb's signature, a request for a replacement boiler, whose last service had provoked a teeth-sucking groan of disbelief from a plumber who was about nineteen. This, Catherine knew, would never make it beyond the post room at Regent's Park, there being a standing instruction that all mail from Slough House addressed to Finance be binned unopened. Besides, if you started replacing worn-out parts round here, where would it stop? Any overhaul would include herself, and she wasn't sure she'd survive an upgrade.

She went back into Lamb's office, the pile of forms in her arms. All over the world banks were becoming coinless, cars driverless, offices paper-free. Here in Slough House they were taking up the slack, as if in Newtonian response to refinements made elsewhere: an equal and opposite surfeit of unnecessary busywork.

Lamb was where they'd left him: arse in chair, feet on desk. Through holes in his socks, his toes tasted freedom. He was smoking, and though Catherine suspected him capable of doing this in his sleep, she'd yet to prove it. She slapped the papers onto his desk, or at least, onto the clutter that littered his desk. A self-defeating gesture, because once they slipped onto the floor they'd be archived as far as Lamb was concerned. He had a three-second rule about paperwork: that long on the carpet, it was good as filed.

Without opening his eyes, he said, 'I sense your disapproval.'

'If you ever sense my anything else,' she said, 'one of us has been replaced.'

'They spend their whole lives hoping for something to do,' he said. 'And you want to spoil their fun?'

'We should leave Harkness to the Park.'

'Yeah, that happened last time. And they let him walk.'

'And what's your plan, exactly? Always supposing you track him down, with all this genius expertise at your disposal?'

This time he opened his eyes. 'I thought it was my job to remind you they're a bunch of useless twats,' he said. 'Not the other way round.'

'They're not entirely useless,' she said, but even to her own ears, her protest sounded insincere.

Lamb took the cigarette from his mouth and examined it as if it were an alien artefact. Then he flicked it at his wastepaper basket, scoring a direct hit. 'Last time Frank Harkness showed his face, he sent one of his sockpuppets round with a gun.'

'I hadn't forgotten.'

'He's got the blood of my joes on his hands.'

'Funny how they're joes once they're dead.'

A thin spiral of smoke rose from the wastepaper basket.

Lamb said, 'Maybe you're right. Maybe he's just got the blood of more useless twats on his hands. But they were my useless twats. And I hadn't necessarily finished with them.'

'You'll get River killed.'

'Standish, I could chain him to his desk and lock the door. You really think that'll prevent him going after Harkness?'

She wasn't in the mood to admit he might be right about anything. Nor inclined to warn him that he'd set his bin on fire: if nothing else, burning Slough House to the ground would see the paperwork off.

Speaking of which, the papers she'd set down for him began their inevitable slide floorwards. Catherine caught them before they became airborne; automatically tapped them into alignment before tucking them under her arm. It was as if the role into which she'd been cast was an iron maiden, retaining its shape even as she was screaming for release. And her mind flipped forward a few hours: the journey home, the bottle of wine. Its glass body smooth to the touch. All those memories, waiting to be released.

He was watching her, his lip curled in its automatic sneer. What was it like being him? Pointless even to speculate. 'You've been seething for a while,' he said. 'You ever going to actually combust, or just keep us all in suspense?'

She didn't know what he was talking about, or at least, that was the impression she tried to convey. 'You need to sign these,' she said. 'Now would be good. And with your actual name this time. Nobody was amused by the last lot.'

'I'm surprised they even read them.' Lamb reached out a fat palm, and she handed him the forms. While he signed them with a blue Biro – its plastic casing bitten through: he destroyed a dozen a week, not using more than one for actual writing – he continued scrutinising her. 'Cartwright hasn't done any work for longer than I can remember,' he said, 'and the fact that you keep typing up whatever garbage he hands you doesn't make them official reports. You know and I know and Cartwright knows that ninety-nine per cent of what we do here is to provide practice for Regent's Park's document shredders, but that won't help him if I call him upstairs now and can him on the spot.'

'Do you plan to do that?'

'Not today. Today he'll actually be putting some effort in, which will make such an almighty change I'm half expecting spring to break out, with fucking butterflies and stuff. He's probably tap-dancing with cartoon rabbits as I speak.'

'You seriously think River'll be able to trace him?'

'I seriously think if we dangle River from a piece of string, Harkness will show his face sooner or later, which is the only reason for keeping Cartwright in place I can think of offhand. That doesn't involve using him as a toilet brush. What's Guy want leave for?'

So much, thought Catherine, for his disregard for what he was signing.

She said, 'I can only imagine she needs respite from the unrelenting comedy.'

'Yeah, I thought it was probably that. Does she know I can dock her a week's pay for taking leave without proper notice?'

'You really can't.'

'Yeah, but does she know that?'

Catherine shrugged. She'd fought enough of Louisa's battles for one day. She held her hand out and Lamb surrendered the forms. All she needed to do now was dispatch them, wait a day, then begin the process again, with nothing achieved in the meantime. Well, Louisa would get her leave, she supposed. On her way to the door a thought struck her. 'Wicinski. Lech. Should he even have access to the internet?'

'He's already Kevin Spaceyed his career,' Lamb said. 'If he wants to go for the full Rolf Harris, he's a braver man than me.'

'I'm not sure theirs were online offences.'

'Well, I'd have said Damian Green,' said Lamb. 'But I didn't want to have to add a footnote.'

He magicked a cigarette from somewhere, plugged it between his lips, then bent and retrieved a smouldering twist of paper from the bin. He blew on it until it caught flame, and used it to light the cigarette. Then he wafted it to ash, dumped it back in the bin, and poured the dregs of a cup of tea on the budding bonfire. A thick plume of smoke filled the room.

'They're not all joes,' he said.

'. . . Who aren't?'

But Lamb had closed his eyes, and didn't answer.

Before returning to her room Catherine went downstairs and wordlessly dropped the holiday request on Louisa's desk. On her way back she passed Ho leaving the kitchen: a slice of pizza hung from his mouth, and he was carrying a plastic bottle in his left hand, his right still bandaged up. He said nothing. He was probably working out how best to trace Harkness's car, she surmised, though he was in fact thinking about mousetraps, how there was a thing about if you invented a better mousetrap, the world would beat a path to your door. Frankly, though, Roddy couldn't see how mousetraps could be bettered, the one he'd found in Wicinski's bin being an unimprovably effective way of silencing the bastards. Not to mention damaging fingers. How was he supposed to navigate the keyboard jungle with his hand taped up? It was like attaching bells to a ninja. You were robbing him of his greatest strength.

When he got back to his office Wicinski was there, but not working;

staring, rather, at Roddy. So that was the way it was. *Okay*, thought Ho. *You and me. Right here, right now.* One hand tied behind his back, kind of, but that wouldn't slow him down: a back-flip, a left-handed throat jab . . . His arm was suddenly wet because he'd crushed his plastic bottle, flushing its contents over his wrist, in reaction to which he'd bitten through his pizza, half of which dropped to the floor. Shit. He put the bottle on his desk, retrieved his lunch, Wicinski's eyes never wavering. *You wanna piece of me?* thought Roddy. *Wanna try your luck?* Bigger men than Wicinski had been mentally ground to paste by the Rodster. He removed a small brown pellet of dirt from his pizza – he was always finding pellet-shaped bits of dirt here, just like the ones he found at home: strange – and flicked it away. Not about to let the staring weirdo spoil his lunch.

He logged on and picked up where he'd left off. One-handed he might be, but snatching data from Hampstead's Mickey Mouse street-warden company was easy as kicking a puppy: the algorithm he'd triggered before going to warm his pizza had finished its job already, decoding the password. He copied it, flipped to the command screen and pasted it where the prompt demanded: bingo. Free and total access to all stored data, so now he could spend as long as he liked watching raw footage of cars parked on various roads in Hampstead, across a four-month time span. He'd like to see Wicinski pull that off. The Rodster, on the other hand; give the Rodster anything with a monitor and a keyboard, he'd be watching rough cuts of the next *Star Wars* movie before you'd opened the popcorn.

Still sticky-fingered, he fed today's date into the search box, and his left-hand screen fragmented into thirty-two boxes, each providing a live feed from one of Hampstead's traffic control cameras. And this was Roddy working single-handed, he reminded himself; his primo digits out of action, though flexible enough to shovel what remained of his pizza slice into his mouth. Back to the command screen: let's skip back a couple of hours, see what was happening then. He could feel the new boy's eyes on him. Maybe Lamb hadn't given him anything to do; maybe Lamb had just told him to observe and learn, which was fair enough, but let's face it: the only lesson he'd be taking home today was how far short of Roddy Ho's skill sets he fell. Watch and weep, new boy, watch and weep. Roddy was viewing footage from this morning now, thirty-two boxes' worth, each flipping into a new channel every few seconds because there was a lot of CCTV in Hampstead: a *lot*. Like everywhere else in London, when you walked the streets you were auditioning for the non-speaking role of passer-by.

Or perhaps trying out as a stuntman.

Because *there*: blink and you'd miss it. Sixth screen along, third row down. He paused everything, moved the clock back thirty seconds, maximised the box that had caught his eye and ran it again. River Cartwright, jumping onto a moving car and clinging on for maybe seven seconds? Six? Roddy was going to time it, bet on that, but meanwhile he was enjoying the spectacle: the world's worst suicide attempt. The car couldn't have been going more than twenty. It was kind of a pity Cartwright had fallen off soon as he did, because if he'd managed another second or two, he'd have been dumped slap in the middle of the junction. And as far as Roddy was concerned, there was nothing wrong with River Cartwright that being involved in a major traffic pile-up wouldn't put right.

A small detail entertainment-wise, but a crucial one so far as his task went, was that the numberplate of the car Cartwright was attempting to sledge showed up bright and clear in the frame.

He finished his energy drink, and tossed the empty into the bin. Tracing a plate, assigning an identity to the vague shape behind the wheel, was something he could do in his sleep; such a lowly task he didn't feel down to doing it himself, so he emailed a screenshot to Shirley Dander: let someone else do some work for a change. Wicinski was still staring, so he leaned back in his chair and swivelled the monitor to show off his success.

'Congratulations,' Wicinski said after a while. 'Data theft. Quite the hot-button crime.'

'For national security,' Roddy reminded him.

'Which might have mattered once. But this is a post-Brexit, post-truth, fake news world, and something I've noticed is, people are pissed off.' Wicinski smiled, but not in a good way. 'Hate figures are the new black. People find a spook like you watching their every move, you'll be the poster-boy for every anti-government pressure group going.'

And this was exactly the kind of shit the HotRod was used to: the frank admiration disguised as contempt; the derision that masked drooling envy. Life in Slough House, he was surrounded by no-hopers, trying not to let him see they were grabbing for his coat tails. Whatever coat tails were.

Ho said, 'Who's gunna find out?' Wicinski was starting to irritate him. Also, a bit of meatball or something was lodged between two molars, and with his right hand currently inflexible, he was going to have Voldemort's own job freeing the damn thing.

'Yeah,' said Wicinski. 'That's what everyone says. Right up until somebody blows the whistle.'

'Last time someone tried something like that, Lamb found out about it first.'

'Yeah? And then what?'

Roddy couldn't remember. Hadn't been good, though. And besides, he himself, the Dyno-Rod, was pretty pitiless in vengeance mode too. Not so long back, he'd heaved a would-be killer through a window. Well: details were hazy. But he'd been there, and the would-be killer had wound up dead on the pavement. Do the math.

He returned to his screens. Wicinski's gaze, he knew, remained fixed upon him: a dark-eyed stare intended to unnerve. Which, okay, was starting to do that, but not because the RodMan scared easy – hell: he'd been sharing a building with J. K. Coe for a year, and he was a genuine psycho – it was more about Wicinski's past having been wiped from Service records. That was spooky. What they knew he'd done was enough to put you off the guy. So whatever he'd done that someone wanted covered up, well, that must be seriously dark.

The chunk of meatball came loose of its own accord, and Roddy's mouth filled with what tasted like beef.

Blowing the whistle, he thought. Was that an actual threat? Could be. That was the trouble with the slow horses; they were constantly rattling their cages, checking the bars still held. If it weren't for Roddy himself, his calming influence, the idiots would have burned the building to the ground long ago.

The stuff he and Lamb had to put up with. Good job he had Wicinski's number . . . First suspicious move from you and the Rodster'll tie you in knots, thought Roddy. Lead you down the garden path, drown you in the pond. He could picture himself going over this with Lamb; the older man's shoulders heaving. *What I could have done with ten men like you in the old days*, Lamb was saying. *Ten joes like you, I'd have run rings round the Kremlin.* Eyes narrowing with suppressed pleasure, Roddy registered the ping of an arriving email but didn't open it, so remained unaware that Shirley Dander had tracked Harkness's car to a national hire chain; an office in Southampton. The vehicle was an Audi; the customer one Jay Featherstone, who'd used a Canadian passport. Until someone got a look at its photo, and confirmed it was the man himself and not a proxy, she couldn't be sure she'd tagged Harkness; that it was a hire car, even, didn't mean it hadn't subsequently been snatched. But if the customer were legit and the car stolen from him he'd have reported it by now, unless he had good reason not to, like being dead or something – too many variables, Shirley decided. Time being, they might as well assume Frank Harkness was disguised as a Canadian, which could mean wearing a plaid shirt and carrying a hockey stick, but more likely meant he'd be using his normal voice, wearing normal clothes, and banking on no one knowing the difference. In Southampton, or anywhere else that wasn't Toronto, that seemed a safe bet.

Anyway: her part was done. Cartwright could haul up the paperwork and say whether it was daddy. And then – if she'd read the signs aright – Lamb might just let them off the leash, which would make for a late

Christmas present. Harkness had killed Marcus, or primed the hand that did so. Thinking that thought had Shirley clenching her own hand: making a fist, letting it go. Making a fist. She'd shared this office with Marcus once. They'd had their moments, but never come to blows. And in the end, they'd been partners.

She had to avert her eyes from the wall, remembering this. The wall against which Marcus's life had ended; his final thoughts sprayed upon it like illegible graffiti.

Making a fist, letting it go. Making a fist again. Letting it go.

Shirley had attended court-mandated anger management sessions not long back, and the sessions had been successful in the sense that she didn't have to go to them any more, but unsuccessful in the sense that she'd punched someone in a nightclub earlier in the week, and while this had, as it happened, been the manager, that probably didn't count. The whole thing had been a misunderstanding – he had thought she was accusing his staff of selling drugs; in fact she'd been complaining that they weren't – but she had to be honest with herself: not resorting to violence during misunderstandings had been a key feature of the anger management course. And if, in her defence, it had been a hell of a punch – straight uppercut, no tell – that wasn't really, when you got down to it, an actual defence. Punching someone who didn't see it coming lost you points for self-control. Whether or not they were a dick didn't enter into it, apparently.

Then again, the course hadn't been an entire waste of time. At least she knew what bullshit she was expected to spout next time someone got to ask her: *And how did that make you feel?*

Buoyed by this positive thinking, she checked her email: yep, Cartwright had requested a copy of the relevant paperwork from the car hire firm, a 'request' phrased as delicately as a grip on the company's lapels. There weren't many advantages to Slough House, but the fact that nobody knew its status as Service pariah was one, making it possible to play the national security card with civilians. Just don't get tweeted about while doing it. Cartwright had been promised a response within thirty minutes, which in most offices translated as an hour and a half; time to grab some food, Shirley thought, a Pavlovian reaction to a glimpse of J. K. Coe passing her door, carrying something wrapped in greaseproof paper. He took it up to the office he shared with River Cartwright, who as usual offered no greeting. They'd reached this kind of détente, Coe supposed you could call it; a working arrangement whereby either might as well have been alone for all the rapport in evidence. Which suited Coe.

He sat, took a bite from his sandwich, and set the face recognition program running again. He'd have left it on while fetching lunch – that was what computers were for; to do stuff for you while you did other stuff – but experience had taught him that the program froze every twenty minutes, unless you paused it. The footage it was currently trawling through was of yesterday's ferry arrivals at Southampton: the foot passengers. Until confirmation came that the man who'd hired the car there was the same man driving it in Hampstead – Frank Harkness – this could be a waste of time, but if you were after a working definition of life as a slow horse, that would do. Which, again, suited Coe. His was a precarious balance. His own trauma lay far in the past, or so the calendar said; it didn't feel like ancient history though, not when memory woke him in the small hours. And the glimpses he'd had since of what he was capable of himself didn't make for comfortable contemplation either: he was, it seemed, the sort of person who would shoot an unarmed, manacled man, an action you only had to perform once for it to become a defining characteristic. Not the person he'd assumed he was. Another, more recent outing had suggested him capable of heroism too, at least in the eyes of others, though Coe knew that when he'd shot an armed terrorist dead in Derbyshire, he'd been in the grip of something – call it a manic curiosity – over which he'd had little control; the overwhelming urge to see what a dead terrorist looked like, close up. Given all that, wasting time was as good a way of getting through it as any.

The picture on his screen juddered, halted, and the dialogue box conjured a message: *Refer to Annex C.* This referred to a database of known mercenaries – legit, grey area and downright nasty – and the highlighted face belonged to a man with the pitted skin of an acne survivor, and eyes that revealed nothing. They didn't usually, in Coe's experience. Those with something to hide knew not to put it in their windows. The man's hair was short enough to qualify as military; his gear – a black polo-neck under a thigh-length winter coat, combat trousers, boots; a duffel bag over one shoulder – ticked the same boxes. Way too young to be Harkness so not on Coe's agenda, and besides, he couldn't find the match on Annex C while running face recog; not on hardware that was creaky when scooters were hip. Coe put his sandwich down, scribbled a reminder on its wrapper, then hit return, allowing the program to restart. The way it trip-hopped face to face, superimposing geometric shapes upon each, was as mesmerising as a screensaver, and about as productive. What would the program make of him, he wondered? He barely recognised himself any more, that was for sure. And then the program stalled again, and he thought he'd over-pushed it, but no; after a quivery moment another dialogue box appeared. *Refer to Annex A.*

Thinning fair hair, noticeable cheekbones. A middle-aged face on a capable-looking body.

'Cartwright?' he said.

Cartwright grunted.

'This him?'

Cartwright looked up, came over, squatted by Coe's desk. After a while he said, 'Where's this?'

'Southampton. Ferry arrivals. Yesterday.'

'It's him.' He tapped the screen. 'Annex A?'

Coe said, 'Big and bad.'

'Well don't access it. No need to let the Park know we're looking.'

Three bags full, thought Coe.

'Almost certainly Jay Featherstone, then,' said River Cartwright, even as his own computer pinged incoming paperwork from the car hire firm.

From upstairs came a familiar explosion: a Jackson Lamb coughing fit, though by the noise, you'd be forgiven for assuming he was giving birth. The two men shared an uneasy moment, one broken by a voice from the doorway: Louisa Guy, delivering a farewell.

'You're away?'

'Leave.'

'With this going on?' said River.

But Louisa was already halfway down the stairs.

Coe glanced to the window. It was dark outside, the pavements bracing themselves for overnight frost. Soon there'd be snow, and the country in the grip of its annual pantomime: cancelled trains, motionless airports, unnavigable roads. He hit return on his keyboard and the program chuntered back to life, sorting through the rest of Southampton's arrivals: the weary, the footsore. It had already found what Coe was looking for, had pinned Frank Harkness to its memory-board, but why stop there? He was dimly aware that the coughing upstairs had subsided; that Cartwright had returned to his desk. Other aural irritations continued: the burping of radiators, the passive-aggressive grumbling of the fridge. A slamming door would be Shirley Dander; the scraping of a chair, Roddy Ho. He had grown used to this, both the discordant soundtrack and the occasional harmonies it hid; had learned to find comfort in continuity, though knew full well that the only reliable constant was fracture, that eventually everything broke. Which might happen as easily in the snow as at any other time.

And his computer blipped once more, as another Annex C match was made.

6

'Why didn't I know that Frank Harkness was in-country?'

A wobble drifted across Richard Pynne's features, as if a TV screen had briefly lost its hold. Pynne – inevitably Dick the Prick, but less and less often in his hearing – was the nearest Di Taverner had had to a favourite since the days of the late James Webb, whose legacy was a snatch of Service wisdom: *Don't nail your colours to two different masts*. Or, as the corridor version had it, Don't get fucking shot. The latter outcome wasn't a direct result of the former infraction in Spider's case, but might as well have been, and Pynne was assiduous in maintaining an undivided loyalty where Lady Di was concerned. A large young man with shaven head and thick-framed spectacles, he would have looked at home in Shoreditch, making energetic visits to pop-up coffee boutiques and craft beer spaces, but instead was shift manager on the hub, maintaining daily workflow and ensuring the efficient manning, resource-utilisation rather, of the floor's workstations. He had his eyes on a Third Desk role of course, overseeing field ops, but so did everyone else. Then again, not everyone else had regular sit-downs with Di Taverner; nor had anyone – far as he knew – been assigned a low-risk, home-soil, agent-running gig. So: officially admin for the moment but groomed for stardom, that was Richard Pynne. Which was a fair bit of background to cover before responding to one short question, but Pynne was ever conscious of his status, and hated it to be thought, for even a minute, that he wasn't on top of his brief.

Frank Harkness.

'I'll check on it,' he said.

'You know who he is?'

The question direct, and here was another Service gem: You never lied to Diana Taverner until you were sure you could get away with it.

'. . . He's not on my radar.'

'Then you need a bigger dish.' Taverner pursed her lips, as if trying to banish a bitter taste. 'He's former CIA. One-time liaison with the Park. And then spent a couple of decades running a deep-cover mercenary outfit from a French chateau.'

'And he's in-country now,' said Pynne. 'Should we worry?'

'Well, he made a farce out of what should have been a solemn moment, but it's possible he was just passing and saw no reason not to. Check with the DGSI, though. He was playing flics and robbers in their back yard long enough, they ought to have stuck a flag in him. Maybe we can get some actual collaboration, instead of indulging in pissing contests.' She paused. 'And collaboration, well. They're French, they won't need reminding how that works.'

'I'll choose my words carefully, shall I?'

Di Taverner allowed herself a brief smile. 'Soon as you can. But first, an update on Snow White.'

Which was the codename for the operation Pynne had been given: home-soil, low-risk.

There was little to report. Hannah Weiss, Pynne's joe, was a minor double: believed by the BND – the German intelligence service – to have infiltrated the British Civil Service on its behalf, she had in fact infiltrated the BND for the British intelligence service. That was what Regent's Park thought, anyway. Pynne was her handler, but truth was she needed little handling; beyond her recent shift to the office of the minister in charge of Brexit negotiations – 'in charge' being used in its loosest possible sense, there – she'd made no demands on him. They met once every three weeks, meetings that were easily the high point of Dick Pynne's calendar: an attractive young woman, an expense-account coffee, the sense that his career was in the ascendancy. He kind of wished those sessions had an audience, though had to admit that that might have compromised the whole Secret Service aspect of proceedings.

Taverner asked him, 'Anything new on BND protocols?'

There wasn't. Hannah's German handler similarly made contact every three weeks, though he splashed for lunch, being on a better expenses deal than Dick, and also, as mentioned, German. That aside, the running of a joe in the field seemed to differ little on the two sides of this currently friendly divide; had probably differed little since joes and fields were first discovered. Hannah brought back to Dick the details of these debriefings, at which – to maintain the appearance that she was working for German intelligence – she fed Peter Kahlmann, Dick's opposite number, various Brexit-related titbits to accompany his schnitzel –

('I hope you're not descending to racial stereotypes,' Lady Di put in. 'They eat at Fischer's. He likes the schnitzel.')

—all of which had been carefully vetted to ensure minimum damage to British interests, however glittery they might seem. The idea was to boost German confidence while negotiations were ongoing; encourage them to overplay their hand, or at least to underestimate British resolve. There were limits, though. Dick's suggestion that they sow a rumour that the Brexit minister was approaching mental breakdown, and likely to cave early on crucial points, had been vetoed on grounds that were, he was informed, 'outwith his need to know'.

'And what about Hannah herself? How's she bearing up?'

'I think she rather enjoys it.'

He knew he did.

'Okay, thanks, Richard. Good meeting.'

Not ten minutes later, back at his desk, Richard Pynne watched Oliver Nash, chair of the Limitations Committee, working his way across the floor, heading for Lady Di's office.

She called Clare Harper while driving home, that final comment in the coffee shop – *You were fucking Min, weren't you? I'd have hoped that counted for something* – carefully unmentioned, as if it were an elderly relative's flatulence.

'Okay,' Louisa said. 'Tell me about Lucas's recent movements.'

Like she was a private detective, or a GP.

'Just the normal. School, friends, his bedroom . . . Nothing out of the ordinary.'

'And he doesn't have a girlfriend?'

'You know what they're like these days. He has friends who are girls. But no one special, no.'

These days weren't so distant from her own, Louisa thought; not in real terms. But hell. The difference.

'What's his number?' she asked. 'I might be able to get it traced. That's what you were hoping for, isn't it?'

'He didn't take his phone with him.'

She might as well have said he'd left his kidneys behind. Louisa didn't know many teenagers, but she couldn't swear she'd ever seen one without a phone in its hand.

'You're sure?'

'It's right here. I'm holding it.'

So okay: short of leaving a banner reading DON'T COME LOOKING, Lucas couldn't have made his intentions clearer. But still. Abandoning home and mother was one thing, but his phone? If this was adolescent dramatics, it was an extreme case.

She said, 'Can you check on his recent activity? Or—'

'I don't have his—'

'—Password, right.' There were people Louisa could ask, who could crack a phone's password faster than a teenager could crack its screen, but the most obvious was Roddy Ho, and she didn't want to go that route. Asking Ho for a favour was like chewing someone else's gum.

'What about his computer? Or is that passworded too?'

'No. House rules. But they don't use email much. It's all texts and Snapchat. And his browser history's the usual stuff, social media and music sites. He clears it pretty regularly.'

Even Louisa did that, and she didn't have a mother on the premises. She said, 'Send me the list of sites he'd been looking at?'

'I've told you, there's nothing unusual there.'

'And yet I'm the one you asked for help.'

She heard a noise in the background, a boy's voice. That would be . . . Andrew.

Clare said, 'I'm sorry.'

'I understand.'

'You can't. You don't have children.'

No, but she'd noticed most mothers were fond of them. Why was that so difficult for Clare to get her head round? But Louisa simply recited her email address so Clare could send her Lucas's browsing history, then fretted at a traffic light, hating the stop-start of her commute. But at least that was over for the next week. Because she was going to do this, it seemed. Whether for Min, for herself, for Clare, even for Lucas: that was background fade now. She was going to do this.

Clare was saying, 'Thank you.'

'I'm not promising anything.'

'No, but . . . Thank you.'

Louisa ended the call, promising to get back to Clare later.

When she reached home the first thing she did was fire up her laptop and examine Lucas Harper's online history. Clare had sent his browsing tree as a screenshot, and a quick glance revealed nothing to excite maternal discomfort – Lucas was a cricket fan, like his father; had obsessively checked stats, as if hunting for a glimmer of hope in the recent Ashes debacle; and he spent time on YouTube and Facebook, like everyone else. Also Amazon, and other online retailers: clothes and sporting goods, mostly. Wikipedia. Google.

A couple of sites fitted no obvious parameters, though. One was for a catering company, Paul's Pantry. 'For all your party needs.' It was based in Pegsea, Pembrokeshire. *That's in Wales*, she remembered Clare saying. The other was for a property in the same county; a place called Caerwyss Hall, which offered all the facilities your company required for a weekend getaway, including conference rooms, swimming pool, assault course, stables, quad bikes, spa and gym. The thought of her company — specifically, of Jackson Lamb — making use of all or any of these momentarily swamped any other consideration, but once she'd banished such images, she commenced wondering why Lucas had been interested. Paul's Pantry, she guessed, had been where he'd worked over Christmas. Maybe this had been one of their catering events.

She rang Clare again to check. 'Does the name Caerwyss Hall ring bells?'

'It's near Pegsea. One of those big manor-house places that's gone corporate? Weekend retreats and team-building. Where everyone has to pretend they get on, and nobody hates anyone else.'

'Hell on earth,' Louisa agreed. While they talked, she was looking up the Wiki pages Lucas had visited. 'Lucas worked for Paul's Pantry, right? Did he help cater an event there?'

'Yes. The day after Boxing Day. It was good money.'

But he'd looked at the site since then, so he hadn't been checking up ahead of the job, to know what to expect.

The Wiki harvest was a curious collection. Some well-known names. Some obscure companies. What on earth was Bullingdon Fopp? Was this what teenagers did to pass the time: surf below-the-skyline entities from the financial news pages? It didn't seem likely. She said, 'What about his interests? I can see he likes sport. What about politics?'

'Not really. He was interested in causes, all young people are, or should be. He got uptight about the whole Me Too thing. But Labour–Tory politics, no, it turned him off. Each as bad as the other, he reckoned.'

Louisa was scrolling through Caerwyss Hall's website, scanning their About Us page. The usual puffery, and pull-quotes from users. *Our team has gone from strength to strength. We were delighted with the care and support on offer.* And there, halfway down the page, Bullingdon Fopp again. A PR company. No quote offered, but the company was listed as a customer.

'And sport, yeah. He's a fitness fanatic.'

She nodded, pointlessly. Was feeling unfit herself today, well short of her 10,000 steps. She scrolled back to the top of the page, wondering why Lucas had been so interested in Caerwyss Hall, and what had led him to research the name of one of its corporate clients.

As if she'd been reading her mind, Clare went on, 'He logs his daily exercise, and if he's fallen short during the week, he makes up at weekends. Goes on runs to get his mileage up. That sort of thing.'

Louisa paused. 'Does he have a Fitbit?'

'God, yes. He's obsessed with it.'

'And did he take it with him?'

'I imagine so. I haven't see it lying around.'

'Okay,' said Louisa. 'I don't suppose you can lay your hands on the paperwork, by any chance?'

In Slough House, the afternoon was doing what the afternoon did: outstaying its welcome. River had printed the photocopied passport from Southampton, the supposed Canadian called Jay Featherstone, and pinned it to his office wall. This was his father. He had no fond childhood memories to draw on, because he hadn't met the man until last year, but he hadn't forgotten how Harkness had dumped him in the Thames on that occasion. More delaying tactic than murder attempt, to be fair, but Frank's absence during River's childhood had presumably left certain gaps in his knowledge, such as whether his son could swim, so you couldn't write it off as horseplay. Then again, River couldn't swear his mother knew that much. Talk about a fucked-up family. They had enough raw material to float a psychotherapy practice.

He was rolling a pea-sized ball of Blu Tak between finger and thumb, and he flicked it now at Frank's photo. It hit the paper, hung for a second, then dropped to the floor.

The name Jay Featherstone was all they had. Lamb had vetoed contacting border control: there was no need to alert anyone – he meant the Park – that they were looking. Not that they'd need alerting. Di Taverner had been at the funeral, and would no more expect Lamb to shrug Harkness's presence off than she'd expect him to fly, or brush his teeth. But that was par for the course; much of life at Slough House was determined by the push-me/pull-you relationship between those two. River would suggest they get a room, provided the room was soundproofed, locked, and had an alligator in it.

'So what do we do?' he'd asked earlier, when they'd gathered in Lamb's room once more, pooling what they knew. It had already been pooled by email, of course, but Lamb shunned emails; would have communicated entirely by dead-letter drop if he could. The stack of phone books holding up his desk lamp testified to his analogue preferences. 'You can break a man's ribs with a telephone directory,' he'd once observed. 'Try doing that with a rolled-up copy of the internet.'

'I assume we have some idea where our mock Canadian has got to?' Lamb had said. 'Not that I approve of mocking Canadians. That'd be like shooting kittens in a barrel.'

River said, 'We have a credit card from the car hire firm.'

'He used it to book a room at a Travelodge,' said Ho.

'Classy bastard,' said Lamb. 'Where?'

Shirley said, 'Stevenage.'

'It's as if you're working in harmony,' Lamb said. 'Like a fucking Coke commercial.' He belched, possibly a Pavlovian thing. 'You'll be wanting a group huddle next.'

'He's the reason Marcus was killed,' Catherine said quietly.

'Who was Marcus?' Lech asked.

They all stared at him.

'Jesus,' he said. 'Pardon me for breathing.'

'They're not being unfriendly because you're new,' Lamb explained kindly. 'They're being unfriendly because you get your kicks watching kiddy porn.'

'We should go there,' River had said. 'Stevenage.'

'Yeah, we should, if there was the remotest possibility he'd still be there,' said Lamb. 'But it's probably best we don't bother, on account of not being complete morons. Present company excepted.' He was holding a cigarette. He hadn't been, a second before, but this was something the slow horses were used to: between endless examples of fat bastardy, there was the odd moment of slick trickery too. 'So. Any ideas as to what he's up to?'

'Stevenage,' said Shirley. 'I'm ruling tourism out.'

'Yeah, Stevenage was regrouping,' said Lamb. 'His business lies elsewhere. Where's your mother?'

This to River, who started. He said, 'Brighton. You don't think—'

'Maybe.' Lamb plugged the unlit cigarette into his mouth, and for a moment looked lost in thought.

'Because if she's in danger—'

'But maybe not. No, if it was her he was after, he'd not have needed to scope out Grandpa's funeral to find her. He's a lifetime spook. I imagine he knows about directory enquiries.' He looked up, and River saw something in his eyes that wasn't usually there. 'I'd thought he might have wanted to see you, but that's not likely either, is it? No, there's something else.'

They waited, but whatever it was, he hadn't grasped it yet.

Shirley said, 'That new guy was there. Nash? The Limitations Committee's new boss.'

She mimed someone looking down a sniper scope. It wasn't a very good mime, but the context was obvious enough that it didn't have to be.

River said, 'Frank Harkness has a screw loose, sure. But he has no reason to want to whack the head of the Service's steering committee.'

A match flared, and the smell of burning tobacco filled the room. 'We all know Cartwright here's biased, on account of, you know, DNA and stuff, but he has a point.' Lamb shifted in his chair, and swung his unshod feet onto his desk. 'Last time Frank was here he was mopping up his own mess, but it was a mess he made trying to protect this country's interests, not destroy them.'

'Big difference,' Shirley pointed out.

Lamb grunted, then frowned. 'I'd be the first to admit I have trouble telling you apart,' he said. 'But is there someone missing?'

'Louisa's on leave,' Catherine reminded him.

'All right for some, eh? I suppose we should be grateful there's not an emergency on. Like, you know, a homicidal spook on the loose.'

'She probably decided it was Park business. And that Slough House had no reason getting involved.'

'Nice going. Here's me bending over backwards to boost the morale of this shiftless bunch of spastics, and you have to undermine them. I don't know why I bother, I really don't.'

He took a drag on his cigarette, then scowled at the glowing end, as if concerned it would give his position away.

Coe spoke. 'He wasn't alone,' he said.

Lamb put a spare finger into his ear, wriggled it about, and removed something he peered at then wiped on his sock. 'That's better, touch of tinnitus. Unless . . .' He looked enquiringly around. 'He didn't speak, did he?'

'There were three men with him.'

'Let's pretend we'd like a little detail.'

Coe said, 'I ran face recognition on the Southampton arrivals. There were three other hits on the same ferry. All on the Park's Annex C.'

Lamb's look of perplexity was a pantomime dame's, appealing to an audience for help with a lunatic.

Surprisingly, it was Lech Wicinski who came to his aid. 'Minor players,' he said. 'Mercenaries, informants, known associates. That kind of thing.'

'What you might call the grey area,' River said.

'So the kind of pool Harkness might go paddling in,' Lamb said. He pointed his cigarette at Coe. 'Any visible contact?'

'No.'

'But a big coincidence if they weren't a team. Unless Brittany Ferries were running a special. Three lowlifes for the price of two. You check this Annex Whatever?'

'All have records as private contractors. Military.'

'So Harkness has a team in country. Gadfuckingzooks.' Lamb shook his head, but River saw a gleam in his eye. That pretence about not knowing what Annex C was; the general air of marvelling at the world's dirty linen. Fat slob he might be, but joe blood ran in Lamb's veins. Had stained his hands.

Now he said to Coe, 'Nice to see you using your brain, instead of spreading someone else's over the landscape. You have names for this crew?'

'Anton Moser. Lars Becker. Cyril Dupont.'

'That was all just noise to me, but I assume the rest of you have taken note.' Lamb sat upright suddenly, swinging his feet floorwards. 'Anything else?'

'Harkness is Annex A,' said Coe.

'Meaning, I presume, that he's regarded as toxic?'

Coe nodded.

'And yet he walks among us. Seems like the deal he swung last time still holds good.'

'Which means,' Catherine pointed out, 'that he's untouchable.'

'You again? I'm starting to wonder whose side you're on.' He flipped his cigarette stub into the air – a new trick, this – and it dropped neatly into the half-full mug of tea on his desktop. 'Harkness might have a hands-off agreement with the Park. But he doesn't have one with me.'

Me either, River thought. Me either.

'So,' said Lamb. He surveyed the gathering. 'To answer Cartwright's impertinent little whine five minutes back, what we do now is find out if

Dozy, Beaky and Titch were at that same Travelodge with Harkness. And if not, where are they now? That sound like it falls within your skillset, grasshopper?'

He was looking at Roddy Ho, who gave a twitchy smirk in response. 'Yeah, sure.'

'How splendid. Wrap it up by teatime and I'll see about getting you a gerbil, to replace that girlfriend of yours.'

Shirley scowled. 'How come he gets special treatment?'

'Fact of life, Dander. Us minorities pull together.'

'. . . You're a minority?'

Lamb looked pained. 'I'm half lesbian on my mother's side. Or does that count for nothing?'

That was then. Now, River stood and approached the photocopy on the wall. Jay Featherstone – Frank Harkness. He'd inherited some of his father's looks; the mole on his upper lip was his own, but the colouring was hand-me-down, and the general facial structure, his shape, his essence, was there in his father's features. Along with what else? All his life, he'd thought he'd inherited his ambition from his grandfather, and the stories the O.B. had plied him with throughout his youth. He hadn't known that being a spook was a dynastic thing. That his father lived in those same shadows.

Half without meaning to, he slammed his fist side on against Frank's face. A little payment on account, though Frank's expression didn't change, and all River gained from the moment was a throbbing in his hand.

He knew Coe was watching as he returned to his desk, just as he knew that if he glanced Coe's way, Coe would be focused on something else.

River sat down again, and got on with brooding.

If you want your enemy to fail, give him something important to do. This stratagem – known for obscure historical reasons as 'The Boris' – was one Di Taverner set store by, and if Oliver Nash wasn't exactly an enemy, he was the kind of ally you wanted ground into submission whenever possible.

Technically, the Chair of the Limitations Committee argued First Desk's case before Treasury and the Cabinet in general; in practice, as one of Diana's predecessors had pointed out, chairs can wobble. Sometimes you had to saw a length off a leg. And Di Taverner had no qualms about cutting Nash off at the knees, but there were ways and means. It made sense to balance the cruel with the kind.

Nash made his entrance with his usual lack of aplomb; dexterity he might have in spades when it came to diplomatic wrangling, but in actual physical terms, he had the grace of a boat going sideways. Lady Di had visions of him crashing through her glass wall, gifting the boys and girls on the hub a legend they'd never forget, but apart from a brief tussle with the visitor's chair, and a nudge to her desk which rattled its drawers, he made harbour without incident. Despite the weather, he looked warm. It occurred her that he always did, but then, he carried enough padding to make an Arctic outing plausible.

Seated, comfortable, he spoke. 'This morning.'

'I thought the vicar spoke well,' she said. 'Nice balance between service for his country and tactful lack of detail. You know Cartwright's neighbours thought he was in Transport?'

'Wonder what they made of the acrobatics. A disgruntled commuter paying his disrespects?'

'Families,' said Diana. 'I put it about that the grandson's a little . . . emotional.'

'"A little emotional"? What would having a breakdown look like? Digging the corpse up and doing a waltz?'

She allowed him a small nod.

'So who was he, Diana? And what was he doing at Cartwright's funeral?'

'His name's Frank Harkness, and I have no idea.'

'One of us?'

'An American.'

'Oh, Christ. CIA?'

'Former.'

'*Former*? They use formers for wet work. Jesus, they didn't have Cartwright killed, did they?'

'Unlikely. The head of CIA's a voice of sanity in the US at the moment. Then again, it's all relative. Would you like coffee, by the way? I should have asked.'

'Thank you. And maybe a biscuit? I skipped lunch.'

Nash's battle with his waistline was approaching mythical status at Regent's Park, though 'battle' might be overstating it, given Nash's half-hearted approach to hostilities. His strategy mostly consisted of carrying on as normal and hoping the situation would improve. Besides, his definition of 'skipping' didn't differ wildly from 'postponing'; lunch might have been omitted from his diary, but an afternoon biscuit frenzy would soon have things back on track.

While waiting for the promised refreshments to arrive, he said, 'Several people warned me about taking on this role, you know. They seemed to think there were easier ways of securing a seat in the Lords.'

'Oh, we're on the side of the angels, Oliver. You just have to remember that angels do God's dirty work.'

Nash nodded. 'So if I wanted to know what was going on without knowing anything I'd have cause to wish I didn't, how much would you tell me?'

Not much more than a paragraph, was Taverner's considered opinion. The details of Harkness's last UK appearance, shortly after the Westacres bombing, were still under wraps – not so much buried in the files for thirty years as left blowing in the wind, to be scattered for all time – and while Nash was entitled to be fully briefed, he was wise not to press the point. Deniability was next to godliness in Westminster's corridors, and godliness itself second only to unassailable majority. And the last time anyone had seen one of those, the resulting messiah complex was still being grumbled

110

about in The Hague.

But Nash was an ally, so here was something he could do: sit on a piece of information and make sure it never hatched.

'He worked liaison, between Langley and the Park. Only a little, and a long time ago. But afterwards, once he went freelance, he made use of certain . . . assets.'

A tray was brought in, and Nash's mood improved.

'It turned out he'd helped himself from our dressing-up box before putting certain events in train,' Taverner continued when they had the room again. 'Which made bringing charges a tricky business. It could so easily have looked like we'd been incompetent.'

Than which, as both knew, there were few looks more damning. It was a rare historical car crash that forensic reconstruction couldn't make seem a successful emergency stop. And as in any line of business, a succeeding CEO who couldn't make a bygone cock-up look like an opportunity missed wasn't fit for management, and should take her retirement package, her annual bonus, her golden handshake and her non-disclosure kickback and tiptoe from the boardroom in disgrace. So no, Taverner wasn't worried that she might seem incompetent; Claude Whelan had been in charge during the Westacres atrocity, and the associated buck had been branded with his initials long before it came to a halt. What Taverner would prefer not to become public was the nature of the deals she'd made to ensure that that particular deceleration didn't inflict whiplash on her too.

Nash reached for a second Hobnob, making quite a good fist of looking like he was doing this unconsciously, his mind on other things. 'And is that coming back to bite us? Because I don't want to wake up tomorrow and find nasty headlines on my iPad. I didn't much like it when they came neatly folded on good old-fashioned broadsheets.'

'No editor's going to print that St Len's is the Spooks' Chapel,' she said. 'Not unless they want to find out what it's like having their own mobiles monitored. So no, a minor brouhaha at a family event is all that happened.

It'll stay that way.'

'And Harkness?'

'Wheels are in motion.'

'Just so long as they don't come off.' Nash leaned back in his chair. Were it not for the smudge of chocolate on his upper lip, he'd have looked the model of an executive decision maker. 'Because the Service isn't in good odour at present. Too many missteps, too few triumphs. While acknowledging that your own tenure's still in its infancy, the PM isn't convinced that a corner's yet been turned.'

'She's rejected my working paper,' Taverner said flatly.

'It's not a good time, Diana. The cupboard is bare. Now is not the moment for a root-and-branch overhaul of operational practices, however crucial you feel that might be.' He glanced at the plate of biscuits, but successfully glanced away again. 'Between ourselves, playing wait and see might be no bad thing. The PM's stamp of approval hardly comes with a lifetime guarantee. It's no secret she wasn't so much made leader as handed a janitor's uniform. Once Brexit's been finalised, and her job looks less like an excrement baguette, someone more competent will step into her breeches. Then, perhaps, the ball will be back in your court.'

'Our court, don't you mean?'

'I'm on your side, Diana. You know that.'

'Good to hear. But we don't just need new balls, we need our racquet restrung. I'm trying to safeguard the nation, Oliver. That's not a good area to penny-pinch on. And it's not as if we're currently standing shoulder to shoulder with our sister services.'

'Our European allies aren't going to throw us to the wolves just because we're looking for trading partners elsewhere.'

'Maybe not. But nor are they going to let us sit at their tables if they think we're best buddies with China, or Kazakhstan, or whoever we end up swapping glass beads with. The borders have shifted. We need good, old-fashioned, on-the-ground intelligence, backed up with the appropriate hardware. We can't be keeping our fingers crossed that the neighbours'll lend us theirs when the chips are down.'

'The people have spoken, Diana.'

'Did they speak? Or just scream in frustration?'

'Save it for a dinner party. The government of the day, elected by the people, indicates the path we have to tread. Currently, that's the path of make and do.'

'And the government of the day doesn't always choose the wisest route.'

'Which are words best kept between these walls. You're First Desk now, Diana. That carries responsibilities above and beyond the operational. Caretaker or not, the PM has a right to expect your loyalty.'

'Don't worry, I'm not planning a coup.'

'Good to know.'

'I'll let her own party do that.'

'You're not filling me with confidence.'

She said, 'Blowing off steam. That's all.' She dipped her head ever so slightly. 'Thanks for arguing the case, anyway.'

'Yes, well. Let me handle the politics.' He looked at his watch, noticed the dusting of crumbs on his sleeve, and brushed himself in irritation. 'Time I was away. Be brave and true, and all that sort of thing.'

'Oliver.'

She smiled him out of the room, thinking: *The Boris*. Give your enemy something important to do.

It did no harm to have Oliver Nash think he was in charge.

'No way,' said Emma Flyte.

'You owe me one,' said Louisa.

'No I don't. Where on earth did you get that idea?'

Louisa said, 'I just thought it might sway you if I said that.'

'Huh.'

Emma was at home. Even a week into unemployment it felt strange, not going to work. First day, she'd pounded her phone: contacts contacts contacts. Putting the word out that she was on the market. She imagined networks lighting up, like an old-fashioned switchboard; messages relayed from one source to another; information absorbed, mulled over, passed on. There'd be speculation – *how come the Service let her go?* – but one of the benefits of the covert world was, there was no shortage of alibis. *The details can't be made public. I'm sure you understand.* Wouldn't stop the gossip, because nothing ever did, but gossip at least guaranteed she'd be on everyone's agenda for a while. Lots of places – big interests – *expensive* concerns – would be happy with an ex-Met, ex-Regent's Park cop on their books. So far, though, her calls remained unreturned.

Didn't matter. Give it a week, give it two, the serious players would come to her. For the moment she just had to play the waiting game.

The trouble was, it was a game she was really bad at. The week had been purgatory: household chores, bloody books, staring at the TV until its programmes became nervous. Having nothing to do was driving her crazy. A call from Louisa was a relief.

They weren't friends, exactly. They were friendly, though. And now she was no longer Park, perhaps they could take things to the next level; like, do stuff together without getting into a fight. Time would tell.

But whatever happened next, this phantom favour wasn't going to be it.

'It would be a quick in, quick out.'

'It's Regent's Park, not Tesco's.'

'That's what I meant. Those self-service checkouts take forever. Anyway, if you're too chicken—'

'Fuck off, Louisa.'

'—too *scaredy pants* to venture into the lions' den, you could always get Devon to do it. I'm sure he'd be only too happy to do you a favour. And twice as happy if he knew he was doing me one at the same time.'

'You realise he's gay?'

There was a slight pause. Then Louisa said, 'Yeah, I knew that.'

'You didn't, did you?'

'Course I did. Doesn't mean he won't want to do us both a favour.'

'Except it wouldn't be doing me a favour, because I have no interest in persuading someone on the hub to break the law. Can I run that past you again? What you're asking is against the law.'

'Used to happen all the time when I was at the Park.'

'And remind me where you are now?'

'. . . Point taken.'

'It's not only a sackable offence. I genuinely think Lady Di would have someone shot.'

Louisa said, 'I knew that really. Just thought it was worth taking a punt.'

Emma said, 'Are you drinking?'

'Glass of wine.'

'Gimme a sec.' She didn't know why she said that: she took the phone with her as she went into her kitchen, found a glass, and poured herself a healthy slug of malbec. Benefits of unemployment: you didn't have to worry about next morning's head. The disadvantage was, of course, that if it went on too long, she'd be swapping the malbec for Thunderbird. And that wasn't a good look at all.

Glass full, she said, 'How's things?'

'Same as.'

'That bad, huh?'

'You heard David Cartwright died?'

'Yes. How's whatsisname taking it?'

'River. Much as you'd expect. I'll pass on your regards, shall I?'

'Just make sure he knows I forgot his name.' Emma sipped her wine. Mid-week drinking had a certain vibe, she decided. Maybe those folk sleeping in doorways had a point. 'What about the fat bastard?'

'You seriously want to know?'

'I'm hoping you'll say he's at death's door.'

Louisa said, 'I doubt Death would answer. It'd hide behind the sofa, pretending to be out.'

'Good point. Who you looking for?'

'Missing kid.'

'How old?'

'Seventeen.'

'Girl?'

'No.'

'How come you're looking?'

'It's complicated.'

'You're shagging the dad?'

There was a pause. Then Louisa said, 'Long time ago.'

More to it than that, Emma could tell. She took another sip of wine, let it roll around her mouth, then said, 'And you think you can trace this kid by his Fitbit?'

'Not personally. But the thing is, he's still wearing it. And given they're internet-enabled, and I've got its registration number—'

'Then someone with the right kit should be able to pinpoint—'

'His exact location, yeah.'

'Well, you're probably right. But I'm not going to bluff my way onto the hub and ask one of the worker bees to break fifteen different laws for me. They didn't like me when I worked there. They're not going to do me any favours now.'

'Sure they liked you.'

'They were scared of me.'

'There's a difference?'

Emma conceded the point by finishing her wine.

She said, 'Why don't you ask your tame keyboard muppet? I seem to remember there's nothing he can't do with a computer. Or that was the

116

impression he liked to give.'

'Yeah, no, the thing is, if I ask Roddy to do it, it would be like I owed him a favour.'

'It would be precisely you owing him a favour,' Emma pointed out.

'Which is worse,' Louisa agreed. 'On account of I work in the same building as him. Though that does, in fact, give me an idea . . .'

Emma waited, but nothing more was forthcoming.

'You still there?'

'I was hoping,' Louisa told her, 'that you'd work the next bit out for yourself. Hence my dramatic pause.'

'. . . God, no.'

'Pretty sure he'd jump at the chance to get in your pants. Good books is what I just said. Ignore whatever you thought you heard.'

'I am *not* going to go begging favours from Roddy Ho.'

'Awww, you remember his name. That is so cute.'

'Louisa—'

'Plus you're bored out of your skull. You know you are.'

'This was your plan all along, wasn't it? You knew there was no chance in hell I'd go into the Park for you. And you're hoping because I'd say no to that, I'd be more likely to say yes to this.'

'I have no idea what you mean. Plan? We're having a girly chat.'

'One in which you play me like a . . . xylophone.'

'Yeah, I can't play the xylophone. Listen, Emma, seriously? I really need to find this kid. And I don't think Ho will do it for me. He's been kind of pissed off since, you know. That whole fake girlfriend thing.'

Emma looked at her empty glass. She was being played, no question. It was true, though, that she was bored out of her skull.

She said, 'I do this for you, you'll explain what "complicated" means?'

Louisa said, 'To the last syllable.'

Emma picked the glass up, walked back to her kitchen. 'Okay,' she said. 'You want to read out that registration number?'

7

That evening – while River was turning off his computer at Slough House, then rebooting immediately, thinking *ten more minutes*; just ten more minutes running Jay Featherstone's hire car through ANPR, in case it had registered while he was powering down – Richard Pynne stopped for a drink on his way home. He needed it. Instead of researching Frank Harkness, his afternoon had been one of crisis management: a Park operative had dropped off the map. A contractor, her role was to supervise the incineration of shredded documents, the crushing of superannuated hard drives, and to some she was little more than a glorified janitor, but not to Pynne. The way he saw it, she regularly laid hands on broken secrets. Who was to say they couldn't be reassembled? So when it had been brought to his attention that she wasn't at work, and when the resulting knock on her door revealed a vacant flat, it was clear she'd taken her jigsaws to auction. Thus her photo was red-flagged, and took the UK airports' hit parade by storm; meanwhile, Dick put a team onto assembling a menu of recently sledgehammered work product, a task which involved most of the hub. And it went well, or as well as these things ever do: by seven, he'd been ready to deliver to Lady Di a list of operations to be regarded as tainted when someone handed him a Post-it the contractor had stuck to her manager's desk that morning: she had the flu and was going home. Further investigation revealed she'd changed address without updating her personal details. All of which went to show, as Richard emphasised in his end-of-day report, that procedures should be rigidly adhered to. There was a reason red tape existed; it was so things didn't fall apart. And now he needed a drink.

It was a corner pub off Great Portland Street, with a battle-scarred mirror behind the bar in which he could keep an eye out for undue interest. The afternoon's false alarm didn't mean real alarms couldn't happen, and since leaving the Park he'd had that uneasy sense of hearing footsteps in synch with his own. There were tricks you could pull – double back to check a shop window, pause to fix a shoelace, halt at a bus stop – and he'd tried each in turn. But if he had a tail, it failed to wag. Now inside, he ordered a gin and tonic; made it a double. However exemplary his actions of the afternoon, he didn't want to dwell on them. Nor was he keen to know what the boys and girls of the hub would be chatting about over their own after-work cordials.

He wished he were meeting Hannah. Amazing how a hint, a swift deflection, could turn disaster into weatherbeaten triumph. *Bit of a flap this afternoon. Nothing I can talk about . . .* When he looked up, Lech Wicinski was on the stool next to him. 'Hey, Dick.'

'What the fuck?'

'I was passing. Saw you through the window.'

Pynne turned automatically to the window, then back to Wicinski. 'You shouldn't be here. Shouldn't be talking to me.'

'What are you, royalty?'

Good as, Pynne thought. Given their respective status. He shook his head. 'Lech. Remember your letter? From HR? No contact, not with anyone from the Park, while—'

'Yes, I remember. It's a fucking earworm. But you know what?' Wicinski waved a finger and the barman approached; he ordered a pint, then picked up where he'd left off. 'I don't much care.'

Red tape held things together. Once people like Wicinski started cutting through it, it would be a full-time job maintaining integrity. That wasn't the reason he'd been let go, obviously, but he wasn't doing himself any favours.

Now he said, 'It turns out I don't have many friends at the Park.'

'Many? Try none. That was some pretty sick shit you were looking at.'

'It wasn't me.'

'There'll be a hearing. You know how this works.'

'I don't, actually. I've never been in this situation before.' His pint arrived, and he forked over a tenner. 'You know what they say about you on the hub, Dick? That you're one pocket protector away from being a geography teacher.'

'Very amusing.'

The barman laid Wicinski's change on the counter.

Pynne watched the mirror while this was happening. The two of them, side by side; you might mistake them for friends. That was how appearances worked: they pulled you one way, reality went another. He slid a hand into his overcoat pocket and said, 'Why were you following me?'

'Because, like I say, you have a rep. Geography teacher.'

'And what, you were lost?'

'Meaning you like things done the way they should be done. And I realised something earlier today. I don't need a friend. I need someone who wants things done properly.'

Pynne drained his G&T, in perfect unison with his reflection. He was okay with the way he looked. Calm. In control. 'Fronted by a pissed-off junior, but not letting it get to him. Hear what the man had to say, then blow his candle out. Gently.

'They will be,' he said. 'The hearing happens later this week. Lady Di, Oliver Nash. There'll be evidence.'

'But I won't be there to state my case.'

'It's not a court of law. It's Regent's Park.' His hand still in his pocket, he fondled his Service rape alarm, as they were called. Anyone tried to slip a hand between your thighs, you pressed the button. 'That being so, let's both save our breath and you get back on home to, remind me. Sara?'

'Keep her out of this.'

'Sure thing. We done yet?'

'No. I want you to do something. Not for me, not just for me, but because it's the right thing to do.'

'Hurry it up.'

'A couple of weeks ago, I ran a search and hit a flagged name. A person of interest. I think I triggered something. I think I was being shut down.'

'This is paranoia, Lech.'

'Well in the circumstances I'm entitled, don't you think?'

'I—'

'Dick, listen. Could you follow up on that name? Please? It's Peter Kahlmann, that's K-A-H-L-M-A-N-N. Peter. But don't run the usual checks, or it'll be noticed. I was thinking maybe put in a request through GCHQ, with the wanted ads?'

Wicinski meant the list of trigger words the monitoring agency updated daily, as it reaped the national chatter. Emails and phone calls, online conversations: plucking syllables out of static. And since communications between the Service and GCHQ didn't always flow smoothly, chances were, the same flags wouldn't be in place on their respective targets. Especially if the flag in question was internal to the Park. Pynne knew all this. He didn't need it spelled out.

'Before the hearing. This is evidence, Dick. It might be evidence.'

The man should listen to himself. There was desperation in his voice; a whiny, needling pitch to make any listener flinch.

Pynne signalled for a refill, and while it was coming pulled the alarm from his pocket. He set it on the bar. 'You should know, I just pressed this.'

'Jesus, man—'

'So it'd be best all round if you left now.'

For a moment, it was a toss-up: Wicinski was going to throw a punch; Wicinski was going to make one last plea. In the end, the coin dropped nowhere. The man just shook his head, said 'Fuck you,' and got up to go.

'Lech?'

Wicinski paused.

'I'm not saying I believe you. But I'll do the right thing.'

Wicinski remained motionless for another half-second, then nodded, and went out the door.

Pynne put his unpressed alarm back in his pocket as his G&T arrived.

I'll do the right thing, he thought, but that didn't involve running stray names through spook channels. Not after having disappointed Di Taverner once today already. The last thing she'd said to him after this afternoon's fiasco still rankled: 'Seriously, Richard, just go home now.' He had some distance to make up there; to shred that memory, or take a hammer to its hard drive.

And now he had Lech Wicinski to deal with too. But that was okay. That was one problem he could fix.

He was halfway down his glass already. Definitely needed that. Seeing it off with one grand swallow, he nodded a farewell to the barman, and followed Taverner's final instruction at last.

Catherine Standish, too, was homeward bound. She had stayed late at Slough House, unsure, as so often, whether the work she was engaged in demanded prolonged attention, or whether her delayed departure had been a form of self-punishment. Being the last one out, locking up behind her, provoked a raw awareness, one she usually held at bay. But walking through the rank little yard into the alley, she couldn't help but think: *This.* This was more than her workspace, it had become her life, a life now dwindled to a series of dull tasks which, because of her meticulous wiring, she performed to a standard beyond anyone's expectation, after which the usual weary journey home to the usual empty flat. A decade ago, fifteen years, this was a better future than she might have had call to expect. But twenty years ago, thirty, and it was a ruin of a life, stripped of ambition and hope. A vision of it granted to her then would have rocked her firmament. Might have driven her to drink.

She left the Tube a stop early, called at the Wine Citadel, and bought a Barolo. An understated label of which she approved. A good wine spoke for itself. It went into a plastic bag, and should have been an anonymous weight in her hand, but somehow wasn't. There was something about a full bottle, the way it responded to gravity, that couldn't be mistaken for anything else. It was like carrying a big brass key, which would open the biggest door ever heard of.

It was cold on the street – not long now, and this weather would have its way with her bones. She'd creak on waking, slow to a crawl on frosty pavements. There were so many things age could do to you; so few you could do in return. In the end, she supposed, you just stayed on your feet as long as you were able, then took the rest lying down.

Her apartment block was set back from the road, shielded by a hedge; its lobby, when she reached it, was empty and chill. Her heels clacked on its tiles. If she dropped her plastic bag its contents would shatter and the floor become swampy with cinematic blood . . . The image made her tighten her grip. Some losses were more unthinkable than others.

And then the lift, and its slow rise; and then her own floor, with streetlight streaming through the window at the far end. Her key already in her hand. Her next automatic gesture already in motion.

As soon as she opened the door, she knew the flat was not empty.

She stepped into her sitting room with her coat on, her bag hanging from her hand. The corner lamp was on a timer, and performing its usual magic; throwing its glow at the rows of bottles, allowing them to beam back fractured light, so the room became the inside of a genie's lantern. This light spoke of blood, and stained the air with a ruby mist. Walking into it, she felt as if she were stepping underwater, and the two possible outcomes of such an action – that she would drown; that she would float – remained in perpetual tussle. This was where she lived, the edge on which she balanced. And its one enduring comfort was, she balanced there alone.

'What the hell are you doing here?'

'I believe the kids call it chillaxing,' said Lamb. The heating had come on, but he wore his coat; his shoes were puddled on the carpet in front of him. He wasn't drinking, oddly enough. He was cradling a bottle, though;

looked as if he were nursing it, one meaty hand wrapped around its label. She recognised it regardless – a Montepulciano; a low-end choice, but a parent doesn't judge.

'Leave now,' she said. 'This moment.'

'You're miffed because I didn't bring a bottle.'

'This is trespass. This is the worst—'

She couldn't speak. She couldn't find the words; they were all trapped behind glass, which was only to be broken in the event of emergency. And while this felt like one of those, she was unable to reach out and perform the required damage.

Something changed; a shift in the light. It was Lamb's phone, she realised. Lamb's phone was resting on the arm of his chair – her chair – and it had just winked out, fading into sleep. Which meant he'd been using it within the last few minutes.

Lamb, using his phone. That might be the strangest thing of all in this strange moment.

He said, 'No, really, take your coat off. Make yourself at home.'

'You have no right to be here. None at all.'

'Well Christ, I know that. I used a stolen key, for fuck's sake. That was a clue.'

'I could call the police.'

'Yeah, they'll think they've caught a smuggler.' He waved an arm: it didn't matter which direction. There were bottles, full bottles, stacked against each wall. They were lined along the bookshelves; parading on the mantelpiece. They were in battle formation on the coffee table, prepared to fend off boarders. 'Or are you opening an off-licence?'

'I haven't drunk.'

'I know.'

'You think I wouldn't be able to hide it?'

'Maybe for the first half hour. But second bottle in you'd be under a trucker, we both know that.'

'And you're here to save me?'

'Fuck, no. I'm here to push you over the edge.' He lobbed the bottle he'd been cradling at her and instinctively she dropped the bag and let the airborne missile fall into her arms. The bag hit the carpet with a thud. No damage done.

Lamb plucked another from the stack next to his chair. 'Bouchard père et fils,' he read. 'Yeah, that'll rinse the taste of derelict from your gums.'

'And that's your party trick, is it?' she said. 'You're going to throw bottles at me until I crack and open one.'

'Hey, they're your bottles. I'm just the middleman.' He glanced around. 'Hope you got a discount for bulk. You could buy a house for what this cost. I mean, in Sunderland. But still.'

She walked into her kitchen, trembling. She took her coat off and hung it on a chair: it slid to the floor, and she let it. She grabbed a glass and filled it from the tap. Drank. Refilled it. Drank again.

What had she been planning? She didn't know. It was madness, to surround herself with this temptation; madness, but a kind of security too. The possibility of a single glass would always hover over her; might be enough to lead her to the cliff. But this – the Aladdin's cave she'd wrought – was something else, beyond mere temptation. It was the promise of absolute carnage. Lamb was right: two bottles in, there'd be no bottom to the depths she might fall. The life that had dwindled to a series of dull tasks would look like paradise over her shoulder. So why was she flirting with destruction? She heard a bass rumble, and returned to her living room. Lamb had succumbed to one of the coughing fits that had plagued him lately. Red-faced, sweating, he was bent double, one meaty hand covering his mouth, the other curled into a fist and thumping the arm of the chair. He might have been wrestling with demons.

Catherine watched. This would wear itself out. It always did. She supposed she could use his temporary uselessness to go through his pockets and take back the key to her flat he'd acquired. Or steal his shoes, walk around in them for a while. And she shook her head at the thought: God, no. Anything but that.

Maybe just beat him to death with a bottle.

He was returning to normal, the coughing subsiding. The fist became an open palm. Through it all, he'd not relinquished the bottle: it was clamped between his thighs, upright. Another image she didn't want taking root.

When he'd finished, she handed him the glass she was still holding. He drained it, wiped a hand across his damp forehead, and glared at her.

'That's not going anywhere, is it?' she said.

'Chest infection.'

'You're sure? It sounds like your whole body's in revolt.'

'Antibiotics'll clear it up.'

'They tend not to work with drink taken.'

'They're drugs, they're not fucking Irishmen.' He studied his hand for a moment, then wiped it on his coat, 'And let's not forget, I'm not the one with the death wish.'

'Which you're here to help trigger.'

'I hate indecisive types, don't you? Shit or get off the pot.'

'It's time for you to go.'

'And this wino's trolley dash of yours, you're doing it for one reason only.'

'Jackson Lamb, amateur psychologist. I almost want to record this. But mostly I just want you to shut up and go away.'

She might as well not have spoken. 'It's because Taverner told you I killed Charles Partner. Your sainted boss, who was a fucking traitor, by the way. She told you that, and it's been eating you up ever since.'

Lamb rotated the bottle in his hands as he spoke, and she stared as its label became visible, was obscured, became visible again. One bottle among many, but for some reason it had secured her full attention.

'Because every day you come into work, open my mail, bring me my tea, and these are all things you used to do for him, back in the good old days.'

The good old days, when she'd have opened that bottle without a second thought; when its contents would have measured out the first half of an evening, the half spent wondering whether she'd have a quiet night, or maybe get a little drunk. Just to take the edge off.

'And I'm the one blew his brains out.'

And that's what she had to live with. She'd grown used to Lamb over the years; used to the idea that this half of her life, the dry half, was to be spent in the employment of a gross, unpredictable bastard who had, like it or not, saved her. Without him she'd have been discarded after Partner's death, and who knew if her fledgling sobriety would have survived that? So buried somewhere deep in what she felt for Lamb was gratitude, because he was the reason her raft remained afloat. And then she learned that he'd killed Partner. The darkest stain of all, and the one that had taken longest to come to light.

'That's what Taverner told you.'

'And you're here to tell me that's not true,' she said.

'No,' said Lamb. 'I'm here to tell you how it happened.'

Good job he had Wicinski's number . . . First suspicious move and the Rodster'll tie you in knots.

So yeah: good times. The RodMan had Wicinski's number, and was currently watching a visual simulacrum of it – its avatar a steaming turd – hanging steady just off Great Portland Street, an address Google Maps indicated was a pub. Stopping for a drink, huh? Hanging with your mates? But why there, Wicinski? Why a pub nowhere near your place of work, your home address? Oh yeah, Roddy-O's got *your* number.

He had Lamb's number too, and had just used it.

Good times.

Roddy was at home, in front of a bank of monitors, four of them: thirty-two-inch plasma screens, their combined weight not much more than a couple of the pizza boxes stacked on the floor. It was new kit, bought with the dosh his insurance company had coughed up after the robbery; a robbery carried out by the Service's security team, though this was a detail Roddy hadn't felt it necessary to include on the claim forms. It had been a major aggravation. But live and learn: one of his screens was now rigged to a CCTV camera above his front door. Even the Rodster could be caught unawares, but not twice.

The room was middle storey and had a mostly glass wall: previous occupants had used it as a kind of urban conservatory, which went to show that no matter what your postcode, you couldn't rule out hippy neighbours. As a result of the same incident which had seen his computer kit go walkies, Roddy had had to have one of the big windows replaced. He'd managed to undercut the original quote by some distance, a triumph slightly mitigated by the way it now rattled a lot when the wind blew, and a fair bit when it didn't. But then, he was generally plugged into his sound system while he worked, and no rattle could interrupt *that* mess. He'd been listening to the classics lately – Guns n' Roses; Deep Purple – an indication of growing maturity. There was a specially wistful drum solo on *Live in Japan*. That shit had escaped him when he was younger.

The turd avatar just sat there, steaming. Drinking solo, or a meatspace chat? Roddy couldn't tell.

He took a long pull on an energy drink, which was electric blue and promised enhanced mental receptivity. Even the RamRod took what help he could get: no shame when you were a 24/7 guy, which Roddy was, except for when he was asleep. The turd, meanwhile, just sat there. One day, Roddy thought, a little investment, a little more hardware, he'd be able to activate screen vision when tagging a mobile, and see who his target was mixing with, and what was going down. Give him extra edge, if that was possible. *More edge than a cliff, babes*, he imagined himself saying. (He really needed someone to say this stuff to.) More edge than a polyhedron. But better look that one up first.

And it wasn't like he didn't have a lot of stuff going on. This Wicinski business had interrupted his current project, one that had occupied him for weeks. Essentially, Roddy was on a mission to protect the vulnerable – because what would be the point of his skills if he didn't use them to good effect? It would be like Thor using his hammer to put up shelves – and his chosen group ('Ho's Hos') was made up of a random selection of models from clothing and perfume ads in lifestyle magazines: a diverse range of 17–23-year-old women. They were his #MeToo group, because that was a big thing now, and each of them, every time he looked at their picture, he thought: *Yep, me too. I definitely would.* That was basically how selection was made. And what the protection was, he showed these women how trackable they were – how they laid themselves open to the attention of predators, who could easily find their personal details, their home addresses, their real-life situations.

True, when the Rodmeister said 'trackable' he meant provided you had access to sophisticated technology, but that was the thing about saddos: there was always going to be one who was both savvy and kitted out.

He shook his head, and fished a handful of M&Ms from the packet in front of him. Ho's Hos. And how he looked after them was, he began with a basic assumption, that each would have a presence on social media, the chances of which he put at a conservative hundred per cent. After that, it was straightforward image recognition, which was where the technology came in. Matching a Facebook profile, a Twitter glimpse, to a photo shoot: basically, once you'd scanned and uploaded the image and made a cup of tea, your job was done. And sometimes, too, other photos came to light; other photo shoots these perfume and clothery girls had signed up for, which might or might not involve perfume but had little to do with clothing. These too he downloaded and saved and printed out: all part of the dossier-building. And once a dossier was thick enough, Roddy dispatched it directly to the girl in question – first class delivery; no penny-pinching – so she'd know she had a well-wisher; someone intent on alerting her to the dangers a saddo predator could represent. He did this anonymously. Heroes work in the dark. But he liked to think of these girls – women – receiving his packages, and realising how much care and attention had gone into them; how focused some unknown but totally woke stranger was on their well-being, to compile these warnings about their vulnerability. He imagined their grateful tears as they reconsidered their online options. Fewer selfies emailed to boyfriends. A little less online sharing. A bit more wary in general, really, and as he thought about that something shifted on one of his monitors. Not the Wicinski turd; that remained static. The CCTV feed. There was someone at his door.

A blonde woman in a long dark coat.

Roddy blinked.

Nah, couldn't be.

Couldn't be.

But it was.

He headed downstairs, pausing at the hallway mirror. Looking good, man. Looking fine. He practised a quick boyish grin: not the full wattage, because he didn't want to cause damage. 'Phasers to stun,' he murmured, then opened the door.

On Emma Flyte, former head Dog.

'Mr Ho.'

'Hey.'

She gave him a puzzled look. 'Are you all right? You seem to be in pain.'

'No, I'm fine.'

'Okay.'

'. . . I was grinning, that's all.'

'Oh . . . Mind if I come in?'

He switched the boyish grin off. Stick to business, to start with. But really, like, yeah, right: business. She was no longer head Dog; no longer Park. No kind of business could bring her to Roddy's door.

131

'I don't mean to be rude, but your mouth is open.'

Closing it, he led the way inside.

Downstairs was a kitchen and a living room he barely used – storage, mostly; lifestyle like Roddy's, you wound up with a lot of cardboard boxes – so he went straight up the stairs, and she followed. Stood in the doorway of his workspace a moment, taking it in. A faint burble leaked from his abandoned headphones, and a louder hum from the monitors. The feed from the street showed his empty doorstep, a quiet pavement.

Flyte said, 'You remember me, I take it?'

Roddy gave a curt but meaningful nod, and wiped dribble off his chin. Sure, babes. I remember you. Until recently she'd been in charge of the Service's internal security: chicks did all sorts of important stuff these days, which was great. And he'd encountered her before, of course. There'd been an interrogation situation, long story, but clearly he'd piqued her interest. Kind of inevitable. Of course, the downside of being in that role, head of security, was she couldn't get involved with active personnel. Had to keep herself aloof. Anyway, here she was, no longer in the job. And here she was, in Roddy's house.

'I do indeed.' Smooth. 'Can I offer you a drink?' He consulted a mental list of his fridge's contents. 'I have Malibu.' Women dig Malibu, so Roddy always kept a bottle handy. Better check the best-by date, though.

'No thanks.' She looked at the monitor displaying the central London street map. 'You're running a surveillance.'

He nodded. Man of few words.

'From your own house.'

He nodded again.

'That's not strictly allowed, is it?'

He shrugged. Then decided a fuller answer was called for. 'I don't always play by the book,' he said.

Flyte nodded, as if she'd heard that about him.

'It's kind of interesting, actually,' he said. 'That little, uh . . . that avatar—'

'The pile of shit.'

'Um, yeah. He's somewhere he shouldn't be.'

shall not, until investigations have been completed to the satisfaction of this department, have contact with colleagues

Flyte said, 'That's not far from the Park.'

'Yeah.'

'One of your crew?'

'That's right.'

She shook her head, momentarily lost in admiration.

And she was awesome, thought Roddy. The blonde hair, the dark blue eyes, the creamy skin: she could have played a robot on *Westworld*. Not to mention walk straight into Ho's Hos, no audition required. Bump an existing member, even. As it happened, he knew for a fact there were no dodgy photos of her on the internet. A very careful lady.

He wondered whether it was too soon to call her babes. Kim – his ex-girlfriend – had liked it when he called her that. An empowerment thing.

She said, 'You'll have heard I'm no longer in the Service.'

Roddy gave his curt but meaningful nod again.

'No. What I meant was, you'll have *heard* I'm no longer in the Service.'

Oh – *kayyy* . . .

She said, 'Sometimes it's best to have certain stories get around. If it's generally thought I'm no longer on the job, then I have greater . . . flexibility.'

Roddy nodded again. Emma Flyte's flexibility was something he'd given thought to in the past; the fact that she was here, now, talking about it, made the day special.

'But it also means I have to work behind the lines. Using resources I don't have to account for. Doing things I might have to deny later. Are we on the same page here, Roddy?'

'Sure thing.'

[*Babes.*]

'And seeing how you're one of those guys who doesn't play by the rule book, well. Maybe you could help me out with something.'

And this was his moment. This was where he'd shine. So he forgot about his Rules of Cool, laid aside his trademark Treat 'em Mean protocol, and instead flashed on the maximum wattage Roddy Ho bedroom smile, way before she'd done much to deserve it.

Because sometimes, just turning up was enough.

'Babes,' he said. 'I can help you out with anything.'

And the look on her face told him that, as usual, he'd said exactly the right thing.

Lamb said, 'Once upon a time, I was Charles Partner's joe.'

Catherine closed her eyes, and felt the dark sparkling: all her glass. All her bottles. And now Lamb among them, like a dragon nestling in someone else's gold, ensuring that it would never be pure again. She'd have to get rid of them, every last one. And she wasn't sure she was ready to do that.

He was right, the bastard. The bastard was right. This fortress, the one that might so easily topple and crush her, she'd built it because of what Diana Taverner had said.

Tell me, Catherine. Something I've always wondered. Did Lamb ever tell you how Charles Partner really died?

She forced herself to speak. 'This isn't something I want to talk about.'

'Who cares? You were off your face at the time. Anything that didn't escape your attention came in a glass or had its hand up your skirt.'

'I was sober when he died. When you killed him.'

'I'm talking about the year before.'

And now she opened her eyes.

She was on her sofa, facing a bookshelf obscured by bottles; a view so distantly familiar it was a postcard from her past, when she had no control over the direction her evenings would take. When she might find herself trapped by a drunken bore; so boring, she'd find him a fascination; so drunk herself, she'd sleep with him.

'I was running joes of my own by then. The Wall was down and all kinds of nasties came crawling out. It was a full-time job keeping up with the acronyms. And there were the retirees, the assets, those we'd recruited from the other side, so they could risk their lives and betray their country. Starting to see a theme here?'

She didn't want to be involved. Didn't want to hear this; wasn't going to participate.

'There was one we called Bogart. Middle-ranking Stasi officer who'd come to us long before cracks started appearing. This wasn't someone looking to save their skin. Or get rich. Remember that. It's important later.' He picked up his phone, which was still resting on the arm of the chair, and stuffed it into his coat pocket. When his hand came free again it was holding a cigarette.

She said nothing.

'You're not gunna tell me I can't?'

'You foul my living space just by being here. Cigarette smoke's not going to make a difference.'

He thought about that for a moment, then shrugged and tucked the cigarette behind his ear.

She wondered if he'd just wanted to make her speak.

'When the Wall fell, Bogart was offered the passport package. New life, new house, new car, the usual shit. Turned it down. Said the time for betrayal was over. From now on it was about rebuilding the country, and that meant cutting the cord. No more dead letter drops, no more cut-outs, no further contact. And we all lived happily everfuckingafter. Gives you a nice warm feeling inside, doesn't it?'

River had told her about the evenings he'd spend with his grandfather, David Cartwright – the O.B. – back when the old man was still in the light, and she had a vivid picture of the pair, sharing a history only one of them had lived through. This was a grotesque parody of that. And the strangest detail, the ungraspable fact, was that Lamb wasn't drinking. Wasn't smoking.

'Except the Cold War didn't really end. It just hid behind closed doors, like Trump in a tantrum. So when Partner decided his own passport package wasn't good enough, and a Civil Service pension wouldn't keep him in the luxury he had in mind, well, it wasn't hard to find buyers for old news. Such as who'd been chipping away at the brickwork when they should have been shoring it up.'

He fell silent. Maybe he was imagining a fire he could stare into. The best on offer was the winelight glimmer of the bottles.

'So Partner betrayed Bogart,' she said, when the silence became too much.

She might not have spoken. 'There were quarterly sit-downs back then,' he said. 'I'd come back to the Park and spend days with Cartwright, going through the diary, what happened when, who did what. Before he went picking daisies, that man had a mania for detail. Study the small cogs, and you'll see which way the big wheels turn. Shame he couldn't see what was happening under his fucking nose.'

'Nor did you.'

Lamb put his unlit cigarette in his mouth.

He spoke around it. 'Dates and places, but never names. Wall or no wall, Berlin was a zoo, so we still played Berlin Rules. Even First Desk didn't get to know a source's identity, because that was the law. So in retirement Bogart remained Bogart, and only I knew who Bogart was, and Cartwright was fine with that, as he should have been.'

There came a noise from the corridor; someone leaving the lift. Footsteps down the hallway, a door opening, closing. It was unremarkable enough that it might have gone unheard, but Berlin Rules were now in play. Off-stage noise was enemy action. Any footfall might be the last thing you heard.

When all was quiet, he continued.

'Ever go drinking with your old boss? Might have been a contest. He could put it away. Thirst like a fucking camel. Unless he was pouring it under the table.'

She'd thought many things about Jackson Lamb, most of them bad. But it had never occurred to her he'd been a teenage girl. 'So that's it?' she said. 'Charles Partner got you drunk, and you told him who Bogart was?'

The look he gave would have turned a younger woman to stone.

'Or enough,' she said, 'that he could work it out and sell the name?'

'He didn't have to.' Lamb's words were hard as bullets. 'He only had to sell a single syllable.'

That made no sense, until it did. What single syllable could make a difference? Only one Catherine could think of.

She.

Lamb wasn't looking at her now, or at anything else. He might have been the genie hiding in the lamp, contemplating all the wishes he'd heard down the years.

'I didn't think he'd noticed. End of the week, I went back to Berlin. Nothing happened until the following month.'

He inhaled dirty air through an unlit tube. His lungs must be dishrags, thought Catherine. Like something you'd pull from a blocked kitchen sink.

'There were only three female Stasi officers of that rank in that department at the time Bogart was operating,' he said. 'It wouldn't have been difficult to identify her. Bit of due diligence. A few weeks at most.'

He looked at the cigarette in his hand, rolled it between his fingers.

'But they weren't fucking perfectionists, were they? So they did all three. No possibility of error, no overtime involved. Hard not to admire the practical approach.'

And then the cigarette disappeared. Up his sleeve, she wondered? Or had he just made it vanish; cast it back into the past he was staring into?

'Ever seen someone hanged with piano wire? For extra points, you tie something heavy to the victim's feet. An iron is good. Leave the body long enough, the head comes clean off.'

'You saw them?'

'No. But I got to hear about it.'

'What did you do?'

'I heaved my fucking guts out.'

'Afterwards.'

'What do you think? I reported back to Cartwright. Because he was the brains of the Service.'

'You told him you'd leaked Bogart's gender, and now Bogart was dead. You joined the dots. You pointed him at Partner.'

And then you shot Partner in his bathtub, she thought. Where I found him.

The memory of it tasted fresh, and probably always would.

Lamb lifted the bottle from between his thighs, and re-examined its label. For a moment she thought he was about to draw its cork with his teeth, but instead he leaned over and replaced it next to its neighbours. And Catherine had to fight a sudden urge to grab it and crack its seal herself. Isn't that what she'd been working up to? She'd been teetering on the edge so long that not to fall would disappoint. Not to drink, not to succumb: that would be an act of betrayal.

But she wasn't going to do so with Lamb as a witness.

And then something he'd said struck her.

'This happened the previous year, you said. The year before you killed him.'

He looked at her, his skin mottled in the hazy light.

'So why did you wait so long? Friend or not, mentor or not, he was a traitor. He had your asset murdered. For money. So why'd you wait, Jackson? Were you hoping you were wrong?'

The cigarette was back, dancing between the fingers of his hand like a miniature baton he'd failed to pass on. Always, he'd be left holding it.

He said, 'I knew I wasn't. Cartwright responded like it was news he'd been waiting to hear, straightforward confirmation. And where the rest of us saw blood and teeth, he saw opportunity. If Partner was dirty, that could be put to use. And that's what happened for the next year. He made Partner work for us again, without Partner knowing it.'

'He fed him misinformation,' said Catherine.

'Oh yes. But nothing you could put a pin in and stick to a board. Whispers, just. That a goldmine had opened up in joe country. That we had a new asset in the enemy camp. He couldn't tell Partner who it was, and Partner couldn't ask, but let's just say that when the next round of promotions hit the Kremlin, we'd have a top-shelf source of a quality we'd never had before.'

'Cartwright was targeting someone. Destroying them with a rumour.'

'Someone bound for greatness.' The cigarette was tap-dancing across his digits, but that aside, she'd never seen Jackson Lamb stiller. Even his breathing seemed silent. 'You wouldn't remember the name. A one-time bright spark who Cartwright thought too bright, too sparky. You don't want the opposition fielding their best players. And any leg you break in the dressing-room, that's time saved on the pitch.'

The last time she'd seen David Cartwright he'd been a scared old man, nervy of shadows. Perhaps it was true what they said about age: that in its darker corners lurk the monsters of our own making.

'The following year I was called back to London. And that's when it happened.'

When you shot Charles Partner in his bathtub, she thought again. Where I found him.

'Cartwright's timing was immaculate, I'll give him that. Moscow wouldn't believe for an instant that Partner killed himself. The way they saw it, it was proof positive he was onto something, and we whacked him before he could sell it.'

'Did it work?'

Lamb looked away, at the makeshift glass wall. He must have been able to see his reflection shining back at him; a fly's-eye view of his own gross shape.

'Well, the bright spark was fucked right enough. Molly Doran could probably tell you where he is now, and it's probably the Russian equivalent of Slough House, but he hasn't bothered the world since. He must still be wondering what hit him.'

'Quite the little triumph for the Park, then.' Catherine closed her eyes and saw it again: Partner's body in the bathtub; the contents of his head a red mess on the porcelain. A pulpy mixture, like trodden grapes. Some memories seared themselves on your mind, like a shadow on a wall after a nuclear flash.

'Yeah, that depends, doesn't it? Because the role he'd been lined up for, that was a biggie. Director of the FSB, which is what they called the KGB after the makeover. Only with boyo shafted, Yeltsin had to turn to his second choice. Care to hazard a guess who that was?'

Her vision shimmered, unless it was the light faltering. '. . . No. No, that can't be true.'

'Makes you think, doesn't it?' He sneered. 'Maybe David Cartwright wasn't the mastermind he pretended to be. Unless he had his own reasons for giving Vladimir Putin a leg up. On Spook Street, it's hard to know what to believe.'

Catherine stared at him in horror.

'But me, I think it's the law of unintended consequences. For other examples, see the history of the fucking world.'

Lamb put the unlit cigarette in his mouth again.

'They gave me Slough House once the shitstorm died down, and you know what they say. My gaff, my rules. And you know what rule one is. Nobody messes with my stuff. I don't know what Frank Harkness is up to, and I don't care. He left bodies in my yard, and he'll pay for that. And if the Park's pulling his strings, they'd better have another puppet ready. Whatever game they're playing, he's off the board.'

He stood so suddenly she thought the world had shifted; that the building was tumbling, and he'd been thrown loose. With the wave of an arm, he took in her treasures. 'So all of this, Standish, all this dancing about with your personal demons, nobody cares. Least of all me. Drink or don't, but make your fucking mind up and do it quick. Because I have better things to worry about than how far you're gunna fall, and what kind of splash you'll make when you hit the bottom.'

She found a voice somewhere, and used it. 'Always a comfort to have you around.'

'Just doing my job.'

She sat while he forced his feet back into his shoes and clumped from her flat. All around her the bottles whispered, their rose-blood colouring staining the air. When all was quiet again she stood and walked to the window. Lamb was down there, on the street, but he disappeared into shadow as she watched. Where he belonged, she thought.

It occurred to her that he'd neither opened a bottle, nor taken one with him. But there were other things to think about, and she didn't dwell on it long.

Louisa was on her third glass of wine, taking it slowly. On the TV, a rather camp chef was constructing a masterpiece involving squid ink and shredded kale. In Louisa's sink was the pan she'd boiled pasta in and an empty tub of pesto.

She muted the sound when her phone rang.

'You work with that guy?' Emma Flyte asked. 'I mean, spend time with him on a daily basis?'

'He's not that bad when you get to know him.'

'Seriously?'

'No, of course not seriously. He's a dick. You just notice less after a while, that's all.'

Emma said, 'That's not an experiment I plan to undergo.'

'Still time to change your mind. Always an opening at Slough House.'

She could hear Emma shudder and it almost made her smile. Almost.

'But you got what you were after, right?'

'What *you* were after,' Emma corrected her. 'And it's going to cost you. I haven't decided yet, but it might involve a spa day. I need some kind of corrosive cleaning process after that.'

'But he traced the Fitbit.'

'He traced the Fitbit.'

This time Louisa did smile. Day one – not even day one: she'd been at work today. Tomorrow was day one. And already she'd found Lucas. How cool was she?

'So where is it?' she asked.

Emma said, 'I'll text you the actual coordinates. But big picture, it's in a town called Pegsea, in Pembrokeshire.'

'Okay,' said Louisa.

'That's in Wales,' Emma added.

'I know. Somebody told me.'

Afterwards, she zapped the TV off and considered her options, but not for long. Bottom line was, she was due a stupid idea. Her lifestyle choices of the past six months had been reassuringly sober, and mostly couched as a series of negatives: I will not go to bars by myself; I will not hook up with strangers. I will not spend four hundred quid on a pair of boots. Okay, that last one she'd reneged on, but if you were going to backslide, you might as well do it in killer footwear. And she hadn't hooked up with any strangers lately.

Looked like she was going to Wales, then.

She checked her weather app, and confirmed what she suspected: that it had been snowing in Pembrokeshire, with more on the way.

Good job she had a new winter jacket.

Finishing her wine, she went to pack.

Something in his bones had always sung of doom. But nothing in the lyrics had ever suggested this: that he'd be sleeping in his clothes in his office, while his life fell apart around him.

Child porn? You were looking at child porn?

He hadn't been. He had tried to tell her that. Whatever was happening, it was something he'd been thrown into, not something he'd dug for himself.

So why didn't you say? Why hide it from me, we're going to be married, Lech, why did you hide this from me if you're innocent, if it's not true?

For obvious reasons. For obvious fucking reasons, Sara. Because it's child porn, Jesus Christ – even the words rip a hole in your guts.

And besides, he thought. *And besides. You know me. You love me. How can you* possibly *believe that I'd—*

Richard Pynne, he thought. As soon as he'd left the pub, Pynne must have been on the phone. *Let's both save our breath and you get back on home to, remind me. Sara?*

Which was what he'd done, got back on home, after a long walk through the late-night, ghost-blown streets. A day in Slough House, with its damp dissatisfactions, needed flushing out of the system.

And then he was back at the flat, to find Sara in furious tears.

Most of their conversation was thankfully a blur, a mishmash of italicised outrage and grief. He hadn't packed a bag; hadn't been offered the chance. But he'd walked out at last, through a door that had been standing open half an hour, its cold warning blowing right through him. And then the streets again, and the weight of his angry thoughts, and nowhere to go except here. Slough House.

This time of night, it ached like a rheumatic joint. Lech could hear its floorboards wheeze, its pipework bang. It was a warehouse of memories, all of them bad, and now it was having dreams. And he was caught up in them; every time sleep came near, one limb or other thrashed out in alarm. It was as if he were standing on a flight of stairs, his balance fragile as an egg. He mustn't fall. But staying where he was filled him with terror.

Weak light, lamppost light, swam through the window. On the street something clattered to the ground. On the staircase, a shadow broke loose and entered the room.

Lamb.

He moved without a sound, though that was hard to fathom given his bulk, and for a while hovered in front of the desk, his gaze unblinking, unreadable, until at last he shook his head and reached for the landline. He lifted the receiver, punched some numbers, waited a while, then spoke. 'Yeah, customer for you.' He held the receiver out to Lech. 'Samaritans,' he said. 'Quid a minute in the kitty when you're done.'

Lech stared.

Lamb shrugged. 'Or just leave it in your will. Up to you.'

He dropped the receiver, left the room and headed upstairs.

Lech looked at the phone, still live, still softly crooning.

Then he ripped it from its socket and hurled it at the wall.

8

It was snowing by the time Louisa crossed into Wales.

She had set out early; had virtuously breakfasted on muesli and apricots, and packed a bag with nut-based energy bars, carrots, and a pack of what claimed to be yoghurt-covered raisins, though could easily be mouse shit past its best. All of which was more than enough to counterbalance the pair of breakfast McMuffins she picked up later. Roddy Ho had traced Lucas Harper's Fitbit to Pegsea; the map coordinates Emma had pinged her would match, she guessed, Bryn-y-Wharg, or that was how she'd heard it over the phone – the cottage Clare and her boys used twice a year. That being established, she might have easily spent the rest of her sudden holiday hunkered in her flat, working her way through *The Good Wife*. But a fuse had been lit. On the motorway, racing into a cold front, she'd been keenly aware of not being at her desk, compiling a list of suspect library users; of not attending one of Lamb's morale-shafting meetings. Slough House cast a long shadow, but not that long. Here, the sky was a blank page. Traffic was steady, the radio crackly with weather warnings.

If Lucas wasn't at the cottage, she'd get an update on the Fitbit's whereabouts via Emma – might cost her another spa day, but now that Emma had established comms with Roddy Ho, she might as well keep ploughing that furrow. Last thing Louisa wanted was to owe Roddy a favour herself, especially one involving the name Harper. All pennies dropped eventually, even down wells like Roddy Ho, and she didn't want Min's ghost raised among the slow horses. Questions asked. Memories stirred.

Not that there was a shortage of ghosts round Slough House.

A little while back, River had thought he'd received a call from Sidonie Baker. This was fine, as far as it went; Sid had been a slow horse, and what was wrong with a former colleague getting in touch? Except that Sid

Baker was dead: shot in the head, carted away in an ambulance, and that was the last anyone saw of her. She'd been a slow horse, yes – except, somehow, not quite; there was a rumour she'd been planted in Slough House; a rumour which, if true, made her Park, and if she were Park, she might not be dead after all. Because Park couldn't bring you back to life, but it could cover up the fact that you'd never actually died, and what it really really liked to bury was the notion that a mistake had been made, ever. Having an agent go down on a London street with a bullet in her head definitely fell under 'mistake'. So when no record of Sid Baker ever having been admitted to that hospital, in that ambulance, came to light: well, that could mean she'd been whisked away, couldn't it, River wanted to know. Could mean she was still among the living.

Or it could just mean that the Park had found something better to do with the body: for instance, not have it appear in a headline, anywhere, ever.

And what Louisa thought about it was, she didn't know. Probably Sid was dead, and it was best to work on that assumption, because otherwise you'd jump every time the phone rang, or spend your life looking through windows. She hadn't said as much to River, though perhaps should have done. *Get your mourning over.* Couldn't say it now. River had been in a turmoil even before his grandfather died, and he was unlikely to have calmed down now Frank had shown his face again.

But that was in a different country. Because here she was, in Wales.

The snow worsened, and the last twenty minutes of her journey took almost an hour. Satnav was a stranger here, and led her up a few false roads, but in the end there it was, Bryn-y-Wharg, a whitewashed cottage at the top end of a steep lane perpendicular to the main road through the village. Similar properties lined the lane, down one side of which a row of cars was parked, iced with snow an inch thick. It was early afternoon but streetlamps were already lit, flakes swirling round them like a plague of moths. The cottage itself was dark, its windows blank. Louisa parked opposite, where the lane widened before angling around a church wall, and sat reconsidering the day's decisions. She'd kitted up well: she had walking boots and the ski jacket she'd bought before Christmas, when a previous snowfall had blanketed the capital. Even so, she was in new territory, looking for someone she wouldn't recognise, and had nowhere to stay. But this was the choice she'd made. Getting out from under Jackson Lamb's meaty presence; breathing clean cold air, and enjoying being a stranger. Being somewhere new gave you licence. You could reinvent yourself, adjust to a different reality.

And it wasn't like she'd made a life-or-death choice or anything.

Snow drifted across her windscreen. The temperature in the car was rapidly falling.

Louisa grabbed her jacket from the passenger seat, struggled into it, and stepped out into the world.

Secrecy was the Service's watchword, but leaking like a sieve was what it did best. When the leaked material was classified the leaker was tracked down and strung up, or so the handbook required, but gossip was and always had been fair game – who'd lunched who, and where, and how often – and Di Taverner knew better than to attempt to fix that. So when she had a meeting off the books she tagged it personal time in her calendar, happy for her staff to weave erotic legends around her absence, just so long as that kept them from any darker truth.

This lunchtime she was in a club off Wigmore Street, whose members-only dining room was a throwback to what passed for pastoral in the public school imagination: actual wooden benches ran alongside two long tables, gazed down upon by portraits of stern, academically garbed homunculi. This arrangement might have led to communal feasting and lively interaction, but in fact fostered cliquery, which was its main purpose. Diners paired off, or clustered in small groups, with intervening spaces across which to pass the salt, or shuttle a basket of rolls. The occasional woman, suffered as a legislative necessity, was treated with that degree of reverence which borders on contempt, and never realises how transparent it is. The dress code tended towards the baggy.

Most voices bounced off the ceiling; the louder they were, the shallower their content. But underneath that was the bass murmur of business being done.

Di Taverner enjoyed her rare visits, partly because it was always salutary to observe the Establishment with its braces loosened, and partly because it amused her to be one of the few who knew the club to be the brainchild of one Margaret Lessiter, a college contemporary of hers, who had been trading off the blinkered self-regard of men since freshers' week.

There were few diners, the cold weather keeping them away. For the young, winter brings a glow to the cheek; for those of Lady Di's vintage, a certain amount of upkeep is required outside the normal temperature range. She disappeared briefly on arrival; on her reappearance her face was fresh, her features unravaged, and she sat at the far end of one of the benches barely acknowledging the scant others present, whose conversation was muted, but organic – there was a rule about mobile phones, and the rule was: no mobile phones. These remained out of sight; dismantled too, in Di Taverner's case, both battery and SIM card removed. Though she was always struck, on performing such measures, that the increased security they offered was partly offset by a heightened awareness of the vulnerability that demanded such measures in the first place.

For some reason this observation reminded her of her erstwhile boss, Claude Whelan. He'd have enjoyed it. Absent friends, she thought; though, as with the majority of her relationships, it was only absence that made friendship feasible.

The menu did not require study – experience had taught her that the risotto came in smaller quantities than the shepherd's pie, and was therefore preferable – so she sat unoccupied for five minutes. Her lunch-date's lateness did not surprise her. Maintaining his own clock was in keeping with a larger, all-encompassing solipsism; part of a package that had been returned to sender so often that a less arrogant soul might have wondered whether it were correctly addressed. When he at last showed up, it was with no obvious sense of hurry, and he paused to speak to others before joining her. One of those who rose to greet him looked vaguely familiar to Taverner, but in a generic way, as if he'd once belonged to a boy band who'd troubled the charts for a while, but whose disparate units made no impact whatsoever. He offered his card to Taverner's lunch companion, who took it with every sign of enthusiasm, and who was still clutching it as he arrived at her side, where he tore it in two and dropped it on the table.

'One-time policy adviser to David Cameron,' he said in explanation. 'The poor bastard. Who wants that on their CV?'

'Looking for a new role, is he?'

'For a whole new identity, if he has any sense.' He studied her. 'Ravishing as always, Diana. Can't think why you insist on meeting in public.'

'Oh, I'm sure you can.'

Peter Judd smiled in his usual wolfish way.

Still a wolf then; still a beast. True, now that he was less in the public eye he had pulled back on his more obviously camera-friendly habits, like riding a bicycle and spouting Latin. The line he'd once walked had been redrawn, and was no longer a highwire, strung between the City and Westminster Palace; more an invisible thread, connecting interests that were likely subterranean. Former home secretary and one-time scourge of the liberal left, with a personal life not so much lock-up-your-daughters as scorch your earth and erect watchtowers, he was now a private citizen, which, given what he managed to get up to when a public servant, didn't inspire confidence. This being so, Taverner had found it wise to keep a quiet eye on him since he'd left office. Officially at least he was keeping his nose clean, running a PR business, which took a little image-adjustment: Peter Judd had always spent more time jamming bushels over other people's lamps than dimming his own, and an image of him scrubbing his clients' paths to the limelight didn't come easily. People could change, though. It was all she could do not to bark with laughter as that little gem came to mind.

'You're looking very . . . prosperous, Peter.'

'Everyone looks prosperous this time of year. It's why gym membership goes up.' He patted his stomach as he sat, having walked round the bench to be facing her. 'Beach-ready by Easter, don't worry. You appear pretty trim, though. Power agrees with you.'

'I don't think of it as power. I think of it as service.'

He nodded. 'That's damn good. Did you write it yourself?'

'I do hope we're not going to spend all lunchtime sparring. I'm passing up a perfectly good maintenance and upkeep review meeting for this.'

'I'm flattered. Have you ordered?'

She hadn't; they dealt with that. And once the waitress – waitperson, she wondered? Waitstaff? – had retreated, she said, 'So. "Bullingdon Fopp"? Really?'

'Don't pretend you're not amused.'

'Oh, I am. I just wonder you have any clients.'

'Lorry loads. Private jet loads, I should say. Everyone wants to be in on the joke. Because it's no joke. You know how this works, Diana. No network like a college network. Surely First Desk of the intelligence services doesn't need reminding of that. Especially not one with a Cambridge degree.'

'Funny. But only because it was long before my time.'

'Old treacheries cast long shadows. Here's our wine.'

It was poured, and the bottle left in an ice bucket within easy reach.

'And the private sector's a happy hunting ground?' she asked. 'It still feels strange, not seeing your name on the front pages.'

'Consider it a . . . sabbatical.'

Her glass failed to reach her lips. 'A comeback? Seriously? With your history?'

'You want to know the thing about history?' he said. 'History is over. That's its purpose. A few years in the wilderness, breaking bread with the lepers, and you can return rinsed and pure, your sins not so much forgiven as wiped from the public memory. Oh, the occasional high-minded journalist might dig up some long-forgotten peccadillo, but it's one of the blessings of an electorate with a low attention span that once you're out of jail and passed go, you're golden.' He sipped wine. 'Short of kiddy fiddling or animal cruelty, obviously.'

'"Long-forgotten peccadillo"? Orchestrating a coup, near as damn it? Not to mention the attempted hit on a member of the security services.'

'I do miss Seb,' Judd admitted. 'He had a skill set you don't often find in your run-of-the-mill valet.'

'Yes, I'm sure Jackson Lamb would sympathise with your loss,' said Lady Di. 'Though I doubt he'd tell you what he did with the body.'

'That's the way Seb would have wanted it,' said Judd philosophically. 'A nice professional job. No prolonged farewells.'

'Whatever you think of the electorate's short-term memory,' she said, 'I think you can confidently expect Lamb to harbour a grudge. And I'm not sure he'll be happy to see you back in the high life.'

'Lamb can be dealt with, if perhaps less . . . extremely than was attempted last time. I'm sure he has skeletons in his closet.'

'You have more faith in his discretion than I do. I expect Lamb has skeletons at his breakfast table. But that doesn't mean he rattles easily.'

Judd waved an airy hand. 'He's a detail. One of many. Meanwhile, I'm eating a lot of rubber chicken. The political returnee's equivalent of humble pie. And calling in favours, of course. As I said before, no network like a college network. And our new prime minister is – well. Let's just say we go way back.'

Something about the wide-eyed innocence of this statement triggered Taverner's shagdar.

'. . . You're kidding.'

'It never ceases to please me how women who like to appear so in charge in public like nothing better than to be supplicant behind closed doors.'

'Oh, God.'

'Mind you,' he added thoughtfully, 'we don't hear the phrase "strong and stable leadership" anything like as often as we used to. Most of her public appearances, she looks like a woman who's forgotten her safe word.'

The food was arriving. She held her tongue while the plates were set in front of them, and suffered Judd's polite harassment of the waitress – definitely waitress in this context – before speaking again.

'And that's why you invited me to lunch? To let me know you're on the comeback trail? Frankly, Peter, however that goes, I can't see our professional futures being entwined any time soon. And as for private encounters, well. I'm as sentimental as the next girl, but there are some primrose paths best trodden only once, don't you think?'

'And yet I'm sure I'll be scaling those blue remembered hills, in memory at least, for years to come.' He picked up his fork. 'But no. No, my dear. I alert you to my career intentions only because you'll find out about them anyway, and long before the press gets its boots on, I've no doubt. No, I had other things in mind. Something you need to hear.'

'Our opinions as to what I do and don't need are likely to differ,' Diana said. 'But speak your mind. And then I'll decide whether I'm going to have a second glass of this rather ordinary white before I return to work.'

'Forthright as ever.' He kept his eyes on her as he dug his fork into the mashed potato topping of his pie. 'In the first instance, I'm here to demonstrate my bona fides,' he said, unable to resist stressing the word: *boner*. Old habits die hard. 'There's been some . . . activity you should know about.'

'What kind of activity?'

'The kind that falls within your remit, I'm afraid. Yes, national security would be involved. Ideally in a blanket-dropping sort of way.'

'You're going to have to use plain English.'

'In plain English,' said Peter Judd, 'it seems that some rather bad people are about to commit naughty deeds on your patch. Perhaps you'd like me to continue?'

She nodded, and he did.

The barn was old, and gaps between its slats ensured a steady draught. It contained a stew of ancient smells too – rotted animal waste and mulched down hay – and through a hole in its roof a twirling pillar of snow descended, as if a snowman were attempting to rise from the hard-earth floor. But Anton Moser had slept in worse, and there was no reason to suppose he wouldn't sleep in worse again.

They'd arrived – himself, Lars Becker, Cyril Dupont – the day before, having spent the previous night in Stevenage, awaiting instructions. Secret agent bullshit, but Anton had worked for an actual secret service in the past, and knew better than to complain. Besides, he'd take a Travelodge over a barn any night, especially in the snow. All around the landscape was altering, hills smoothing out to a series of uninterrupted mounds, above and behind which the sky loomed huge. On the map the barn was a tiny square by a scrabbly patch of woodland; in reality it had fallen into disuse years ago. The oil patches by the door had dried up, and the few bits of equipment still in evidence, a pitchfork and a pair of shovels, were rusty souvenirs. The ladder to the loft was missing rungs. This hadn't stopped Anton bedding down there, where the animal smells were less pronounced. Probably fewer rats too, unless rats could climb faulty ladders. Anton didn't know. Animals were a closed book.

They were a mile out of town, and a little more than a mile from the coast. It was mostly cliff edge, but he wasn't expecting a sea exfiltration. It would be one of those jobs where you leave a body in a ditch and drive back to the city. By the time the locals found it Anton would back in Cologne, doing what he did best, which was resting between jobs.

'Yo, Anton? You jerking off up there or what?'

'Yeah. I was thinking about those sheep we saw.'

'Ones with the little horns?'

'No, the other kind. The little sexy ones.'

'You're a fuckin' pervert,' said Lars. 'They were under age.'

Anton sat up, stretched. Checked his watch. Two, a little after. It was already dark: nothing but the cloud-covered sky offering light. The sun would probably show up in three or four months. Until then, the locals lit torches, or stayed indoors. Anton didn't understand that shit. He'd grown up bleak, and how he'd fixed that situation was, he'd started walking soon as he was able, and never glanced back.

And look at him now, he thought. Just look at him now.

The job was straightforward. Two colleagues, both of whom he'd worked with before, and a boss – Frank Harkness – who was something of a legend: ex CIA, and then a long career nobody knew much about, which was exactly the sort of reference employers approved of. The man himself had showed up an hour before and done a walk-around, checking the barn, checking the terrain: that was who he was. Always assuming, even in Wales, miles from anywhere, that this was joe country. What Anton thought was, this was sheep country, but being careful was the difference between a long career and a bootless corpse.

Recce done, Frank gave them a heads-up.

'There's been a complication, but nothing you can't handle. The target now has professional help.'

'Yowser,' said Cyril.

'So you might actually have to earn your wages. I hope that's not too alarming a prospect.'

Anton scratched his ankle. He was starting to think all this hay, or its ancient remnants, was having an allergic effect. He was itching like a bastard. 'This help. They in the game?'

'It's nobody you'll have bunked down with, if that's what you're worrying about.'

It wasn't, but it was good to set the picture straight. This job, sometimes you ended up going toe to toe with a former colleague, which

154

caused problems for your sentimental types. The way Anton approached this, he didn't make friends much. This saved heartache down the road.

Frank said, 'It seems the kid's father was a spook, and his mother reached out to a colleague. The colleague's a lady spook, and doesn't represent a huge threat. There's a department where Five keep their screw-ups, and that's where she's from. Slough House. The operatives get called slow horses, and there's a reason for that. But still. She's Five, however low on the food chain, and that means she's in the game. So if she turns up, take her out. We'll worry about the right and wrong ways to treat a lady afterwards.'

'I know how to treat a lady,' Cyril said. 'We should invite her back here, get her to pull a train. Would warm this shithole up.'

Frank ignored that. 'I've got art,' he said. 'Gatecrashed a gathering.' He produced his phone, called up a photo, passed it around, Cyril first.

Cyril made an *unk-unk* noise and wrapped a hand round his crotch.

And Cyril, thought Anton, really should get in touch with himself. Always first to brag about getting some action; always last out of the showers when bunking with a crew. It was the twenty-first century, for Christ's sake. Nobody gave a damn which way he swung, so long as he could lay down supporting fire in a landing zone. Anton, personally, would carry a rifle for gay rights, so long as he got paid. Didn't matter to him. Generally turned out, of course, that those writing the cheques were sticklers for traditional values. But what could you do?

Meanwhile, *unk-unk*.

The phone reached him, and the woman was a looker, sure, especially after a couple of days in a barn. Brunette but with blonde highlights; nice figure in a formal-looking outfit. Dark eyes. But there were several things you couldn't tell about a woman just by looking, and one was how she'd handle herself in a firefight. This chick was spook-trained. Damaged goods, but you always had to factor in dumb luck. So if she showed up in any of the wrong places, Anton wouldn't hesitate to mess up her highlights.

Frank said, 'Three hours till boots up. I want you in place ninety minutes before the kid shows, and I don't want any complaints about the weather. Make it clean, make it tidy, and leave the body in a nice deep drift. Any luck, it'll be June before anyone finds him. Questions?'

'This lady spook,' Cyril said. 'She be armed?'

'Doubtful.'

'Because—'

'No guns. It's got to look accidental. I'll say it again. Questions?'

Nobody had questions.

'I'm heading into town, where I plan to enjoy a nice hot meal. We'll regroup here at twenty-two hundred, where you will tell me there were no problems. Becker, you've got the command. Gentlemen.'

Frank Harkness left the barn, and a moment later they heard his car start, then rumble off through steadily falling snow.

'Becker, you've got the command,' Anton said.

Lars's salute turned into a finger, stoutly raised.

'Three hours from now, we'll be lucky to get anywhere without a plough,' Cyril grumbled. 'It's fucking Narnia out there.'

'We're getting paid, aren't we?' Lars said.

Anton scratched his damn ankles again, and decided to heat up some soup.

Heading out into weather like this, they'd need something hot inside them.

The other diners had left, after a protracted session of backslapping. More than once, the shop-soiled boy wonder who'd pressed his card on Peter Judd glanced their way, hoping for a farewell wave, or a job offer, but to Judd, as to the public at large, he'd ceased to exist.

Diana's risotto was a congealing mess, though she'd nibbled an asparagus tip or two. Judd's shepherd's pie, on the other hand, was now mostly a gravy-traced outline.

This hadn't stopped his flow of words.

'One of my clients runs a factory in the north-west. It specialises in, let's say, machine parts.'

'Let's.'

'Very technical, sophisticated—'

'I know which factory you're referring to, Peter. I know precisely what you mean by "machine parts". And I even know the name of the man who, behind a positive thesaurus of false-flag identities, actually owns said factory. So you might as well cut to the chase.'

'You're well informed.'

'I'm head of the Secret Service. I thought we'd established that.'

He bowed, ever so slightly. 'Said man, then, in the cause of public relations, occasionally arranges discreet get-togethers, in remotish locations. Those involved shun the limelight. But at the same time they expect a certain amount of . . . razzmatazz. An indication that their custom is not unappreciated. That, whatever the public perception of such arrangements, their business is not only legal but a necessary fillip to the economy of our own and other nations.'

'Spare me the editorial. They're arms dealers, not gentleman warriors.'

Judd gave the slightest of smiles, refilled their glasses, then inserted the empty bottle upside down in its bucket. 'And to make sure such gatherings go smoothly, our friend likes to make sure they're also attended by personages of quality. The kind whose presence impresses both domestic and foreign parties, and ensures that negotiations are conducted in an atmosphere free from unseemly rancour.'

'Which is where you come in.'

'I've sat at table with government leaders the world over, you know that. My address book positively oozes quality. The proper one, I mean. Not the little red one.'

Which positively oozed available company, no doubt.

'Go on.'

'There was a particular occasion,' he said, 'just before the new year. Which, as you might imagine, required a certain celebratory atmosphere.'

'Are we talking hookers and cocaine, by any chance?'

'It's not impossible.'

'Funny, isn't it,' she said. 'No matter how sophisticated and technical the machine parts on offer, it's always girls and drugs that oil the wheels. So what went wrong?'

'Nothing drastic.'

'Then why are we discussing this? I'm already aware that nasty deals are the market's lifeblood, and I don't need you to tell me how, once we're sundered from Europe, we're going to be bedding down with some unpleasant customers. Be that as it may, I don't pick fights outside these borders. If the deal you're talking about broke no laws, and no one ended up dead in a bathroom, then I don't need to hear the details.'

'And yet here we are. May I continue?'

She didn't bother hiding her sigh. 'If you must.'

'On the occasion we're discussing, which took place in Pembrokeshire, at a place called Caerwyss Hall, the personage of note in attendance was, let's say, exceptionally high born.'

'Does he have a name?'

'On such occasions, he prefers to go by a number. Number Seven, in fact.'

'How tiresomely like a Bond villain.'

'Well, in his case, the number has significance. It being how close in line to the seat of power he was at the time.'

He waited while tumblers rolled in her eyes.

'. . . Oh, Christ.'

'Yes.'

'Are you telling me that the Duke of bloody—'

'*Hush.*' He put a hand on her wrist; squeezed it. 'No names. Here or anywhere else.'

She said, 'Remove that. Now.'

Judd did so.

'Number Seven has been an invaluable asset for decades, an ambassador for growth and wealth generation. But it's in nobody's interests that his work on behalf of certain sectors of British industry becomes a topic of public chatter. Regardless of the huge amount of wealth generated, and the resulting benefit to Her Majesty's Revenue and Customs.'

'Or, in his case, Mummy's Revenue and—'

'Yes, yes, very funny.'

Diana realised her glass was empty. She hadn't noticed draining it. 'You just told me nothing went wrong. Please underline that for me.'

'Nothing went wrong,' he said. 'As such.'

'Oh, God in heaven.'

'But there was a boy.'

'A boy? I know he likes them young, but I thought—'

'No. One of the staff catering the event. Apparently he was the curious type, and saw something he shouldn't have. And while I wasn't actually present the entire time the, ah, conference was taking place—'

'Conference.'

'—Yes, conference, I was nominally its convenor, since my firm made all the arrangements. So this boy decided I was his first phone call.'

'What did he want?'

'Fifty thousand.'

'And what did he see?'

Judd said, 'Well, we could probably call it fifty thousands' worth, in the circumstances. I mean, the bar bill came to more than that.'

'I assume he had some kind of recording.'

'He made no such claim. He simply asserted knowledge of Number Seven's presence at what he called an orgy, and suggested I might like to buy his silence. Before, as he put it, things went viral.'

'And have you paid?'

'Not yet.'

'But you plan to?'

Judd picked up his empty glass and revolved it slowly in his hand. Unusually, he seemed unwilling to look at her while doing so. For Peter Judd, any physical action undertaken in the presence of a woman was foreplay; doubly so if the action involved food or drink. Or plucking his nasal hairs, in all likelihood. But now, his gaze directed elsewhere, he said, 'I may have made a . . . tactical error.'

'A tactical error,' she said flatly.

'It happens.'

'I know it happens, Peter. I know it even happens to you. But hearing you admit it, well. That's on the level of a Tour de France winner testing clean.'

'I decided the best thing to do was throw a scare into the boy.'

'Of course you did.'

'And that it might be best if I weren't immediately involved. Given my current intentions.'

'You mean, given your plans to re-enter politics, you'd rather not be dragging a traumatised teenager in your wake? I see your old nous hasn't deserted you.'

'So I, ah, referred the matter upwards.'

'You resorted to prayer.'

'Not exactly.'

'No, I didn't think so. Who? One of the parties at this *conference*, right?'

He nodded.

'And they are?'

'Let's say they're a nation state currently looking to consolidate their power base.'

'By eradicating opposition within their borders, no doubt.'

'I'm a democrat, Diana. And I believe in the sovereignty of nations.'

'How wonderful for all concerned. What did they do?'

'They may have brought in hired help,' he said. 'Professionals.'

'Mercenaries.'

Judd nodded, once.

'So,' Taverner said. 'We have a teenage boy who witnessed God only knows what depravities involving sex, drugs and a senior royal, as a sideshow to an arms deal. And one of the parties to the deal plans to kill him before he can make this public.'

'You can't be sure they intend to kill—'

'And Peter Judd is having a crisis of conscience. I think that's the detail that really frightens me.' She picked up her glass, put it down again. Nothing in it. 'Okay, you've got my attention. What arrangements were made? For paying off the boy, I mean.'

'A handover near where it happened, in Pembrokeshire. As the boy suggested.' The hint of a sneer crossed his face. 'I rather suspect he wanted me to think he's local.'

'So you managed to identify him.'

'Well it wasn't complicated, Diana. And even in Seb's absence, I do have staff.' He paused. 'There is a slight further, what shall I call it? Further *wrinkle* you should know about.'

She sighed. 'Enlighten me.'

'His father was one of yours.'

'One of my what?'

'A *spook*, Diana. He was in Five. Deceased now, but in his time, yes. Name of Harper.'

Di Taverner said, 'It never stops, does it?' She thought a moment. 'The only Harper I recall was one of Lamb's. A slow horse.'

Judd said nothing.

'Which means Lamb will almost certainly find a way of complicating matters.'

'There's no reason he should find out about this.'

'Not having a reason is one of the things Lamb does best.' She looked him in the eye. 'I'm still unconvinced by the crisis of conscience.'

'Maybe I just wanted to do you a favour.'

'With an eye on my owing you one.'

'And Number Seven remaining firmly in the shadows. Whatever the outcome.'

Di Taverner said, 'Oh, absolutely. We must safeguard our national treasures.'

She rose to go.

Judd said, 'We have more to discuss.'

'I don't have time.'

'I don't mean now. Once this matter has been . . . disposed of.'

'I'm not in the mood for cloak and dagger, Peter.'

'Aren't you? I rather thought that was your thing.' He stood too. 'We'll talk more. To your advantage. Trust me.'

She laughed. 'Trust you? Oh, Peter. You say the funniest things.'

He leaned across as if to embrace her, but she was already on the move.

Snow had blurred the boundaries between road and verge, casting all it covered in a strange new light. Louisa parked at the top of a lane running down to a crossroads, fields in all directions, and before her headlights died noted that the fenceposts they illuminated were the aftermath of battle: a row of spears, protruding from graves. And then just fenceposts again. With the car quiet the world became huge, and mostly dark, though a dark blanketed by soft white numbness. There'd been no traffic on the road. Locals knew better than to venture out in this.

Earlier, she'd called Emma from a pub on Pegsea's high street. Emma, it would be fair to say, hadn't been delighted with her updated request.

'You want me to talk to him again?'

'You can do it on the phone this time.'

'That's still talking. You get that, right? That talking to someone on the phone is still talking?'

'But it beats being up close and personal.'

'You're actually in Wales now?'

'Yep.'

'You're insane. I heard on the radio they were expecting another six inches.'

'Probably a man said that. In which case it'll be more like two.'

'What's it doing now?'

She'd looked out of the window. 'You ever see *The Day After Tomorrow*?'

'God.'

'Look, I know Roddy. If he tracked this thing for you last night, he'll still be tracking it now. It'll take him like five seconds to update the coordinates. Five seconds. Max. And I need this, Emma. The kid's not at the cottage. Doesn't look like he's been there.'

'God,' said Emma again. Then: 'Two spa days. And you come with me.'

'Deal.'

'I'll need both,' Emma grumbled. 'Just to get the feel of his eyes off my skin.'

She called back within the hour. Roddy Ho, Louisa surmised, was keen to impress Emma Flyte.

'Okay,' Emma had said. 'Did we say four spa days?'

'Cumulatively,' Louisa agreed. 'He manage it?'

'You got a pencil?'

The coordinates Emma gave her were for Lucas Harper's Fitbit, in real time.

'And he's pretty static.'

'Hope he's not dead in a ditch.'

There was a pause.

Emma said, 'Is that a likely scenario?'

'Just a turn of phrase.'

'What are you getting into here?'

'Nothing. He's a missing kid, that's all. I've never even met him.'

'And yet there you are, in Wales.'

'Like I said. I knew his father.'

The numbers squiggled on the scrap of paper in front of her meant nothing by themselves. Were meaningless, without a map to make them solid.

'Call me later,' Emma said. 'When you find him.'

'Okay.'

'Or if you don't. Call me anyway. Nine o'clock.'

'Nine o'clock,' Louisa agreed.

And now she was here, an hour short of that deadline; her map app – map app, she liked that; it looped in her mind: *map app, map app* – having pinpointed the Fitbit as being within a couple of hundred yards. She'd been expecting a building, a pub most likely, but there was nothing; just a junction at the foot of a slope, around which some trees had gathered. More woodland lay across the snow-covered fields. And somewhere beyond them was the sea.

A crossroads in the dark. An insignificant junction: what on earth was Lucas Harper doing there? And where was he, anyway? Emma's words came back to her, *What are you getting into?* That Lucas didn't want to be found was a given, else why would he leave his phone behind? But even so, this was a strange hiding place. It looked like somewhere you'd arrange a handover, or an ambush. Maybe better to approach on foot, as quietly as she could manage. And maybe better not to be totally unprepared.

From the boot she took her tiny backpack and her all-purpose tool: a monkey wrench, once used in battle by Shirley Dander. And as long as she was being careful, best not to stride down the middle of the road. She'd walk by the fenceposts, where the snow was deeper, but a scraggly runt of a hedge offered cover. But as she made her way down the slope, something snagged at her: *fuck!* – her new ski jacket. A triangular tear on the right breast now, a flap of fabric hanging loose. This was what you got, doing favours for strangers. Damn it to hell, she thought. Damn it to hell.

Wrench in hand, and thoroughly pissed off, Louisa Guy made her way down the slope to the tree-marked junction below.

Part Two
Wild Geese

9

When his buzzer buzzed, breaking sleep, River assumed it was a malfunction. His buzzer never buzzed. Buzzers were for friends he didn't have; maybe bringing a bottle, or asking if he fancied a walk. For a life in which he'd throw sticks for dogs and wear a loosely knotted scarf, like in a movie montage. But before he could get his head any further round that, his buzzer buzzed again.

There was little noise outside. This would have been worth celebrating, any other time: there was a nightclub nearby, and the quietest moments River enjoyed after dark were in those brief interludes that followed someone getting stabbed, or a bottle being smashed. Here, though, was the lull between the last Uber and the first delivery truck, a respite he generally observed by sleeping through it. Whoever this was better have a good excuse.

He wore jogging bottoms and a grey T-shirt. Bare feet. Frigid floor.

The spy who walked round in the cold.

Through his intercom he could hear someone waiting by the building's entrance. 'It's six o'clock in the morning,' he told them.

'It's Emma Flyte.'

He hadn't expected that. Mind you, he hadn't expected anything: that was more or less the definition of surprise.

'Mind if I come in?'

'I didn't think you lot asked.'

'You might not have heard. I'm no longer at the Park.'

'Oh, right, yeah.' He shook his head: still half asleep. 'I knew that.'

'So . . .'

He pushed the button that unlocked the building.

She appeared at the top of the stairs moments later, and walked through the door he was holding without looking impressed. River couldn't blame her. He wasn't impressed himself, and his standards were doubtless lower than hers. The flat, a one-bed, was shabbily decorated, and scored low on ambience and everything else, not to mention being further east than he imagined she usually ventured, though as soon as he caught that thought he corrected himself: Emma Flyte was ex-Met. She might look like a model, but she'd walked a beat. Had dragged villains from grubbier dwellings than this.

It was easy to fall into the trap of underestimating beautiful women. And best to avoid doing so while wearing jogging bottoms.

While he was thinking all this, she'd taken control of the room. 'Louisa's gone off the radar,' she said.

'Louisa's gone on leave,' he told her. 'I mean, don't get me wrong, I love Service jargon. But she filled in a form and everything.'

'Thanks, I knew that. And probably wouldn't be here if that's what I'd meant. Nice as your place is.'

'My cleaner's not been well.'

'Looks like your cleaner got old and died. Possibly of shock when decimal currency came in. But like I say, not what I'm here for. Louisa called me yesterday, asking for a favour. She promised to check in later. She didn't.'

River nodded, mostly to get circulation going in his head. 'Okay. I— Do you want coffee?'

'Do you have any?'

'I'm not sure.'

'Then let's pretend you didn't bother asking. Did she tell you where she was going?'

'She didn't tell me anything. She just waved goodbye on her way out. What favour did she ask?'

'She wanted me to run a trace.'

'Car? Phone?'

'Fitbit,' Emma said.

'. . . Yeah, okay. Not sure I've come across that before, but . . .'

'But you're basically wearing a GPS.'

'So it can be done, I get that. But you're no longer at the Park. You just said.'

'Top marks, paying attention. No, I'm not. I didn't run this through the hub. Point of fact, I got your colleague onto it.'

'. . . Ho?'

'Ho.'

'You asked Roddy Ho a favour?'

'You don't think he'd do me one?'

'I think he'd roll over and waggle his legs in the air. I just wouldn't have thought that was something you'd want to see.'

Emma said, 'Louisa said she needed it done. Can we move on? The Fitbit belongs to one Lucas Harper. That name ring bells?'

'Harper?'

'Lucas.'

'Min Harper was a colleague,' River said slowly. 'He and Louisa were . . . together.'

'Were?'

'He died.'

'Okay . . . And Lucas?'

'Min had children,' said River. 'Lucas might be one of them. Where did he turn out to be?'

'Pegsea,' said Emma. 'Pembrokeshire.'

'That's in Wales.'

'I believe so.'

'And you told Louisa this, and then she went dark?'

'That's right, you like a bit of jargon. No, it didn't happen that quickly. After I spoke to her, she drove off to Wales. Then later she asked for an update, and I got Roddy—'

'Ho.'

'—to confirm the location. I passed that on to Louisa too, the map reference, so she could find Lucas. And the last thing she said was—'

'That she'd call back.'

'Once she'd found him. But she didn't. And I've called her a dozen times. Goes straight to voicemail.'

River rubbed his eyes. Most of the night he'd lain awake, thinking about his father: what Frank was up to, why he'd reappeared. What move he might make next. Yesterday, while – it turned out – Louisa had been driving to Wales, he'd gone to Stevenage, to examine the Travelodge Frank had checked in to. Nothing. No clues, no tracks. The best he'd managed was a list of number plates: all the cars that had registered there that week. He'd not given Louisa a thought, beyond the disgruntlement he'd felt at her taking off, just when it looked like they might see action.

'Cartwright?'

'I'm thinking.'

'I can tell that requires your total attention. But is there any chance you could speed it up?'

He made a decision. 'What's it doing outside?'

'Getting ready to snow. In fact, it's only just marginally warmer out there than it is in here. How much detail do you want?'

'Keep your hair on. I was wondering what to wear.'

'You're planning on getting up? That's good.'

He said, 'Louisa's had her moments. She might have met someone in a pub and forgotten she said she'd call. But . . .'

'But?'

'But not if she was on a job. Especially not if the job involved Min.'

'Yes, I wondered about that. So I woke Ho an hour ago, and got him to run another trace.'

River waited.

Emma said, 'The Fitbit's not moved in the last few hours. Nor has Louisa's phone. And they're both in the same place. Which appears to be a roadside ditch.'

The current head of Tricks and Toys – the Park's gadget section, which also oversaw tech issues; like a high-street phone outlet had merged with a party shop – was a forty something redheaded black woman named Terrance. Richard Pynne was confident the red hair was a chemical intervention, and pretty sure Terrance couldn't be her first name, but that was what everyone called her, and though he made a mental note after each encounter to check her personnel file, had never followed through. T&T, anyway, he kept at broomstick's length ever since he'd queried the timekeeping of a junior glitch-monkey – the guy was arriving twenty to thirty minutes late on a daily basis: there was leeway, and then there was taking the piss – and that same afternoon found his Oyster card inexplicably fundless. Sometimes you were outgunned. But his long-term plan was to wait for the next round of development appraisals, then shaft the little bastard with a poison-tipped memo.

But right this minute, bright and early Friday morning, he was in a corridor, and here was Terrance buttonholing him.

'I've finished with the rogue laptop.'

It took Pynne a moment to work out which laptop she meant.

'And?'

'And my report's in your inbox.'

'You couldn't give me the bullet points?'

She could, she did, and like every IT professional everywhere, ensured it was unlikely he'd grasp her meaning first time round. By the third dumbed-down repetition, though, he thought they were, if not on the same page, somewhere in the same chapter.

He said, 'So what I'm understanding here, what I'm taking away is, you can't categorically state, one hundred per cent, that the material found on the hard drive was downloaded by the certified user.'

'That's right.'

Which punched a hole in the case against Lech Wicinski. It wasn't just his laptop they were talking about, it was his culpability.

'And if it were introduced by a third party, there's no way of knowing who.'

'Except it would have to be a savvy operator. The protection on our gear's world standard,' Terrance said. 'Bypassing it's a lot more complicated than dicking with someone's Oyster card.'

Pynne thought, on the whole, he'd let that one go.

'So not just a potential bad actor. A potential *state* bad actor?'

'Would be my guess.'

'And would you have a shortlist? Who'd have the, ah, chops to pull this off?'

She said, 'China, India, for sure. The Russians, probably.'

'Americans?'

'Nah.'

He said, 'What about the Germans?'

'Hmm. Possibly.'

'. . . Thanks.'

'But I'm not saying for definite it happened that way. Twenty per cent chance, maximum.'

'Okay.'

'Which is still way too big to let pass. I'm going to have to go for a rebuild on the firewall. Which will require an overspend.'

'Okay,' he said again. 'Thanks. But listen. When you're applying for the funding, don't mention this in your business case. It's highly classified. Highly.'

'Right,' Terrance said. 'So I've got to apply for funds to patch a possible hole in our firewall which I'm not allowed to mention when applying for the funds.'

Pynne allowed that it wasn't ideal.

'Nah,' she said. 'Regent's Park. Business as usual.'

She went on her way.

Pynne returned to his office, and deleted the email she'd sent him.

Two hours later River was on his fourth coffee: this one supposedly a double-shot Americano, though he'd had more kick from a cough drop. He was at a counter pressed up against a café window, the stool too high for comfort: he had to sit sideways, because his knees wouldn't fit. Shirley Dander didn't have the same difficulty, on account of having, as she put it, a lower centre of gravity: lot of syllables for shortarse, he remembered thinking first time he'd heard that. He'd called her once Emma Flyte had left, not because she was top of the list of people he'd call in an emergency, but because he had no such list. He was going to have to do something constructive about his life soon, but at the moment was too busy negotiating his way through it.

Shirley's demands were predictable enough: a cappuccino and a sausage sandwich, the latter so lathered in ketchup, she looked like an extra from a zombie movie two bites in. That was for turning up. Getting her to listen to what Flyte had said was more of a struggle.

'So she's missing.'

'Yes.'

'In Wales.'

'Yes.'

'What the fuck's she doing in Wales? It's just sheep and windmills.'

River, who wasn't certain about the windmills, said, 'She was looking for someone.'

'Someone Welsh?'

'Someone specific. Min Harper's son, in fact.'

'Min Harper?'

'Uh-huh.'

Shirley thought about that for a moment.

Outside, the first few flakes of London snow were drifting down. By the time the third or fourth one hit the ground, buses would be returning to their depots.

'Flyte told you this?'

'Yes.'

'She's seriously hot.'

'And reliable.'

Shirley considered this. 'I don't necessarily need them reliable,' she said. 'But I do like them hot.'

'She says Louisa's phone hasn't moved in however long it's been. Twelve hours? She's worried.'

'Maybe Louisa's asleep.'

'She said she'd check in with Emma.'

'Maybe she forgot.'

'And she's not picking up calls. And Flyte reckoned her phone might be in a ditch.'

'How could she tell?'

'Roddy tracked its coordinates.'

'Can you be that accurate? To, like, the nearest inch?'

'I don't know.'

'Because it doesn't sound likely to me. Maybe they're just accurate to the nearest motel. In which case probably Louisa's found this kid, and is road-testing him for his old man's sake.'

'You're kind of sick, you know that?'

In response, Shirley banged on the window.

The café was the other side of the road and a little way down from Slough House, between a hardware store and a Costcutters, and until recently had been vacant for six months, prior to which it had been an almost identical café but with different-coloured chairs. Its sole attraction for the slow horses was its proximity, which was the reason J. K. Coe was walking past now, garbed in his usual hoodie despite the cold, his head invisible, his hands jammed into pockets. When Shirley thumped the window he started. River only imagined, but it wasn't that big a leap, Coe's fist appearing with a blade in its grip. Coe was a sleeping dog: if you were going to startle him, River thought, it was as well to have a pane of glass in between.

Meanwhile Coe had stopped in his tracks and was staring at them.

'Do you think he recognises us?' River said, his lips barely moving.

Shirley gestured to Coe to join them. 'Being a psycho doesn't make him a bad person,' she said.

'No,' agreed River. 'It's being a bad person makes him that.'

Coe entered like someone expecting a hostile welcome.

Shirley said, 'Louisa's gone missing in Wales. Are you getting coffee? Can you get me another?'

Coe looked at River. 'Wales?'

'If you're at the channel, look up and left,' River explained.

Coe ignored that. 'It's snowing.'

'I noticed.'

'It's snowing worse in Wales.'

Shirley and River shared a look. 'I think,' Shirley said slowly, 'I *think* he might mean that everyone in Wales right now has technically gone missing. On account of the snow.'

Coe shrugged.

'That's good input, thanks,' said River.

Coe shrugged again.

'I was talking to Shirley.'

They watched as Coe left the café and continued on his way to Slough House.

'Sometimes I think he's just plain weird,' Shirley said. 'And at other times I totally get him.'

'Well he's fuck all use either way,' said River.

'What are you going to do?'

'I don't know.'

'Wales'll be, like, closed by now.'

'I know.'

'And Frank's out there somewhere. We're just waiting to find out where.'

River didn't answer. Yes, Frank was out there somewhere, posing as a Canadian, or had been. But his hire car had dropped off the map, and he'd have a new ID by now. Given the run of the hub, they'd pinpoint his whereabouts in hours, but with the resources at their disposal River might as well be on Slough House's roof, using a kitchen roll holder as a telescope.

And meanwhile Louisa was missing. And Louisa was his friend.

Unless she was just on a jolly, and had lost her phone.

'Flyte admitted it might not be an actual ditch,' he said. 'I think she just wanted me to treat it like an emergency.'

'Well, if Louisa has been in a freezing ditch all night, the emergency part's probably over by now,' said Shirley.

'Thanks.'

'Hey, she's your friend. She's always been arsey with me.'

'What if it were Marcus?'

'He'd have been a lot easier to find in the snow,' Shirley conceded.

Seems River wasn't the only one spending too long in Lamb's company.

They finished their coffees and walked to Slough House, the weather gathering pace: nothing lying yet, the ground still eating it up, but give it time, give it time. He'd speak to Lamb, he decided. If Lamb thought a joe was in peril—

And then Coe was approaching, emerging from the alley round back of Slough House.

'Wales,' he said.

'What about it?' said Shirley.

'Those plates from Stevenage.' He was talking to River. 'I ran them through ANPR.'

'And one of them's now in Wales,' said River.

'Two of them,' said Coe, but River was already gone.

The walkway round Regent's Park's rooftop was narrow, and cradled by the overhanging tiles of a steeply angled roof on one side and an eight-inch wall on the other. A route allowing for maintenance work, it had never been intended for casual use, but the view it offered meant that most of the Park's regulars made the occasional foray up here, a tradition memorialised by the innumerable cigarette ends trodden underfoot. Diana Taverner led the way from the access door to the building's north-east corner and paused by a squat turret, an outlet of some sort, from whose wire grille a metallic odour drifted. Snow was starting to pattern the tiles. Between a gutter and the overhang, a spider was tuning its web.

Behind her, Oliver Nash said, 'Is this really necessary?'

'I like it up here,' Taverner said, not looking round. 'Reminds me what's at stake.'

'A very London-centric attitude, if you don't mind my saying so.' He was hanging back as much as he could without it looking like he was doing so.

They weren't that high, but they were high enough. There were few soft landings in the city. The view was metal and glass, weeping concrete, a distant splash of golden stone. From where she stood, Taverner could read the date carved into the brow of the building opposite: 1893. Many older constructions carried such badges. Newer ones didn't, as if less sure of their place in history, or the future. Buildings are more vulnerable than they used to be. One of the reasons she was here.

'Diana?'

'Would you rather go back down?'

His every feature screaming *Yes*, Oliver Nash shook his head. 'Let's get on with whatever game you're playing, shall we? Before we both freeze our balls off.'

'Nicely put.' She turned. 'I want to trigger the Fugue Protocol.'

'. . . I see.'

It rather seemed he didn't.

'Oliver?'

'The Fugue Protocol. And that's, um, that's . . .' He stopped. 'You'll have to forgive me.'

'Of course.'

'I'm normally on top of my brief.'

'Yes.'

'It's just that there's such an awful lot of—'

'We have Wi-Fi, Oliver. If you want to verify your standing orders, go right ahead.'

'Thank you.'

With a show of reluctance, he produced his phone. Diana watched while he called up the Service intranet, entered his code, and burrowed into his office's back story: duties and expectations, liabilities, known unknowns. His appointment, unlike hers, had not arrived ballasted by a decade's preparation.

'The Fugue Protocol,' he said at length. 'Yes, I remember now.'

Funny how you always remember right at the end, a little voice squeaked inside her.

'A home-soil operation, with no oversight.'

'That's correct.'

'You want to go under the bridge.'

'There. Anyone would take you for a lifer.'

'There's no need to mock.'

'Just lightening the mood. Are you up to speed with the implications?'

He was still squinting at his phone, its text a little undernourished for close reading. 'And you don't wish to provide a reason why.'

'That would be the nub, yes.'

Nash pursed his lips. 'Somewhat unorthodox, don't you think?'

'It's precisely orthodox. That's why it's a protocol. With a specific procedure attached.'

'Designed for extreme levels of emergency,' he said. 'For use in conditions of extreme secrecy. So in the wrong hands – forgive me. In the wrong *circumstances*, a tool for any manner of black mischief.'

'I'm in this post because I'm trusted, Oliver. This is one of those moments when you have to rely on that trust, and let go of the tiller.'

He looked out over London's rooftops, perhaps seeing in their boxed and fluted shapes, their haphazard geometry, the same thing she had seen a moment ago. The very modern problem cities shared: that they were always left out in the open.

'I trust you. What I'm less . . . *sanguine* about is the current state of the coffers. No oversight means an uncontrolled spend. And we are not currently in a position where I'm comfortable with that.'

'The whole point of the Fugue Protocol is that it supersedes such considerations.'

'Not to mention bypassing the steering committee. And the Minister. Which is the reason you're seeking to trigger it, am I right? No oversight. That's the key here.'

'The protocol exists for a very good reason.'

'As do its safeguards.' He was looking at his phone again, scrolling through the standing instructions. 'Misuse carries severe penalties, Diana.'

'Yes, thank you. I'm aware of that.'

'And yet, it says here, I have to say this out loud. Wilful and deliberate misinformation – wilful and deliberate, that's a tautology, yes? No matter. Wilful and deliberate misinformation in response to the listed questions could result in prosecution. Being First Desk won't help you.'

'If I weren't First Desk, I couldn't trigger the protocol. It's a bespoke arrangement.'

'Yes, well. Are you sure you want to do this?'

I'm standing on a roof on a January morning, she wanted to say. How serious do you need me to get? But she simply nodded, and waited for him to find the pertinent section of text.

He did so.

'One. Is there a clear and present danger – that's an American phrase, isn't it?' He shook his head. 'Really, I'm not sure we should be borrowing

– oh, never mind. Not the issue.' He cleared his throat. 'Is there a clear and present danger, or has a credible threat been made, to the government and/or its constituent parts, by which I can only presume is meant persons holding offices of state?'

'No.'

He raised an eyebrow. 'Really? I was rather expecting you to say yes there.'

'There are further questions, Oliver.'

'Oh. Right. Yes.' He glanced about, as if expecting a prompt from the wings, then raised his phone to his eyeline again. 'Two. Is there a clear or present danger, or has a credible threat been made, against the person of Her Majesty and/or any member of the royal household, most particularly, but not limited to, immediate family members?'

She said, 'Define threat.'

'That's not an answer. We both know what threat means. Danger to life and limb.'

'I'd have thought a greater latitude was implied.'

The height, the cold, the falling snow: all of these things sharpened Nash's tone. 'Diana. Are you in possession of information suggesting that an attempt may be made on the life or liberty of a member of the royal family? A yes or no answer is required.'

'. . . No.'

'You don't sound certain.'

'I'm alert to the severe penalties you mentioned. What if the danger were reputational?'

He eyed her suspiciously. 'That would be a political matter.'

'A political threat.'

'Which falls outside the bounds of the protocol. Your office is apolitical, Diana. You know that.'

'Of course.'

'Is this the reason you initiated this charade? You believe there's been some kind of non-physical threat to a member of the royal household?'

She thought for a moment, then nodded.

'If you have information regarding anything of the kind, any political shenanigans, it's your duty to bring it to Committee. I shouldn't have to remind you of this.'

'And I shouldn't need to remind you that sources need protection, and that the Committee has been known to leak.'

'Not while I've been chair, it hasn't.'

'Forgive me, Oliver. But my memory goes back further than the last six months. If I bring my concerns to the Committee, they'll require verification, and that will mean giving up my source. Which is not acceptable.'

'I can't authorise you to go free range.'

'Pity.'

'And there's no sense in me reading the rest of these questions out, is there? I'm not authorising the protocol on those grounds, and you have no other grounds to offer. Is that correct?'

She nodded.

'I can't help thinking there's something going on here, Diana.'

'It's the Secret Service, Oliver. There's always something going on.'

'I'll have to minute this.'

'Of course.'

'And it's going to look a little . . . sensationalist of you. If you don't mind my saying so.'

'Do what you have to do.'

'I'm going in now.'

'Good idea.'

She let Nash lead the way back, but paused before following him onto the staircase. Behind her London yawned, then hunched its shoulders. The snow was falling harder, and the sky was iron grey.

The morning had grown old before its time.

And before long, the afternoon was giving up the ghost.

'Let me drive,' Shirley said.

'We're taking shifts, remember?'

'But you're going so slowly!'

'We're in a traffic jam,' River pointed out.

There were three of them. J. K. Coe was in the shotgun seat, staring out of the passenger window. Shirley was behind River, and gripping his headrest: he could feel her tension.

'If you're not gunna get a move on,' she said, 'at least play some music.'

But every radio station so far she'd vetoed on grounds of being lame. And the only CD he could find was called *Metal for Muthas*, and he'd sooner gouge his own eyes out.

'It's like travelling with a teenager,' he said.

'Is not!'

River glanced sideways, but Coe was wired into his iPod, and might as well have been back in Slough House.

The M4 was at a standstill not twenty miles clear of Hillingdon: a lorry had shed its load across the westbound lanes. Radio reports hadn't specified what this was, but River was guessing quick-drying cement. No fatalities, apparently, which Shirley did not take well. Causing her inconvenience should be a capital offence.

Even on the motorway, snow was starting to lie. The country to either side was disappearing under its cloak: a landscape of lumpy fields and pissed-off cattle.

This wasn't what an emergency dash was supposed to look like.

Back at Slough House, he'd gone straight to Lamb's room, the others in his wake. Lamb was at his desk, shoeless, his electric heater pumping out an exhausted warmth that filled the air with the smell of fried dust.

'Louisa's in Wales. I'm going after her.'

'Did I wake up in a fucking romcom?' said Lamb.

'I think she's in danger.'

'Because that would explain the snow,' continued Lamb. 'And the lack of black faces.' He slid a hand inside his shirt. 'Come to think of it, did I wake up in Wales?'

'What makes you think she's in danger?' Catherine said, arriving from her own room.

River said, 'Coe traced two of the cars from the Travelodge where Harkness and his crew stayed. Both crossed the Severn Bridge Wednesday evening.'

'So. Some people drove from Stevenage to Wales,' Catherine said.

'Same time Louisa heads there?'

'Coincidences happen.'

'What's she doing in Wales, anyway?' Lamb asked. 'I assumed she was on the shag. Has she seriously been through everyone closer than that?'

'She's looking for Min Harper's kid.'

For once, Lamb said nothing.

River said, 'Tell me it's a coincidence that Harkness and his crew are exactly where Louisa went.'

'Well,' Catherine said. 'The same country. If it was even them.'

'Wales, though. It's not a huge place.'

'It's exactly the size it is, isn't it?' Shirley said. 'Reports are always saying something's "an area the size of Wales". And that's exactly the size Wales is.'

This was met with a short silence.

Lamb said, 'And to think I had you down as incapable of coherent thought.'

Roderick Ho had appeared. 'Louisa's phone hasn't moved all night. When Emma was at my place, she was asking.'

'. . . Emma Flyte?'

'Yeah. She was at my place.'

Shirley put her head in her hands.

Lamb said, 'So Louisa's looking for Harper's boy in Wales, and you think Frank and his crew are after Louisa. There's a slight flaw in this.'

'Which is?'

'That you're an idiot. If Frank was after Louisa, what stopped him taking her at the funeral? Your Wile E. Coyote impersonation? No, if Frank and his crew are in Wales, it's not Louisa they're after. So unless it's a coincidence, like Madame Guillotine here says, it must be Harper's boy.' He paused. 'And I don't believe in coincidence.'

River said, 'Why would they want Lucas Harper?'

'Well, if he's anything like his old man, because he's lost something that belongs to them. On the other hand, let's assume for the moment there's stuff going on we don't know about. That'll be harder for me than for you, but the least you can do is make an effort.'

He produced a cigarette from inside his shirt, and plugged it into his mouth.

'And it would explain what Frank was doing at the funeral,' he went on. 'He wasn't there to see you. He was there to check out Louisa. He must have known she was looking for the kid.'

Catherine said, 'How?'

'Golly, good question. Oh hang on, I know. We're fucking spooks.' He lit his cigarette. 'If I was after the boy, I'd have kept tabs on his mother. Tapped her phone. Presumably she got in touch with Louisa?'

'Don't know,' River said.

'Big surprise. So once that's happened, first thing Harkness does is put a tag on Louisa, to make sure she doesn't fuck up his plans. That would involve having her picture, which is why he was at the funeral. Stop me if I'm going too fast.'

'And Louisa found the boy,' said Coe. 'Or knows where to look.'

'See? Norman Bates is keeping up.'

Ho said, 'I found the boy through his Fitbit. Emma asked me to.'

'She's almost certainly after your body,' Lamb said. 'Probably needs a draught excluder.' He blew out smoke. 'Okay, sounds like you're off to Wales. How do you plan to get there?'

'My car's off the road,' Shirley said quickly.

'And I haven't got one,' said River.

Everyone looked at Coe.

'Mine's at home. An hour away.'

Everyone looked at Ho.

Ho said, 'I don't want to go to Wales.'

'We don't want you to come,' Shirley explained.

'But we're going to need your car keys,' said River.

Lamb said to Coe, 'Try not to kill anyone.'

Coe shrugged.

'On our side, I mean.'

'Why do you need my car keys?' Ho asked suspiciously.

When they'd all clattered out of the office, Catherine said, 'And this is wise?'

'Said the drunk with the wine cellar in her living room.'

'If Louisa's in trouble, we need to call the Park. Or the police. Ho said her phone's not moved all night.'

'Neither did mine,' said Lamb. 'And I was alive last time I checked.'

'Did you ask for a second opinion?'

He ignored that. 'We've been over this. The Park can't be trusted where Harkness is concerned because its fingerprints are all over his lunatic fucking misdeeds. And I'm not watching him walk away again.'

'But you're not going to Wales yourself.'

'Christ no. I'm on a crusade, not a one-star minibreak.'

'And what if Louisa's already dead?'

Lamb became absent for a moment, as if a light had winked off. It winked back on again. 'She's probably okay. Going dark's protocol in joe country.'

But he stamped on the floor, to summon River back upstairs.

Catherine raised an eyebrow.

'What kind of boss would I be,' he said, 'if I dispatched the office junior without a going-away present?'

'A normal one?' she suggested, and just avoided colliding with River as she vanished back into her own room.

That going-away present was in River's pocket now, weighing his jacket down.

Traffic shunted forwards, and came to a halt again. The lane heading back to London was moving freely, if with wariness; the snow was drawing black lines on the road where tyres had cut through it. It occurred to River that the lanes up ahead, the far side of the spilled load, might be inches thick by now. But we'll plough that furrow when we come to it.

'Yellow car,' said Shirley.

'What?'

But she didn't explain.

And the snow kept falling.

On a normal day London was bright and busy, full of open spaces and well-lit squares. But it was also trap streets and ghost stations; a spook realm below the real. Think of the city as a coded text beneath an innocent page, thought Richard Pynne; a hidden string of silent letters, spelling out missing words. Every footfall on every paving stone tapped out meaning few could read.

Pynne had never wanted to be a joe, preferring to view the world from a desk, confident that these desks would become bigger, their views more panoramic, as his career skyrocketed. But it couldn't be denied that moments like this carried excitement; a pleasure that was necessarily furtive, borderline sexual. It helped that it was Hannah he was on his way to see, and that the meeting was unlogged – at the Park, he'd diarised the hour as UPB, urgent personal business; standard code for dentist or clap clinic. For now he was wrapped in a legend, and London was enemy ground.

Ground slowly whitening under a soft wet blanket of snow.

He waited behind Embankment Station, and when he saw her approaching ostentatiously checked his watch; not to show her she was late, but to indicate to anyone watching that they were an ordinary couple, and she was late.

'You got here.'

She looked amused. 'Is there any reason I shouldn't have?'

'No. None. I only meant . . .' What he'd meant was lost before he'd said it. He looked around: nobody in sight. Nobody important. A man fussing about with a sheet of cardboard. Two young women, hand in hand. He said to Hannah, 'Would you like to get coffee?'

'I don't have time. You said it was important?'

'It's about Peter.'

Peter Kahlmann, her BND handler. The man who thought he was running a German spy in the British Civil Service.

'What about him?'

'Has he . . . said anything lately?'

'Has he said anything? What does that mean?'

'Has anything unusual happened?'

'No, Richard. Nothing unusual has happened.'

'So no security worries? He hasn't asked if anyone's been . . . checking up on him?'

'You've asked me this before.'

'And now I'm asking you again.'

'And the answer's the same, no, nothing. He's a tired old man, that's all. I'm his last job. He just wants to take my reports, which are full of useless rubbish as you know, because you write them, and then go back to his nice warm flat and listen to Radio 3. As far as he's aware I'm someone's idea of a prank, a tiny little mole in Whitehall, beaming back gossipy bullshit. That's all.'

Instead of, thought Richard, a tiny little mole in the

189

Bundesnachrichtendienst, beaming back snippets of tradecraft.

Hannah eyed him kindly. 'What's the matter? Really?'

'It's probably nothing.'

'But not actually nothing.'

'No . . .' She was his joe, he was her handler, and there were no secrets between joe and handler. Or at least, not where a joe's safety was concerned. That was sacred text: a handler protected his joe.

He said, 'It's just that something happened. Back at the Park. An analyst ran Kahlmann's name through several databases.'

'You told me that. Why is it important? Analysts analyse things. It's what they do.'

'But not long after, this particular analyst, well . . . he was compromised.'

'Because he was checking up on Peter Kahlmann?'

'. . . I don't know. It's possible.'

'So you think that the BND value me so highly that they'd nobble anyone who probes too close?'

'I value you.'

'Glad to hear it. But if I was valuable to them, they'd not have given me to Kahlmann in the first place. They'd have assigned someone of a higher calibre. Someone keen to do a proper job.' She punched him lightly on the shoulder. 'I'm small fry, I know that. I don't have esteem issues, don't worry.'

And that was the truth of it, he thought with relief. As far as the BND was concerned, Hannah was a little fish, a sleeper who might never wake, but merely murmur messages from the edge of slumber. Pillow talk from Whitehall's dormitory – gossipy bullshit, like she said. Not someone the BND would risk a diplomatic incident to protect. Which meant Snow White would remain his and his alone: their secret meetings, their familiar haunts, their special relationship. Kahlmann was a nobody, which meant that Lech Wicinski's fall from grace was his own guilty problem, nothing more.

This was good, because at the disciplinary hearing earlier, back in the Park, he'd given Di Taverner a truncated version of T&T's report on Wicinski's laptop.

'The material can't have been planted remotely.'

'Is that a hundred per cent?'

'. . . As good as.'

Nash, who spent half his life in the Park these days, had made his standard harrumphing noise. 'So then. Matter resolved.

Taverner said, 'I'll speak to HR. Have his papers drawn up. And a report filed with the Met, obviously.'

Which had alarmed Pynne, but not as much as it did Nash.

'No, I'm not sure that's wise.' His mouth twisted: nasty taste. 'It's a touchy subject down the corridor, viewing pornography at work. Ended a promising career, let's not forget. One of the PM's closest allies.'

'Well, she should choose her allies more carefully. Sticky fingers aren't a good look anywhere. Round the Cabinet table, they're a positive embarrassment.'

'Be that as it may, public awareness that a member of the security services was watching porn, *illegal* porn, when he should have been safeguarding the national interests, well. It's a lose-lose situation. No, it's best if the police are kept out of this.'

'Which will strengthen his hand,' said Pynne.

'Leaving aside the somewhat unsavoury image that brings to mind,' said Lady Di, 'care to elucidate?'

'If we sack him but don't inform the police,' said Pynne, 'he'll know we're frightened of the publicity. So he might go public himself. Claim innocence.'

'Whereas if we keep him where he is,' said Nash, 'he'll stay quiet. For fear we'll inform the Met if he misbehaves.'

'Fine,' said Lady Di. 'He's a slow horse. Thank you, Richard.'

So all was well. Maybe he'd finessed it, but it was the right outcome.

He said to Hannah, 'You're right. Forgive me. I worry about you, that's all.'

'There's no need, Richard. Really. We're good.'

His pilfered hour was up. Without quite planning to, he leaned and kissed her cheek.

She smiled and squeezed his arm. 'See you soon.'

He headed into the station. When he looked back she was still standing there, waving at him. He waved back, and disappeared from sight.

Then Hannah walked round to the Embankment, and into the small park behind the Savoy, where Peter Kahlmann – real name, Martin Kreutzmer – was waiting with a bouquet of roses.

'Peter!'

'I like to spoil you.'

And he did. In flagrant contravention of every espionage protocol she'd ever read about, or seen in films, Peter would show up at undercover trysts bearing boxes of chocolates, or abduct her as she left work, and whisk her off to a West End show: best seats in the house. If the Peter Kahlmann she described to Richard Pynne was a worn-out salaryman, the reality was a favourite uncle, the one who'd got down on all fours and pretended to be a bear. The risk was, someone would notice he really was a bear after all. Because if Regent's Park discovered that Kahlmann was actually Martin Kreutzmer, then what had been assumed to be a minor fun-and-games op would have been escalated to Serious Business, for Martin was a name on Spook Street, and anything he was invested in demanded a closer look.

Yet here he was, handing out roses in the snow.

'They import them from Africa.'

'They're lovely. The perfect accessory for a clandestine meeting.'

'Everyone will assume I'm a dirty old man,' he said, taking her arm. 'They'll write their own story, and pay no attention to who we really are.'

They walked through the park, collars up against the cold.

'So,' he said. 'What did Young Lochinvar want?'

'He's still worried about that analyst,' said Hannah. 'The one who ran your cover name.'

'A development?'

'I don't think so. He's a worrier, that's all.'

'Nobody's perfect,' he assured her.

She told him all she'd gleaned from Pynne lately: about Diana Taverner, and her struggle to keep hold of the Service's steering wheel.

'They have so many committees,' she said. 'So many meetings. And the budget's tight. Richard thinks she's worried control will be taken away from her, and vested in a board. She's spent years waiting to take over, he says. And now they're looking to change the whole power structure.'

'But she's a survivor.'

'You know her?'

'I know the type. When the game stops going their way, they change the game. She's waiting for her moment, that's all.'

Hannah said, 'I think Richard knew this analyst.'

'Were they friends?'

'I don't think he has friends.'

'Apart from you,' said Martin.

That made her laugh.

They parted on a lane leading up to the Strand, Hannah cradling the flowers as if they were an infant. Like any fond lover Martin Kreutzmer walked backwards the first few steps, extending his farewell, but his smile faded once he'd turned. On the Strand he headed left, for Trafalgar Square, where a murmuration of tourists, undeterred by the cold, weaved around one another in constant motion. Martin liked the pointless busyness of it. He found it conducive to thought.

He had assumed that the analyst, whose name Hannah had wheedled from Pynne over cocktails, had been sufficiently spiked; exiled to MI5's equivalent of Robben Island, where he'd spend the rest of his career wondering what just happened. Now, it seemed more was required. If Lech Wicinski continued to fuss, and Pynne looked beyond his own infatuation with Hannah, the operation would fall apart, and with it, Martin's career. It wouldn't just be his loss of a promising agent, and the glimpses into life at Regent's Park her handler leaked. It would be the favours Martin had called in to compromise Wicinski: persuading a colleague to corrupt the analyst's laptop had been well outside his remit. But it had been for Hannah's sake, he reminded himself. Hannah was his joe. And a handler protected his joe.

Maybe, too, he should curb his own natural excesses. This wasn't, after all, just fun and games. Time to bring Hannah into the adult world: no more roses, no more outings.

As for Wicinski, his days of roses were also over. Because let's face it: Martin Kreutzmer had already crossed one boundary. Be foolish not to cross another if that was what it took.

It was a pity, really. Lech Wicinski had only been doing his job. Still: that was life in joe country. Martin patted his pockets, remembered he didn't smoke, and waded into the tourist pack, swiftly becoming invisible.

10

The key safe was a small plastic box, the size of a cigarette packet, fastened to the outside wall at ankle height. To remove the key, you brushed it clean of snow, then clicked open the lid and keyed a code on a rackety plastic number-board. Or, if you didn't have the code, you raised your booted foot and brought it down hard, removing safe and contents in one ugly crunch. Then scrabbled about in the snow before finding the key half a yard away. Picked it up with trembling fingers. Slotted it into the cottage door on the third attempt.

That's if you were Lucas Harper.

Downstairs was kitchen and living room combined, with a wood-burning stove; upstairs was a bathroom and two bedrooms. It was as familiar to him as his own home; he'd been staying here with his family since a toddler, year in, year out. The family was smaller now, of course. Last night, after the handover had gone wrong – what should have been a straightforward swap: their money, his promise of silence – after the flurry of violence that ensued, and the hours spent hiding in darkness, this was the sanctuary that came to mind. Not in use this week, thank God . . . The world was a scarier place than he'd known. He could be lying dead, face down in the snow.

Late afternoon. Friday? He'd barely slept, hadn't turned a light on. When a car rolled past he'd dropped to the floor, made himself tiny in the darkness. Like the toddler he'd once been, in this same holiday cottage.

The car had struggled round the inclined corner and faded. But Lucas had stayed hidden for five minutes before climbing back onto the sofa.

Your money's right here. But you're going to have to come closer.

He'd been clear on the phone. The money was to be left at the crossroads, chosen because it was just a mark on a map, a few trees and a signpost. There'd be no contact of any kind. He wasn't an idiot. His dad had been a spy.

I need to hear you say the words. That you'll never tell anyone what you saw that night.

What he'd seen had been a chance to secure a future. To make some cash.

The man had been short, but bulky; dark-skinned. European looking and sounding, though Lucas couldn't put a country to it. His hair had a corkscrew curl, his chin was thickly stubbled, and when he'd stepped from the trees it was as if he'd just appeared, fully formed; a woodsprite out of *Lord of the Rings*. Lucas had been watching the copse for an hour, and had seen no movement. Not until the man had wanted to be seen. That knowledge seemed to form in his gut; a knot of fear that sprang as suddenly into being as the man himself.

Who wasn't, Lucas noted, carrying a rucksack. Lucas had specified a rucksack – what easier way to carry fifty grand?

Come on, Lucas. Don't make this harder than it has to be, hey?

That was when he'd known he was in trouble.

Lucas drew his knees up and rested his forehead. The temperature was dropping by the minute, but he didn't dare turn the heating on. The boiler made a whooshing sound on ignition, then rumbled steadily. The neighbours might notice, and come to investigate . . .

He'd used a payphone to make the deal; had disguised his voice. They shouldn't have his name – if they'd found out who he was, it wasn't so they could congratulate him while handing over the money. No, it meant they had no intention of paying him . . . All of that, crashing through his mind as soon as the man called him *Lucas.*

His hands were gripping his calves now, and he could feel the muscles taut beneath the skin. Last night, those muscles had melted . . . Adrenalin should have given him wings: that was the evolutionary code. In fear for his life, he should have moved like a gazelle. Instead he had struggled on legs heavy as tree trunks, while the man hadn't even bothered to give chase. When Lucas glanced back he was still by the signpost, a grin on his face.

And way behind him, beyond the next hill, an approaching glow, as if a rocket were launching.

Lucas had tried to run, but the snow wouldn't let him, sent him sprawling after three steps. Before he'd regained his feet the car broached the crest of the road, headlights on full, and then it was heading into the dip, pausing at the crossroads to collect the man, and then on the move again, up the rise, gaining on Lucas without even trying. The snowy road lit up and noise flooded his head, the engine's roar, and the crunching of snow beneath wheels. They meant to run him down. He'd be like one of those rabbits you found by the roadside, clipped by traffic: almost intact but for one comical section, cartooned flat. He'd be a punctuation mark in the snow. When the woman appeared from nowhere, reaching out from the ditch, he'd thought this was how it happened: that the last moment of your life involved being snatched clear of it. But when he hit the ground and the car screamed past, he knew he was alive.

The car stopped, and the man from the crossroads peeled out, came running back.

The woman rose and swung her arm just as he arrived. Whatever she was holding hit his head with an organic-sounding *whump*.

She turned back to Lucas. 'Run.'

He didn't need encouragement.

The road ahead was blocked by the car, so he ran back down to the crossroads, finding it easier now, his limbs adjusting to this new reality. At the signpost he'd turn right: there was a footpath, leading into woods. With enough of a start, he'd find a hiding place there. These thoughts fell into place like a puzzle solving itself. All he need do was keep moving . . . He dared a look behind. The lit-up car was an island in the darkness, around which shadows danced, one of them the woman who'd just saved him. Something flashed in her hand. As Lucas watched she swung out again but missed her target and slipped in the snow. Before she could reach her feet—

All thought fled as a shape appeared at the living room window.

Lucas froze in place. The shadow hovered, and pressed itself against the glass. When it moved Lucas rolled onto the carpet, then crawled to the door. He crouched beneath the diamond-shaped glass in its upper half, an ear pressed to the wood, while someone shifted on the doorstep, snow creaking beneath their weight. The key safe, he thought. Its absence had left a mark on the outside wall. If you knew what you were looking at, it was a neon sign screaming *Trespassers*.

He clenched every muscle in his body, and when the doorbell rang he was ready for it, and managed not to yelp.

But the whisper behind him almost made him jump out of his skin.

'*Don't.*'

And then a hand was clamped across his mouth.

In the car, things were not going well.

'Where are we?' Shirley asked, having just woken up.

'We're in Wales.'

'Yeah, mastermind. I can see that.' (There was no way she could see that.) 'I meant where exactly?'

They were on the B4298, and it didn't help her mood being told.

'So . . .' She tailed off.

'So are we nearly there yet?' River prompted.

'I didn't say that.'

'But you wanted to.'

'We can't go much further,' Coe said.

'It'll be fine.'

'No it won't. It's snowing, I've twice lost traction. Visibility's a yard and a half. We're going to end up in a ditch.'

'Whose idea was this?'

'I didn't notice you coming up with a better one,' River said. 'So . . .

Not going much further. What would that mean?'

Coe said, 'Stopping.'

It had been slow going even once they'd passed the jackknifed lorry. The canyons carved by preceding cars should have made their passage simpler, but in fact had them skidding on compressed snow. Shirley's turn at the wheel had been particularly lively, accompanied by an uninterrupted stream of invective, directed mostly, but not exclusively, at other road users. River had wondered whether she'd dipped into a pocket stash when their attention was elsewhere, but decided that if she had, the invective would have been less inventive. Coke had a way of making its adherents imagine themselves masters of the universe, while robbing them of original thought.

'Yeah, mastermind,' she said now. 'It would mean stopping.'

But Coe had a point. The snow was falling as thickly as ever, with a thoroughness bordering on the sociopathic. Around them, traffic had eased to almost nothing, either because of the smaller roads they'd turned onto, or because not everybody, Shirley's commentary notwithstanding, was a fucking idiot. And here they were on a B-road which might as well have been way further down the alphabet: bare empty fields either side.

River peered at the map on his knee with a keyring torch. 'I meant in terms of shelter.'

'I'm hungry,' said Shirley.

Coe muttered something under his breath.

River said, 'Did we pass a turning a little way back? On the right?'

'Uh-huh.'

'Okay, so if we're where I think we are, we're about halfway between the two nearest towns.'

'What's that in miles?'

'About four either way.'

'Crap on a cupcake,' Shirley said. 'Four miles? We can't stop here.'

A sudden light dazzled all three: a dip in the road, and a monstrous truck heading the opposite way. Without slowing it blasted past, rocking them in their tracks, leaving the car shaking like a rabbit in a predator's wake.

'Christ!' said Coe.

'Fuck!' said River.

'Is there a McDonald's nearby?' said Shirley.

When his heart was back to normal, River said, 'They don't mark them on the map yet. But I'm pretty confident there isn't.'

'Did anyone bring food?'

'You've eaten it all.'

'Have you checked the glove box?'

'I'm not going into Ho's glove box,' River said. 'Not without protection.'

'Just open it. There might be chocolate.'

So he opened it and there were, in fact, gloves in there. But nothing else.

'He probably thinks it's a law,' Shirley said.

Coe said, 'Here's a layby.'

'We're not seriously stopping?'

They seriously were.

Coe killed the engine. 'We were going three miles an hour,' he said. 'We're nearly doing more than that now.'

They weren't alone, though it took a moment to register this. Another car a few yards in front; a bigger shape in front of that, which would be a lorry. The lack of streetlights, and the falling snow, cast everything in otherworldly shapes, and the only immediate noise was each other: rustling in winter clothing.

Beyond that, just the muffled sound of a smothered world.

River had a single bar on his phone.

He stepped out, struck by the extra effort everything took in the snow. Partly the cold, partly the differences in depth and distance that the covering provided.

Lamb answered on the first ring.

'Let me guess. You're lost.'

'We know where we are,' said River. 'We just can't see any of it.'

'Every time I think I've plumbed the depths of your cackhandedness, you go ahead and surprise me.' River heard a striking match. 'Still got your going-away present?'

'Yes.'

'Good. Shoot yourself in the head. Then Shirley. Then the mad monk.'

'Definitely the order I'd choose,' River said. 'Has Louisa called?'

Lamb hesitated. 'No.'

'Because we can't get closer. Not tonight.'

'How far away are you?'

'Best guess, four miles.'

'You can't walk it?'

'Not in this.'

He heard an inhalation. Lamb could hold a lungful longer than anyone he'd known. In any other context, it might show how healthy he was.

Lamb said, 'Either she was dead before you set off, or she just went dark. So there's only a fifty per cent chance things are any different now.'

Which comforted River as much as statistics ever did. 'I'm wondering if we're doing the right thing. Whether we should have alerted the Park.'

'Last time Harkness went on a rampage, they swept up after him. For all we know, he's still on their tab.'

'Yes, but—'

'Yes but nothing.' Lamb exhaled, and River could almost smell his smoky breath. 'Cats don't care, the tooth fairy takes backhanders from dentists, and the Park does not have your best interests at heart. Sorry to crush your illusions.'

'I still think we might have made the wrong play.'

'Which is why you're the one freezing your knackers off, while I'm dickbraining your efforts from a cosy chair,' said Lamb. 'That's like masterminding,' he added, 'but with idiots. And oh, yeah, Ho was asking how his car is.'

'We let Shirley drive,' River said. 'How does he think it is?'

He pretended he'd lost the signal, but stood for another moment in the freezing cold before climbing back into the car. It had been his choice to come, he reminded himself. Not the first time that a decision made in an angry moment had felt less sensible when the mercury dropped. Which he could live with, mostly, except this time it was Louisa who might end up paying the bill. Or might already have done. And he was four miles distant from knowing which.

The snow was maybe tapering off, but that might be wishful thinking.

Frank said, 'So, that went well.'

'She hit Cyril with a monkey wrench.'

'Did I ask for details? I needed a kid in a ditch. Three of you and a car, and you couldn't manage that much.'

Anton had thought: *Yeah, and where were you?*, but didn't think it wise to say it out loud.

Fact was, they'd focused on the wrong target. When the woman appeared, she'd made it clear she was dangerous by dropping Cyril. That got their attention. The kid, meanwhile, had legged it. It had been dark: no streetlights. Two minutes' start, and it was like the night had swallowed him whole. Following footprints in the snow sounded easy enough, but this was pitch black, and soon they were in a wood. They weren't fucking Apaches.

And while that was going on, Frank the Legend had been nowhere, so Anton wasn't thrilled to hear him explain how they'd screwed up.

They were back in the barn. Would still be out there, ploughing on, but Cyril had keeled over, complaining about flashing lights, of which there weren't any. Lars, team medic, had held up fingers. Cyril proved good at spotting when the answer was three, but he might have been guessing. People usually held up three fingers: Anton had no clue why.

Frank said, 'If I'd known you needed help, I'd have come along. But I figured you were professional enough to deal with a teenager.'

Anton said, 'Yes, and you want to be careful messing about in the snow, your age.'

'You say something?'

'If we'd had guns, it would have been over before the woman arrived.'

Frank said, 'Yeah, but it would have made the whole accidental death scenario less plausible.'

And how plausible is it looking now, Anton wondered.

Frank said, 'Fuck it. It is what it is. So okay, boots on. Weather like this, there's a chance the kid hasn't cleared the area yet. If he's gone to ground, he'll have headed somewhere familiar. That gives us three possibles.' He pulled a page from a tiny red notebook, tore it in two, and passed one half to Lars, the other to Anton. 'He worked for a firm called Paul's Pantry, owner one Paul Ronson. Lars, check it out. And the place where he stayed with his family. Anton, that's you. And Cyril . . . Have a fucking lie down. You look like a local.'

'He could be back in London by now. Or at a police station.'

'Saying what? That some people he tried to blackmail didn't like it? No, he's a kid and he'll do what kids do. He'll hide under the bed and hope we've gone away.'

'Staging an accident,' Lars said, 'is a lot more complicated after last night.'

'Which is why, for one day only, I'm Father Christmas.' Frank walked through the open barn door, into the snow flurry. His car was a smooth-angled sculpture already. He destroyed the effect by opening the boot and pulling out a black holdall, from which he produced two handguns: Sig Sauers. One he handed to Anton; the other to Lars.

'What about me?' said Cyril.

'You made the naughty list. State you're in, I wouldn't trust you with an electric toothbrush,' said Frank. 'Stay here. And try not to get hit by any more wrenches.'

Anton did what he always did when handed a gun: he checked its load and its moving parts. Lars did the same. The sound made the barn a war zone, briefly.

'Spare magazines?'

'You're in Wales, for God's sake. Unless they've weaponised sheep, you're already outgunning everyone you'll meet.'

'Farmers have guns,' Lars pointed out.

'So avoid farmers.'

'What are your plans?' Anton said. 'If you don't mind us asking.'

'I'll check out Caerwyss Hall,' said Frank. 'Which is the other place we know the kid's familiar with. That all right with you?'

Anton shrugged.

'Okay, let's roll. If we're going to go noisy, you'll need to clear the decks afterward. So torch this place when we're done. Capisce?'

'We'll manage.'

'Try not to screw up this time.'

With Frank gone, they slipped into German.

'We have one car,' said Lars.

'I know. I've counted it.'

'So—'

'So we drive into town, park, and do the rest on foot. Meet back at the car afterwards. Shall I write that down?'

'You're the same kind of prick he is.'

'But thirty years younger,' said Anton. 'Imagine my future.' He looked at Cyril. 'You all right on your own? You want a night-light?'

'If you find the woman,' said Cyril, still blurring his words, 'bring her back here. I've a tool of my own to knock her round with.'

'If we find the woman, we'll waste her,' said Anton, meaning it. His balls still ached from her knee. 'And you can save your tool for a rainy day.'

He tucked the gun into his belt, beneath his coat. Lars did likewise.

When they left the barn Cyril was trying to light the stove, but kept breaking matches.

It didn't look like torching the place was going to be an issue.

Louisa removed her hand from Lucas's mouth, slipped past him, and pressed her eye to the peephole.

On the doorstep stood Emma Flyte.

She opened the door, pulled Emma in and closed it again. 'They sent *you*?'

Emma unbuttoned her coat and shook her head vigorously. Droplets flew. 'Nice to see you too.'

'Emma!'

'Nobody sent me. I came looking for your phone.'

'But how—'

'Trains,' said Emma patiently. 'They're still running. Or were. And only taking twice as long as usual.' She looked at Lucas. 'You're Lucas Harper, right?'

The boy nodded, unable to speak.

'Well, looks like she found you.' She turned back to Louisa. 'You were meant to call.'

'You came all this way because I didn't phone?'

'A lot of cases, that would be passive-aggressive behaviour,' Emma admitted. 'But, you know. Our line of work.' She was surveying the open-plan room. Lights off, no heating. An attempt at vacancy. 'You're hiding.'

'Could we move away from the windows?'

Which proved Emma's point.

She followed Louisa into the room. It was warmer than outside, but you needed a stopwatch.

Louisa was nursing her left arm. Lucas Harper had scratches across his cheek.

'What happened?'

'Like you said. I found him.'

'I am still here, you know!'

Both women looked at Lucas.

Emma said, 'This is going to work best if only one of you tells it.'

'Who are you?'

'A friend of the woman who hurt her arm helping you.' She turned back to Louisa. 'Is that broken?'

'I don't think so.'

'Accident?'

'Well, I think he planned to break it. So in that sense, yes.'

'I sometimes wonder if Lamb gives you all lessons in smartarsery. How bad does it hurt?'

Louisa said, 'It's still in its socket. I might have damaged a tendon.'

Because when she'd slipped in the snow, the second man – not the one she'd copped with the wrench – had dropped and straddled her. Nine times out of ten that would have been it, but with her free hand she'd scooped snow and mashed it into his face, making him rear back; making him, more crucially, open his legs wide enough for her to ram her knee into his crotch. Ten times out of ten, that was always it. Then he was sprawled in the snow and she was scrambling for the wrench, her fingers just making contact when the third man, who'd been driving, leaped on her from behind, pulling her arm back almost to breaking point. Instead of resisting she'd rolled with it, using his momentum against him, and suddenly he was on his back, Louisa on top, and she raised her head and butted his face. He let go of her arm and she pulled free, tasting blood, her legs not wanting to work, though she forced them. Then she was heading down the dark road, haring after Lucas.

'We were out all night,' she said. 'Hiding in the wood.'

'Where you ditched your phone.'

'And Lucas's Fitbit. I wasn't taking chances.'

'And yet here you are.' Emma looked at the boy. 'You okay?'

He nodded.

'Glad to hear it. How much trouble are you in?'

'It's not my fault.'

'It never is.' She turned back to Louisa. 'Where's your car?'

'They slashed the tyres.'

'Yeah, well, probably doesn't matter. The roads are a mess. But get your coats on anyway. Where's the nearest police station?'

'We can't go to the police,' said Lucas.

'He's right,' Louisa said. 'Besides, I called it in. The Park will respond.'

'Well, they're taking their time. And meanwhile, we can't stay here. Because it was the first place I came looking.'

'Yeah, how did you—'

'I used to be a cop, remember?'

'And they let you keep your crystal ball?'

'Cartwright told me who Min Harper was. So I had Devon access his personnel file. Turns out he called the Park from here once, so the address was on his contact list. That took me literally three minutes. Even the guy you clocked with a wrench probably isn't going to take much longer. So, like I say . . .'

'Except they don't know who Lucas is.'

'You're sure about that?'

Lucas said, 'He knew my name. The guy at the crossroads.'

Louisa said, 'You told them who you were?'

'No.'

'But they found out anyway. Christ . . . We shouldn't be here.'

'As I said.'

Louisa was already grabbing her coat from the back of a chair.

'It's dark,' Lucas said. 'And we don't have a car. Where are we going?'

He looked, thought Emma, about twelve.

She said, 'They're not looking for three of us. We'll check into a hotel, a B&B, whatever, and make a plan.' She looked at Louisa. 'Which will involve telling me exactly what's going on.'

Before Louisa could reply, a fist ploughed through the diamond-shaped window in the front door.

He didn't have to be here, Lech Wicinski reminded himself. He could be in a hotel. There was, come to think of it, one down the road; a strangely modern building in which he suspected guests were crammed into capsules overnight, like corpses in cold lockers. But that would be better than this. At the back of a cupboard he'd found a blanket, which looked like it might have been a picnic accessory between the wars, and was slumped in his chair like a pensioner on a promenade, blanket draped over him. And still he was cold and uncomfortable; and still he stayed, because making for a hotel would involve human intercourse, and Lech would rather wake up dead tomorrow than make small talk now. For the moment, Slough House was his refuge. Which, like any other, had its price.

'You look like a slug in a kaftan.'

Lamb, leaving. But finding time to look in as he made his way downstairs.

Lech said, 'Just finishing some stuff up.'

Lamb snorted. 'Well, if it gets too cold . . .'

Tell me how to work the boiler, thought Lech. Please.

'. . . You'll fucking freeze.'

And then he was gone. Lech expected to hear him on the stairs, whose response to any tread was an irritated didgeridoo solo, but he might as well have dematerialised once out of sight.

Except for the sound of the back door closing; a double *thunk* exacerbated by the chill air it passed through to reach his ears.

So now he was alone.

He called Sara again, but was blocked. Thought about dialling from the landline, but realised the futility of that: this wasn't a technical fault to be worked around. Not like she'd be relieved he'd got through. He closed his eyes and let weariness wash over him, while outside, the snow did what various bands of homicidal lunatics had failed to do over the years, and brought London to a halt. Come morning, the city's boots would have tracked through every virgin inch, churning white to grey and yellow and black, but for now peace had fallen, as if the city were forgetting all the nervous accidents that went into its daily recreation of itself. Only the occasional car passed along Aldersgate Street, though the nearby traffic lights continued their unflappable sequence, tinting the window panes red, amber and green. Under their hypnotic spell Lech dozed, his exhausted brain mimicking London's hibernation. When he woke, the office was colder, but nothing else had changed. Though he realised he might be hungry.

That would make sense: he hadn't eaten in forever. And didn't want to now, or at least, didn't want to undergo the brute mechanics of it – the shovelling into his system of edible products – still less the various exchanges such a transaction might require: *Will sir be dining alone?* Sir will be ending his life with the cutlery if he's forced to answer that.

But there was a row of miserable shops over the road, and they would be open. There was an equation of despair in which retail outlets find their level, and the worse the fare on offer – the fly-raddled kebabs, the chicken wings on the turn – the more likely that a miserable clientele would require twenty-four-hour access. He would cross the road, buy food, come back, eat, sleep. The sooner he did this, the more time would pass.

So he stood, let the blanket drop to the floor, and went down the stairs. The door to the back yard jammed. Lech had to lean on it heavily, and felt it scrape as it gave way. And then he was outside, in the snow; some flakes still falling, but just as an afterthought. All damage done, he thought. It didn't look like damage – even the battered green wheelie bin had assumed a kind of mammalian grace under its soft covering, and was the shape of a landed whale – but damage was what it was; a slow battering ram that, once it receded, would leave splintered wood and crumbled tarmac in its wake. Which suited Lech's mood. His stomach growled. He opened the door to the alleyway, stepped through it, and a fist slammed into his face, turning the white world black. He staggered, felt his heel catch on something, and fell into the snow.

And caught the briefest flash of light on a blade as his attacker stepped into the yard, pulling the door closed behind him.

Emma dived for the door before the intruding hand could find the latch, slamming the chain into place almost before the coloured glass splinters hit the floor. But not fast enough to avoid being grabbed by her coat, and pulled hard against the woodwork.

Louisa jumped towards her, but Emma shouted 'Back door! Now!'

Lucas was already on his way; Louisa hesitated, but only half a beat.

'Open it,' said a voice.

Emma fumbled for the latch, but only to fix it into the locked position.

'Now!'

She pulled back as abruptly as she could, and threw herself to her left. The grip didn't weaken, but she slipped her arms from her sleeves as she fell, and the hand was left holding her coat, which dropped to the floor as the figure receded. Next moment the door shook as a foot slammed against it. There was a soft, slumping noise as snow fell from the roof; then another plaster-crumbling thud when the figure kicked again.

It was a holiday cottage, not a safe house. A few more like that, there'd be broken wood on the carpet.

Emma snatched up her coat and ran.

The back door led into a garden, one raked so sharply that steps ascended to the lawn. Ahead of her, Louisa was scaling a seven-foot wall that Lucas, presumably, had already vaulted: Louisa's injury slowed her down, but before Emma reached her she was over too, her white ski jacket making her seem an escaping snowman. The wall was brick and bulging with age. Emma threw her coat over, found what passed for a foothold and propelled herself upward, hauling herself onto the wall's upper edge before risking a backwards glance. A man was emerging from the cottage, pointing a gun. She'd dropped onto the other side before he fired. If he fired. She heard nothing. Then again, her head was full of snow; she'd landed face down, flat on the ground.

When she looked up, everyone around her was dead.

Shirley had disappeared behind the hedge bordering the layby, having a piss, River hoped, but possibly snorting coke. Coe had remained behind the steering wheel, giving a good impression of a man who didn't care where he was. But he wasn't dressed for the weather, and if River had been in the business of giving a toss, he'd have been mildly concerned for Coe's welfare: it wasn't going to get warmer soon.

On the other hand, his own clothing didn't match the conditions. His jacket was little more than an anorak.

And this was just another of the drawbacks of being a slow horse. The sort of thing his grandfather would have warned him about, once: that their enforced inertia, the mind-mushing sameness of their days, meant that any hint of action and they leaped at it, and damn the consequences . . . Frank would be laughing, he thought. If Frank could see him now he'd shake his head, laugh, and look for another river to drop him into. So it would be best to make sure Frank didn't see him; that the first Frank knew of his presence was when he felt River's hands round his neck . . .

Jesus. Was that what he intended? To kill his father?

A ripple ran through Coe, as if River had wandered across his grave en route to Frank's. Then the door opened, and Shirley was back.

'I checked out the hostiles,' she said. 'Car's empty. But the lorry's not. It's got a nice warm cabin, quite roomy. And there's a man eating hot food and watching TV.'

'How roomy?'

'Bigger than my flat. I told him there were three of us here.'

'And?'

'And he asked if any of us were women,' Shirley said.

'Did you let him live?'

'I'm going back later, to stuff him in his microwave.'

Coe opened his eyes. 'I'll check the boot.'

'Maybe Ho keeps his spare pizzas in there,' Shirley said hopefully, but when Coe returned all he had was a large cardboard box, which had once contained a plasma screen and now held only sheets of filmy-grey packaging.

'Bedding?' River asked.

Coe shrugged.

'We'd better huddle,' River said.

'No way am I fucking huddling,' said Shirley.

'Fine. Freeze to death.'

'I would genuinely prefer that.'

'Can we have your coat, then? Since you're going to freeze anyway.'

'Fuck off.'

River and Coe looked at each other, it dawning on both that any huddling was going to be an all-male affair.

'I don't like being touched,' Coe said at last.

'Huddling isn't touching. It's . . . survival.'

They rearranged themselves, Shirley in the front, slamming the door loud enough that nobody was in doubt as to her state of mind. Coe hovered in the snow a moment, handing the sheets of packing foam to River before tearing the cardboard box along one seam to open it out. When he got back in he arranged this over them: a stiff, graceless blanket laid over the spongy wrappings.

'Where's mine?' Shirley asked.

'It's for huddlers only.'

'Bastards.'

'Your choice.'

After a minute's thought, much of it audible, Shirley got out and climbed back in next to River. 'Lamb finds out about this, he'll shit,' she said. 'Loudly and often.' She twisted sideways. 'And that better be a gun in your pocket.'

River didn't reply.

'Jesus . . . You've got a gun in your pocket?'

'Lamb gave it to me.'

'That is so fucking . . . He never gives me anything!'

'Possibly he thinks you're a little excitable.'

'He probably meant us to share.'

'I'm pretty certain that was the last thing on his mind.'

Shirley said, 'Yeah, well, if you have any big psychological block about shooting your father, I've got dibs.'

'We have to find him first.'

Coe said, 'We should get some sleep.'

They fell quiet, if you didn't count Shirley's stomach.

J. K. Coe remained awake, though, his head against the glass. The world outside had vanished, and he liked this – the absence of everything, as if all feeling and event had been subtracted from existence. Here on this side of the door, he had River Cartwright's sleeping form slumped against his shoulder; they were jammed thigh to thigh, and he could feel River's pulse, a steady echo of his own. And just beyond River Shirley Dander, who, in sleep, seemed to pump out warmth, as if the fires that burned within her never rested. Coe could sympathise, though he wasn't sure it was heat his own demons thrived on. He thought they preferred the cold.

He closed his eyes at last, and summoned up the sound of a piano; a tune so fragile, it could wander trackless through the snow. He wasn't clear that this was sleep, but it was near enough that his breathing became regular, and whatever gremlin stalked his thoughts ceased its fidgeting and let him be.

They were woken hours later by a snowplough lumbering past.

When Emma looked up, everyone around her was dead.

'Christ . . .'

And then Louisa was there too, using her good arm to help haul her to her feet among the gravestones.

'This way.'

Because there was only one route: through the churchyard to the gates.

Lucas was ahead, though he had stopped to look back, unsure what to do next. And behind them, the other side of the wall she'd just cleared, was a man with a gun.

She was breathing okay, despite the rough landing; felt clear-headed, despite these mad few minutes. And her cop instincts were kicking in, undamaged by her years as head Dog. Whatever was going on here, the boy was at its centre.

She pulled free of Louisa. 'Go.'

'Be careful.'

Emma nodded, but Louisa was already off, running in a crouch, as if fearful of snipers.

A pair of black-gloved hands appeared on top of the wall, and Emma dropped behind a gravestone. Scuffmarks in the snow should have betrayed her: in the daylight they'd be a neon arrow. But there wasn't even any moon; just a faint silvery hint behind the clouds. And if he was moving fast enough—

He was.

Was almost past her before she was ready, oblivious to the tracks on the path. There was no gun in sight; he must have tucked it in a holster, but that was an observation made in movement. Already, she'd uncoiled like a jack from its box, using the headstone to propel her as if kicking off in a pool, but even then only just caught his leg below the knee. Enough to send him sprawling, but his heel clipped her forehead as he fell, causing lights to go on suddenly. She pulled back before his foot could catch her again, this time deliberately, and was upright first. If he hadn't been reaching for his gun he'd have tipped her over while she stood one-legged, but that crucial second was all it took for her to bring her other foot down on him, a sudden memory – where did this come from? – of a brick crashing into her riot shield one hot day in Tottenham. That same feeling of resistance. This time, Emma was the brick. He rolled with the blow, and wherever his gun was it was going to take close personal contact to relieve him of it, and she didn't think she'd broken him quite. Better to quit while she was ahead. All of this had taken moments, like an edgy edit in an action film. Louisa and Lucas had disappeared through the gate. She took off after them, shrugging herself into her black coat, which swirled behind her like a vampire's cloak; the drops of blood on the snow crumbs from an interrupted feast.

11

The first task of snow is to make everything new; its second, to make the same scene creak with age. By early Saturday morning London's snow was loosening its grip, sliding from rooftops with the noise the wind makes catching a parachute. On the roads gritters had left rusty scattershot patterns in their wake, and grey lumps had formed where tyres had pulverised drifts. Noises, too, were returning to normal, the streets' acoustics adjusting themselves. Every footfall was helping return the city's streets to their unadorned state, while yesterday's snowflakes learned the lesson London offers all who settle there: that while all are unique, most appear identical, both before and after being trodden on.

Catherine Standish noticed all these things, and none of them, on her way to Slough House. They were background music, winter's tune, and she'd heard it before. On the Tube people appeared chirpier, in the manner of those who'd survived an unexpected seizure, but these too she blanked out. There weren't many of them anyway. It was early; it was a weekend. She wouldn't be heading to work herself if half of Slough House weren't in joe country. Most of the night she'd lain awake, wondering whether her own wobble – her months' long teeter on the lip of sobriety – had foreshadowed a greater tumble, and she'd arrive at work to find each office shrouded in black crêpe, the house disintegrating. She wasn't one for omens, but Lamb appeared to think bills were falling due. And if he wasn't always as right about things as he thought he was, there were times when his bullish nature guaranteed the outcomes he expected, as though the world knew better than to thwart him when his blood was up.

The image arrested her. Her last sight of Lamb's blood had been on a mottled handkerchief on his desk top, the souvenir of a coughing fit.

A chest infection. That's what he'd said. He was taking antibiotics. Catherine thought about that for a while, then thought about Lamb at a doctor's surgery, and scratched the image immediately. Thought about him talking to a Service quack, and scratched that too. Thought, instead, about him self-diagnosing and acquiring under-the-counter meds from a contact in a pub: that ticked the right boxes. He'd been smoking himself into the grave for as long as she'd known him – it was basically a race between the fags and the booze – and maybe he was right, maybe this was an infection, and drugs would clear it up, but you never knew. It should not be possible to live like Jackson Lamb and avoid consequence. But that was a thing about life: it had been known to favour bastards.

In the alley behind Slough House, footprints led in both directions. Sometimes people wandered round in the dark, looking for somewhere to relieve themselves, or to indulge a brief tremble. Catherine was no prude – how could she be, with her history? – but hoped she'd never cemented a temporary friendship between bins. That was the thing about the past, though. You could never tell what your previous selves had been capable of. Brushing away speculation, brushing snow from its handle, she pushed open the wooden door to the back yard. London always led to this. You passed through its streets in all kinds of weather, but always ended up in this dismal cramped yard, the glum odour of failure seeping from its walls. Or you did if you were Catherine Standish. Another cheerful note to start the day on, and her heart skipped a beat as something groaned.

She let her bag drop, but not before reaching into it for her tightly rolled umbrella. Ridiculous, yes, but once before she'd been snatched from a London street, and not letting that happen twice was high on her list of absolutes. But when she turned there was nobody; just the memory of her own breath hanging like a forgetful ghost, unsure where it should be.

The groan repeated itself.

Her heart was back to normal, and an observer would have assumed she was calm. This was her strength; that in most situations, she swiftly adjusted to her mean, which was that, since the majority of bad things that were going to happen to her lay in her past, there was no great call to fear the present. Besides, the groan was a groan, which meant this bad thing had happened to someone else. And it was coming from the bin; the green wheelie bin whose covering of snow was less thick than on the upturned bucket, whose presence in the yard had always been a mystery. So the bin had been opened since the snow began, and given that the chances of a slow horse emptying an office bin unbadgered were on the thin side, this hadn't happened for the purposes of rubbish disposal – and why was she running through all this in her mind? There was somebody in the bin, and they sounded injured. Either a derelict had wandered in looking for shelter, or a random stranger had dropped from a helicopter, or—

Or whatever.

She flung the lid back with difficulty, and peered in, and found him nestled in the rubbish like a Sumatran rat, among takeaway cartons and throwaway cups, and damp newspapers that should have been recycled, and cigarette cartons that should never have been bought. His eyes, wide open, looked through her to the sky. Sweet Jesus. He'd been caught in a trap left in someone else's bin, and behind the filth she could make out jagged graffiti on his face.

Once more, she was not alone. Someone had stepped into the yard behind her.

Catherine didn't need to turn. A tinny leakage filled the air, as if bad music were dribbling from someone's ears, or the headphones meant to install it.

'Roderick,' she said.

'. . . Huh?'

'Roderick,' she repeated, turning and clapping her hands to rid them of snow. 'What happy timing. Perhaps you'd help Mr Wicinski out of the bin.'

And then, when Roddy looked like he was having trouble putting those words together, Catherine poked him sharply on the shoulder. 'That wasn't a suggestion. Do it now.'

So Roddy, with no great panache, gave it a go.

The happy news the snowplough left was that the road was largely cleared.

There was, however, a downside.

'It tried to fucking bury us,' said an outraged Shirley.

'Maybe if you keep swearing, the snow'll melt off,' River suggested. He and Coe were scraping the plough's leavings from Ho's car using the cardboard sheets that had seen service as bedding. 'In which case, you know. Carry on. Don't lend a hand or anything.'

'I'm busy,' she snarled.

The plough was long gone, and its driver too far away to hear the words 'muff-sucking cum-bucket', even if they'd have meant much to him, or indeed, anyone but Shirley. Whose voice in the still morning air had the clarity of a church bell, though you'd be more likely to respond to an invitation to prayer from a Dalek.

The lorry driver stuck his head out of his window. 'Can you keep it down? I'm trying to shave.'

Shirley turned her Gorgon face on. 'I've two words for you, so listen carefully. Fuck. Right. Off.'

'. . . That's three words.'

'You're not listening, you're counting. Don't make me come over there.'

The man's head withdrew.

River sighed.

'Don't you start,' she warned him. She looked back in the direction of the parked lorry. 'And he'd better have jam in that fucking cabin. Because if he speaks again, he is toast.'

Job done, Coe had cast his cardboard sheet aside and was studying his phone, which River assumed meant he was working on a problem. This turned out to be geographical.

'Louisa's phone is this side of Pegsea,' he said.

'How do you know?' growled Shirley.

Coe stared at her. 'Because I have the coordinates,' he said at last. 'And a map.'

'. . . Okay. Jesus. Just checking.'

'So what are we waiting for?' said River, climbing back into the car.

They were waiting for Coe to finish plotting his course, which he did in silence, standing in the cold.

Shirley was scrumpling up the foam sheeting. 'Last night must be the most action Ho's back seat's ever seen,' she said.

'It's the most I've seen in a while,' River admitted.

'You'd better not have been doing anything while I was asleep,' said Shirley. 'Because if you did, and I find out, you're a dead man.'

'Trust me,' River said. 'Even if I had a list, you wouldn't be on it.'

Coe got into the driver's seat.

'And that goes double for him,' said Shirley. 'You messed with him in the night, he'll be pissed. And he hasn't killed anyone in ages.'

'Far as you know,' Coe said.

'. . . Was that a joke?'

'I don't do jokes.'

'Could we get a move on?'

Coe started the car. 'I have a plan,' he said.

Coming from anyone else that would be reassuring, but like Shirley said, Coe hadn't killed anyone in a while, and it wasn't clear to River that that wasn't simple lack of opportunity. Last time he'd found himself in a village setting Coe had face-painted a pavement. The face belonged to a terrorist, true, but it had been an over-the-top reaction that didn't say much for the man's mental handbrake. And here they were out of town again. It was possible, River reflected, that Coe followed the rock-star-on-tour guideline, and thought nothing counted outside the M25. In which case, it was as well the only gun they had was in River's pocket.

'Gunna tell us what it is?' Shirley asked.

'Not yet.'

'Why?'

'Because if we find Louisa's body, it's moot,' said Coe, and put the car into gear.

The ploughed road was rocky going, but at least they were on the move once more.

As they left the lorry driver waved a two-fingered salute, but River decided not to mention this to Shirley.

There were better ways of waking, but at least this was waking . . . The man last night had had a gun. That's what Emma had said, and she was all kinds of reliable, being a former cop, a former Dog, and a woman who took no shit. So the man last night had had a gun, which indicated intent: had he caught them, they'd not be waking at all. Louisa had already known that finding Lucas had led her into dangerous water, but she'd hoped it reasonably shallow. How wrong could you get?

Emma had left the man in the churchyard, and the three of them had run through the town, crossing the deserted main road and heading towards the estuary: no plan involved. The air was heavy with unreality. Snow had made everything strange, casting the town back centuries, and everyone had taken shelter – everyone bar a cat on a wall, its hateful eyes glinting.

There were footpaths by the estuary, with enough tree cover to be free from snow. A sign by an open gate warned of possible flooding, but this seemed more acceptable than an armed man. Who wasn't on their trail yet – behind them was only the cat, now a black shape in the middle of the road, picking its way townward with slow, exaggerated steps. And then they were among the trees, and the road might as well have been miles away; a distant glow from an alien settlement.

A car chose that moment to chug slowly along the high street, its engine a reminder of a different age, which hadn't yet come to pass.

They were still running, Lucas in front, Emma at the rear; deliberately, Louisa knew. She was in good shape, could have outrun either, but this was Emma being a cop again, taking others under her wing. Which irritated Louisa, but not as much as the memory of Emma telling her to run, and Louisa doing just that. Not waiting to help. Not bringing the bad guy down together. Just running, as if she were afraid the two of them acting in concert would be less effective than Emma solo. As if she were afraid.

But she hadn't been afraid last night, she reminded herself. She'd taken on a carful of bad actors, armed with only a wrench.

By the water's edge, just visible through the trees, were boats; dim heaps in the darkness which might have lain there years. Lucas was sprinting ahead – and then wasn't; dropped from sight as if down a hole, which was more or less what had happened.

When she reached him he was already scrambling to his feet, but something in his eyes made her turn away, knowing he'd not want her to see him sob.

Emma arrived.

'Any sign?' Louisa asked.

'I think we left him in the town.'

But it wasn't a big town, and there weren't many places the three of them could be.

'What should we do?' said Lucas.

He was very young suddenly; a twelve-year-old, too small for his boots. Mud on his face.

'Police,' said Emma.

Louisa touched her elbow. 'No. Trust me.'

'Yeah, I tried that. And look where we are.'

Lucas said, 'What's that?', and pointed into the trees.

That was a shed some yards off the path, so nestled in darkness, it looked like one more shadow among many; the kind of place, in a fairy tale, that would house a cobbler or troublesome elf. This one, when Louisa forced the door – a padlock hanging from a hasp that had lost two screws – turned out to contain a stack of traffic bollards and collapsible signs warning of Men Working Ahead. Presumably this was a seasonal activity: it didn't look like Men had Worked anywhere near here since the clocks went back.

'Is this wise?' Emma asked.

'What's your better idea?'

Police, Emma's look repeated, but she didn't say it out loud.

They gathered inside, and it didn't get bigger, but once Louisa had shifted the signs, there was room to sit on the floor. Lucas, clearly, needed this – fear had carried him this far, but the fall had knocked the flight out of him, and all he wanted now was to be in the dark, unseen.

'It's okay,' she told him. 'It's going to be okay.'

He didn't answer.

Emma said, 'Well, let's not get ahead of ourselves. It might be okay. But given I've no idea what's going on, I'm not handing out guarantees.'

'Thanks,' Louisa said. 'He needed to hear that.'

'I'm cool,' Lucas said, without sounding it.

She was reminded of Min, and it was sudden and painful.

There was a window, but it was half-obscured by a stack of poles whose function Louisa couldn't guess at. And it was cobwebbed and filthy, and they were surrounded by trees . . . In the gloom, they were vague shapes, Lucas cross-legged on the floor, Louisa half-kneeling by his side. Emma standing. What little light there was reflected off her hair. It was like sharing a cupboard with a guardian angel. Outside, all seemed quiet; a thought that hadn't finished forming when something scratched at the window.

'Jesus!'

'It's a branch,' Emma said, a heartbeat later. 'Tapping on the pane.'

Even the trees wanted to come inside. That's what kind of night it was.

'Are we safe here?' Lucas asked.

Before Emma could respond with the truth, Louisa said, 'We'll be fine for a while.'

'How many of them?' Emma said.

'Last night, three. I put one of them down. He'll have got up again by now.'

'Three's not many,' said Emma, half to herself. 'Maybe you're right. We'll be fine for a while.' And then she had looked down at Lucas. 'So. Let's start with why three men want to kill you.'

. . . That had been last night. It was morning now, and Louisa had woken, which was good news; had fallen asleep in half the space she needed, which wasn't. Beside her, Lucas slept. Emma was nowhere. Louisa got to her feet, feeling like an origami figure being unfolded, and reached for the door. It was light outside; a thin, watery light that made her want to say *gruel*. Emma was there. In her long dark coat, her blonde hair loose, she looked like she'd stepped from a trailer, ready for her close-up. And this was after a night in a shed. It wasn't like Louisa was jealous, but seriously? Fuck.

Emma said, 'Get some sleep?'

'A bit. Got a signal?'

'Don't know. Haven't got a phone.'

'. . . You what?'

Emma said, 'It must have fallen out of my pocket. Probably when I tossed my coat over that wall.'

'Ah, shit.' Louisa looked up the footpath towards town. 'Like it or not, you're a slow horse now. Any signs of life?'

'A dog walker twenty minutes ago. Are you okay? You're moving like a crash dummy.'

'I'm too old to sleep in a shed,' Louisa said. 'Or too young. One or the other.'

Emma nodded. 'What Lucas said. Did his story change since he first told you?'

'Not so I noticed. I think he's telling the truth.'

'Yeah, well. The whole men with guns bit does add weight.'

Lucas had been staying in a B&B further up the coast, he'd told them. Had thought it wise to be in the area a few days before the arranged handover, 'to check things out'.

He'd looked so much like Min, saying that. And if Min had indeed said that, the first thing Louisa would have done was come up with a contingency plan.

'And what was the result of this . . . "checking out"?' Emma asked.

Lucas, miserably, said, 'I thought it would all be okay.'

'You wanted money for your silence,' Emma had said. 'For not telling anyone what you saw.'

Lucas had nodded.

'Okay then. Tell us what you saw.'

So he had.

What Anton had this morning was a sore fucking face.

'You know what's good for that?' Lars had asked.

Lars. Team medic.

'Not getting stomped on.'

Ha-de-fucking-ha.

Second night running they'd been out in the open, chasing their tails. The kid could be anywhere, but Anton didn't think so. He thought they were both still in the area, waiting for a clear shot at an exit. The county might as well have locked its doors and put the empties out. The trains weren't running, and the roads were a joke.

'Besides, she's Park. A joe in the field survives hostile contact, he calls it in and digs a hole. She, in this case. And waits for back-up.'

'Which is who stomped your face, right?'

Anton had spent the night with a mouthful of snow, anaesthetising himself. But while stomping his face might look like back-up, it hadn't felt like back-up, if he could get Lars to appreciate the difference.

'She wasn't armed,' he said.

'Just as well.'

'Yeah yeah yeah. If she'd come from the Park, she'd have come strapped on.'

Lars wasn't buying. 'On a home visit? It's Wales, not Ukraine.'

'Could be High Street Kensington,' Anton assured him. 'In response to a joe sending up a flare, the Park would send guns. Not a blonde.'

He hadn't always worked the grey area – eight years in the BND after six in the military, and one thing you learned on Spook Strasse was, folk drove on different sides, but the highway code stayed the same. The Americans wore fake smiles and the Russians rubber gloves, but the processes for taking care of your own were pretty much fixed across all divides.

'She's not their exit route, in other words,' he said. 'Just an added complication.'

They were a mile outside the village, not far from Caerwyss Hall; the car pulled onto a verge. Driving was slow, like learning to ice skate. The fields all around were smooth plains, and the trees against the morning skyline looked like Christmas decorations. Snow, though. Soft and fluffy on the outside, but ruthless as a shark. It was the fucking Disney Corp by other means.

'Two chicks,' Lars grumbled. 'What is this? *Charlie's Angels?*'

Anton hoped not. Charlie had three.

'Women have a natural advantage,' he said. 'First contact, you tend to pull your punches.'

'It's working so far.'

'Second time round, it's a different story.' Anton's knuckles clicked in the cold still air. The gun in his jacket was a reassuring weight.

'You're sure then,' Lars said. 'They're still in the area.'

Anton was, for all the reasons he'd just said.

'Just as well,' said Lars. 'Because here comes Frank. You can repeat all that to him.'

The Fugue Protocol, thought Lady Di.

She was in her office, Saturday morning. Some jobs don't respect private life.

The Fugue Protocol: it was a back-door process, dependent on the cooperation of whoever was chairing Limitations. So there'd never been a hope in hell it would be approved, Oliver Nash being far too circumspect to license anything which might cause increased laundry bills round the Cabinet table. Even Oliver, though, had had his antennae up. *I can't help thinking there's something going on here, Diana . . .*

It's the Secret Service, Oliver. There's always something going on.

No Fugue, then, but that was fine, because all she'd wanted was her minuted application, so that once the cat hit the fan, spraying blood and fur on the walls, she'd be able to say *See? I could have stopped this.* It didn't take genius to work out that Frank Harkness's presence was part of the deal Peter Judd had warned her about – that he was here to squash whatever had happened at Caerwyss Hall – and nor was it a secret that Lamb was gunning for him. Which he might think he was doing below the radar, but for all Lamb's streetsmarts, he was behind the techno curve. It was one thing setting his social retard on pulling up CCTV records; quite another to expect this to happen unobserved. That particular shit was out of the bag: Diana knew damn well the slow horses had been tracking Harkness's footprint since his arrival in Southampton, and given their generally poor impulse control, they'd no doubt be haring after him first chance they got. He had, after all, left blood on their carpet last time round.

So yes, things could get messy, and when that happened, whatever you were trying to cover up generally became headline fodder, which in this case meant the duke's name being spattered across world headlines. Again. Not in the UK, obviously, where most editors tugged their foreskins when the Palace required, but damage would be done: nothing pissed the public off more than privilege caught with its pants down, and nothing pissed off Lady Di's own lords and masters more than a pissed-off electorate.

And as with any corporate behemoth, shit cascaded downwards:

The Service isn't in good odour at present. Too many mis-steps, too few triumphs
. . .

But let's see how Downing Street enjoyed a scandal that could easily have been avoided.

I applied for Fugue. I could have handled this. But I was turned down.

And then, maybe then, they'd start to listen when she outlined what the Service needed if it were to prosper and protect this increasingly isolated island state.

She stood, left her office, walked the hub. This was her routine: to make sure the boys and girls – they were always girls, always boys; it was the local language – knew that whatever happened, she was available. There was chatter coming in from Russian sources; a whisper of a potential hack on a high-street bank. Which might mean it was going to happen, or might mean somebody somewhere was bored, or might mean something entirely different was in the wind, and she was being encouraged to look the wrong way . . .

Josie stopped her. 'You wanted to know if anything untoward came in from Pembrokeshire way?'

She made it sound like the Wild West.

'Tell me.'

'We got a coded message Thursday night, from a civilian mobile. But the recording stayed stored. Didn't hit the screen until this morning.'

She handed Taverner a printout: a go-dark notice. One that decoded to *Hostile contact*.

'Why the delay?'

'Because the ID doesn't match any existing protocol. Whoever it's from, it's not one of ours.'

'Have you checked the number?'

'I was just about to.'

'Don't bother,' said Taverner, folding the printout. 'Someone's playing Cowboys and Indians without permission, that's all. You can file it under forget. Thanks, Josie.'

There was always the possibility, she supposed, resuming her circuit, that Lamb's crew might pack the mess away without drawing attention to themselves, or to whatever shenanigans had prompted the blackmail effort. On the other hand, if they were sending up distress signals, it didn't seem things were going their way. And you could usually rely on the slow horses to make a bad situation worse . . .

What she needed, as she'd told Nash more than once, was a root-and-branch overhaul of operational practices.

She was prepared for a certain amount of collateral damage in order for that to happen.

Slough House was absorbing another memory.

The man looked *sick*, thought Roddy Ho.

And not in a good way.

Handy job the Rodster had been there to hoik him from that wheelie bin, because no way would he have made it out on his own. So Standish had held the lid while Roddy stood on an upturned bucket and reached down to grab Wicinski's arms. You could tell he wasn't dead – the groaning was a clue – but he wasn't cooperating, and frankly the RodMan would as soon have left him where he was, but he kept on reaching, and Wicinski kept not cooperating, and the upturned bucket wasn't all that stable, and probably, if you weren't an expert, it might have looked like Roddy fell into the bin himself. Fact was, though, he'd worked out that this was the most efficient way of getting the job done. It was all about leverage, in the end.

That was when Lamb turned up.

'Trump on a treadmill.'

His head appeared over the lip of the bin like the sun over the horizon.

'There are better places to learn how to swim.'

Roddy would have capped that, but he had something in his mouth he was eager to dispose of.

And then Lamb had reached in, exactly the way Roddy had done, except he grabbed Wicinski by the arms and hauled him up and out before throwing him over one shoulder.

Unseen, Catherine Standish had said, 'Careful.'

'I am being careful. This is me being fucking careful.'

Roddy had risen to unsteady feet on a floor of unsteady rubbish in time to see Jackson Lamb disappearing inside Slough House, carrying Lech Wicinski like a rolled-up carpet.

The door didn't even stick. Maybe, just this once, it didn't dare.

Roddy had followed five minutes later, once he'd got out of the bin. In his office he found Wicinski laid on the floor, because sitting in a chair was outside his range, like expecting a bowl of jelly to change a lightbulb. He looked shocking. Not just the filth he was caked in but the blood filming his face, which Standish was dabbing at with a damp cloth. It wasn't a laughing matter – apart from anything else, it was making a mess of the carpet – but still, it was a bit funny, because whatever had happened to Wicinski had happened a *lot*. Anyone tried to jump the RodMan in that fashion, they'd better have a hard-on for hospital food.

Lamb was in Roddy's chair, using Roddy's keyboard as an ashtray. The sleeves of his overcoat were wet, and across one shoulder was a smear of something someone hadn't thought worth eating.

He said, 'I left you in the bin. Can't you take a hint?'

Bantz, thought Roddy.

Then Catherine said, 'Oh, Lord above . . .'

'What?'

It wasn't immediately clear whether Lamb was answering a prayer or asking a question.

But Catherine said it again, 'Oh, God, no,' still on her knees by Wicinski, dabbing at his face, then squeezing the cloth into a bowl. The run-off was foul; Wicinski's face a little whiter, though there were marks that weren't coming off; that looked like they'd been scored into his cheeks . . .

Lamb squashed his cigarette into Roddy's desk, and rose.

Catherine looked directly up at him. 'They've written on him.'

And she'd got that right, Roddy thought. They'd scribbled on the man with a razor. All across his cheeks, as if they were using him as a memo pad: a brief reminder to themselves, and the whole of the rest of the world.

P-A-E on one side.

D-O on the other.

Can't even fucking spell, Roddy thought.

The snow lay unruffled on the field, as far as they could tell.

'She might be under all that,' Shirley said. 'It might not have snowed until after.'

After what, River didn't ask.

Shirley elaborated anyway. 'What I'm saying, her phone might still be in her pocket.'

'It was already snowing when she went quiet,' said River. 'So there'd be tracks across the field.'

'Not necessarily. It's snowed more since.'

But there'd be bumps and ridges, thought River. Wouldn't there? If Louisa was somewhere in that field, or in the ditch that ran alongside it, traces of her passage would be visible; a coded message scribbled on the landscape.

He said, 'The plough's been past, so there's no clues on the road.'

They all knew that anyway, but he needed to be saying something. In case it was true, and Louisa was out in that field somewhere, lying quietly beneath the snow.

'What's that?' asked Coe.

He was looking ahead, at where the road crested against the skyline.

They drove on to where the parked car sat on a verge, half buried by the plough's passing.

'Louisa's,' said Shirley.

River was already on the roadside, scraping snow from the parked car's windows; tenting his hand to peer in. 'It's empty.'

Shirley had joined him, and went round back to open the boot. 'Tell you what,' she said. 'She keeps a monkey wrench in here usually. It's not there now.'

River had a shrewd idea how Shirley knew about the wrench, and what use she might have put it to in the past. He tried the driver's door, and found it unlocked. But the car was still empty, and there were no scrawled messages, no clues, to be seen.

Shirley slipped under his outstretched arm and popped open the glove box. A pair of sunglasses dropped out. 'When did they make it illegal to carry chocolate?' she grumbled.

'We know Louisa was here,' he said. 'We know she dumped her phone nearby, next to the Fitbit she was looking for. But if she was under all that snow, there'd be traces of it happening. I think she got rid of it on purpose. She was going dark.'

'Which is protocol,' said J. K. Coe, 'after hostile contact.'

'And she's got her monkey wrench with her,' said Shirley. 'Which means the hostiles might have suffered some contact themselves.'

And if one of those hostiles was Frank Harkness, River hoped the wrench had left a trough in his head. But he couldn't see it happening: Frank was too cagey to be caught off guard by a blunt instrument. Though maybe all he meant was, he'd come off second best to Frank himself, and in some hollow corner of his soul, didn't want to believe Louisa was capable of doing better.

Shit.

He shut the car door. It was freezing to the touch; rather like himself. A night in a car and no breakfast. Who could blame him for his thoughts?

'You said you had a plan,' he said to Coe. 'Care to share it with the rest of us?'

'Not a plan as such.'

'But anything's better than nothing, right?'

Shirley said, 'Does it involve food?'

'Shut up, will you, Shirl?'

'Shut up yourself.'

'That's a good idea,' said Coe. 'We could fight.'

'. . . Maybe later,' Shirley conceded.

'Your plan,' said River.

Coe waggled his phone. 'Map of the area.'

'And?'

'If she's gone dark, she'll have looked for shelter. Uninhabited shelter. There are farm buildings marked on here. Barns.'

'Louisa?' said Shirley. 'In a barn?'

'Well, I can't see her building a treehouse,' River said. 'You got a better idea?'

'Coming here wasn't a great one to start with,' Shirley said. 'I'm giving up on ideas for the time being.'

'We'll need to split up,' Coe said.

'Bags the wheels,' said Shirley.

River said to Coe, 'I'll take Louisa's.'

'With four flats?'

Jesus, right. He hadn't noticed for the snow.

'Okay then,' he said again. 'So two of us are walking. Where are these barns?'

Coe turned his phone to face them. Its screen showed white, with a tracery of grey lines, and could as easily have been a photograph of their surroundings as a map.

'Yeah, I'm gunna need more instructions,' said Shirley.

River took a closer look, and said, 'This the kind of thing you mean?' He pointed at an oblong shape tucked into the corner of a larger oblong shape. A dwelling in a field, which odds on was a barn.

'Uh-huh.'

He tweaked the picture, made it smaller. The coastline appeared.

'I'll take that direction.'

Coe nodded, then turned to Shirley.

'Whatever.'

'Okay. Go back the way we came, then take the first left. You'll come to a wood. There are buildings just beyond it.'

'Sounds like a farm.'

'Might be.'

'Will there be dogs?'

'Dogs are a bit like fast-food restaurants,' Coe said 'Most maps haven't got round to including them yet.'

'I thought you didn't do jokes,' Shirley reminded him. Then she said, 'You know what bothers me?'

Though both men, having spent a day in her uninterrupted company, had worked up a comprehensive list of things that bothered Shirley, neither volunteered a probable top ten.

'What bothers me is how come she never called it in. I thought that's what you did after what you just said. Hostile contact. You call it in before you go dark.'

It had been bothering River too.

If it worried J. K. Coe, he hid it well. 'We're going that way,' he said, pointing down the road. 'We split at the next junction.'

River looked at Shirley, who was climbing into Ho's car. 'Be careful.'

'Is that "be careful" as in "here, why don't you take the gun"?'

'No,' said River.

The two men set off down the road on foot, while Shirley executed a four-hundred-point turn. It was snowing again by the time she was headed in the right direction.

So here came Frank, and yes, he made Anton repeat everything he'd just said. And then stood gazing across the landscape: at the little town not far below, blinking into light, and the estuary beyond, on which boats were now bobbing on the rising tide. Earlier, they'd lain on the snow-dusted silt like discarded toys. The whole country, come to that, had the air of a forgotten nursery.

He said, 'So they haven't skipped the area yet.'

'I don't think so.'

'You don't think so because thinking so means you've screwed up, and screwing up means you don't get paid.'

'Hey, we're here, on the ground. We get paid.'

'Yeah, take it to a fucking tribunal. Two nights they've been hiding up a tree. You're supposed to be good at this.'

'There's a lot of countryside,' said Lars. 'And there are only two of us.'

'Where's Cyril?'

Cyril was still back at the barn. Concussion or not, he was having a laugh.

Frank shook his head. He'd been up all night too, scouting the woods around Caerwyss Hall, holding to the notion that a spooked kid trying to lose himself would head for familiar territory. His own original plan had been simpler: give the kid the cash, and tag the bag. That way they could pick him up soon as they liked. But the decision hadn't been his to make. That was the trouble with the rich: they looked to stay that way by keeping both hands on their money. Or maybe they just didn't trust Frank to bring it back afterwards.

It was snowing again. If you stared directly up at the sky, it was like watching a cathedral collapse very slowly.

He said, 'Well, if they'd gone to the cops, we'd know about it by now. There'd have been activity. So they're staying dark, and back-up's not in a hurry to get here. I haven't heard any choppers, have you?' They hadn't. 'Like

I said, this is Slough House. Maybe the Park figures it's cheaper to cut 'em loose, save the cost of a pension down the line. But if the cavalry don't turn up soon they're gonna figure that out for themselves. That's when they'll make their run.'

Anton glanced at Lars, but Lars was paying close attention.

Frank went on, 'You lost them in the town last night. They're not gonna try and head out of town on a footpath, not in this weather. The road only goes two ways. It heads towards the coast, which is basically a dead end, or it heads back towards civilisation. They'll figure we've got that one blocked.'

'The three of us?'

'Oh, pardon me, did you fill in a questionnaire? Because how else would they know how many of us there are?'

Anton didn't answer.

Frank said, 'So let's try being methodical. You're on the lam, there's snow everywhere, you're up to your fucking eyeballs. Where you gonna hide?'

'Find an empty house.'

'But you get spotted breaking in, that's like sending up a flare. And you clearly don't want the cops out, or else that's where you'd have gone in the first place.'

'Needle in a fuckin' haystack,' Anton said.

'And you know how to find one of those?'

'Burn the haystack,' Anton muttered.

Frank said, 'There's boats on the estuary. And boats mean boathouses. And there are barns. You found one, right? How hard can it be? They've spent last night holed up in a handy barn, and once the roads loosen up, and traffic starts moving, they'll make tracks. We need to find them before that happens.'

'We need more men.'

'Yeah, and who's gonna pay them? So stop whining and look at barns and boats. Start from the pick-up point and work inland. I'll do the same, heading towards the coast. Lars, do the estuary. Call in every hour. And call Cyril, tell him to get off his fucking sickbed. That all okay with you?' He was looking at Anton. 'Or you got a better plan?'

Anton said, 'Let's just do it, shall we?'

They got back into their cars, Frank waiting a moment until the others had headed off down the road. He could do without Anton's bitching, but it wasn't like he wasn't used to it. In his previous life – an independent – he'd worked with the same guys for years, guys whose thinking he'd known as well as his own. That was then. Now, he was hired to do jobs and given the men to go with them; men with military backgrounds for the most part, and prison history often as not; and men like Anton, who'd done covert work too, on the blunter side. Door-kickers, not strategists, but that didn't stop them thinking they should be the ones giving orders. And sooner or later he'd meet one who'd do more than just shake his tree, but it wasn't going to be Anton. They both knew that.

Still, it would be best not to turn his back too often. Spooks, when you got down to it, couldn't be trusted. Frank should know.

He drove slowly down the lane, past fields that were white, and growing whiter.

12

'There's stables out back of the Hall,' Lucas had told them. This had been in the shed the night before. Cobwebbed patchy dark, with every movement magnified in the gloom, becoming a nest of spiders, or an inquisitive rat. 'I went there for a smoke sometimes.'

'A doobie?'

He rolled his eyes. 'Yeah, if you're like *sixty*.'

Sitting on the roof; legs dangling down. Not an approved Health & Safety seating posture, but then again, smoking dope in general didn't make many H&S lists.

It had been just before New Year; a party at Caerwyss Hall. A corporate event catered by Paul's Pantry, the outfit run by a friend of Lucas's mother's – both women caught the inverted commas round *friend*. The corporate client was a PR firm called Bullingdon Fopp, whose CEO was one Peter Judd, a bigtime political player once, and still regarded by some as a Lost Leader. Fair enough in Louisa's view, if where you wanted to be led was a mash-up of *The Handmaid's Tale* and *It's a Knockout*.

'We were supposed to be off the premises, but I didn't want to go back to the cottage. There was just Mum and Andrew. It was boring.'

This was before the snow rolled in, and the cold was the damp, bronchial kind, where everything seems to be breathing out: plant life, telegraph poles, garden furniture. The moon was a well-kept secret. The single bulb above the door of the kit room opposite was the only illumination, and it cast everything as an etching from a storybook: all the detail Lucas could see, shapes and curves and corners, became wavy grey lines the harder he looked at them.

That might have been the dope, of course. It was a lot stronger now than when Louisa had last drawn a toke.

He'd been thinking about America, he told them. He wanted to go to America. A road trip. See for real what he'd seen in the movies. But it took money. Everything took money, even uni. And it wasn't like dope was free.

In the telling he'd forgotten they were there, and had slipped into the cadence of the stoned.

From his vantage point, Lucas had had a clear view of the cobbled yard below. There was a gleaming new Land Rover at one end, its mud-splashes looking like decals: an expensive bit of rough. That had been the weekend's theme, all these rich men pretending they were handy, and even as he'd had the thought he heard voices. A lot of voices.

'So I killed the spliff and moved back. Didn't want them to see me.'

Because nobody was supposed to be there after dinner. The staff had cleared the dishes; the bottles were lined up on the sideboard. The rich had the run of the property. Whatever games they played, that was their business.

Or pleasure. Whispers in the kitchen suggested girls were bused in after dark.

He said, 'I couldn't see what was going on, but there was a lot of laughing and talking. And then it got lighter. There was a spotlight on the Land Rover roof, and they'd turned it on.'

There'd been the sound of something being dragged across cobbles.

Someone whistled the Lone Ranger tune, and everybody laughed.

'And then it went quiet.'

A tense quiet. The crowd had become an audience.

'And then a whirring noise, and a *thunk*. And everyone cheered.'

Good shot, sir!

Lucas had crawled to the edge, and looked down. There were maybe ten of them below, all men. And they'd set a target on a tripod at one end of the yard, and someone had fired what looked like a crossbow, and the *thunk* had been the bolt biting its mark: not a bullseye – anything but – but a solid pounding into the outer red ring.

'Good shot?' Emma wondered aloud.

So Lucas told them who had fired it.

'Oh, sweet Jesus . . .'

Not just a bunch of rich businessmen fooling with dangerous toys when drunk, but a bunch of rich businessmen with a royal playmate. Even this late in history, it changed the settings.

Lucas had said, 'They carried on for half an hour or so, and then it got too cold so they went inside.'

'And that was it?'

No. That wasn't it.

When it was quiet he'd fired up again and lay a while longer. He was on a Greyhound bus in his mind, zipping past endless fields of wheat. Middle of nowhere.

That was when they'd come back with the girl.

There was nothing you could do, Catherine had thought, to make these offices worse. The threadbare carpets, worn in patches, revealed a floor which did not inspire confidence, and the walls bulged inwards in places, as if planning to obliterate all they contained. Paintwork blurred into various stains daubed in accident or anger – coffee splashes, curry sauces – and corners were black with mould. Even the air: even the air felt like it had come in here to hide. No, this was as bad as things got. A flamethrower would only improve matters.

But it turned out she'd been wrong. You could make things worse. You could dump a damaged body between two desks, and have it lie on the floor, its head on a lifeless cushion. You could look down on a man whose face had been used to sharpen a blade.

PAEDO.

There'd been no charge, no trial. Just punishment. And now this.

Hard to refute the statement your own face made.

She said, 'You need medical attention.'

'No.'

'I'll get you a cab. I'll come with you. If you don't get those cuts seen to—'

'No.'

'—they'll scar.'

He looked at her, his dark face darker than ever.

'You can't live with that carved into your cheeks.'

'I'm not going to a hospital. Not looking like this.'

'Not a hospital, then,' she said. 'Lamb will know someone.'

'No.'

Two different kinds of pain, meeting head on. A crash no part of him was going to walk away from.

'I'll leave you to think about it. But think hard. If you've a chance of getting those cuts to heal, you have to act soon.'

And how had this come to pass, she wondered, leaving him. At what point had she become Slough House's conscience? Guiding the slow horses towards their better choices, when her own lately had been courting disaster?

The morning was wearing on. The only word from Wales was an occasional call from River: no sign of Louisa, though her car had turned up. Lamb had relayed this without comment. Louisa's car, abandoned, meant nothing. Perhaps she'd just grown sick of it, and left it by the side of the road.

We're spies, Standish. All kinds of outlandish shit goes on.

Lamb was drinking, which was early even for him. The only other concession he'd made to being indoors was taking his shoes off. His feet were on his desk and he was scowling at the wall so hard Catherine felt sorry for it. Imagine absorbing Lamb's moods, day after day. Then again, where did that leave her?

She said, 'He won't get it seen to.'

'Surprise me again.'

'He'll carry those marks forever if he doesn't do something.'

Without looking at her Lamb said, 'He's not gunna let anyone see them. It'd be like turning up at a christening holding a dildo. Everyone'll assume the worst.'

'So what's his alternative?'

Lamb said, 'Nothing you want to dwell on.'

'You think he really did it?'

'Not any more.'

'What's made you change your mind?'

'I haven't.'

She said, 'Someone should record you for training purposes. How not to have a conversation.' She sat. 'The words "not any more" suggest a change of attitude.'

'Yeah, well, in this case they mean I hadn't given it any thought till now.'

'He arrives with paperwork saying he's been viewing child pornography, and you hadn't given it a thought?'

'You're all fuck-ups, Standish. The manner of your fuck-uppery's irrelevant.' He was holding a lit cigarette. How did that happen? 'Far as Wicinski was concerned, the bit that worried me was him using his office laptop. I mean, I work with idiots. But that's Olympic standard.'

'So you weren't bothered what he was here for,' she said. 'Didn't stop you goading him.'

He looked offended. 'Course not. You think I'm made of stone?'

'And now you've decided he's innocent.'

'Because anytime anybody really, really wants me to believe something, I turn it upside down and rattle it hard.' He raised his teacup to his lips. Talisker, Catherine knew. And give him credit, he wasn't hiding the fact. He simply hadn't been bothered to hunt down a glass. 'The only people who know about Mr Solidarnosc's supposed tastes in wank-matter are here or at the Park. Or they're a third party who fitted him up. And given Coe's not on the premises, I'm focusing on options two and three.'

'Why would the Park crucify an innocent man?'

'Why would the Park ever do anything? But I'll tell you what last night's carve-a-Pole was all about. Someone's sending a message.'

'What message?'

'Oh, do keep up,' said Lamb. 'The message was "paedo". What do you want, pictures?'

'But—'

'But fuck,' said Lamb. 'If you can remember what that's like.' He stabbed his cigarette to death on the nearest surface. 'Whoever did it wants everyone to focus on what Wicinski supposedly did. And not on whatever it was he actually did that made them fit him up in the first place.'

'So not the Park, then.'

'Not the Park,' said Lamb. 'Because if they wanted him out of the picture, he'd be gone. No, they sent him here because they thought he did what they told us he did. So whoever fucked him up in the first place must be pretty good. I mean, I'm told those laptops are bastards to hack. They have passwords and everything.'

'So not the Park,' Catherine repeated. 'And yet they knew where to come looking for him.'

'I keep forgetting you have a brain. Though in my defence, you don't use it often.'

'It could have been a colleague. Someone who believed he was looking at child porn.' She'd believed it herself, hadn't she? 'It's the kind of thing that gets people riled.'

'Villagers with pitchforks. Or sink-estate morons. But a trained professional would have just broken his legs. No, the whole physical graffiti thing's misdirection.' He drained his teacup. 'Feel free to tell him that. Might cheer him up.'

'How come he was here, anyway?'

'He's been sleeping in the office.'

She should have known that. Time was, nothing happened in Slough House she didn't have an inkling of.

'Why?'

Lamb said, 'Because his girlfriend kicked him out. Turns out she didn't like sharing her bed with a kiddy fiddler.'

'So she knew too.'

Lamb said, 'Yeah, but I can't see her jumping him in the dark. A woman scorned, and all that. She'd have done it in the high street with a TV crew watching.'

'And how did she find out? I get the impression Lech's not one for baring his soul.'

Lamb said, 'She had a phone call.'

Catherine stared.

He said, 'What?'

'You bastard.'

Another cigarette appeared. Another flame flared.

'You told his fiancée? You couldn't let him work things out for himself?'

'Not a lot to work out, Standish. I mean, there were only two ways she could go with the information. And the clever money was always gunna be on her flipping her wig.' His cigarette tip burned brightly. 'No one's that broad-minded.'

'But why tell her? Good God, what made it your—'

'Ho traced him. He's been meeting someone from the Park. Which I assume means he's been keeping them up to speed with what we're doing, which, if you'll recall, I very specifically didn't want happening. And I don't like repeating myself.'

'So you screwed him over.'

'No, I reminded him whose side he's on.'

'By removing his sole support.'

'He doesn't have to like it,' Lamb said. 'He just has to know it's the way things are.'

Catherine didn't know what to say. A man downstairs had had his life, now his face, dismantled.

'I've got joes in the field,' he said. 'If Wicinski was running his mouth off, he was putting them at risk.'

'I think that's a first,' she said.

'What is?'

'You, justifying your actions.'

'It's Spook Street, not *Sesame Street*. If he was scared of getting hurt, he should have stuck with his roots and been a plumber.'

'He's an analyst. I doubt he knew he was signing up for the front line.'

'That's why they have small print. So crybabies can't say they weren't warned.'

'Jesus wept!' She shook her head. 'Every time I think you've scraped the barrel . . .'

He opened his desk drawer and found his Talisker.

She said, 'You've got joes in the field because somebody messed with your stuff. Isn't that what you said the other night? Frank Harkness stamped dog dirt into your carpets and walked away, and that's been burning you up ever since.'

'Are you charging for this? Because I never pay for therapy unless it includes a handjob.'

She said, 'Just because this is all you've got doesn't make it worth destroying people's lives for.'

'Then what does?'

'You should call the kids in before someone else gets hurt. As soon as they've found Louisa.' She stood. 'And not everyone who lives on a council estate is a moron.'

'I deal in broad strokes. From where I'm sitting, everyone's a moron.'

Before leaving, she turned to look at him once more. He was pouring out whisky, his measure defined by the limits of the teacup. She couldn't see his eyes. Didn't want to.

'And think about this, too,' she said. 'Lech's one of yours now. And someone just messed with him. What are you going to do about that?'

She didn't wait for a reply.

Her own office was shrouded in gloom, its skylight muffled by snow. But she didn't turn the light on. Instead she sat, much as Lamb always did, in the dark, and wondered what grief was heading their way next.

One of the men said, 'Smell that?'

'. . .What?'

'Someone's been smoking a joint.'

The spliff was a straw-thin corpse in Lucas's hand, but its odour had drifted out, and sunk to the cobbles below.

'. . . Don't worry, my friend. We'll find you one later.'

A girl's voice next. 'Where's the thing?'

'She wants to see your thing.'

'Show her your thing.'

'Trust me, she's seen it. Up close and personal, isn't that right, my darling?'

The girl's laughter had a brittle edge. 'No, the *thing*.'

'Here we go, darling.'

There were sounds Lucas couldn't identify, mechanical and clunky.

As carefully as he could, he peeped over the edge of the roof.

The spotlight was on again, illuminating the target, but there were fewer people than before. Something else had changed too – they were drunker, more manic. A coked-up energy floating free.

There was only one girl. She was slight, and despite the cold wore an abbreviated silvery dress, flashing like a glitterball in the headlights. She'd been handed the crossbow, and it looked huge in her arms. How old was she, anyway? His age? The men were far older and uniformly dressed in evening wear. There were five of them, and they watched the girl in a hungry way: fifty, he said, when Louisa asked. Or sixty. Balding men, or grey-templed.

She almost dropped the weapon, but managed to get it level. One of the men stood behind her, a hand on her waist. He was whispering into her ear.

When she loosed the bolt it went wild, careening into the dark.

The men collapsed in laughter.

She stamped her foot, but was laughing too. 'I wasn't *ready*!'

The crossbow was lifted from her hands, and another bolt fitted.

'Just pretend you're pointing a finger.'

She wasn't pretending hard enough. The second bolt, too, was swallowed by the night.

This time, the crossbow wasn't handed back to her.

Someone had lit a cigar, and its smoke rose skyward.

'Okay, chicken,' another man said. 'Your turn . . .'

She was laughing along with them when they took her across to the target.

Again, that whistling . . . The Lone Ranger. No, the William Tell Overture, Lucas remembered.

And then he thought, *Shit, no* . . .

The same thing must have occurred to the girl, because her laughter stopped as if a tap had been turned off.

'What are you doing?'

'Just a little fun. Nothing to worry about.'

'He's a great shot. Like a magician.'

'But what are you doing?'

'A bit of fun. You like a bit of fun, don't you?'

'No, please don't do that—'

Lucas couldn't see what was happening.

'—no please don't, you're hurting me—'

'Of course we're not.'

Her scream was cut short.

When the men moved away, he could see that they'd fastened her to the struts of the target with belts, and had stuffed a handkerchief into her mouth. As soon as they were clear she threw herself to the ground, taking the target with her, trapping herself like a tortoise. Most of the men laughed. One returned and lifted her to her feet, set her so she was leaning against the target once more. Lucas couldn't hear what he said: just a word or two, carried upwards with the cigar smoke.

Careful . . . very still.

When he backed away, the girl remained upright.

Her short dress shimmered in the spotlight's glare.

One of the men had disappeared into the dark, in the direction of the house, and for a moment Lucas thought he'd gone for help, to fetch a grown-up, but when he reappeared he was holding, what, a fucking *pumpkin?* A pumpkin, pilfered from the kitchen. While the others watched, laughing, he put it on the girl's head.

It fell off.

'Tell her to stop shaking!'

Lucas couldn't hear what he said to the girl, but whatever it was, he said it with a hand on her chin, looking straight into her eyes.

When he replaced the pumpkin on her head, it fell off.

Someone left the group, wandered into the shadows of the barn. He re-emerged with a roll of tape in his hands, holding it like a trophy. There were cheers, and more laughter, which continued as the pumpkin was strapped to the girl's head. She was shaking, and it slipped to one side, and when the nearest of the men returned and set it straight again, he tapped her on the cheek with three fingers – not a slap exactly; more a warning.

'I should have done something,' Lucas said.

Louisa said, 'It wouldn't have gone well. There were five of them. And they were drunk.'

But Emma had said nothing.

In the darkness of the shed, with some night-creature rustling around outside, the boy had continued his story.

Lars, as instructed, had headed down to the estuary. Snow was falling, and as he crossed the main road through town he saw no one. Twenty minutes earlier he'd passed the woman's car, which he'd disabled the other night, and while kicked-up snow showed someone had been checking it out, there was no Police Aware sticker on the windscreen. Right now, nobody was aware of anything much. People were sticking to their firesides, their TV screens. The shops were shuttered, and schools were closed. He'd heard that on the radio, which had also advised him to remain indoors unless his journey was absolutely necessary.

Which it kind of was.

It should have been an in-and-out job; had been sold to him as such. He hadn't been given background, which was fine: if that stuff mattered, it wouldn't be in the background, and besides, all stories were the same in the end. This particular version, someone had seen something he shouldn't, and wanted paying to keep quiet about it. Fine if what he'd seen had been the neighbour kissing the milkman, and what he'd wanted was a little of the same; less fine if the mark was in the arms business, and the tag was fifty grand. Because there was a strict policy in that line of work: you did not allow anybody to take one bite from your apple. Because one bite led to two, and two bites later the whole fucking tree was gone. No, some orchards were best left alone, because they were owned by people who knew people like Frank Harkness, who in turn knew people like Lars. And people like Lars, he'd be first to admit, didn't care whose apples they were safeguarding, as long as the money was right.

Add to that the bruised cheek from where the woman had headbutted him that first night, and what you had was what the movies called a situation. One which, if it hadn't been for the fucking snow, would be over already.

Instead, another woman had turned up: a blonde in a long dark coat who was also handy, apparently. The whole thing was beyond a joke.

He reached the bottom of the road that bisected what passed for a high street, and it became a tree-shrouded dirt lane, a wooden gate effecting a boundary between the two, next to a signpost suggesting occasional flooding. Trees covered the track towards the estuary, so the snow became a whisper rather than a shout, a series of grace notes nestled in tree joints. The ground was muddy, offering a smorgasbord of prints, both boot and animal. Maybe a Boy Scout would have studied this longer. Lars just walked on, eyes peeled.

The first woman had been wearing a white ski jacket, which would have little camo-value here. The blonde, though, was dressed in black, and if she knew what she was doing, might get close.

But this was farming country. Gunshots wouldn't startle the locals; especially gunshots muffled by snow-covered trees.

He walked on, sticking to the track.

Somewhere up ahead, he heard voices.

It could have been worse. The girl could have been killed.

The bolt had sliced flesh from her arm, spraying a theatrical gout of blood into the air – Lucas had stumbled telling this part, as if the description were beyond him, though the memory was fixed; the blood black in the spotlight's gleam, the pattering as it hit the ground. Girl and target collapsed, the girl screaming through the gag. The pumpkin came loose, and rolled into shadow. And the excited buzz the men had been sharing climaxed in a two-second silence, while drunken coked-up brains assessed damage and formed contingency plans.

Then the man who'd fired the bow laughed, a werewolf bark, and the others joined in.

Five minutes' later, the weeping girl had been led away.

His story over, Lucas had subsided into silence.

And here, now, in the morning, Emma said, 'Any normal kid would have gone to the police.'

'Think about the people he saw,' said Louisa. 'A royal, for God's sake. And Judd used to be Home Secretary. In charge of the police, remember? And – what was that?'

Both became still.

The noise had come from down the track; a soft padding on a path littered with twigs and dead leaves.

Emma put her hand on Louisa's elbow, but Louisa shook her head. Two short jabs of the finger: one towards Emma, the other to the shed. *Stay here. Watch the boy.*

Then she stepped off through the trees.

The door opened.

He'd been lying on the floor in Shirley Dander's room, into which grey light fizzled from a sky with the clarity of a stained tablecloth. The carpet smelled of dust and ancient spillage. It was Slough House in close-up, worn and mouldy, and if he lay long enough he'd seep into its fabric; become another spore in its culture of damaged mediocrity. Thoughts he put on hold as the opening of the door was followed by a heavy incoming tread.

Lamb said, 'You still alive?'

Lech said nothing.

Lamb kicked him, not gently.

'Fuck you!'

'I'll take that as a yes.'

Lamb threw himself into a chair, as if the chair had done him some great disservice in the past, and was suddenly smoking. Had a bottle too, which must have been in his overcoat pocket. Two glasses appeared from another pocket, and he poured a small measure into one and pushed it in Lech's direction.

The other, he filled halfway to the brim.

'That's quite the barcode you've been given.'

Lech said nothing.

Lamb sighed. 'If I have to kick you every time I want a reply, my foot'll be black and fucking blue before we're done. Now get off the floor and drink that.'

He didn't want a drink, but suddenly he did. And nobody else was offering.

There was a visitor's chair this side of Dander's desk, which was a mystery all of its own – visitors weren't a thing round here – but came in handy as a means of hauling himself up. When he lowered himself into it, Lamb was staring at him with an expression which, in anyone else, he'd take for contempt. But Lech had come to suspect that Lamb's default expressions – boredom, dislike, irritation – were a series of masks, not so much intended to disguise the way he felt as to make you think he felt anything at all. So he sneered back, feeling his cheeks split under the cotton wool padding Catherine had taped to them. 'What's this, then? Pastoral care?'

'Which would make you what? A sheep?' Lamb pretended to think about that. 'Dumb, defenceless, and leaking a trail of shit. Sounds about right. Drink your medicine.'

Lech reached for the glass. Even as its contents scorched to his stomach, he remembered not having eaten since yesterday lunchtime; his late-night excursion in search of food having ended in pain and darkness.

'Jesus, go easy. I've only half a bottle left.'

But when Lech slapped the glass back down on the desk, Lamb refilled it with the precise same single measure.

'You had a meet with someone from the Park,' he said, before Lech could take another drink.

'. . . How do you know?'

'Let's pretend I'm a spy. A pub off Great Portland Street. Who?'

Lech said, 'His name's Pynne. Richard Pynne.'

'Good mate?'

'Not even.'

'Glad to hear it, given how quickly you gave him up. What were you offering?'

'How do you mean?'

'You want a ticket home. You idiots always think you're special, and if you ask nicely enough the Park'll spread its legs. But you need to offer something first. Flowers, chocolates, sexy underwear. I'm just wondering how cheap you are.'

Lech said, 'I offered him nothing.'

'I'm supposed to believe that?'

He shrugged, reached for his glass, and drained it. Not so burny, the second time. That was how life worked: after a while, you got used to anything.

Lamb's glass was empty too.

Lech reached for the Talisker, and Lamb made no attempt to stop him. He poured a single measure into his own glass, then waggled the bottle in Lamb's direction.

Lamb pushed his glass closer.

Starting to pour, Lech said, 'I don't care what you believe, you fat fuck. I offered him nothing.' He kept pouring. 'I was looking for information, not giving it away.' The whisky reached the brim of Lamb's glass, but Lech didn't let that stop him. It streamed down the sides, pooled on the desk, ran in rivulets for the edge. 'Hoping to find out who put me in this shithole.' He shook the last drip from the bottle, and tossed it into a corner. 'That clear enough?'

Lamb kept his eyes fixed on Lech's as he reached for his glass, and lofted it daintily between finger and thumb without spilling a drop.

'And how did that work out?' he said.

'He knew fuck-all.'

'Told you fuck-all, you mean. There's a difference. Because he's back at the Park and you're stuck in this shithole, looking like a half-arsed invisible man.' Lamb moved his head nearer the raised glass and – still without taking his eyes off Lech – tipped the whisky into his mouth. He barely appeared to swallow, but something happened, because the glass was empty, and his other hand was steering his cigarette to his lips. He inhaled, then leaned closer. 'Speaking of which, let's have a look.'

'At what?'

'What do you think?' The words came out as separate blocks of smoke. He scribbled them away with a wave of his hand. 'Let's pretend I'm looking for clues. You know, the assailant was left handed. Has an interest in classical calligraphy. That kind of thing.'

'You're a bastard, aren't you?'

'Yeah. But they said that about Sherlock Holmes.'

Lech stared at him.

Lamb said, 'Why do you care? Standish says you won't get it seen to. So you'll have to get used to being stared at.' He squashed his cigarette out on the inside of his empty glass, then lobbed it into the same corner Lech had thrown the bottle into. 'Living artwork like yourself.'

'I—'

'Just take the fucking plasters off.'

Slowly, carefully, Lech did so.

Lamb lit another cigarette, and for a full minute after Lech had peeled the second plaster away said nothing. His cigarette tip glowed and faded, glowed again. The painkillers Catherine had given Lech were doing their job, but his cheeks pulsed in time to that cigarette. He imagined the letters burning scarlet, like hot coals glimpsed beneath ash.

'Probably wise not to get stitches,' Lamb said at last. 'You'd have a face like a fucking sampler. What did you ask Richard Pynne?'

Lech said, 'I ran a name, Peter Kahlmann. That's the only thing I can think of, the only thing I did before all this happened.'

'And it tripped a wire?'

'It was flagged.'

'Off-limits, then. Seems harsh, though, doesn't it? Take your life apart for a breach of protocol.' Lamb shook his head, as though bemused by the cruelties of fate, and stood. He was still wearing his coat. Lech wasn't sure he'd ever seen him take it off. 'How's your insurance?'

Lech didn't reply.

'Because I doubt your work bennies'll cover plastic surgery.' Lamb jammed his hands in his pockets. 'You owe me a bottle of Talisker. Don't make the mistake of thinking I'm kidding. But here. In case a third way occurs to you. Other than stitches or surgery.' He pulled something from his pocket and put it on the desk. 'I'll want it back, mind.'

He left the room and headed downstairs rather than up.

After a while, Lech reached for Lamb's gift and weighed it in his hand. Heavier than it looked. Good quality. A real old-school implement, in fact, with a handle that might be silver.

When he unfolded it, the razor's blade glinted meanly in the pallid light.

Somewhere under a pile of snow – in a wood, in a field, by a stile – was the monkey wrench she'd used to clock one of the bad actors that first night. She'd have liked it now. Women carrying blunt instruments were taken more seriously. It was the #MeToo equivalent of wearing plastic-framed glasses, but without the hipster connotations.

At the time, though, it had been weighing her down, and flight had been her major concern.

She moved through the trees as quietly as she could, but underfoot was a mess of twigs and leaves; the same carpet that had given away the enemy presence – it was always enemy presence; that was the rule. In joe country, any stranger was a hostile.

Emma had disappeared from view already. The shed was a blocky dark presence in a thicket; a casual glance, and you wouldn't know it was there. But it wasn't the casual glance that worried her; it was the expert appraisal. The noise came again – a rustle, but one with deliberate pace to it; a measured rustle, not a careless breeze. A rustler who had paused to measure his impact on the surroundings.

Louisa waited. The estuary lay behind, a hundred yards or so; the tide was in, and had filled the basin with a shiny grey light that glimmered between trees. Every other direction was shades of brown and white. The sound that had alarmed her came from the path, she thought, but it was hard to tell.

It happened again: a low-down noise. Someone easing forward, but keeping low, close to the ground.

What mattered, she thought, was that she lead them away from Lucas.

She had to assume he had a gun, and with that thought dropped to one knee, and groped around for rustic weaponry. No club-shaped sticks appeared. No handy brick-sized rocks. A few loose stones was all. She took them anyway, thinking *David and Goliath*. This jacket, white and puffy: would it stop a bullet? Wouldn't even slow one down. But best not to think about that.

One stone, smooth and brilliant, she kept in her hand. The others she slipped into her pocket.

When she reached the track she fell to a crouch. The path stretched for a hundred yards before veering left; in the other direction, the way they'd come last night, the sightline was no more than twenty. The ground was rough and pitted, and there was an odd stretch, tramline straight, three inches wide, where snow lay. An oddity caused by the shape of the overhead trees, she assumed, not wanting to pay attention to quirks of nature; wanting to focus on that rustling sound which came again now, to her left. Her grip on the stones tightened. Whoever was approaching didn't sound loud enough to be a person, which meant they were a person trying not to sound loud; a person who knew where to place their feet. She could all but see him, fading into sight like a professional, his gun in a two-fisted grip. Her jacket might as well have had gold and red circles imprinted upon it. And then the fox came trotting round the corner, its movement a bare rustle in the morning light; the scrappy bundle in its mouth a living thing until two minutes ago. It barely glanced at her as it passed. Some dangers were more noteworthy than others.

Louisa breathed out, shook her head, and went back to rejoin Emma.

The voices belonged to a man, a woman. The woman was leaning against a tree and the man was up in her face. It didn't look pretty but that was okay: he wasn't looking for pretty, or its opposite. Neither of these people mattered. They were, though, in his way.

He made to head past, but the man spoke.

'What you looking at?'

Lars raised his hands in polite surrender. 'Just out for a walk.'

'Yeah, well walk somewhere else, all right?'

Lars looked at the woman. She didn't seem surprised at her companion's belligerence. Wearied by it, if anything.

He said, 'I don't suppose you've seen my friends? Two women? One wearing white, the other black? And a teenage boy?'

The man stepped away from the woman. 'Am I here spying on women? Is that what you're asking?'

'It wasn't what I was asking, no.'

'Just as bloody well, right? Because I'm minding my own business, okay? Which is what you should be doing too.'

'Yes, fine. Okay.'

'You foreign? You sound foreign?'

'Well,' said Lars. 'I'm not from round here. That's true.'

'Maybe that's why you don't speak fucking English. Because I told you to piss off out of it, but you're still here. So what you plan to do about that?'

'I plan to piss off now,' said Lars.

'Glad to hear it.'

'And I'm sorry about your nose.'

'What you mean, you're sorry about my—'

Lars broke the man's nose with as little movement as possible, though the man more than made up for Lars's economy by going into a jig, accompanying himself with a high-pitched squeal. Throughout all this, the woman, to her credit, gave only a single yelp, which Lars decided to interpret as appreciative. He beckoned her closer. 'Make sure he keeps his head up,' he said. 'Here.' He guided the woman's hand so it was tilting the man's chin. 'Like this, okay?'

She nodded, mutely.

'And tell him not to be such a dick, yes?'

Though it was possible the man had figured this out for himself in the last ten seconds.

He walked on down the path and then stopped and turned. The woman had let go of her boyfriend's head and was holding her mobile in trembling hands. He sighed, went back, took it from her and hurled it into the woods. Then he set off back down the track at a steady jog, alert for the two women, the boy, and anywhere they might be hiding.

Someone had hung an air-freshener above the frosted window, which had been painted shut years ago. Catherine Standish, he expected. Hard to know whether to admire her persistence or scorn the futility of her gestures. Presumably she was responsible, too, for the bottle of bleach next to the toilet, and the clean hand towel on a rail by the sink. But there'd been nothing she could do about the limescale scarring on the sink itself, and the mirror screwed into the wall was a battle-flecked mess. He was coming to recognise the process: you could resist all you liked its mildewed embrace, but Slough House would eat your best efforts in the end, its inch-by-inch victory as metronomic as the dripping of that tap.

Lech looked in the mirror. He'd barely use this to shave in, its surface was so pitted and green. But even here, his new wounds lit the room; the letters rearranging themselves in the absurd logic of reflection, but still legible, unmistakable; trumpeting their meaning the way sense jumps out of those wordsearch puzzles. *PAEDO*. He might as well be hoisting a flag

He thought: How could he walk into a casualty ward, a doctor's surgery, and ask for help with this? *It's not true. It isn't true.* He'd be begging for belief, in exactly the same way he'd be begging for belief if it were true. Didn't doctors report stuff like this to the police? Jesus . . . His hands were fists. Even he wanted to batter his face into fragments. As if, by smashing his reflection, he could destroy what was written there; erase the lie destroying his life.

And it hurt. It hurt like hell.

From his pocket, he retrieved the razor Lamb had given him. Silver handle, with a fleur-de-lys design. Something from another age: like pocket watches and fountain pens. Lamb himself clearly didn't use it: his jaw was a stubbly mess. But he kept a tool like this: what did that tell you? Having asked the question, Lech supplied the obvious answer. Who fucking cared? This wasn't about Lamb.

The letters glowed scarlet in the mirror. They were radioactive. Toxic spill.

He opened the razor, and stared at the blade.

Maybe if he just never shaved again. His beard was thick and, left untamed, would cover his face like knotweed. It would drive people crazy, trying to read the letters through the undergrowth . . . But if he chose that path, he might as well pick out a bus shelter to bed down in. Stuff his possessions into carrier bags.

Already his throat was crawling with stubble. But it was such a puny defence, wasn't it? A blade like this, you could slice your way through it, stubble and throat, Adam's apple, in seconds.

Give Lamb this: the fat bastard knew what he was talking about.

In case a third way occurs to you. Other than stitches or surgery.

He could not live with this word carved into his cheeks.

Lech lifted the razor and did what he had to do.

13

The thing about someone else's car was, it was automatically an all-terrain vehicle.

That went double when it was Ho's.

Shirley was glad to be alone after a day and a half in company. J. K. Coe was okay, because he could go hours without speaking, and was interesting on account of being on the freaky side. River Cartwright, though, was seven blends of vanilla. When she was bored at work, which was most of the time, she replayed *Bourne* or *Bond* scenes, with Cartwright bringing his own special talents to the role. Like the bit in *The Spy Who Loved Me*, when Bond skis over a cliff, and drops for what feels like forever before his Union Jack parachute opens. Cartwright would drop forever too, before his lunch came flying out of a wrongly packed bag. Bit cruel, but hell: it was the Secret Service, not Secret Santa. Lamb had explained that when making them work late Christmas Eve.

With this on her mind, she almost didn't see the turn-off until too late. The usual markers had been obliterated, but the fenceposts whose tips punctuated the snow broke rhythm abruptly, leaving a gap, so she swung Ho's newly branded ATV ninety degrees onto an upward-inclined lane which hadn't been used since the first snow fell, judging by the lack of tracks. Or that was the plan. Fucking Ho's car, though: as reliable as its owner. Instead of following the lane upwards it basically ploughed into a snowdrift, and if it hadn't been for the airbag she'd have cracked her head on the windscreen.

There was a possibility, too, that she'd just driven into a ditch.

She sat for five minutes then wrestled her way free, which was an adventure in itself. The snow came past her knees, and the air was biting cold. Her footwear was sturdy – Shirley was a Doc Martens girl – and her jeans were actual proper jeans, without stupid designer rips, but her anorak's skin was plucked and pitted from a recent encounter outside a nightclub, when a stuccoed wall had been used as a vertical mattress . . . She wondered about going through Ho's boot, maybe hoisting an accident triangle on the road, or planting it on the car roof like a birthday candle, but in the end settled for sending the *Metal for Muthas* CD flying across the snow-covered field like a frisbee, before slamming the door shut.

This might not be the right lane, or even a lane at all, but she was on it now. Might as well follow the incline to the crest, and see if she could spot Coe's farm buildings from up there.

So off she plodded, a short dark figure on a big white canvas, leaving a trail behind her that was slowly swallowed as snow continued to fall.

J. K. Coe was cold, but preferred it that way. Warm was sleepy; warm was soft. Warm lost you focus, then bad things happened. He still remembered the person he'd once been, who had returned home after a normal day to find himself a sudden prisoner, fastened to a chair in a plastic-clad room, while a naked man threatened to unzip him with a carving knife. His worst moment, one that hadn't actually happened, was hearing the wet slap of his organs hitting the floor. That's what you could expect when warm and comfortable. In the cold, he was sharp as a blade. And his hand dropped to his pocket with the word, reminding him of the short sweet knife it carried.

He checked the map on his phone. Dotted lines and blank white spaces: for once, the diagram matched the reality, which was open spaces with a faint grid laid over it; wire strung between fence posts, marking boundaries. Leafless trees like Holocaust sculptures. Behind him, on the main road and coastward-bound, a small figure that was River Cartwright. Cartwright, Coe thought, had twofold motivation today. Find his friend, and find Frank Harkness. Well, 'find'. He wanted to kill Harkness. He didn't know whether Cartwright realised that himself yet, but it was clear as daylight to Coe.

Not that he cared. There'd been a time when he'd have resisted leaving Slough House. Would have clung to his desk: staring at a screen, out of a window – didn't matter. Time was what you were up against, and J. K. Coe had a strategy: you just coasted through it – ignored its bumps, all the wayward topography it hurled at you in the shape of other people, random events, bad memory. You kept your gaze blank, paid as little attention as was compatible with functioning, and the world moved on. Sooner or later, you got to the end of the day. Then you could manage the dark for a while, breathe slowly, and prepare for it all to start again.

But he'd come to realise that surrender was also an option. If you went along with whatever was expected – got in the car; marched where you were pointed – time passed just as quickly. It didn't matter, in the end, whether Coe was at his desk in Slough House or on an all but invisible track leading to a barn on a snowy Welsh hillside. Just so long as he wasn't strapped to a kitchen chair, waiting for the splash as his innards met a plastic-wrapped surface.

He stopped, shook his head. The image cleared.

Then he stamped his feet. Cold was good; cold kept you sharp. But his feet weren't getting the message.

Next time he looked back, Cartwright had disappeared.

Snow was drifting down; not a blizzard, but one of those unstoppable forces that would end up carrying off walls and bridges. In time, its cold began to feel like a different kind of warmth. That couldn't be a good thing, he decided, as he cut through a copse to find, when he emerged on the other side, a barn.

It sat in the corner of a field, as its skeleton outline on his phone suggested. Its reality was more solid than that empty box, but there wasn't much in it: even from a distance, J. K. Coe could see holes in its roof. It was a fundamental rule of construction: left to itself, any building will strive to become its base elements once more; in this case, wood and nails. Slow horses knew this. Slough House was a constant reminder that neglect was one of the few things you didn't have to work at to achieve an impeccably high standard.

He had all those thoughts, and this one too: that there was a man leaning against the barn's outer wall, watching his approach.

A mile to the coast? Call it a mile.

A mile then, but it felt like three.

River's legs were aching long before he saw the first sign, COAST PATH, and an arrow indicating he should keep right on. And if he walked far enough, he might hit cartoon gravity; the kind where you don't start falling until you notice you've run out of ground. He wondered how high the path was, how far the drop to the sea, and whether the landing would be rocks or water. And if the latter, how long you could be expected to last after impact, in temperatures like this. So many different ways to die arising from the same mistake. That could almost be a mission statement. If not for the Service as a whole, at least for Slough House.

The only vehicle he'd seen had been a car lumbering past in the opposite direction. Its driver, an elderly female, had stared at him but maintained her lumpy pace. The dog peering out of her rear window had laughed at River walking in the snow.

He wondered where Louisa was. The slashed tyres were a good sign. They'd not have disabled her car if they'd already disabled Louisa. So at some point, at least, she'd been active and evading the enemy.

Somewhat unexpectedly he had a signal, so he called Lamb.

'Found her yet?'

'Wales is quite big, it turns out.'

Lamb said, 'Yeah, I've problems of my own. Are you still in a layby or have you got off your collective arses yet?'

'We found where she dumped her phone.'

'But not the phone itself.'

'We didn't pack a JCB. It looks like she tossed it. That or . . .' He tailed off.

Lamb said, 'I'm not a fucking infant. If she's lying dead in a field, she's been there a while, that's what you're saying?'

'Yeah.'

'Well, let's hope not. If I've lost a joe while she's on leave, I'll never hear the end of it.' River heard the clicking of a lighter, and the sandpaper rasp of a cigarette being lit. Then Lamb said, 'You've mentioned the snow. Any signs of wolves?'

'Wolves? It's Wales, not . . . Mongolia.'

''Cause I'm wondering if that's what you've been chucked to. If Guy went dark, she'd have called it in first, and the Park would have responded. In which case you should be knee-deep in back-up by now. Alpha types, unlike you and your loser colleagues.'

River said, 'I've only had a signal about half the time. And if she rang the distress number, she wouldn't get a human response. It goes to a recording.'

'I really did want a lecture on Park processes. Can you explain their time sheets now?'

'All I'm saying, she might not have known she didn't get through. She could have dumped her phone and gone dark without the Park knowing about it.'

Lamb said, 'That's exactly the kind of arsehole outcome I've got used to.'

Behind him, there was traffic noise; the aquarium swoosh of a big car passing.

'You're outside?' said River. He hadn't meant to sound surprised, but, well, Lamb? Outside?

'Visiting an old friend.'

River wasn't sure which was the less likely scenario: that Lamb had an old friend, or that he might ever make a new one. 'My battery's nearly done,' he said. 'I'll call when I can. Any news from there?'

He wasn't sure why he asked, except that something had to have happened, if Lamb had left his room.

'Wicinski cut himself shaving. Or someone did.'

Whatever that was about, River didn't have the battery power to pursue it. 'Hanging up now,' he said, and disconnected.

Five minutes later, the snow deeper here than on the road, he was on the coastal path.

'Just a fox,' Louisa said, back at the shed.

Emma, less concerned about local wildlife than the general situation, said, 'You should have been out of here the first night. Stolen a car.'

'The roads were shit. You couldn't see two feet in front of you. Besides, I was exhausted. And they didn't have guns then.' She rubbed her arm. It was hurting still, and she was tired and thirsty. Some nut-based energy bars, carrots and a pack of raisins yesterday, and not much sleep. 'I thought they were local thugs, paid to throw a scare around. That was before Lucas told me what he'd seen. Who he'd seen.'

Emma said, 'A prince of the bloody realm. Thanks so much for involving me in this.'

'I'm pretty sure it wasn't him I hit with the wrench,' said Louisa. 'If that makes you feel better.'

'I doubt he even knows about this. He's probably known nothing about anything his whole life, except that every so often he has a problem, and someone makes it go away. But on the whole, he probably doesn't get to hear about the problem.'

'You think he's why we've had no response from the Park?'

'If anyone was coming they'd be here, weather or not. And it wouldn't have taken two minutes to find you, given the cottage was on Harper's contact list. So yes, I imagine he's the reason why.'

'We're on our own, then.'

'Looks like. Unless your Lamb gets his act together.'

Which had been known to happen, thought Louisa.

She said, 'What do you think happened to the girl?'

'I expect they paid her off.'

'At least they didn't kill her.'

'If they had, Lucas would never have got off that roof,' Emma said. 'They'd have sanitised the area. Look, there were three of them that first night, right? And they were waiting for Lucas to walk into their arms. So maybe three is all there is.'

'There'll be someone directing operations.'

'Four, then. Still not enough to cover everywhere.'

'What are you thinking?'

'What I've thought from the start. Police. Judd might have been Home Secretary once, but a town this size, this far from London? I doubt he could fix a parking ticket.'

'You want us to walk up to the front door?'

'Maybe not all three of us.'

'It's bang in the middle of town. It's a risk.'

'Which goes both ways. What are they going to do? Gun me down in the high street?'

'"Me"?'

'They had a look at you when you were Wonder Womaning them with your monkey wrench. Only one of them saw me. And not for long.'

'I'm not sure I like this.'

'Which bit especially? Hiding in the wood, not having food, or men with guns?'

It was true that there wasn't much upside.

'You're noticeable, though,' Louisa said. 'A three-word description would do it.'

Emma had already produced an elastic band from her coat pocket; her hair was tied back before Louisa finished speaking.

'Maybe I should rub mud into it,' said Louisa.

'In your dreams.'

'Then maybe,' said Louisa, 'we should swap coats.'

What Shirley needed was snowshoes.

No: what she needed was a yacht, moored somewhere far away.

But all she had was one small twist of speed, for an emergency.

Truth was, she'd had six emergencies since yesterday but no privacy, and while she had few qualms about getting into it with River Cartwright ('Excuse me? Weekend?'), she wasn't a hundred per cent confident of J. K. Coe's reaction. A thing about psychopaths: you couldn't tell which side of an issue they'd come down. Little bit of discretion there, then. One of her overlooked virtues, her opinion.

She paused, removed a glove with her teeth, and rummaged in her back pocket, at last producing a cellophane wrap with barely anything in it. The rough equivalent of what, a double espresso? . . . Not long back, she'd tried experimenting with drugs. The experiment had been to see how long she could go without using them, and, having established to her satisfaction that the answer was 'Quite long enough, thanks,' had gone back to doing whatever she wanted, whenever she liked.

And it wasn't a problem. It wasn't like she answered to anyone, except Jackson Lamb, and he gave no kinds of fuck. Marcus, sure, would have had objections. Marcus wouldn't approve of her taking speed, not on an op. True, this felt more like a misguided office outing, but still, he'd have had a point . . . She missed Marcus. So perhaps she should honour his memory by keeping the speed until this was over, and she almost certainly would have done so, had she not already taken it while engaged in mental debate. But it showed, anyway, that she was capable of moral disputation. Another overlooked virtue. She was practically a saint.

New-found energy buzzing, Shirley crested the hill and found more whiteness: a sky bigger than London's, and not shy about it. And on the downward slope to her left, a darker shape, behind snow-draped trees. A pitched roof.

You'll come to a wood. There are buildings just beyond it.

And that was what she'd found, only instead of driving up the lane, she'd parked early and walked. The kind of thing that could pass as a tactic, if you were describing it to someone else. You want to get the drop on someone, you don't approach their front door on foot. You find an alternative route.

Shirley Dander, she thought. Queen of fucking everything.

Let's see what's going on round there.

Snowshoeless, she made her way towards the trees.

The first 'shed' turned out to be a gun emplacement: a brick shelter half-buried underground, with narrow slits facing the sea, and littered with crushed cans, crisp packets, crumpled silver foil, and sooty embers; with mulled odours of urine, beer and tobacco. Hard to say whether it had been used as living quarters or party-space. Either way, it didn't say much for the local amenities.

River emerged to a now-familiar canvas: the sky, the sea, the cliffside and fields, all varying shades of white.

Despite the weather, he wasn't the first here this morning. Snow was kicked up in front of him. Maybe the woman he'd seen in her car, with her comedian of a dog . . . Something underfoot rolled and he went down on one knee in the snow, like a pilgrim. It would be so easy – so easy to miss your step, and pitch headlong into a short future. Looking for someone else was tricky when looking where you were going demanded your full attention.

Louisa wouldn't have come this way unless she had no choice. The path dipped and dawdled, and even in fair weather must have been hard going where it negotiated the ragged edge. And if you fell, to answer his earlier question, you wouldn't drop straight into the sea; you'd bounce off the sloping face then land on a rocky outcrop far below. River didn't want to guess how far. Didn't actually want to be this close to the edge while he speculated. Pretty clearly, though, whatever hostile contact she'd encountered, there were ways and means out here of disposing of bodies.

On the other hand, this was Louisa. If an encounter with her involved someone going over a cliff, you couldn't rule out it being the hostile. Not entirely.

He brought back to mind the map on Coe's phone. The gun emplacement had been the first marked construction on this path, the next being a few hundred yards further on. After that there was a hike of maybe a mile to the lighthouse. He had no plans to walk that far, not along a path little more than a suggestion. But the next outbuilding, he'd take a look at.

And then the figure appeared, coming River's way; moving at a lick suggesting it didn't find the ground problematic. And familiar enough to warrant River checking the reassuring weight in his pocket.

The figure came to a halt five yards away.

It pulled the hood of its parka down.

'So you found me,' said Frank.

'Hi,' said Coe.

He wondered if that syllable sounded as false in the air as it did in his head. He was not someone who said Hi to strangers. One look should tell anyone that much.

It earned a response, though: 'Hello.'

'I think I'm lost.'

'So do I,' said the man.

He was dressed like a soldier – combat boots, khaki trousers, a belt packed with Action-Man accessories, and fingerless gloves: okay, a bit hipsterish for the military, but probably an advantage when it came to triggerwork. Annex C material, then – legit/grey area/downright nasty – but even as Coe fed in the details, the soldier's frosting of teenage acne had given him away. He was one of those whose face Coe's program had recognised, coming through Southampton's ferry terminal. Cyril Dupont.

Coe had a good memory for names, for faces. An attribute which would have been a boon in his career, if his career hadn't terminated in trauma and after-shock.

The soldier said, 'Where were you heading?'

'Pegsea.'

'That's back the way you've come.'

'Oh. Right.'

His accent was what Coe would have expected: French, but with an American slant. Annex C, he guessed, put you on the kind of career plan where languages were thrown together like socks in a tumble dryer.

He was talking again. 'You're not much of a traveller, are you?'

'What makes you say that?'

The soldier made a vague gesture, head to toe. 'You're not dressed for the weather.'

'I don't feel the cold.'

'You won't feel your fucking toes in five minutes. Your boots. They're ridiculous.'

Coe looked down at his boots. They looked wet, true, with that salty residue boots get when you wander in the snow too long. But ridiculous was a bit strong.

Then again, the soldier's footwear was serious. Boots you could walk the mouth of hell with, frozen over or not.

He wasn't here for macho fashion tips, though. 'I'm looking for a friend.'

'Well you're shit out of luck. Because I don't want to be your friend, and there's nobody else here.'

He sounded woozy, thought Coe. As if he'd walked into a wall, going faster than average. His boots might be combat-ready, but Coe wouldn't have put money on him being able to lace them without help. Which was useful information, because this man knew Coe wasn't a tourist. Sometime soon, that was going to have to be acknowledged.

Coe couldn't see far into the barn, and there might have been any number of others in there, huddled quiet as mice, or their corpses stacked like firewood.

Best all round would be if he left now and regrouped with the others, but that option had been removed from the table. There was no way this guy was going to let Coe walk away, ridiculous boots or not.

The real question was whether he had a gun.

Well, thought Coe, maybe he did, maybe he didn't. The answer wouldn't be long in coming. And some moments you just arrived at, he supposed. His desk in Slough House seemed very far away. But sitting there would be another route to the same destination in the long run.

He rubbed a cheek grown numb in the cold and said, 'You're Cyril, right?'

'I'm not wearing that scuzzy thing,' Emma Flyte had said, and meant it. A white Puffa jacket, visibly torn at the breast, and overdue a launder. 'Why would you think I would?'

'Because they're looking for a blonde in a dark overcoat.'

Emma wasn't convinced a swap would help, though conceded that her disinclination to wear white came into it.

Whatever: more important things.

She left Louisa at the shed and headed towards the town, creaky at the joints. She hadn't slept more than ten minutes, and was reminded of her early days in the Met, when a shift-change would skew her rhythms. But that hadn't killed her. Then again, she hadn't been evading armed men, or not often. The track wasn't wide, and she kept to the middle to avoid snagging on upright brambles. To her left, through the trees, she caught glimpses of the estuary, slowly blanketing under snow. And then the track swung through a thicker patch of trees, and she lost it.

The road wasn't far. Five minutes? But she hadn't encountered anyone yet, the snow keeping people indoors.

She'd need to find someone, though; ask where the police station was, unless she got lucky, and it was bang in the middle of the high street. Failing that, she could revisit the graveyard and retrieve her mobile. Even if the Park had thrown a towel over the birdcage, Devon Welles would take her calls . . . That's what it had come to, she reminded herself. Jobless, out of favour, and relying on Mates' Rules for back-up. Something Louisa had said came to mind.

Like it or not, you're a slow horse now.

Yes, well. We'll see about that.

A man rounded the corner ten yards ahead, coming her way.

One of the bad guys.

She kept walking, because the alternative was to turn and run, or plough through the undergrowth and end up draped across a bush like so much laundry. Besides, this one hadn't laid eyes on her before; would be working from whatever description the man she'd put down last night had fed him, but already his eyes were narrowing, and it might just be that he had a thing for blondes, or he might be computing information. Either way, it was best to derail him.

She slapped her hand on her thigh and whistled so loudly he flinched.

'Seen my dog?'

'What kind?' he asked, closing the gap between them, but before she could invent a breed his fist slammed into her cheek.

Emma's head filled with static.

The ground was harder than it looked.

Frank said, 'So you found me.'

'Looks like.'

'Not that I made it difficult. A hire car? I mean, Jesus, son. Did you wonder why I didn't just get hold of a biplane and drag a banner behind me?'

River said, 'Every time I get one up on you, you make it sound like that was your plan all along.'

'It's called parenting.'

Even in the snow, the whitewashed backdrop of the coastal sky, River could see Frank's grin; his American teeth just another shade of white.

He gestured in the direction Frank had come. 'Louisa's not back there, then,' he said. 'In whatever it is. A shed?'

'A byre, I think they call it.'

'Whatever, you're still looking for her. And the boy.'

'Unless I left them dead. You want to go check?'

River shook his head. 'If you'd killed them, you'd not come back the same way. Bad tradecraft.'

'Ah, that's adorable. Listening to words like that in your mouth, it makes up for everything I missed when you were a kid. Like hearing you go *brrm brrm* when you played with a car.'

River ended up in the Thames last time Frank got him mad. Probably best not to get riled now.

He said, 'I thought you had principles. Stupid, misguided, lunatic principles, but still. But now you're a hired gun, right? The kid Louisa was looking for, you're looking for him too. What did he see?'

Frank laughed. 'What he *saw*, River, he was asking fifty grand to keep quiet about. You think I'm gonna tell you for free?'

'So that's your job. You're saving someone fifty thousand pounds.'

'Jesus, listen to yourself. *I* cost more than that, son. I'm not saving anyone anything. Except the trouble of doing this themselves.' He crossed his gloved hands across his chest and slapped himself, scattering snowflakes. 'Don't ever let anyone take a piece of what's yours, because they'll always come back for the rest. Basic rule of business.'

'And that's what you are now? A businessman?'

'Means to an end. I'm still fighting the good fight, River. It's just, I have to fight a lot of bad ones too, to pay the bills. We're not all on the government tit.'

He moved a step closer saying this.

River sighed, and pulled out the gun Lamb had given him.

Frank did his best to look shocked. 'Seriously?'

'Whatever you're holding, take it out very carefully and toss it over the edge.'

'There are seals down there. You want to give them a loaded weapon?'

'If it makes you feel better, leave the safety on.'

Frank grinned again, wider than before. Then he unzipped his parka a notch, and slipped a hand inside.

He let it stay there longer than River was comfortable with.

'Frank,' he said, 'let's be clear about something. If I have to shoot you dead, I'm willing to do that.'

'We need to talk about your boundaries, son.' But he withdrew the hand, and with it what looked to River like a Glock, a match to his own. 'You're sure?'

'I'm sure.'

Frank lofted the gun to his left, and it disappeared over the cliff edge. River didn't hear a splash, but hadn't expected to.

It was a long way down.

Frank said, 'Your mother's looking well, by the way.'

'Leave her out of this.'

'That's the trouble with this family. Lack of communication. Never did tell you I was sorry about the old man, did I?'

'You're not.'

'Yeah, that's the reason I didn't tell you. You talk to me about principles? One day you should take a long hard look at what your grandpa got up to. That'll complete your education in a hurry.'

He came another step closer.

'Near enough,' said River.

'You planning on shooting me?'

'I haven't ruled it out.'

'So that's your back-up. What's plan A look like?'

'You come back with me to London.'

'What, to "answer charges"?'

River said, 'Last time you showed up, I lost a colleague.'

'I know about your colleagues, son. You should be thanking me.'

'Stop calling me that.'

Frank shrugged. 'I can stop. Doesn't alter the facts, River – and by the way, "River"? I just want you to know I had nothing to do with that. I'd have called you Jack, or Steve. But anyway, River? We're getting to the point where we have to make choices. Because I'm not going back to London with you, and I'm not gonna let you shoot me. So, you know. Crunch time.'

'How many people do you have?'

'You think I'm gonna tell you that?'

River fired. The bullet churned snow an inch from Frank Harkness's foot: to tell the truth, River hadn't been sure he'd miss. But at this stage in his growth and personal development, he wasn't bothered if he shot a few of his father's toes off.

'Jesus Christ!'

But he sounded impressed.

River said, 'How many?'

'Three,' said Frank. 'Happy now?'

'Where?'

'Two down by the estuary and one right behind you.'

River fired again.

'Will you stop doing that?'

Truth was, he wasn't sure. Now he'd started shooting at his father's feet, the temptation was to move up to his knees.

Frank said, 'I have three guys. You already know that, I'm sure. And none of them will walk up to you with open arms, like I just did. Now, can I ask you something? How much is the rent on that shitty flat you're in? On the shitty side of London?'

'What?'

'Simple question, son. You're busting your nut for a job that's given up on you. You earn fuck-all and you're going nowhere. I told you that a year ago, and you're still at it, doing the scut-work and living off crumbs. I'm surprised your mother hasn't had words with you, tell the truth.'

River said, 'And yet, I'm the one pointing the gun.'

'Ah, shit, the only reason Lamb's let you off the leash is 'cause he wants a piece of me, right? Otherwise you'd be back in your kennel, filling out forms, and going home to a fucking hovel. You're never going back to the Park, River. Has that penny not dropped? You're never going back, and you're always going to be earning shit money doing brain-numbing work. Unless you open your eyes and start grabbing some opportunities.'

'What, like hunting down children?'

'I won't lie to you. Some jobs stink worse than others. But you want to make the world a safer place, right? Because you're not doing that in Slough House. All that's for is keeping a few idiots off the streets. And you're better than that, we both know it.'

River said, 'You're offering me a job? Are you out of your fucking mind? The reason I'm here is to keep you from doing what you've been paid to do. To murder a kid, remember?'

'One job out of many. Couple months back, I got to take some really bad actors off the board, and I mean *really* bad. And those guys won't be wiring any bombs again, you can trust me on that. So sure, every so often, I have to get my hands dirty. But not all that dirty. This kid, he's just looking for an easy score. He's hardly an angel.'

'Okay, great. Let's find him and shoot him in the head.'

'Come on. I'd never make you do anything you're not comfortable with. And besides, all this, it's a means to an end, son. All I'm after is some stake money. Get back to my real job.'

'Which is making the world a safer place.'

'And not doing it from a shitty flat on the shitty side of London.' Frank shrugged. 'The money's out of this world. Just saying.'

River gave this some thought, was disconcerted to discover that the idea of earning serious money wasn't entirely unwelcome, and eased his conscience by shooting Frank in the foot. Or in the boot anyway, taking the tip of his Quechua off. Frank needed a cobbler more than a doctor, but still: the look on his face made River rich for a second.

He said, 'That was my final answer, if you were wondering.'

'That's a shame. Because it was my final offer.' Frank balanced on one foot for a moment, while he examined the damage. There was no blood River could see, which would have made it an excellent shot had he been as scrupulous in intent as in execution. As it was, blind lucky was probably the phrase.

Frank planted his foot on the ground once more, and looked to his left again. 'Long way down,' he said.

Then he made his move.

Shirley had slipped through the trees, negotiated a stile half submerged in a snowdrift, and was now round back of the barn, if barn was what it was. She'd had in mind a wooden structure, and this was brick; but that aside, it ticked the right boxes, smelling bad and being nowhere. There were voices, too; a low mumbling exchange whose words she couldn't make out. Didn't sound like Louisa, but Louisa, if Shirley were honest, had never been top of her search list. If Frank Harkness were in the area, that was different. Harkness hadn't actually pulled the trigger on Marcus, but he'd aimed and loaded the gun. And Shirley didn't have a gun herself, but if Harkness was using this would-be barn as a hideout, she wasn't going to let him walk away.

Somewhere inside her, a voice, not unlike Marcus's, was pointing out what a bad idea this was.

And given time, she'd have listened. That was the thing about Marcus: he could be convincing, when he wasn't pouring his life savings into the nearest fruit machine. And he knew a thing or two about action, having spent the upward-trajectory part of his career kicking down doors and shouting threats. So he'd have thought twice about wandering into a potential combat zone with nothing in his hands except that tingly feeling you get when your fingers are freezing.

On the other hand, consider the source. Marcus was dead, which, if it didn't nullify every opinion he'd ever had, made him easier to ignore.

At least find a stick.

She looked around. No sticks as such, but the stile had a loose plank, which she made looser without much difficulty. If it was a little unwieldy in her hands – too short, too thick – imagine how much more so it would be in your face. That was a rejoinder to Marcus, who'd just sighed, unless it had been the wind in the trees. The voices inside the barn had continued uninterrupted. Just a quiet burble, as if a strategy were being discussed, or orders delivered. And meanwhile snow was falling, and here she was, on her own, with a chunk of wood in her hand. The sensible thing would be to stay hidden until whoever it was emerged, and if it were the Annex C team, as identified by J. K. Coe, to track them from a distance until she was able to reconnect with the others.

And not, for example, try to get the drop on them before they realised she was here.

Because that would be a good way to get killed. One Shirley; at least two bad guys. Not impossible odds, but unlikely to attract the clever money. On the other hand, she still had accelerants surfing through her veins, and even without that stimulus, recognised the moment for what it was; one of those that never failed to light her candle. Brief bulletins from her past flashed to mind: capsizing a Klieg light onto a parked van; firing a volley of bullets into a derelict building. Standing with her back to a church door while a crowd pressed forward, nearly crushing her to death. Anything could have happened to her by now. Those were only some of the things that had. And you never knew what was coming next.

And besides, a blaze of glory would do her fine. It wasn't like there'd be universal grief if she never came back. A few Hoxton bartenders would miss her, along with some coke-dealing bouncers, but Shirley had been sharing her bed with an unslept-in space for too long, and there'd be no one waiting up for her key in the door. And anyway: shut up. Frank Harkness

279

might be a badass, but Shirley was no Girl Guide. And there were times when an inability to manage anger had an upside.

Okay, Marcus, she whispered. *Partner.* Let's see how much dust we kick up this time.

Stubby length of wood in her hand, Shirley edged round the barn towards the front.

The ground had been harder than it looked, but she was off it now. She'd been expecting a kick in the ribs but he'd been relatively gentle, if you didn't count the punch in the head. Instead he'd produced a gun and crouched next to her, barrelling it into her neck. From a distance, you'd assume she'd tripped and he was offering aid.

'Where's the kid?'

Emma shook her head.

'We both know how this goes. You don't want to tell me, and I don't want to hurt you. But at least one of those things will happen. Let's not make it both.'

She thought that was pretty good for what sounded like a second language.

Her hands were pressed against the cold earth. She tried to grasp a handful, because every weapon counts, but it was too hard, too compact.

He said, 'Let's try this. You decided to split up. You were going for help? So I know they're back there, the way you came. Take me to them. This can all be over really fast.'

She shook her head.

He said, 'It's only the boy we're after. I don't even have to kill him. Just convince him he made a mistake in pretending he saw something, whatever it was. You want to hear something funny? I don't even know what. Not my business.'

It would all have sounded a lot more reasonable without the gun poking into her neck.

'What do you say?'

She shook her head.

He sighed, and dropped the relatively gentle approach, banging the side of her head with the weapon so that Emma saw flashes: lightning brightening the trees, as if an angel were passing. But the light faded, and no heavenly messenger arrived. Pity. A flaming sword would have been nice.

'I can keep this up for longer than you,' he said. 'Nobody's coming. Don't kid yourself about that. The place is deserted.'

Emma's mouth had filled for some reason. Head trauma. Side effect. Little phrases, mostly relevant. She wanted to spit, but had to swallow. It didn't taste like blood.

'One more time. Where is he?'

It was probably worth being hit again.

In the event, it didn't feel like it.

The way Anton saw it, the clock wasn't so much running as sprinting – if they didn't find the kid soon, it wouldn't be a matter of keeping him quiet so much as buying his memoirs in paperback.

One kid, two women. It shouldn't have turned into Stalingrad.

He was in his second barn, and finding no sign of recent habitation. The first had been occupied, but only by a local woman and some of her cows: she'd been perturbed to see him, but not because he was a strange man on a violent mission; rather because it was snowing and he looked lost. Did he need feeding? For a moment, the possibility of a different life had floated before Anton, as if a doorway had appeared in the snow: he could step through it and enter a different existence. But none of that was really on the cards, so he just said something about needing to get back, and crossed that barn off his list.

And now he was in this one, and it didn't look so different except for being empty. It contained an animal smell, though, as if it too had recently sheltered cows. He wondered where they were now. And then reached for his phone to check in with Lars, but stopped halfway.

A noise outside, round back.

He eased his gun free instead, and stood with his back to the wall by the side of the open doors.

Louisa said, 'Okay, time to go.'

Lucas stood in the doorway of the shed, and looked out on the world as if it had just got bigger.

'Aren't we waiting here?'

It seemed safe to him because they'd spent hours here. Anywhere you slept unharmed became sanctuary. But if the men looking for them had any kind of plan, it would involve checking places off a list, and they'd only be looking in those places they hadn't searched yet. Louisa could have told him this, but didn't think it would help. What Lucas needed was instructions; the knowledge that somebody else was in charge.

'No. We'll go further along the estuary. If they come this way, it'll most likely be from the other direction.'

From the town, she thought. The way Emma had gone.

'Maybe there'll be people there,' he said.

There might, but Louisa had the feeling civilian cover wouldn't offer much protection. Just a larger set of targets.

'Come on.'

She was shivering – they both were – but decided that was a good sign. If they weren't, it would mean they'd grown numb. Numb wasn't good. Creaky wasn't great, but she could live with it. Or hoped to have the opportunity to do so.

Hunger, that was the big thing.

She scooped snow from a low branch in passing and ate or drank it, making each individual tooth in her head complain, but at least she wouldn't die of thirst.

'That's kind of disgusting,' Lucas said.

'. . . Seriously? All that's happened these last few days, and me eating snow is disgusting?'

'Trying to keep my standards up,' he muttered, reminding her unbearably of Min.

The pair reached the track and checked both ways. No one in sight.

Coat flapping round her knees, Louisa led the way.

A bird's eye view would have offered this: two dark figures scrambling on a carpet many shades of white.

The bird wouldn't have been interested, though. The bird wouldn't have been out in this weather.

Frank had moved faster than River expected, even given previous experience. And he had moved slower than he should have done, which Frank might have been banking on; that some bone-deep instinct would stay his finger. Most boys didn't shoot their fathers. Most fathers, too, wouldn't have known to feint before lunging; River's bullet tugged at Frank's sleeve before spending itself harmlessly over the sea, and then River was on his back, Frank on top of him, pinning his gun arm down, forearm across his throat, and trying to push his knee up into River's crotch.

'Let go of the gun, kid.'

'Fuck . . . you.'

With his left fist he tried to batter Frank's head, but couldn't get a direct shot: the arm across his throat was blocking his shoulder too, weakening his punches. Frank smiled through them, or bared his teeth anyway; absorbing the damage. *Watch and learn, son.* The unspoken words were on his breath.

'Be easier on both of us . . .'

River's vision was fading to black; dark spots exploding into other, smaller spots. He should have shot Frank while he had the chance. It might not be what the O.B. would have done, but his mother wouldn't have batted an eye.

He moved his lips. Mouthed words.

'I can't hear you . . .'

He tried again.

'Still can't hear you.'

He tried again:

'. . . Dad . . .'

Frank moved closer, to catch River's drift.

River bit his ear.

For moments there was crazy confusion: he could breathe again, but was breathing in blood. And then he was rolling, but not quite free; each locked in the other's embrace, and at last River got something like a decent punch in, and felt his father's cheek beneath his fist, and then felt something else: a swift and sudden moment of release.

A bird's eye view would have offered this: two dark figures scrambling on a carpet many shades of white.

And then only one.

Without admitting he was Cyril, the soldier shifted his weight from one foot to the other, and tilted his chin. He scanned the path behind Coe, checking for reinforcements. Then said, 'Didn't figure you were a walker.'

'I'm on my own,' said Coe. 'Anyone in the barn?'

Cyril shook his head slowly.

'But you've seen them.'

Cyril said, 'You're with the woman? She caught me a good one with a fucking monkey wrench.'

'I wish I'd seen that.'

Cyril pointed to a mark on his temple, more black than blue. 'That right there. I was slurring words the rest of the night.'

'You still are, a bit.'

'I should get my head seen to.'

Coe nodded.

'But you know what it's like, out in the field.'

'I'm not really a field man,' Coe admitted.

'The boss said something, Slough House? That you lot?'

Coe nodded.

'Said you were a bunch of rejects.'

'That's harsh. But fair. And you're a mercenary, right?'

Cyril shrugged. 'It's a living.'

'Pay well?'

'Yeah, it's good. But sometimes there's months between jobs, you know? You have to budget.'

'Hard to get a mortgage,' Coe suggested.

'Well, I move around a lot, anyway.'

'Still, it's an investment. Thought about buy-to-let?'

'I'm a mercenary. Not a pirate.'

This was a good point.

'Anyway,' said Cyril. 'You wouldn't want to live where my sort of work is.' He looked around. 'Here's not bad, mind. You like the countryside?'

Coe shrugged.

Cyril said, 'You should give it a try, man. Air's a lot better, know what I'm saying?'

'There's shit everywhere, though,' Coe said. 'And I gather they have diversity issues.'

'No, that's true.'

They stood for a while, gazing out across snow-laden fields; pretty much everything white – barring Cyril – as far as the eye could see. A bird of prey was hovering, one black smudge, and just for a second Coe wondered what that was like – to balance on the wind, and track your prey from an aerial distance. Drop on it from a direction it barely knew existed.

A lot to be said for an ending you couldn't see coming.

He said, 'Just out of interest, what did the boy do? That made it necessary for you lot to come after him, I mean?'

Cyril said, 'We don't get a prospectus, man.'

'Right.'

'It's just a job.'

'Right.'

A gust of wind had snowflakes dancing in front of Coe's eyes.

'I'm not saying that makes me blameless or anything.'

Coe didn't have an answer for that.

They stood a short while longer, each lost in thought, but that obviously couldn't last forever.

'Well,' Cyril said at last. 'We should probably get on with it.'

He sounded genuinely sorry.

'Guess so,' said Coe.

His hand dropped to his pocket for his blade.

'Where?'

Emma Flyte's thoughts were rattling round her head, loosened by the last two blows.

'Won't ask again . . .'

There was something of the warzone about it. A forest track, if a tame one. Snow falling, if British snow. And this man versed in brutality; in regarding others as damage waiting to happen.

'. . . Shed,' she said.

They'd have gone by now. That was the plan. Emma would head back to town; Louisa and Lucas would move further along the estuary.

'Where?'

She pointed.

The man hauled her to her feet, while what people called stars buzzed at the outskirts of her vision. She'd been punched before: it was never good. This felt worse.

He grabbed her by the collar, turned her round. Force-marched her back the way she'd come.

Emma could feel his gun in her back; a harsh metal reminder of where power lay.

But Louisa and Lucas would be gone by now, she thought again. And the morning was moving on: even here, there'd be people appearing. Walking dogs, taking exercise. Even here, even in the snow.

Not that people would help. Not civilians; unarmed innocents.

'How far?'

She shook her head: didn't know. Time was elastic after you were thumped in the head. Minutes twisted round each other, and hid in each other's pockets.

In her pockets.

Stones.

There were stones in her pockets, which she didn't remember putting there. But of course, they weren't her pockets.

Maybe we should swap coats.

'I'm not wearing that scuzzy thing,' Emma had said, and meant it. A white Puffa jacket, visibly torn at the breast, and overdue a launder. Not her usual look.

On the other hand, Louisa had had a point . . .

'Come on. Faster.'

Emma moved faster, but stumbled deliberately and fell to her knees. Let him think she was already finished.

Instead of hauling her up this time, he took a step backwards.

'Do that again, I'll assume you're faking. Is that what you want?'

What she wanted was a moment – half a moment – where his attention was elsewhere.

'I fell,' she said thickly. Her voice was not her own. 'That's all.'

'On your feet.'

Something slumped to the ground a few yards behind them, but he didn't even blink.

Snow, dropping from high branches in response to a gust of wind.

Climbing to her feet, she slipped a stone from her jacket pocket. In her hand it felt seamless, egg-shaped, brilliant. One of nature's pointless perfections, smoothed by time.

It wasn't the weapon she'd choose to face an armed man with, but in the absence of anything else, it was a comfort.

'Let's go.'

She'd expected a prod from his gun, but he was keeping his distance now.

Emma started walking, her legs genuinely wobbly. Partly because of the blows she'd taken, but partly, too, for fear. This man's job was to eliminate witnesses. He might have been sent here for Lucas, but his brief had expanded now.

She thought about last night, and the moment in the graveyard. Bringing her pursuer down, and the bare second she'd spent wondering whether to go for his gun. She'd decided it was too dangerous: pity. It would have been good to have it now.

Instead of this stone, so smooth, so feeble.

In real life, Goliath crushed David every time.

But don't think of that.

One half moment where his attention was elsewhere . . .

'It's just up ahead,' she said.

And then the man's phone rang.

The stubby length of wood in her hand, Shirley edged her way round the barn. Still there came that murmur of voices, like something heard on the edge of sleep, or a rumour of distant weather.

Something slipped into her eye, and she blinked it away. A snowflake.

It was odd to be here, but that was okay. It was odd to be anywhere, really. You just got used to some places faster than others. Like any slow horse, Shirley hated Slough House, but had grown accustomed to it too. You had to accept that you belonged somewhere, and it wasn't up to you where that was. Memories weren't optional, any more than fate. Marcus had died in Slough House and it was possible she'd die here, on a snow-blown Welsh hillside, checking out a bloody barn. Of course, she could just duck and cover, wait until the danger, if that's even what it was, passed along, but if hiding were in her blood she'd not be here in the first place. Things were what they were. And she couldn't be different now.

Her blood was tickling in her veins. Partly the speed doing its job; partly the knowledge that she was out here on the edge.

Capsizing a Klieg light onto a parked van.

Firing bullets into a derelict building . . .

Moments when she knew she was alive, largely because people around her were trying to change that.

The voices stopped.

Perhaps they'd heard her. Hard to move silently through packed snow, so perhaps they'd heard her, which meant Shirley had to sacrifice stealth for speed, because once you thought someone might be sneaking up on you, you didn't forget about it in a hurry, and they'd be ready for her, another two seconds they'd be swords drawn. So she ran, as best she could, carting the lump of wood two-handed like a rifle, and Marcus would be proud of her if he could see her now; Marcus would think she was a bloody idiot, but still, he'd be proud of her, taking the fight to the enemy; who was, it turned out, a young woman in a donkey jacket and wellies, reaching up for a transistor radio on a hook; the look on her face one of amusement rather than alarm, as if energetic strangers were part of her morning round. In the darkness behind her Shirley could make out the heavy shape of animals, fed and resting among straw; warmth radiating from them in industrial waves.

The young woman shook her head. 'Look at you, where did you spring from? You must be freezing!'

Shirley couldn't speak, but found herself nodding.

'Cat got your tongue? You're another lost one, aren't you? My second this morning.'

She dropped the transistor into her jacket pocket.

'Well, I'm all finished here. And you look like you could do with a slice of toast, am I right?'

Well, Shirley reflected, if this wasn't death, it might at least be heaven.

'You are,' she said. 'I'm starving.'

'Come on, then.'

Shirley tossed the lump of wood aside, and followed her saviour.

It didn't, in the end, take half a moment.

'What?' the man said into his phone and Emma moved; her fist, clamped round the stone, heading towards his face; her elbow angled to knock his gun arm aside in the same movement. Muscle memory suggested she'd done this before; wearing sweats, on a padded mat. A risky move, but they were the only kind available; he wasn't going to let her go, not now she'd had contact with Lucas. *I don't even have to kill him* he'd said, but not in the expectation she'd believe him. Simply because some things always got said; some lies needed the light.

Punch him in the face.

Knock his gun arm aside.

Some of this happened, but not enough.

No special noise was involved; Emma heard not much more than a cough. That, and the overhead branches sawing each other in the wind, and the soft *whumps* their burdens of snow made when they laid them down. The sound winter sunlight makes when it passes through dead leaves.

And then nothing.

14

She supposed she'd get used to wearing Emma's coat sooner or later; probably around the time Emma wanted it back.

Unless Emma fell in love with Louisa's own white Puffa, of course. Never too late to change your image.

Lucas was pulling ahead; not quite walking fast, more like running slowly. Which presupposed that safety lay ahead, whereas all Louisa was confident of was that danger lay behind.

'Lucas . . .'

'What?'

'Let's take it easy.'

In case they had to make a sudden reversal. In case they found themselves walking into the other half of a pincer movement.

She wasn't sure how much more she could manage. Her safe, secure little flat felt a long way away; its bed and fridge like details from a fairy tale.

Way behind her, out of sight along the wooded track, she thought she heard something: a snapping branch, a breaking limb.

And then they were in daylight; ahead of them the estuary, broadening as it greeted the sea, and to their left a steep hill, lumpily white, up which there must be a footpath, because Louisa could make out a stile at the bottom, underneath a signpost loafed with snow. That would lead up to the coastal path. Descending the hill now, trudging carefully, was a bundled-up figure using a stick. And ahead of them was a building; a pub, its wooden sign flapping in the wind. A single car had been there some time, judging by its rich crop of snow. The pub wouldn't be open, but the car suggested there might be someone inside. And Louisa would pay way over the odds for a sandwich, a cup of coffee.

Beyond the pub, on the far side of a low harbour wall, was an expanse of shingle, daubed with seaweed and torn bits of netting. Slushy-looking snow formed turrets at intervals, but mostly the shingle was just wet . . . More stones, Louisa thought, remembering those she'd slipped into her jacket pocket earlier. A little surprise for Emma, there.

A couple stood on the beach, throwing a ball for a spaniel just this side of hysteria. Its ears flapped like a loose-fitting cap.

'Can we go in there?' Lucas asked. He meant the pub.

'Hope so.'

They reached a gate which marked the end of the estuary path. It was hooked to its fence by a loop of tired red rope, and as Louisa released it she looked again at the figure making its way down the cliff path. Hard to tell how far away, with the snow. The usual reference points had been whitened out. But something about the way he moved was familiar; the shape of his body, or his outline . . . It was River Cartwright, she realised. River, descending to the shore. How the hell had he got there? Though the answer was immediate and fully formed: he'd come looking, once she'd gone dark. A thrill of gratitude washed through her, along with a wave of affection for River stronger than she'd known before, and she'd have run towards him if Lucas weren't here; would, at least, have waved her arms above her head in greeting, had she not changed her mind in that same moment: the man was too broad in the shoulders to be River, unless he was just bulked out by the parka he was wearing, but no, he wasn't; he was familiar, and River-like, but he wasn't River.

He was Frank Harkness.

She said to Lucas, 'We need to go back the way we came.'

'. . . Why? What's happened.'

'Don't make it obvious. Let's just look at our watches, then turn round and head back.'

'It's that man, isn't it?'

'Don't look at him, Lucas. Don't draw attention.'

'But we'd be safe in the pub!'

They wouldn't. Not if it was Frank Harkness.

Louisa made a show of looking at her wrist and shaking her head; a small pantomime probably illegible from where Harkness was, even if he were studying them and not watching his own footsteps. But it had to be done, just as she had to tap Lucas on the shoulder, and point back the way they'd come. She let the red loop drop around the fencepost again, and the pair turned and walked back towards the wooded estuary path. They'd wait until they were sheltered by trees before picking up their pace, putting as much distance between themselves and Harkness as they could,

Which meant moving towards whatever might be coming the other way.

Lars stepped out from the trees and glanced back. Covered with snow and leaves and loose branches, the woman's body still looked like what it was: a woman's body, covered with snow and leaves and loose branches. Shit.

But it was done. The choice was to carry on the way she'd been leading him and see if he could find this shed, or admit the job had just gone to hell and regroup, leave. Harkness wouldn't be happy, but that didn't mean he'd disagree. Sometimes, you cut your losses.

He looked at his phone, to see whose call had caused this mess, and rang back, talking as he walked.

Anton said, 'It's a waste of fucking time. They could be anywhere.'

'I found the woman. The second one.'

'Yeah?'

'Yeah,' said Lars, his flat delivery filling in gaps.

It occurred to him he'd already made his choice: he was walking back towards the town. Away from the body.

Regroup; leave.

'What about the kid?'

'I think we've missed the moment.'

Up ahead, he could hear noises, a group of people it sounded like, and he remembered the couple he'd encountered earlier.

Great stuff.

'We might have a problem,' he told Anton, and rang off.

He'd found a stick, an actual walking stick, hung by its crook from a kissing gate, just before the footpath made its descent to the shore. How in hell, he wondered, did you forget your walking stick halfway to wherever you were going? Some kind of senior moment, he supposed, but hey: a stick would be damn handy, heading down to the shingled beach. There were signs warning you not to use the path in dangerous weather, and this counted, but if Frank Harkness had paid attention to warning signs, he'd either not have lived this long or be somewhere else entirely. One of those options betrayed some loose logic, but he was probably due a senior moment himself round about now.

Damn River . . .

He suspected half his left lobe was gone, but he'd done what he could with a handful of snow, and it was no longer bleeding. His parka was dark enough that you couldn't see the gore. And his toes were sticking out of his boot, but he'd wadded up a handkerchief and patched the damage: all in all he looked a mess, but only when you got too close. In Frank's experience that described about half the population, so he wasn't too worried about it.

Snow was easing off but lay in abundance everywhere, and the natural dips and crevices underfoot were rendered smooth and wholesome by its blanket. On the beach below a couple were throwing a ball for their idiot dog, and emerging from the woodland alongside the estuary was another couple: a woman in a long dark coat and a young man, walking quickly, the boy throwing frequent glances over his shoulder. Harkness stopped, leaned on his stick and couldn't help a smile. Sometimes, you didn't need to go hunting. Sometimes you just had to drop anchor and wait with open arms. Louisa Guy was wearing a long dark coat, as if she were headed for another funeral. Yeah, well, life's little ironies. He began walking again, each careful step probed beforehand with the walking stick.

He didn't want any more accidents.

She thought Lucas might be near the end of his rope.

Which was fair enough; she was damn near down to her fingernails herself.

Frank Harkness was behind them. With any luck, somewhere ahead, Emma Flyte would be returning, accompanied by police.

But how a couple of unarmed Welsh bobbies would stack up against Harkness, she didn't want to think about.

Their brief excursion into the outer air had been bewildering, bright and light. Back under the wooded canopy, everything felt damp and soul-sapping.

She was hungrier than she could remember ever being. Lucas – a teenager – must have felt worse.

And frightened.

'Who was he? Did you recognise him?'

'I'm just being careful. We can wait back here for Emma.'

'What if she doesn't come back?'

'She'll come back.'

Of that much, Louisa was sure. Whatever else was going on, Emma would do what she'd said she'd do.

Lucas didn't answer, or not in words. But the noise he made was half whimper, half growl, like a dog that's not yet been kicked once too often.

Louisa felt a pain tear up her side: a cramp. Oh God, not now. 'I need to slow down,' she told him. 'Give me a minute.'

'You're the one who said to hurry!'

He was dancing up and down on the spot.

She took a deep breath, looked around. They'd already come past last night's shed, hidden among the trees. Maybe half a mile further to town? She didn't know. Distances were boomeranging in her mind; she'd spent days in strange country, and was losing her perspective.

'Come on!'

'Lucas,' she said. 'Calm down. Take it easy.'

'They have guns!'

But it was no longer the middle of the night; no longer deserted. There was nobody in sight, but day was staking its claim. There'd been a couple down by the shore; Emma had seen a dog walker earlier. The track was empty in both directions, but still: it held the possibility of people in a way that it hadn't during the hours of darkness.

But she wasn't sure that made total sense. No way was she going to try it out on Lucas.

Who had moved on a few yards. 'Come *on*!'

Yes.

She moved on, but stopped again almost immediately, and looked to her right.

There, beneath a thick cluster of bushes.

It looked like a patch of snow, but how would snow work its way that deep, with all this overhead cover?

'Oh, fucking hell, what is it *now*?'

She said, 'Stay there.'

'What are you—'

But she tuned him out.

There were patches of snow either side of the track. There were occasional packets and parcels at head height and above, on top of bushes and nestling in the crooks of tree branches, but not in a lump on the ground, pulled almost out of sight of the path. Which meant it wasn't snow. A shiver ran through Louisa despite the coat she wore – Emma's coat – despite the competing sources of warmth: tension; adrenalin; fear. What might have been snow, but wasn't, was her own white ski jacket. That information reached her in a sneaky, underhand way, taking root in her brain before her eyes had finished processing.

Tucked further out of sight, the earth scuffed up to cover blonde hair, was the body.

She'd thought she heard something: a snapping branch, a breaking limb.

A suppressed gunshot.

Emma's eyes were open, but all life had fled.

Louisa heard movement behind her, and turned to find Lucas at her shoulder, wide-eyed with horror.

'Don't look,' she said, but it was too late. And she might anyway have been talking to herself: don't look, don't see. Don't know that you'll be remembering this forever.

But Lucas had fled.

There were five of them; the original couple plus three more, all male, and looking for trouble in a way Lars was familiar with. You came off worst in a scuffle – couldn't call it a fight – and first thing you did was round up a posse, plan a rematch with the odds on your side, as if that would make for a fairer result. Though it would, in fact, depend on the posse. Lars didn't think this bunch would give him trouble.

There was Broken Nose himself, of course, who was basically used goods. The woman was there partly because he'd dragged her along, though essentially because of bad choices she'd made earlier in life. And there were three others, dressed for snow, but not enough to disguise their fatboy bodies: people civilians would make room for in a crowded bar, but who to Lars were a casualty ward logbook awaiting transcription: busted knee joints, fractured skulls, pulverised testicles. He even worked out the order he'd take them in. Broken Nose he'd save for last, and snap at least one of his arms.

But he didn't do any of that. He'd stepped off the track when he'd heard them coming; had cut off his call with Anton and disappeared among the trees. Lars was good at this. He could stand next to a pair of oaks, and within a minute become part of the woodwork. That's what it felt like, anyway. And if it wasn't literally true, it was true enough to evade a bunch of fired-up village boys, who went stomping past without detecting his presence.

Once they were gone he rejoined the track and headed for town at a sprint. There was no telling whether those bozos would find the body – he hadn't hidden it well, but nor had he erected a neon sign – but somebody would before long, and it would be wise to be on the road by then.

It didn't look like they'd be taking home a pay packet, but there were worse fates.

He called Anton on the move, and told him to head back to the barn.

Then he rang Cyril.

Louisa went after Lucas.

There was nothing she could do for Emma, a voice inside her head offered; nothing that couldn't be done just as well later. The voice meant well, but should fuck off.

Emma's open eyes, Emma's blonde hair. Emma's chest wound, ensuring nobody would be swapping coats with her again.

But crying was for amateurs. Slow horse or not, Louisa was a pro, and losing Lucas now would mean Emma had died for nothing.

The kid had taken off like he had wings.

He'd headed towards town, which was good in one way, bad in another. Making for the coast would have put him in Harkness's path. But the fact that they hadn't met anyone coming towards them meant that whoever killed Emma had gone back that way too. So Lucas's biggest danger was he'd overtake the man looking for him, and given his speed, you couldn't rule it out.

None of which made for a comforting soundtrack as she ran along the path, its uneven surface sending dangerous messages up her legs, through her knees, every time her feet hit the ground.

Emma's open eyes, Emma's blonde hair.

Emma's chest wound, ensuring nobody would be swapping coats with her again . . .

Her cramp was back, threatening to split her in two. Heart included. But nothing hurt like guilt.

And now there were voices ahead, round a bend in the path.

She should have slowed and taken stock, or so the voice in her head remarked, but by the time she heard it she was already rounding the corner: there were five of them, four men and a women, and they were straggled across the path as if formation had just been broken. By, for example—

'Did a boy just run past?'

'Is he with you? The little bastard—'

Louisa ran on.

Anton called Cyril too, but Cyril wasn't answering.

The slack bastard might be taking another nap, but Anton, pocketing his phone, didn't think so. Sometimes things didn't just happen, they all happened at once. *We might have a problem* Lars had said, and problems bred like fucking mice. So maybe Cyril had run into one too . . .

So torch the barn.

All kinds of evidence there, if anyone got forensic about it.

The second place he'd checked out had been a wash: empty of life bar a loose plank creaking in the wind round back. Now he was walking down the middle of the road, not far from the crossroads where all this should have ended the first night, and there was still no traffic, except for an electric blue Ford Kia – that was definitely the name – which had ploughed into a ditch, and stuck out against the white background like a hitchhiker's thumb. Tracks led from the accident up the snow-covered field, but there was no one in sight.

Not his problem.

They'd torch their own car too. Frank would have a back-up plan in place; if not, there was an escape and evasion kit taped behind the cistern in the Battersea flat of an ex-girlfriend of Anton's. If he couldn't make it that far, it was high time he found another line of business anyway.

And this looked like Lars now, in that very car; half a mile away, approaching the road from the town turn-off. He was making painfully slow progress, mimicking a camel's rickety rhythm over the humped and pitted snow, but even so, he'd get back to the barn before Anton.

Good. That meant he could make a start on the clean-up.

And find out what happened to Cyril.

It was a scene from the Middle Ages, or a Swedish film.

Snow everywhere, and a body on the ground.

It lay in front of the barn doors, blood pooled around its head, as if someone had dropped a can of paint on it from a height, which was farcically unlikely. Its throat was as open as the barn behind it, and some doors, having been opened, can't be closed. There was nothing to do but step through them. Ultimately, that's what this one had done, though he appeared to have thrashed about on the threshold, unwilling to depart.

One of the Annex C characters, thought River Cartwright. Anton, Lars and Cyril. He couldn't remember their full names. But one of them.

Not far away, sitting in the snow with his back against a tree, was J. K. Coe.

River went to join him.

When Frank had gone over the cliff, River had lain breathing heavily for maybe a minute, staring at an empty sky; a huge grey vault of untouchable space. He could still feel Frank's grip on his upper arms, and was unsure of the sequence that had thrown him free. At last, though, he'd got up and approached the cliff edge. When he'd looked over, there'd been no sign of Frank. The drop wasn't sheer, which didn't mean Frank hadn't ended in the water way below, and didn't mean he wasn't spreadeagled on the rocks, camouflaged by his parka. Alternatively, River supposed, he could be clinging on somewhere invisibly, or making his way, handhold by handhold, back up the steep drop, like a family-sized Tom Cruise. If so, River supposed he'd be seeing him again before long. Frank wasn't one for a quiet exit.

He'd hunted about a bit, recovered his gun, and decided to head back inland, find Coe and Shirley. If Louisa and young Harper were hiding out along the coastal path, Frank would have found them. And if he'd found them, he'd have let River know: the man had been incapable of not making speeches. So this was another dead end. He'd walked back along the path, rejoined the road, and navigated his way to the turning Coe had taken; towards the first of the barns he'd identified on his map.

And here he was.

He sat next to Coe, and neither spoke for a long while, until River at last said, 'Okay.' Then said it again, breathing it out slowly, making it a paragraph.

'O – kaaaaaaaaaaaaaaaayyyyyyyyyyyyyyy . . .'

Then he closed J. K. Coe's sightless eyes with his palm.

From a distance, Coe had looked peaceful, as if he were taking a rest after combat, his hands folded across his stomach. Up close, he had clearly been holding his stomach in. The knife – the other man's knife, River guessed – lay on the ground beside him, staining the snow, and if an expert might have been able to choreograph the moments preceding this tableau, it was enough for River to know that Coe had won the battle, having made his way to this tree once the fighting was done. Though even a partisan view would have to admit that, long term, you'd have to call it a draw.

'I'm sorry,' he told his dead colleague, then went through his pockets, removing Coe's ID and phone. Unlike River's, this still had some charge in it.

As if his looting had triggered an alarm, a phone in the other body's pocket chose that moment to ring.

Emma was dead.

When Lucas arrived at the gate marking the end of the estuary footpath, instead of heading straight up to the high street he veered left, along a lane skirting the town's southern edge which a signpost warned led nowhere. He left a broad, scattered mess behind him in the shape of frightened tracks in the snow, but there was nothing he could do about that.

Emma was dead.

He'd explored this town a million times, on boring holidays. Had arrived every year hoping some major refurbishment had taken place – an amusement arcade, a multiplex, an international athletics stadium – and hunting for them had left him familiar with the tiny side streets, all the rubbish business premises. There was a garage along here; not a city-type garage, with a car showroom attached, but an oily little yard where a man in overalls tinkered with bits. His mum had brought the Skoda here once to have a tickling cough in its engine cured: the car had been left out on the lane for her to collect, its keys balanced out of sight on its onside rear wheel.

Emma was dead.

There was no escaping the rhythm of the thought: it was there in the heavy tread of his feet on packed snow, in the pounding of blood in his ears. Emma was dead. Lucas had met her for the first time just the previous night, but that had been long enough to cause her death, because that was the short brutal truth of it: Emma would still be alive if not for Lucas.

And Lucas, too, might be dead soon, because whoever was looking for him was out here somewhere in the snow.

There was a row of cars outside the closed-for-weather garage. Lucas wasn't a great driver, technically wasn't a driver at all, but he'd learned more failing two tests than most people learned passing one, and he could identify a rear onside wheel no trouble. He looked round before checking the first car. The lane curved, so he couldn't see the footpath gate, but nobody had appeared from that direction, and he could see nobody watching from the back windows of the few houses.

The snow was deeper here, as was usual in unregarded spaces. It had gathered almost as high as the wheel arch; still, the keys were there, first time of trying. Perhaps there was something to be said for small-town life; for its reliable beat. Still nobody in sight. If Lucas could get the car to start, if he could drive it as far as the road leading up to the high street, things would get easier. It was a more occupied area. It stood to reason the road surfaces would be clearer, have more traction; that there'd be fewer murderers around. He cleared the windscreen with his arm, and caused a minor avalanche opening the car door. No alarms went off. He dropped the keys, scrabbled about, picked them up, and managed to insert one into the ignition. It trembled a little, but did the job: Emma was dead but the motor was alive. Now what? Now he urged the car into motion, and nearly killed it leaving its parking space.

Most of the tracks headed up into town: the sane, the obvious direction. The alternative was a no-through lane, its lack of access heralded by a traffic sign on the corner. A single set of tracks led that way, presumably belonging to someone from one of the few houses.

Still, Louisa hesitated.

Lucas knew the town, knew its shortcuts and footpaths. Maybe there was a way round here; a cutting between houses that led . . .

Led where? Fucking Narnia? Any shortcuts led straight to the high street, so on she went, up the hill, all her muscles aching now, and her cheeks numb with frozen tears.

When Lars arrived at the barn, his arse felt like he'd been taming a kangaroo, not driving a car, but that thought vanished before he'd jerked to a halt. Cyril lay out front of the barn, and had either drowned in his own blood or marinated himself in it before giving up the ghost. Lars remembered Frank not giving him a gun: *You made the naughty list. Try not to get hit by any more wrenches.* Something sharper than a wrench had done this. Anything blunter would have taken ages.

There was another body too, under a tree. This one looked relatively peaceful, but equally dead. The chances of it being an innocent passer-by who'd got into it with Cyril over illicit barn usage were not high. The average rambler wouldn't have given even a concussed Cyril trouble. Lars went through the body's pockets, and found no phone, no ID, which more or less proved he was spook A citizen generally had a wallet, and always a phone.

Snow was mashed up everywhere, and the place looked like a polar bear's picnic spot. Lars scanned for recent presence, but couldn't tell one set of boot prints from another. A whole bunch led round back of the barn, but they'd all been taking dumps round there. Aside from that, everything came up or down the main track to the road.

But he didn't have time to work it all through. He'd left one corpse behind already, and there were pissed-off locals stomping round the area . . .

Lars had made worse exits from nastier places, but that didn't mean he could afford to hang around now. Pull the bodies into the barn and burn the place; the car too. It would be on search lists soon. Couldn't be too careful.

He was dragging Cyril across the snow when Anton arrived.

The handkerchief he'd field-repaired his boot with was soaked through, and he'd lost all feeling in his toes. The part of his brain that kept a running tally was worrying at this: his head was going to look lopsided with half an ear missing, but losing toes was way more significant if he didn't want to walk with a limp for evermore.

But another part of his brain, the part in charge of telling him to man the fuck up, was calculating how much of a lead his quarry had.

Frank was approaching the end of the estuary path; could see the road leading up to the high street. It was smothered in snow, the cars lining one side comically behatted and bewigged, but there were figures carrying buckets, liberally strewing sand over the road surface. The town was coming alive. He'd already passed a group of locals on the path through the trees; they'd eyed him suspiciously but he'd replied with the hard stare, and no fuss had been made. But his presence had been noted. And would be again once he stepped onto the streets.

Had to be done, though.

He came through the gate, still using the walking stick he'd found earlier, still not admitting to himself how useful it was – he was too old to be scrambling up cliffsides; that was a job for young men and fools – and rested for a moment just short of the right-angled corner where the road dwindled into a lane. And that's where he was when the car went past, bucking and slewing across the snow-packed surface like a drunk on a skateboard, with Lucas Harper at the wheel.

When the corpse's phone rang, River had taken cover. Standard practice: if you were heading back to base, you let whoever was guarding know you were on your way, in case they got jumpy. Being jumpy was no longer in this guy's future, but whoever was calling didn't know that. There were boot prints leading round back of the barn and he followed them rather than make new ones, and though it quickly became obvious what the space had been used for, he had no time to find a better spot: the dead man's phone rang again, and stopped, and a minute later a car made its laborious way up the snowed-on track.

Within the frozen smell of excrement River crouched, listening to an engine idle and cough and then stop altogether. Heard a car door open then shut. Imagined bitter breathing and angry eyes as whoever it was found his dead colleague, then J. K. Coe, under a tree, his insides partly out.

Whatever had haunted Coe these past years, he was safe from it now.

River eased the gun from his pocket.

Whoever it was stopped moving, as if weighing up options. River approved of the strategy – size up the situation before committing yourself – even if he'd be the first to admit it wasn't one he generally adopted himself. He wanted to check the gun, see how many rounds he had left, but it would make too much noise: every snap, every wiggle, would magnify in the cold country air. Just holding it was noisy. And he could barely slip a finger through the trigger guard, but didn't want to remove his glove yet, in case his hand froze before he needed it . . . And then more noise from out front: the guy had formulated a plan, which, by the sound of it, involved dragging the dead inside the barn.

He was halfway through this task when he was joined by someone else, arriving on foot.

One of them was Lars, he gathered from the greeting. J. K. Coe had identified them by name: Lars and Anton and Cyril. So Lars was upright, and either Anton or Cyril was dead. And Frank, of course, had gone over a cliff, but River would have been happier if it had been two cliffs. Frank wasn't the kind to die quietly, and he'd barely made a sound when he'd dropped out of sight.

There were more sounds from inside now, mutterings in German, and noises of dragging and splashing. And then the car started up, and he assumed they were off, and thought: *Okay, this is it*. He checked his gun under cover of the engine: one round left. They'd be in the front seats, so he'd shoot the driver, bluff the passenger onto the ground. That depended on him arriving at the front end of the car before they left, so—

They drove the car into the barn and killed the engine.

River stopped moving.

Splashing noises, he thought.

He could hear the men going out front again, the stamping of boots, a murmur of speech.

The fizzing of matches.

I really shouldn't be here, he thought.

Then the barn exploded.

Louisa reached the high street, looked left, looked right, and saw no Lucas. She wondered if he'd returned to the cottage – a wounded animal move. Go back to what smelled familiar. He'd be hiding in that cupboard under the stairs, or under a duvet in a corner of the bedroom, or—

Or none of those places, because here he came, jackrabbiting up the street in a tortured car.

And behind him, on the pavement, Frank Harkness.

Others, too, because Lucas was making a splash. If he'd driven before, he hadn't done so through snow, and was making the job of it you'd expect. The car wasn't so much moving forward as undergoing a series of irregular detonations, and if the road hadn't been gritted by staff from the nearby healthcare centre, would have either stalled completely or flipped by now. But whatever you called it, progress of a sort was being made, and Lucas hit a sudden spurt as he reached the turn-off to the centre's car park, where the snow was flattened through use, and approached the junction with the high street at twenty miles an hour.

She saw Frank Harkness see her, and even at this distance – he was a hundred yards down the road – could tell there was something wrong with the shape of his head, but it wasn't slowing him down. Here he came.

The people strewing grit had stopped to watch Lucas's erratic performance, and one of them dropped a shovel and raised an angry fist – the car's owner?

Beyond them, way down the bottom of the road, a woman had appeared through the gate to the estuary footpath. She was shouting, waving, summoning help, and Louisa thought *Emma* – Emma's body had been found.

Lucas reached the high-street junction and ploughed straight on into a craft shop window.

Way off in the distance, maybe a mile out of town, a thin black plume of smoke spiralled skywards.

Much nearer than that, uniformed police officers were emerging from their station along the road.

Louisa was first to the crashed car, but only just. Onlookers had formed a cordon round the shop front almost before she'd checked that Lucas, though dazed, appeared unhurt.

One of the police officers approached, while the other pair went haring down the road towards the shouting woman, and the wood where Emma's body lay.

Frank Harkness halted on the opposite pavement. He looked up the road, down the road, then focused on the tumult round the car. To Louisa's eye, he was calculating odds.

Specifically, now, he was looking straight at Louisa.

The police officer was asking Lucas if he was okay, asking the assembled onlookers to move back, but Louisa ignored her and remained where she was, on the pavement next to the driver's door, on a carpet of broken glass and snow.

She was wearing dead Emma's coat, of course, and tapped its breast pocket slowly, never breaking eye contact with Frank.

I'm armed, she was lying. *Don't even think about it.*

He stared at her for a full quarter minute, while all around the small crowd pulsed and wobbled. A siren was starting up somewhere: she guessed an ambulance.

And eventually Frank nodded, a minor tip of the head, then walked off down the road, his walking stick carried level with the pavement: a pointless accessory.

Louisa breathed out at last, and stepped away from the car.

'Explosion' was an exaggeration, but still: there'd been petrol involved, and plenty of timber.

While the barn burned River lay in the snow against a hummock, feeling his back grow colder, his front warmer, and knowing that the two bad actors, Lars and whoever, were heading along the footpath to the coast. One bullet wasn't going to be enough, not out in the open. And somewhere in the flames in front of him, or in the black angry smoke roiling into the sky, J. K. Coe was taking leave of the planet.

If they'd packed up and left the scene, it meant their job was done.

Which meant Louisa and the boy, Min Harper's kid, were presumably ticked boxes by now; their lives scored off the register.

He didn't want to think about Louisa being dead.

For once, just once, he'd like an op that didn't turn into some catastrophic clusterfuck.

He used Coe's phone, because his own was out of charge, and called Shirley.

'Where the hell are you?'

'Who the hell wants to know?'

'It's me. River.'

'Why've you got Coe's phone?'

River said nothing.

Shirley said, 'Shit.'

'Where are you?' he said again.

'Heading back to the main road,' she said, her voice quieter than normal. 'There's a fire up on the hill.'

'That'll be me.'

The flames were still biting chunks out of the morning when he reached the road to find Shirley approaching on foot. Which didn't bode well for Roddy Ho's car, but, never high on River's list of priorities, Ho's vehicular welfare was even less a concern than usual right now.

Shirley was holding something wrapped in kitchen foil.

'What happened to Coe?'

River gestured with his head back up the hillside, to the burning barn.

She looked that way, and he couldn't read the expression on her face. Sometimes, Shirley Dander was an ABC. The rest, she was lost in translation.

She said, 'Did you find Harkness?'

'Uh-huh.'

'And?'

River shrugged.

'What about Louisa?'

'Don't know yet.'

Shirley said, 'Well. She might be okay.' Then she handed him the foil package. 'Here. I got you this.'

'What is it?'

'Sausage sandwich.'

It was warm to the touch.

He said, 'You only brought one? What was Coe going to eat?'

She didn't reply, and he thought, yeah, right. She'd brought it for Coe.

After a while he rang Lamb, and gave him the story.

15

Martin Kreutzmer liked to read the *Guardian*, because it kept him in touch with that strain of self-lacerating smugness which hoped to inherit the earth, but would have no clue what to do with it. Peter Kahlmann, on the other hand – his primary cover – was a *Daily Mail* man through and through, locked in a constant tussle between resentment and prurience, and calling it victory either way. So it was the *Mail* that Martin – Peter – was reading in Fischer's, looking for a story that wasn't there. This was the most interesting kind. When a story was on the front pages you looked for the holes in the headlines, hoping for a glimpse of the truth they covered up. When the story dropped from view altogether, you wondered what diplomatic origami had been at work, folding the paper so it vanished between the creases.

So: a few days ago there'd been some drug-related killings in Pembrokeshire, which was in Wales – bodies in a burned-out barn, a dead woman in a wood. But the speed with which the story had evaporated made Martin suspect Spook Street activity; either an undercover frolic gone enthusiastically wrong, or something deeper. Wales wasn't uncivilised, if you took a charitable view, but the dangerous edge of things was always closer than it looked. Martin had worked undercover, and like anyone who'd done time wearing the opposition's coat he still woke sweating some nights, undone by the fear that he'd betrayed himself in some tiny way. You could be in your own home, your own bed, but there were bandit eyes on you always, and they never blinked, never looked away. After a while, you forgot that other people didn't know this.

He shook his head to clear these thoughts, and was back in Fischer's, on the foothills of Marylebone High Street, the *Mail* a rolled-up truncheon next to him; his lunch freshly delivered to the table.

'Some things few people get to witness, and most of them wish they hadn't. Like jazz dancing. Or the pope's sex face.'

A large man in a dirty overcoat had appeared out of nowhere.

'Or Martin Kreutzmer eating a salad.'

He dropped heavily into the seat opposite Martin, and fixed him with a malevolent glare.

Martin navigated a forkful of greenery into his mouth, and didn't speak until he was ready. 'Jackson Lamb,' he said at last. 'It's been a long time. Though not quite long enough.'

The waiter arrived. 'Can I—'

'No.'

'We're fine,' said Martin. 'Thank you.' The waiter left, and he said, 'There's something different about you. Wait – I know. You got fat and old.'

'And you had a stroke.'

Martin nodded pleasantly, like a man doing 'relaxed' in charades. Only three people knew he'd had a stroke, or that was what he'd thought two seconds ago. It had been a minor thing, a slight tug on the curtain, but enough for a glimpse, if not of what lay beyond, at least of the fact that there was a beyond, and it wasn't going anywhere. Maybe that's why he'd been taking such relish in running Hannah Weiss. But it was also the reason he'd slowed down taking some of life's corners.

'Which'll be why you joined the salad-tossers.'

'It's not a strict diet,' said Martin, who'd been known to order the schnitzel. 'But I'm watching my cholesterol.'

'I can't imagine what that's like,' Lamb said. 'Losing control of your bodily functions.'

He farted, presumably to demonstrate total dominance over his own.

An elderly couple two tables away stared in horror.

Martin Kreutzmer laid knife and fork aside. 'Is this what passes for covert activities these days? No wonder they put you out to grass.'

'Is that what they did to me? I've been wondering.'

He reached across and plucked a crouton from Martin's plate, examined it in what might have been curiosity, then put it back.

'Because it still feels like the Wild West some days. Especially when a bandit's been branding my cattle.'

Martin used his fork to manoeuvre the crouton Lamb had been fondling, and the greenery it nestled among, to the side of his plate.

He hadn't laid eyes on Lamb since Berlin, early nineties, where Lamb had enjoyed all sorts of reputations, each of them circling one fixed point: you didn't fuck with his joes. Years had gone by, a lot of water pissed into from different bridges, but Lamb had the look of a man whose fixed points stayed where he'd put them. And Martin, yes, had branded one of Lamb's cattle. The fact that he'd done it to keep his own joe safe would melt no ice. Nor did he have to be aware of Lamb's reputation to see the violence currently churning below his surface. 'Current mood', as the kids said: 'fuck off and die'.

He said, 'I always thought you'd end up running the Park. If they didn't stick your head on a pike, that is.'

'They're still sharpening the blade. And you're changing the subject.'

'I haven't crossed your borders, old man. Wherever those borders happen to be.' He speared a ribbon of cucumber with his fork. 'I'm out of the game. Maybe you hadn't heard.'

'You? Retired?' Lamb reached for another crouton, and this time put it in his mouth. 'I've read more convincing lies on the side of a bus.'

'Maybe not entirely retired. But a mentoring capacity, you know?'

'"Mentoring"? I have no fucking clue what that means.'

'No, well, there'd be little point in you trying to pass your skills on, Jackson. For a start, nobody's sure what they are. And for another, they don't mesh with current values, do they?'

Lamb spat the crouton into his hand. 'For somebody who reckons they're out of the game, you sound a lot like someone keeping score. Here, do you want this back? I've hardly touched it.'

313

Martin indicated a napkin, neatly folded beside an unused place setting. Lamb placed the soggy crouton on top of it.

'All things considered,' he said, 'I'd sooner have a stroke.'

'A popular opinion, I'm sure. How did you find me, by the way? And don't say Regent's Park pointed a finger. The Park these days, it's a kindergarten. Our generation could march past in full colours, they'd think we were an outing from a care home.'

'Speak for yourself. I walk past Regent's Park, alarms go off.'

'It's the same all over, mind. Broadcasting, light entertainment, even the clergy. It's like we handed the world to the young.'

'Well,' said Lamb. 'They're cheaper, and they don't rape the help as often. But hark at me interrupting. Please, continue talking shite.'

'I was simply making the point that being a dinosaur has its advantages. I've got used to not being recognised.'

'So you fell into a habit,' said Lamb. 'Congratufuckinlations. That the sort of thing you teach your mentalists?'

'I think you mean mentees. But you make your point. You didn't wander in here by chance.'

'Didn't have to. An old friend marked your card a long time ago. And she never throws cards away.'

Understanding dawned. 'Molly Doran,' said Martin. 'How is she?'

'Well, her legs haven't grown back, if that's what you were wondering.'

'It happened in Berlin, didn't it? Her accident. If that's what it was.' Martin reached for his glass of water. 'And she's still at the Park. I didn't know that.'

'They keep her in the basement.' A cigarette had appeared from somewhere, and Lamb was using it as a prop, balancing it on one finger; staring at its filter rather than looking at Martin. 'And she owes me some favours. So I took her the name Peter Kahlmann, which is one that Lech Wicinski mentioned, and what do you know? Up you pop like a teenager's dick. Because you've used the name before.' He let the cigarette drop into his palm. 'That was careless.'

'Once only,' said Martin. 'In ninety-three, it was. Visiting DC.' He shook his head. 'She must have quite some database.'

'If by that you mean brain, yeah. Having fewer extremities helps. Less distance for the blood to travel. So Wicinski pins a tail on your old cover, and suddenly his laptop turns into a seventies DJ's to-do list, which means nobody cares about what else he might have been looking at. And when he reaches out to have his findings double-checked, someone uses his face for needlework practice. You know what that sounds like to me, Martin?' He opened his palm. The cigarette had vanished. 'It sounds to me like someone wanted to keep the focus away from the name Peter Kahlmann. In case anyone found out it was actually you.'

Martin laid his knife and fork together on his plate, in the accepted semaphore for completion. He said, 'Sometimes we play nasty. Even the youngsters have to find that out.'

'Nice that there's a moral attached. He's got a face like a walking parental guidance sticker. Or did have, I should say.'

Martin paused. 'What happened to him?'

'He finished the job you started,' said Lamb. 'You like this place?'

'It has a pleasing pre-war feel.'

'Yeah. It opened in 2014. Are you ready for the bill or what? This thing's not gunna smoke itself.'

On the street there was slush in the gutters, but the snow had mostly disappeared. Lamb lit his cigarette before they were out of the door. He took up a lot of pavement space, but Martin Kreutzmer, well versed in body language, could read between his lines: Lamb was deliberately moving large; making it implausible, to the casual observer, that he might ever move in any other fashion.

The churchyard opposite, a lunchtime haven for office workers, was empty because of the cold and the damp. As they circled it, Lamb halfway through his smoke already, Martin said, 'I had heard about Slough House, but I hadn't realised it would be so . . . insalubrious.'

'Uh-huh,' said Lamb. 'It's kind of grubby too.'

'Not the crowning glory I'd have expected, a career like yours.'

'Is this you making a pitch, Martin? Because you've all the panache of a schoolboy virgin.'

'Well, it doesn't look like you're taking me to the Park. So I wondered if you had some other kind of deal in mind.'

He hoped so, certainly.

You don't fuck with Lamb's joes.

'Besides, I've been reading fairy stories in the paper. Bodies burned in barns, that sort of thing. I suspect the Park has other things on its mind than whatever a semi-retired spook has been doing, even if he's been doing it in London.'

That, anyway – or something like it – was what he'd planned to say, but he'd barely reached the word *barn* before he had another stroke. All feeling left him momentarily, and then came back again, focused on one small spot below his left lower rib. Lamb was holding him upright and lowering him onto one of the empty benches. A taxi sounded its horn, angry at some pedestrian infraction. Birds scattered. He managed to suck air into his lungs, and his vision cleared.

Lamb said, 'You may have touched a sore spot there.'

It was implausible that he might move in ways that weren't large and clumsy. But appearances were deceptive. *It opened in 2014.* The point Lamb had been making.

Lamb said, 'You were burning a barn too, weren't you, Martin? In a manner of speaking. To destroy evidence, or distract attention. Which is itself evidence, because it means you're up to something and you don't want anybody to know what it is. And you're not worried about the Park. Bunch of kindergarteners, right? No, you're worried what they'd say back home, which means you've gone over the edges, and when they discover what a bad boy you've been, well, your future might start looking as *insalubrious* as mine.'

He could feel the dampness of the bench seeping into his bones.

'They don't even know about the stroke, do they? But they'll find out.'

He thought about the sheer pleasure he'd taken in running Hannah.

'And then you'll get to know what being out to grass feels like.'

The pain had subsided to a burnt-out filament. He said, 'It's nothing, Lamb. You'd laugh if I told you. It's fun and games, that's all.'

'I don't care what it is. But you've run up a bill, and I'm calling it in.'

'I'm sorry about your joe. But I didn't kill him.'

'It would be best if you didn't talk about my joes right now.'

'What do you want?'

'I want you to get a message to someone. He used to be on your books.'

'My books?'

'The BND's. I don't really care whose fucking books they are, Martin, I just need to know you can still reach them from the shelf.'

'I carry weight, Jackson. More than you do, judging by your address.'

'We'll talk about my problems once we've established whose bitch you are. You going to be my messenger boy? Or do I burn your playhouse down?'

Martin said, 'I do that, and you bury this whole conversation? Me being Kahlmann? Running an op in London?'

'I don't give a fuck what you're up to.'

'Doesn't that count as treason?'

'Wouldn't be the first time.'

'It sounds like I'm getting off lightly.'

'You haven't heard the message yet,' said Lamb.

'These events in Wales,' said Peter Judd.

'For the record,' Diana Taverner told him, 'I'm not aware of any events having taken place in Wales. Or anywhere else.'

That morning had seen an ill-tempered Oversight meeting, during which Diana's delivery of her planned showstopper – *I applied for Fugue. I could have handled this. But I was turned down* – failed to receive a standing ovation; Oliver Nash, in fact, going so far as to hint that her attempt to initiate the protocol had been made in bad faith, with precisely this result in mind: a potentially headline-grabbing car-wreck caused by someone else's driving. Her intention being, he only just refrained from saying, to bolster her own case for a bigger, sturdier vehicle. But however it was spun, the deaths of two Service personnel – one recently resigned – and a known Annex-C mercenary, in Wales, made the Park look out of control, which hardly burnished the reputation of the woman supposedly at the wheel. The curious relish with which Nash kept repeating 'in *Wales*' suggested that he considered this an added aggravation, which might have tempted Diana to suggest that it was, if anything, a mitigating factor, had she not registered in time the presence of one Llewellyn Jones, a former Home Office minister who could usually be relied upon to be comatose by the ten-minute mark, but whose eyes had unglazed at the mention of his homeland as if a rugby squad had burst into the room bearing daffodils.

'In that case,' Judd said, 'you'll be pleased to hear that they didn't happen anyway.'

She already knew this. The dead were still dead, of course, but that was a detail: one was a Slough House operative, so to all intents and purposes had been declared surplus to requirements, and if Emma Flyte's name had caused raised eyebrows around the committee table, the abruptness of her resignation, which Diana had allowed to be known was due to personal problems, allowed speculation to wander freely. Besides, Flyte had been known for her startlingly good looks. This lent credibility to her involvement in violent altercation, the potential for an unhappy ending being a recognised tax on female beauty. As for the merc, his obsequies boiled down to a red line through an entry on a database, and nobody was going to lose sleep over that.

For housekeeping purposes, the deaths had been ascribed to drug-related warfare between rival gangs, which sounded enough like a bad TV drama to satisfy most sections of the media.

So whatever had happened already hadn't happened, but it was nice to have confirmation, so she simply said, 'I'm pleased to hear it. Care to elucidate?', elucidating being one of Judd's preferred modes of discourse, there being, somehow, a lubricated quality to it.

He was happy to do so.

She drank her coffee while he talked. They were in a café off Fleet Street, at Judd's suggestion – he wanted somewhere with no danger of journalists being present. London was damp and unlovely, but last week's snow was a dim memory she'd already heard referred to as fake weather. Now, there was talk of continued drizzle and bitter winds for days to come, which surprised Di Taverner not one whit. There was always a bitter wind blowing from somewhere. If the weather didn't supply it, you could rely on Whitehall. Meanwhile, Judd was explaining that his clients – those whose company had hosted the party at Caerwyss Hall – were content to draw a veil over the sorry episode. The savage eradication of problems might be their preferred business strategy, but Western democracies weren't really their playground of choice. What should have been the discreet dispatch of a troublesome snoop might easily have become a local bloodbath: brushable under the carpet most places their products were regular best-sellers, but rather more noticeable where there were more second homes than second-hand cars.

'Besides,' said Judd, 'he rang again.'

'The boy?'

'Sounded as if he were reading off an idiotboard. It seems he's experienced a complete, he called it "memory wipe", of all and any events taking place over the New Year. Probably due to an overindulgence in whatever he was smoking at the time. Apologised quite fulsomely. Quite restores one's faith in the younger generation, the whole drug-taking,

319

blackmailing, body-burning episode aside.'

'So he's gone home with his tail between his legs and that's it?'

'Sometimes, we have to accept that wrongdoers walk away unpunished,' offered the man who'd solicited at least one murder, to Diana's certain knowledge.

Others would face consequences. Slough House needed looking at, Nash had made clear that morning. Whatever one of their operatives had been doing away from his desk, let alone in a knife fight with a mercenary in a snowy field, demanded investigation: the department was supposed to be a holding cell for incompetents, he reminded her, not a halfway house for would-be Tarzans.

She didn't tell him she already had plans for Slough House. Or that they'd been put in operation the day she took over First Desk.

The rest of the morning's meeting had been equally frustrating. Diana had expected her revelation that a civil servant working within the Brexit Office had been working for the BND to be met with shock and umbrage, and a concomitant level of gratitude for the Service's diligence in unmasking her. Instead, there was an air of resigned acceptance that Brexit had thrown up yet another source of embarrassment. Much of the business of government for the preceding two years had been to find a scapegoat for the ongoing catastrophe; blaming at least part of the mess on German interference was, on the face of it, attractive, but wouldn't play well with the public, who might with some justification wonder why a foreign agent had been appointed to the office in the first place.

'And she was being run in-country?'

This from Archibald Manners, parliamentary appointee to the committee, and long-time Park-watcher.

'By one Martin Kreutzmer,' she said. 'Something of an old hand.'

'Molly Doran's work, by any chance?'

Diana had allowed that this was so, skipping over Jackson Lamb's role in the proceedings, which, anyway, hadn't weighed more than a two-minute phone call. *You know how your tame lab rats are supposed to keep tabs on foreign talent? Remind me, does that include feeding them Service gossip on a silver fucking tray like this was Downton fucking Abbey?* His follow-up suggestion – that she spend a minute or two ascertaining exactly who the fuck Peter fucking Kahlmann was, the better to feed him his own fucking arse before dropping him off the nearest fucking tower block – quickly became an unsanitised instruction to Richard Pynne, who'd morphed into Richard fucking Pynne in the time it took him to reach her office. Peter fucking Kahlmann, it turned out, was a cover for Martin fucking Kreutzmer, which, if they'd known from the drop, would have made Operation fucking Goldilocks a non-starter. Little Hannah Weiss, their fledgling double, was in fact a triple, a revelation which led, in turn, to the further discovery that Diana Taverner didn't always have to press a button to cause the glass walls of her office to frost over. Sometimes she could do it through sheer force of rage.

Anyway. The committee didn't have to hear about that.

And if Lamb thought this little offering made up for leaving bodies strewn about the Welsh countryside in his futile attempt to have Frank Harkness skinned alive, he was going to be disabused in pretty short order.

'I sense that I don't have your full attention.'

She blinked. 'Peter. I've had a busy morning. I've a busy afternoon ahead. Followed by a busy evening. I'm glad to hear we've had a promise from a psychotic weapons merchant that they're no longer intent on sending armed talent to murder a British citizen, but that having been settled, was there anything else?'

'I rather wanted to discuss the state of the world.'

'. . . Seriously?'

'And how it affects your current role.'

It occurred to her that the café offered no table service. There were no young things in skirts to flirt with, no opportunity to dispense leering largesse. It was no more P. J.'s natural habitat than a Time's Up march. Perhaps he was serious after all.

He said, 'I was listening to the wireless the other evening.'

'It's just the two of us. You can say podcast.'

'One of those discussion programmes the BBC likes to think of as balanced, in that it had a left-leaning liberal debating current affairs with a right-leaning liberal. Long story short, can you guess what they concluded?'

'That things will turn out all right in the end?'

'A predictably smug affair. People have lost faith in government, we were told. Here, in Europe, in the States. But this is simply a correction, the same way the market regulates itself. Democracy hiccupped, that's all. Next time round we'll do better, and our common future will no longer be in the small, incapable hands it currently rests in. I'm quoting, obviously. It was tedious, dinner-party stuff.'

'But thanks for sharing.'

'And yet it touched on the issue I wanted to raise. This being, the current rift between the White House and the federal agencies.'

'Fascinating.' She looked at her watch. 'And yet of no remote relevance.'

'Which mirrors the growing divide between our own government and your Service.'

She sighed. 'If all you're doing is polishing your next blog, you'll be sorry you wasted my time.'

'The PM turned down your request for a root-and-branch overhaul of operational practices.' He raised a hand to forestall her response. 'Don't bother denying it. We both know the PM's a tormented creature. Like one of those soft toys lorry drivers fix to their radiator grilles. That expression she wears, it's terror at all the oncoming vehicles.'

'Picturesque, I'm sure.'

'And once she's gone, who knows, maybe the next PM will be more amenable to your requests. But what about the one after that? And the one after that?'

'Running out of patience.'

'Whoever's in government, whichever party it happens to be, and however lacking in leadership skills and a basic grasp of reality, they're the ones pulling your Service's strings. This despite the fact that no government we've seen over the past ten years has been capable of making the decisions necessary to protect our nation. Take Salisbury. A clear-cut case, evidence stacked a mile high, the guilty party visible for all to see. And yet nothing happens.'

'It's how democracy works.'

'And it's window-dressing. The Cabinet can spend its days talking about high-speed trains or garden bridges and that's fine. But it's not equipped to determine the best way of safeguarding national security because those particular parameters change at dizzying speed. It's an area best left to the professionals. To those who've been engaged on the task on a daily basis their whole careers.'

She said, 'In principle, I wouldn't disagree. But you mentioned a basic grasp on reality, and you've clearly lost your own. Even if the government were to grant the Service autonomy – which it wouldn't do in a thousand years – that would demand a far greater injection of funds than my own rather more modest proposal required. And that, as you pointed out, was rejected on grounds of cost.'

Peter Judd said, 'And yet – leaving that issue aside for the moment – suppose the Service were able to achieve, let's call it a self-sufficient status. Wouldn't that be preferable to the present situation?'

'Effectively, you're talking about a coup.'

'Don't be ridiculous. A coup would be the seizing of power. What I'm talking about is the preservation of the power structure as it is. Democratically elected governments, the rule of law, all the rest of it. Except ...'

'Except with an independent secret service.'

'Acting in the interests of the nation. The best interests, because it alone has a full understanding of where the current sources of danger lie, and the best way of dealing with them. And is thus able to make decisions that the government of the day is not equipped to make, and almost certainly doesn't want to have to. Either because of weak leadership or the keen desire to avoid taking morally questionable positions. Which, as we both know, are frequently the positions one needs to take to prevent harm befalling the innocent.'

'No government would accept that.'

'The government,' said Peter Judd, 'wouldn't have to know.'

'This is insane.'

'Let's step back a little. Full autonomy, yes, is out of the question. But what if you had the resources to operate as required, in situations of critical need, without requiring government approval? Which, as we've established, means government funding? In other words, what if your Service's necessary activities weren't constantly hampered by the need for political acquiescence?'

Put another way, she thought, what if the Fugue Protocol was on the table any time she wanted?

She said, 'Even supposing this daydream were a good idea, where do you imagine the funding would come from. Private enterprise?'

He said nothing.

'Oh, you must be joking!'

'Why?'

'Where would you like me to start?'

'You have to think about the bigger picture. This would be a logical development. Look at the private contractors you already use. Look at the security firms mopping up after foreign adventures. Halliburton. Blackwater. What I'm suggesting is simply the next step on a course that's already plotted.'

'There's a leap between that and privatising the intelligence services!'

'We're not talking about privatisation. Simply an injection of necessary funding from sources with a huge vested interest in national security. They don't want to be hacked, they don't want to be bombed, and they don't want those things to happen anywhere in the cities in which they operate. Now, they have the resources to safeguard their own operations, up to a point, but you have the infrastructure, the legislative authority, the national scope, to tackle those threats at the point of origin. What you don't have is the investment you need, or, with the way things are looking in Europe, support from reliable allies. I'm offering a credible alternative to what we both know is a potentially dire situation. One, I might add, which any sensible government would be looking to implement of its own accord.'

'Even if − Peter. What you're suggesting, it couldn't be made to work.'

'Of course it could. As a staged process. We prove this can be effective in specific, singular instances, and then present it to government as a working model. And trust me, government will listen. The partners I have in mind have their own spheres of influence, and I'm including the political in that. They'd be bringing that to the table too. Not to mention myself, obviously.'

'Because you'd be a part of this.'

'Nothing's set in stone. But you'd require a broker to liaise between the Service and its backers. A conduit, if you will.'

They were sitting in a café off Fleet Street, she reminded herself. This bizarre conversation was taking place in the real world. This morning she'd had a brusque reminder that her position was subject to the oversight and control of others; reminded, too, that allies were also rivals, and trust in as short a supply as money. But this wasn't the answer. She repeated this internally, in case she hadn't heard it the first time: This. Wasn't. The answer.

She said, 'You're not an elected MP. You're a former home secretary. In the public view, that's a little below being a former *Blue Peter* presenter.'

'The public aren't involved, except inasmuch as they'd be beneficiaries. We're talking about a higher good here, Diana.'

'And you're the one who defines what that higher good is?'

'I'm sure we can find common ground. The higher good's a plateau, not a peak.'

It was insane. It couldn't work.

She'd need to hear a lot more detail before she could be persuaded that it was even worth laughing at.

Diana Taverner said, 'It's always interesting chatting with you, Peter. I never know whether to send a thank-you note or a SWAT team afterwards.'

'You'll think about this.'

It wasn't a question.

She left the café without another word. The pavements were damp, the air swimmy with exhaust. Through a gap in the buildings she could see St Paul's, its elegant bulb a reminder that some things endured.

You'll think about this.

She walked back to Regent's Park more slowly than usual.

No more snow had fallen. A thin grey rain, instead, swept the city, and the drains swam with excess run-off, and mains burst with dull predictability. One of these was not far from Slough House, and made a lagoon of a junction, in lieu of fixing which a team of council-liveried characters had erected a roadblock of sandbags and bollards, ensuring that traffic was reduced to a single-lane nightmare, before going off on their summer holidays.

Catherine Standish avoided getting her feet wet by taking the long way round: up the Barbican ramp and over the footbridge. She wore sensible shoes, because who but a fool would wear otherwise on a Monday morning, but had no desire to dampen them unnecessarily. There were inches you could give which, once surrendered, were never won back. Over the weekend, she had emptied each and every one of her bottles into her bath; had kept the shower running while pinkened water swirled round the plughole and was sucked into oblivion, like a memory disappearing inside its own fading details. There were reasons why her sobriety had nearly ended, but those reasons, in the end, were inches best held on to. Her life was not what she might have wanted it to be, but that was no reason for destroying what it was.

Or at least, that was how the measurement currently stood, and for this she was grateful.

In her room she raised the blind, and allowed the new week's watery light to filter in. J. K. Coe had been dead for nine days, and life in Slough House was adjusting to its new mean; his absence did not make things quieter, since he'd often gone days without saying a word, but new ghosts cast pale shadows, and now and again she caught stray glimpses at the corners of her vision. She had not known him well, and it wasn't so much that she missed him as that she wished she'd never known him at all. Loss is easier to bear when it's truly felt. When it's a knee-jerk reaction, it reflects badly on all concerned.

Still, though, she caught glimpses.

Roderick Ho arrived, and Louisa, and River; separately, noisily, unhappily. Louisa, she knew, blamed herself for the recent deaths; River was angry that Frank Harkness had slipped away. Ho was pissed off about his car. The fourth arrival was Lech Wicinski: Catherine was not yet attuned to his movements, but she heard him enter Ho's office, heard their lack of greeting. Shirley was last to turn up. And now we are full. Well, except for the obvious. Catherine was reformatting River's latest report on potential hostile safe house locations, because in addition to being of no obvious worth, it was presented in a variety of fonts, sizes, even colours, a dead giveaway of the cut-and-paste methodology of its compilation. Next time, she thought. Next time. Probably. But for now she gave it a professional veneer, printed it out, slipped it inside a Manila folder, and when she passed into Lamb's room to leave it on his desk nearly dropped it in fright: he was sitting in the dark, a toad shape in shadow, an unlit cigarette in his mouth. His eyes were dark wet stones.

She said, 'I didn't hear you come in,' and heard her own heartbeat in her voice.

He grunted.

There was an empty bottle in front of him, but not his usual Talisker, nor even his usual spirit of choice: it was vodka, or so she assumed. Clear glass, anyway, with Cyrillic script on a red and white label. Yes, vodka. Probably his version of detoxing. By all appearances he'd spent the interval since she'd last seen him drinking: he was oily-faced, red-eyed, and now she was through the door, she could smell the stale days hanging off him. A scrunched pyramid of used tissues on the floor suggested he'd endured one of his coughing fits. He'd been here all night.

She said, 'Come to inspire the troops?'

'Someone's got to be the counterweight. They look to you for guidance, they'll end up hanging round off-licences dressed like Looby Loo.'

A match appeared in his hand, and flared. When he dipped his head to meet it, the light riffed off his hair, briefly haloing him.

'We lost someone,' she said. 'Emma Flyte, too. She was a good woman. They'd still be alive if you hadn't gone after Harkness.'

'Which you warned me against.'

'Don't imagine I wasn't about to remind you.'

'No, you're good at that. Others do the dirty work, you just shoulder the burden.'

'You sent them out against a bunch of professionals. We're lucky any of them came back.'

'Louisa was on her own. On her fucking *holidays*. You think I should have let her deal with Harkness herself?'

'You weren't thinking about her, you were thinking about settling a score. How did that work out?'

'Well, he's dead,' said Lamb. 'I consider that a result.'

His smoke drifted towards her, and she wafted it away as if it were another bad idea.

She said, 'That's not what Louisa said. And she was last to see him.'

Lamb pushed a newspaper across his desk, *The Times*, folded open to foreign news.

Poitiers. Body found. Driving seat, parked car.

328

Single bullet wound to head.

It was barely a paragraph. Associated Press. She imagined, ridiculously, a journo in a raincoat, a press card tucked into his hatband. A camera with a bowl-shaped flash.

She said, 'You've been to Poitiers?'

'Do I fucking look like I've been to Poitiers?'

He looked like he'd been down a well.

'So . . .'

Lamb said, 'I pulled a trigger.'

'Whose trigger?'

'Man named Martin Kreutzmer.' He breathed smoke. 'He's a BND player. Semi-retired, he says, but running an agent here in the Brexit Office, would you believe? Almost like they don't believe we can fuck that one up by ourselves.'

'Imagine.'

'The Park thought she was ours, and that we had a warm body inside the BND. Reality was the other way round. And when Kreutzmer's cover name turned up on a search Wicinski ran, Kreutzmer got to hear because the mole's Park handler told her about it.' He paused. 'Do you want to hear that again? It's not that complicated, but it's so fucking comical it bears repetition.'

Catherine said, 'And Kreutzmer planted the porn on Lech's laptop. To discredit him.'

'But not by himself. He called in favours to get it done, which was a breach of BND protocols. So when Wicinski looked like he was starting to pull at loose threads, Kreutzmer hit him again, hard. To cover his own arse, not just to protect his joe.'

'How do you know all this?'

'Well, Molly Doran told me Kreutzmer was involved. But Kreutzmer himself told me the rest.'

'Because you can be persuasive.'

'And because I had him over a fucking barrel. He wasn't worried about the Park putting him on a plane. He was worried about being fired once it landed.'

Catherine was still standing. She lowered herself into a chair. The only light crawled in through the open office door, and Lamb's face looked like a candleless pumpkin: its holes and hollows lacking any internal flame.

She said, 'And he shot Harkness? Assuming that's who got shot.'

'Harkness was playing with hired talent. And a thing about hired talent? There's always someone'll pay better.'

'You bought them.'

'Not with money. One of his crew, a rat called Anton Moser, remember? Coe identified him.'

She nodded.

Lamb said, 'The mad monk had his moments. It turns out Moser used to bang heads for the BND. Molly has a file. They got rid of him when the heads he banged got too scrambled to debrief. There's such a thing as being too good at your job.'

'Apparently.'

'So he went freelance, and you know what they say about freelance work. There's nobody handing out gold clocks at the end of it.' Lamb ground his cigarette out on his battle-scarred desk. 'So I had Kreutzmer send Moser a message. Let him know there'd be a welcome in the homeland if he did this little favour. A return to the fold.'

'So he murdered Harkness for the chance of a pension?'

'Wait'll you're down to your last tin of sardines, see how you feel about it then. Plus, Harkness was a legend, don't forget. If you're in the business of collecting scalps, that's a nice one to have. Front and centre of the old CV.'

She looked at the paragraph again, and filled in its blanks. A final debrief after the aborted contract in Wales. Payday, even: would they still have been paid, despite the way things had gone? Another bugbear of the freelance life. Whatever the reason, Harkness and Moser in a car, and Moser pulling the trigger; a trigger Lamb had primed, here in London. She had to remind herself, maybe for the millionth time, that this was the world she lived in; that Spook Street wasn't all boring reports in Manila folders. That joe country lay just around the corner.

'And what did you promise Kreutzmer for this?' she asked.

'A free pass.'

'He's running an agent in London, and you gave him a free pass?'

'I said I promised him one. I never said I gave him one.' He'd found another cigarette somewhere. 'And once he'd done his bit' – he gestured towards the newspaper – 'I called Taverner, let her know there's a mole within spitting distance of Number 10. Bet that went down well with the Oversights.'

'Not to mention Kreutzmer.'

'Fuck him. He branded my cattle. That used to be a hanging offence.'

He lit his cigarette.

'He'll be back in Munich by now. His joe'll be at the Park. And whoever they had handling her this end, well, if we're really unlucky, he'll end up downstairs. Maybe I'll make him share a room with Wicinski. What do you reckon?'

'I reckon,' said Catherine, laying a quiet stress on the word, 'that we lost someone. Emma Flyte too. And she was a good woman.'

She still had River's report tucked under her arm, and she laid it on the desk now and left the office, closing the door behind her, leaving Lamb cloistered in his dark.

And meanwhile, on the floor below, River Cartwright is on the phone – unaccountably, uncharacteristically, he wants to hear his mother's voice; wants to hear her talk about his grandfather, whom he is missing. But whatever he wants her to say, he wants her to say it unprompted, and this does not happen. Instead, he suffers the usual flow of self-involved detail

– of lunches enjoyed and conversations won – and all the while his gaze remains on the empty desk by the window, where J. K. Coe once sat. The window has been newly bespattered by bird shit, and he wonders briefly whether Coe would have done anything about this – opened the window and cleaned it off with a rag – before realising how obvious the answer is. Later, River will drop into Louisa's Guy's office on some pretext or other, and will ask 'You okay?' to which Louisa will reply 'Yeah, sure,' not without meaning it exactly; more without addressing the question's undertones. She too has been working the phone; has spoken to Lucas Harper, to Lucas's mother, to Devon Welles, who worked closely with Emma. All these conversations were numb, it seems to her now; an odd adjective for a spoken exchange, but one that fits. And she feels a blank space in her life, where a friendship might have been. She and River will chat a little longer, and they will either agree to have a drink after work or not, depending. If they do, it will not go well. But for the moment, River listens to his mother on the phone, his gaze on the empty desk by the window, where J. K. Coe once sat.

Directly underneath which, on the floor below, sits Shirley Dander, who is currently waiting for her screen to unfreeze, an outcome she knows will remain deferred until she unplugs her computer altogether, then replugs it, and boots up. But for the time being she can sit doing nothing with an alibi for inactivity in front of her, and will continue to do this for as long as humanly possible: through the rest of the morning, for sure; the afternoon too, if possible; the rest of the week, the whole grey year, forever. Something Lamb once said keeps coming to mind – *You lot keep your heads down, do what you're told, and quietly die of boredom, and everyone's happy as an Oxfam worker at a sex party. But start making waves and there are shitstorms waiting to happen* – and she now appreciates its wisdom. For a few moments, behind a barn on a snowy Welsh hillside, she had thought she was ready to make a brilliant departure from life; to avenge Marcus, or die trying. But in reality, it was just another moment in an ongoing series. She isn't ready to die. Wasn't really ready then. And she misses J. K. Coe, because this is something she might have been able to talk to him about, something he might have listened to. But at least her frozen screen isn't going anywhere, and provides a kind of constancy as she sits; her thoughts a flickering menace; her monitor a ponderous slab of light.

Which would invoke in Roderick Ho amused contempt: frozen screen, shit. Freeze a screen in front of the HotRod, you'd see serious melt going on. But then, Roderick Ho is a professional surrounded by amateurs, whose inability to perform the most mundane of tasks – cruise the Web, drop hot beats, remain alive – would be a constant downer, were he the type to nurse disappointments. As it is, he has even risen above the callous disregard with which the others treated his car, though this, it's true, is largely because he might as easily have sunk beneath it for all the notice anyone would take. But while they sit in their various bruised moods, reflecting on their latest failures, Roddy is delving once more into Service records. His researches into Lech Wicinski have yet to be completed: the mysterious wiping of his Service history remains unexplained. Wicinski himself, it has to be said, has also been heavily redacted. This morning he arrived unbandaged, and for the first time Roddy saw that his cheeks are now a furious crosshatching of fresh cuts, new razorings, that have served to obliterate the word carved underneath them. How this happened, and who might be responsible, is a profound mystery to Roddy, but not one he plans to lose sleep over. Instead, he continues quarrying for evidence of Wicinski's past sins, and while he's about it, takes another peek at the dismal records of some of his colleagues. And this is what he's doing when he makes his discovery.

Outside, London sulks. If cities sleep with their lights on, afraid of the dark, they treat the sunlit hours with suspicion, and cast shadows where they can. Many of these fall on Slough House, where they're welcomed as natural camouflage, and having made their way through the dirty windows form a kind of ground-mist on the stairs, through which Roddy Ho wades now, fizzing and bubbling with the news he bears, all the way up to Jackson Lamb's room. It's late morning, and the day is one of smudged margins and ill-defined activities, one thing bleeding into another, the way memories spawn forebodings, but Lamb's stillness is a constant at least, and he remains utterly motionless, barely breathing even, as Roddy explains that all of them, not just Wicinski, but all of them – Roddy Ho, Catherine Standish, River Cartwright, Shirley Dander, Louisa Guy, Jackson Lamb, and all their dead colleagues – all have been wiped from Regent's Park's memory, their histories erased, their pasts blanked out, their Service records expunged. By the time Ho stops talking Catherine is a mute angel at his shoulder, and the others are crowding the landing. They have all heard enough to grasp the gist: their pasts, good and bad, have been cancelled, it seems. What this portends for their future is unclear, and they wait to hear Jackson Lamb's verdict.

But Lamb, in his monstrous calm, says nothing.

Acknowledgements

My thanks, as ever, to the teams at John Murray in London – especially Mark Richards, Yassine Belkacemi and Becky Walsh – and at Soho Press in New York – especially Bronwen Hruska, Juliet Grames, Paul Oliver and Rachel Kowal – for all the hard work and effort they put into making me look good.

And to Juliet Burton and Micheline Steinberg for taking care of business.

And to my mother, my siblings, their attachments and their offspring for being there.

One of the great perks of this job is the opportunity it affords to spend time in the company of writers. Allowing one to stand for many, I'm grateful to Lucy Atkins for support, advice, friendship and innumerable cups of coffee here in Oxford. Happily, I met with similar warmth and friendship far from home while working on this book, from those involved in translating, publishing and selling the slow horses abroad, or whose paths simply crossed mine along the way. So many thanks to, among others, Anik Lapointe, Anna von Planta, Charles Cumming, Claudia Cucchiarato, Daniela Seyfarth, Darrel Bristow-Bovey, Eugene Ashton, Jonathan Ball, Kate Turkington, Peter Cunningham, Philipp Keel, Ruth Geiger, Stephanie Uhlig, and especially Nkanyezi Tshabalala, for making travel a pleasure, when I so often fear it will be an ordeal.

Mostly, though, my debts fall closer to home. Joe country would be nowhere without joes; *Joe Country* would not have been written without Jo. Thanks are not enough.

MH
Oxford
February 2019